The
Long White
Cloud

K. K. Poole

First Published in 2018
by GWL Publishing
an imprint of Great War Literature Publishing LLP

Produced in United Kingdom

ISBN 978-1-910603-45-1 Paperback Edition

GWL Publishing
Forum House
Stirling Road
Chichester PO19 7DN
www.gwlpublishing.co.uk

Image credits:
Trench Map 28.NE Scale: 1:20000 Edition: 8A Published: October 1917 - Trenches corrected to 1 October 1917, reproduced with the permission of the National Library of Scotland.
The Menin Road by Paul Nash, image courtesy of The Google Art Project.

K.K. Poole was born in 1969. He is the son of Australian parents and was educated at Magdalen College School and St. John's College, Oxford. For three successive years he rowed in 'The Boat Race' against Cambridge.

After University, he taught science, coached rowing and gained a doctorate in epilepsy epidemiology before qualifying as a general practitioner in 2003. He is married with three sons.

Dedication

For Ali

Acknowledgements

My thanks to: Alison, my wife, for her quality proofreading, Juliet Solomon for ordering me to 'write another one', Henry Wells for his encouragement, and Wendy Lawrance at GWL Publishing, for her very kind words about this book. Also to the helpful staff at the Dunhill library (Chichester Medical Education Centre) for providing copies of the old BMJ and Lancet articles. Thank you to the Van Eygen family, for making Ypres a place of happy memories for me. Kia Ora to all our Kiwi friends, in particular Renee and Ian: good times, great fishing, and also Rev David Balchin for giving me insights into what it is to be a bombastic minister.

I would like to acknowledge the sacrifice of the New Zealand Expeditionary Force during the First World War: there are all sorts of statistics one can use, but perhaps the simplest approximation is to say that 1 in 5 of the country's entire male population served overseas, and of those, 1 in 5 perished.

A strange thing. After completing the first draft of this book, i.e. *after* I had named one of the central characters McKenzie (a medic attached to the Rifle Brigade), I paid a visit to the Messines Ridge memorial. Inscribed around the stone base of a large cross - perhaps 100 feet in circumference - are the names of 828 New Zealanders whose 'graves are known only to God'. They are listed under their respective units; Machine Gun Corps, Entrenching Battalion, Maori Battalion, and so on. While walking around the memorial, I noticed something incongruous on the pale stone – a solitary black sticker with a silver fern. It was next to the name of a soldier from the Rifle Brigade. The name: McKenzie.

Disclaimer

The Long White Cloud is a work of fiction. However, some of the characters, settings and situations are factual. Small liberties may have been taken with certain elements of these characters' lives, their whereabouts and the timings of events, for the purposes of telling the story.

Ka mate! Ka mate!
Ka ora! Ka ora!

I die! I die!
I live! I live!

First verse of the Haka
(Composed by Chief Te Rauparaha of the Ngati Toa tribe,
circa 1820)

Chapter One

In my dream I could fly.

With a running start I was able to take off from the end of the hospital pier and glide straight up into the night sky. I circled the immense hospital grounds once, to get used to the feeling of being airborne, before heading out over the dark cold body of the English Channel towards the continent. On a south east bearing, if my internal compass was correct.

Above Belgium, the Western Front was lit up by the flashes of hundreds of shell bursts and flares, like a constellation laid out on the black land – a new astronomical discovery all of my own. What would I name it? It would have to be in Latin – perhaps the constellation *'Insanire'*, or *'Mortem'*. Madness or death; either name would do.

I was surprised to see that the town of Ypres was now far behind the front line. A year further forward since I had been taken out of the fight, and there had been a significant advance. Judging by the pyrotechnics on display, the Allies were halfway to Antwerp now. The war was still grinding on though, so how much had really changed? In this war, great reverses could occur and it wouldn't have surprised me at all if that gained ground was lost by Christmas.

The distant rumbling of the explosions at the Front made me fly faster, as if my dream spirit wanted to be somewhere more peaceful, sooner rather than later. I travelled south over the snow-capped peaks of the Alps, down the boot of Italy and out over the Mediterranean towards the city lights of Cairo. I flew low over the Great Pyramid of Cheops, almost clipping its angular summit, pale in the reflected moonlight. Rolling onto my back, I found myself gazing up into the heavens, the three stars of Orion's belt complementing the three stone pyramids of Giza. *Tautoru* was the Maori name for those stars; the three friends. I had learnt that fact from my old friend Reverend Sean Rennie, who knew Maori mythology almost as well as the stories from the Bible. Anyway, this was the moment in my flying dream when I realised the final destination was going to be New Zealand and that my three friends would be waiting for me there – Rennie and his two sons. My subconscious mind was transporting me to a place that might help repair my broken conscious mind – it was a dream with a purpose, a curative dream if you like.

Soon I was over the Suez Canal and the Red Sea, the two bodies of water lightening a touch as dawn approached. The darkness of Europe was behind me now, consigned to the night. Farewell, the constellation of madness.

At last I saw the sun clip the earth's curve, and I banked east towards its welcoming rays.

Years ago, I had travelled this way by ship to a new life in Australia.

It was easy to retrace the route now in the dream; a straight diagonal from Ceylon across the Indian Ocean to the Western Australian coast. I crossed the vivid turquoise waters below in a blur, moving at incredible speed. It was only as the Australian landmass came into view that my pace slowed, allowing me to get a glimpse of the beach at Fremantle, the place where I had first swum in the Indian Ocean with Rennie on the day of our arrival.

Pushing inland, I quickly made Kalgoorlie, the goldfields city of my old adventures. The tin roofs were mirroring the bright sun back up into the sky so dazzlingly that, from my altitude, they looked like tiny jewels dropped onto the ochre earth. Close-up, the place hadn't been as pretty – after dust storms the buildings took on a reddish hue, so that it resembled a town from hell itself.

Over the wild and lonely Nullarbor Plain I flew; a place of Aboriginal magic and mysterious caves. A place of ghosts.

To my right was the southern coastline – the Great Australian Bight; to my left, the seemingly never-ending landmass stretching away to the north. I was accelerating again now – in seconds I traversed the lower half of Eastern Australia. Soon I was out over ocean once again; the Tasman Sea. Another ship's journey being retraced: one I had made in the early months of 1901, on my way to New Zealand's North Island.

And then there it was: 'Aotearoa' – the land of the long white cloud – the place that had become my home.

At the eastern edge of the Coromandel Peninsula, I spotted my friends in a small fishing boat moored off Orokawa beach and started my descent. Now I would get better, I was sure of it. With their help I would become whole again. I would be able to leave D block for good and get my life back on track.

But, as so often happens in good dreams, it ended at the critical moment. Hurtling down towards my waiting friends, a brutal noise sounded all around me and the whole scene evaporated in an instant.

My first thought on waking was how much better life would be if I could dream all the time.

A moment before, I had been nearing the blue New Zealand waters with the sun warm on my face. Now I was back in England, on the cold ward of D Block with someone screaming his head off.

"…AAAAARRRGGGHHH!"

That was the sound that had yanked me out of the dream by the scruff of my neck.

This led me to my second thought… more of a reminder really: I was a patient on this ward and not a doctor manning it.

The third thought was even more sobering than the second: D Block was the asylum.

In 1900 I had stayed in this same hospital after returning from the Boer War, but with one crucial difference: back then I had been a 'normal' patient in 'C block', with other officers recovering from typhoid fever, and not one confined to D block having suffered a mental breakdown.

At that time I had likened the supervised routine – the bells for mealtimes and calls for lights out – to my boarding school days, but now I had been forced to revise that comparison. D-block was another thing altogether; more like a prison. Though I had never been a gaol inmate, I imagined this place must be a fair approximation; strict routines and constant monitoring by the gruff orderlies, a high surrounding wall and locked gates. The clothes we wore – the 'hospital undress' – had that institutional look; a suit made of cheap blue cloth, with a white shirt underneath and a red neck tie. When I had been here as a younger man it had felt like a school uniform, but now with my D block perspective, I thought the clothes were much more like prisoner garb, and may as well have been covered with black arrows.

All the patients in the hospital complex wore the same suit, but on arrival at D Block they took away your tie and shoelaces just in case you were thinking of hanging yourself. It was still hard to believe I was in an asylum with shell-shock. I never imagined it would happen to me, but then a lot of men probably believed the same thing before they had gone to serve in this war.

Another scream sounded: "…AAAAARRRGGGHHH!"

It was a primeval structure of sound, built on a strong foundation of helplessness, with several stories of pain, fear, terror and madness piled on top. For me, the most alarming part of all was how the cries were happening in sequence, one after the other, the sort of repetition you might expect to hear if someone was being burnt at the stake.

"…AAAAARRRGGGHHH!"

Two burly orderlies blundered into the ward and switched on the lights.

I propped myself up onto my elbows, blinking wildly for a few moments before looking across to the place where the sound was coming from. Despite my disorientation, it didn't take me long to work out what had happened.

The bed nearest the door was minus its occupant with only a sad hollow left in the mattress. Underneath the iron bedstead was a man, his white bed sheets crumpled around him like an isolated snow drift.

The poor fellow's name was Cobb and he had been admitted the day before, fresh from the Front, though 'fresh' is probably the wrong choice of word because that makes him sound like a ripe apple, plucked from the orchards and ready for eating. In reality, Cobb was broken and bruised, like a windfall that has hit a dozen branches on the way down and then rotted on the ground. He wasn't alone; every man on the ward was damaged in some way – we were a whole harvest of bad fruit.

He had been ducking under his bed in the daylight hours too, every time someone said the word 'bombs' to him. In the name of scientific research, the doctors had brought in an unwieldy *Pathé* camera and deliberately said the trigger word half a dozen times, to capture the reaction on film again and again.

Like me, Cobb had been dreaming, but instead of flying over Belgium, he'd landed there – back in the place where bombs were exploding, and his dream had fast become a nightmare; one of major proportions I guessed, because he hadn't screamed like this in his daytime episodes.

With the lights on, the screaming had mercifully stopped, replaced by the much gentler sounds of his rapid breathing.

The orderlies knelt down and coaxed him out from under the bed.

Cobb didn't resist – he allowed himself to be led mechanically, like a human puppet, with a docile smile on his otherwise blank face.

His pathetic expression was deeply disturbing. I wondered if that was how I seemed to others. Instead of continuing to watch, I lay back flat and looked straight up at the ceiling, but the lights were too bright and so I closed my eyes again. It was easier that way - it helped to block out some of the insanity surrounding me on this godforsaken ward.

Surely, I thought to myself, if I can dream of fishing boats and not bombs, then I can't be mad. It's not *me* waking everyone with my pitiful screams. Perhaps a lot of mad people thought this way, trying to convince themselves they were fine compared to the *really* mad ones. What couldn't be denied was that I had chosen to inhabit my own internal world, and no-one was allowed in. If that was madness, then so be it.

No-one here even knew who I was.

To the doctors I was one of the craziest, most intractable cases of shell-shock in the whole of D block, and that was saying something. Basically, I was considered a lost cause. I wasn't a screamer like Cobb or some of the others – quite the opposite in fact. No sounds came out of my mouth at all. A whole year had gone by with no change in my condition – to the staff I was just a mute mess of a man with a far-away look in his eye. 'The Quiet Man' they called me on the ward rounds.

When pulled from the mud of the battlefield in October 1917, my uniform had been ripped and damaged beyond all recognition and my cardboard identity discs reduced to a sodden pulp.

For fear of possible gas contamination, the remains of the uniform had then been cut away at the Advanced Dressing Station, leaving me as naked and unidentifiable as the day I was born. Bodily, I was unscathed; almost a miracle after where I had been, a place where bullets from German MGs had curdled the air. In a short handover, the stretcher bearers told the nurse that, since finding me, I had been unable to speak. She nodded briefly, as if it was something she came across quite often. A disconnect had happened. Somewhere in the basement of my mind, the self-preservation mechanism had decreed that various working parts were to be shut down for the foreseeable future.

Later, a haggard doctor with a hundred other wounded men lying outside the Dressing Station had hurriedly scrawled, *'Unknown British Soldier, NYDN'* on my ticket and put me into an ambulance.

NYDN stood for: 'Not Yet Diagnosed, Nervous', and he had written that because medics had been ordered not to use the words 'shell shock'.

For the second time in my life, I was shipped back to the army's main clearing hospital at Netley near Southampton – the 'Royal Victoria'. The first time, to which I have already alluded, was after I had contracted typhoid fever near Bloemfontein in 1900. The coincidence didn't make much of an impression on me at first – the trauma of the Passchendaele Ridge on 12th October 1917 completely clouding my thinking and blotting out my ability to join up the dots. It was only after the days stretched into weeks that the big picture slowly came into full focus; of how, in a seventeen year time-span my life had gone full circle and I was back in the same place where it had all started. God – if indeed he's out there somewhere – must have a very dry sense of humour.

Two MOs from the Royal Army Medical Corps, with a lot more time on their hands than their front-line colleagues, had assessed me upon my arrival at D Block.

"Who… are… you?" one said, slowly and loudly, as if I didn't speak English.

"Lieutenant John Hunston, doctor with the New Zealand Field Ambulance."

At least those were the words which formed in my head – what came out of my mouth was nothing.

"Maybe he can write it down?" the other MO had said.

They had given me a piece of paper and a pencil, and watched as I made an illegible scribble on the page. The medical word for that was agraphia. That's what went through my mind as I saw that all avenues of communication with the outside world had been severed.

"… I can't make it out at all… Why, his handwriting is even worse than yours, Charles."

Ha Ha Ha.

Their joking at my expense lit a fuse under my frustration – I tore up the page, snapped their pencil in half and threw the pieces across the room. Red-faced with rage, I screamed at them noiselessly: *If you bastards had seen what I have seen!*

They diagnosed 'hysterical mutism and agraphia' and held me down, attaching electrodes to my throat and taking it in turns to administer pulses of electricity for twenty minutes at a time. "This is to stimulate speech," one of them kept saying in a rational tone of voice, before blithely going ahead with the shocks.

As a medic myself, I had read in the *BMJ* that the Germans were using these methods; a certain Dr Kaufmann had been carrying out the procedure on soldiers suffering from 'psychical disturbances produced by the war' since 1915. I remembered the article calling it the 'Ueberrumpelung' system, meaning 'unexpected attack', and that it had four main tenets:

1. Preliminary suggestion – preferably carried out in the right 'atmosphere' – i.e. in a hospital where successful cures have been numerous.
2. Powerful electric shocks – this was the 'Ueberrumpelung' part.
3. Maintenance of an atmosphere of strict military discipline – essentially the unquestioning obedience of the patient.
4. Masterfulness and pertinacity – meaning it might take hours to get the result, but it would eventually happen if the physician exerted his 'whole personality'.

Already knowing about 'Ueberrumpelung' meant I was not as surprised as I might have been by their treatment of me. The big surprise was that the British were doing it. Unfortunately, the doctors here couldn't have studied the *BMJ* paper as thoroughly as I had, because as far as I could tell they were only following the second tenet. All of Dr Kaufmann's other suggestions had been cast aside.

This ignorance hadn't stopped my doctors from inventing a new treatment of their own though. After the unsuccessful electric shocks, one of them had put his lit cigarette end onto the tip of my tongue, a procedure I was fairly sure wasn't on any Kaufmann checklist.

When this didn't work, the diagnosis became 'INTRACTABLE hysterical mutism and agraphia'. I had heard one of the doctors say to his colleague: "Great stuff! We'll be able to write this up for the Lancet."

My attempt to laugh at this farce must have convinced them I was unhinged and worthy of more intensive treatment, because then they put hot metal plates to the back of my mouth in another vain attempt to get me to talk.

And all the while they kept making notes for their bloody research.

I hope it's going to be a good Lancet paper, I had thought bitterly, a sarcastic wish cheering me up somewhat because it meant that at least my faculties for cynicism had remained intact. On the inside, I was still my old self.

Soon, they gave up, an outcome convincing me that points 1 and 4 in Kaufmann's system didn't exist here; that is, few successful cures had ever happened on D block, and also that they had no real resolve to keep trying. Point 3 – my unquestioning obedience – had ceased to exist after their initial clumsy interrogation and their laughing at my condition. They only stopped briefly at my bed on the ward rounds now. I hadn't been chosen to star in their horror movie that day. Intractable hysterical mutism wasn't dramatic enough for the camera – after all it was a silent recording. It was the poor buggers with the jerky walks and the paroxysms and the ones who hid under their beds when you shouted 'bombs' who made for the best viewing. In their eyes, Cobb was a star.

To try and forget about all this, I recalled my earlier dream and replayed the incredible flight once more. Not only had I travelled to the far side of the world but I had also gone back in time - almost two years to be specific; to a day when I had been whole and happy.

The lights were switched off and the room quietened again.

Soon, I was asleep and dreaming, going straight back to the fishing boat in blue New Zealand waters. Next to me, my friend Rennie was singing – out of tune and roughly, but at least with enthusiasm and passion – the very opposite to the weary apathy which infected everyone on D-block.

Chapter Two

Off Orokawa beach, North Island, New Zealand
December 25 1916

"I saw three ships come sailing in,
On Christmas day, on Christmas day
I saw three ships come sailing in,
On Christmas day in the…
Oh confound it!"

Reverend Sean Rennie's fishing line had tangled.

For a capable 'fisher of men', he was a truly incapable fisherman. On our trips, he spent most of his time sifting through the mess of line on his lap; the result of one of his many miscasts. It is a testament to Rennie's good character that he didn't let it get to him too much: 'confound it' was certainly the closest he ever came to swearing.

Next to my beleaguered friend, a young man was leaning over the side of the boat, peering down into the waters and frowning hard. When it came to fishing, Manu Rennie had inherited his father's bad luck.

"Nothing's biting tonight," he said, punching the surface of the water with his fist and sending off tiny ripples into the enormity of the Pacific. "Come on, fish – where are you?"

They wouldn't have heard him, or felt the ripples, or however it was that fish detected such things, because the ocean was deep here – a hundred fathoms or more, impenetrable even to the setting sun after only a dozen feet – and they were all the way down. The sea bed was the place where the fish lurked, all good fishermen knew that.

Manu's twin brother, Kahu, down in the stern, set out his own theory:

"Bru, you know what? They are all laughing at your lousy old shrimp bait."

Manu was still leaning over the gunnels and straining to see what was going on down below.

"My shrimps are better bait than your worms," he said.

Kahu laughed and pointed to a white enamel bucket in the bow which contained two fish the size of dinner plates.

"Tell me that those Snapper didn't love my worms."

It was undeniable that so far this afternoon the fishing gods had been with Kahu.

Manu sat back heavily, rocking the boat a little as he did so. He could feel his brother's catch taunting him from the bucket, a silent reminder that he was two nil down.

"Lend me a worm, bru," he said after a while.

Smiling in delight, Kahu opened up his bait box, going through his specimens in turn and explaining in exaggerated detail why each would work better than Manu's shrimps. He was really rubbing it in.

As their banter continued, I focused back on my line.

Things felt the same as usual; the boys carrying on with their brotherly squabbles, Rennie singing his hymns, me trying to feel at peace with the world. This was about as close as I ever got – out in the boat with my best friend and his sons – my godsons – I had to admit, sitting here surrounded by water as the sun went down wasn't a bad way to spend a Christmas Day. Not a bad way at all.

The boys were always vying for supremacy, sometimes overtly and sometimes more subtly. This non-stop fraternal duelling must be hard-wired into the brains of all brothers, perhaps even more so with twins. My twin brother Freddie and I had been the same once.

Most of the time, the competition was jocular, but just occasionally there would be wins and losses which took on a great significance. The first time Freddie had beaten me in a running race was still clear in my memory. Since he was the younger by a few minutes, there was always that natural expectation that the elder brother be the dominant one. As lads we often ran a circuit of the local park, perhaps a mile and a half in distance, and I would always win. Until one day, when I hadn't. One mile in, I had tried to kick away, and this time Freddie had hung on and then replied with a kick of his own, moving ahead. It hadn't even happened on the final straight – he broke me long before that – and he had been merciless, just the way I had always been before. Afterwards, he had said nothing and shown no sign of triumph. We didn't even talk about it. Just beating me was reward enough for him. Though I would later win some of our runs, my reign of total supremacy was over. Of all my adolescent setbacks, that loss had meant the most.

Despite being only fifteen years of age, Manu and Kahu were thickly muscled, each possessing the build of a champion boxer without ever needing to lift a dumbbell. The likenesses between me and Freddie and Rennie's sons – that is, our being twins and having the same competitive streaks – were equally matched by differences. At the same age, we had been as scrawny as scarecrows.

Perhaps the biggest difference was that Manu and Kahu were half Maori, on their mother Materoa's side, and both boys had traditional Maori facial tattoos – *Moko* – to show their ancestry.

The left sides of their faces were un-tattooed, since that half was traditionally associated with paternal ancestry and their father – my old friend Rennie – was one hundred per cent Anglo-Saxon. So it was only on the right side that intricate spirals of blue-black lines covered their foreheads, noses, cheeks and chins. Just by looking at the pattern, other Maori would know what tribe – or *iwi* – the boys were from. In pre-European times, the forty or so Maori tribes in New Zealand had fought one another all the time for territory, but only against distantly related groups. There was a story that in 1837, Hokianga warriors had arrived at a fight between two groups of the Nga Puhi tribe, but after seeing the Moko on display were unable to choose which side to join as they were equally related to both.

The marks were individual signatures, indeed in the early days of land purchases by the colonialist British, the Maori had often drawn their personal Moko patterns on the deeds instead of writing their names.

By having Moko tattooing, Manu and Kahu had made a bold statement about their cultural identity. For one thing, the practice had largely been out of fashion since the wars of the 1800s and tattooing like this was a rare sight nowadays. It turned heads, but the boys weren't afraid to face their past. And by respectfully keeping the left half of their faces clear, they were also saying they were just as proud of their father's bloodline.

Sometimes, when we fished on very calm waters, Manu would study his half Moko reflection in the water and say: "Would you look at that? One half of me has colonised the other half."

We had been in the boat for three hours so far.

Since the fish tended to bite best late in the day, we had come out after Christmas lunch was over.

The boat was anchored half a mile out from Orokawa beach at the best fishing grounds, but the land felt a lot closer than that. The gnarled branches of the Pohutakawa trees lining the sands reached out as if they wanted to grab my fishing rod and show me how it should be done.

People called the Pohutakawa the 'New Zealand Christmas Tree' because they blossomed with red flowers late in November and the flowers stayed right through to the end of December – like nature's own tinsel. I preferred the Maori name, because the trees were not at all like the spruce firs from the Northern Hemisphere that I associated with traditional Christmas trees. The trees were wizened specimens, more reminiscent of olive trees than anything else. To me they had character; they were like venerable old men who, once a year, in a bid to show the world they were still alive and kicking, chose to add a bit of colour to their wardrobe.

Behind the beach and the trees, steep volcanic ridges rose up towards the central mountain chain of the Coromandel peninsula – the peaks running in a line for sixty miles like the spine of a giant stegosaurus.

If I happened to be in an introspective mood, the beauty of this place could feel so overwhelming that I would well up with tears. I think some sights are too much for the rational part of the mind to handle, the images bypassing the judgement filter altogether and heading straight to the tear ducts. I had seen fathers look at their new-born babies and react in the same way; tough men, miners. They would try and hide it, but their reddened eyes would give them away and I would have to pretend not to notice. Whether it is nature or humanity, experiencing raw unadorned reality can sometimes be very moving.

This time, I managed to keep my emotions in check and instead said out loud, "I believe these are what they call the good times."

My remark started Rennie singing again.

"… and what was in those ships all three, on Christmas Day, on Christmas Day? And what was in those ships all three…"

He had undone all the knots now and stood up to re-cast.

Dramatically he raised his arm and threw the rod forward with a flick of the wrist.

"Oh… confound it all!"

He had somehow managed to hook his own jacket at the collar, and the line had tangled again. As he fiddled to free it up, Rennie continued to growl in frustration while the boys and I continued to fish.

Fishing on Christmas Day was a tradition for us.

It had been back in 1911 when Rennie and I had first cooked the catch over a camp-fire on Orokawa beach, the boys only ten years old. Now it was something we all looked forward to for the whole of December.

Bearing this in mind, my friend should have been happier than he was.

Line problems apart, he seemed more vexed than usual – I was sensing a dark undercurrent in my friend's mood. Though he was doing and saying the same as always, there had been a subtle change in his bearing, a tension I couldn't pin down. For the last week this air of gloominess had hung about him: nothing his casual acquaintances would have noticed and probably not even the boys – but it was there. I had known him a long time. Something was definitely on his mind.

Most times we came out fishing, our land-based worries and problems disappeared within the first hour, so for him to still be bothered after three hours told me it must be something serious. To have said 'confound it' was not in itself that unusual, but saying it twice in as many minutes was.

Maybe he was just tired – this time of year was always hard for him, especially Christmas Day. More people than usual crammed themselves into the church with expectant looks on their faces; 'Come on then, Rennie' they seemed to be saying, 'we've decided to come – now, are you going to entertain us, or not?' He wouldn't want to disappoint them; this was his big chance to inspire a new cohort of potential believers. Out of loyalty I would be there of course, sitting at the back and waiting for it to all be over. I wondered what my friend must think of his fair-weather congregation and where they had all been for the past year. But even if such uncharitable notions did break through into that religious head of his, his conscience would have beaten them back with a resounding, 'get thee behind me, Satan!'

Rennie's circuit covered the gold towns of Waihi and Karangahake, spaced three miles apart. Gold towns were ideal places to save souls, because they were full of men harbouring hope for great riches. Kalgoorlie in Western Australia – his previous posting as well as mine – had been a gold town too. The way Rennie saw it, miners just didn't realise that the riches they yearned for were of the soul and not of Mammon. It was his job to help them see that truth.

After his Christmas morning service in Waihi, he cycled out to Karangahake, where he gave the same service again. Deep in a gorge of the Kaimai Mountains and straddling the thunderous Ohinemuri River, Karangahake was a smaller township than Waihi.

On one side of the river were the stamping batteries, crushing ore twenty four hours a day, even on Christmas Day. The 'Talisman' was second only to Waihi's Martha Mine in terms of gold production. Nothing could touch the Martha though – seventy per cent of the region's gold came from there. "There's at least a century's worth of gold in the Martha," the miners would tell me.

On the other side of the Ohinemuri River, perched on the mountain-side, were the shacks and makeshift buildings of Karangahake and the tin-roofed Wesleyan chapel. The noise of the batteries and the roar of the river meant Rennie had to shout to be heard; the same sermon as at Waihi but delivered at twice the volume.

Now, watching him muttering and struggling with his tangled line, it occurred to me that my once indefatigable friend might be finally slowing down.

"I must be getting old," he had said on arriving back at the Manse that day for the roast goose, "because ten years ago I would've been back in time to peel the spuds."

Rennie was forty seven years old now, so I suppose it was to be expected. I was feeling it at forty one; the muscles complaining more than they used to. Physical challenges which would once have been a formality now felt like major feats. It was only going to get worse; I knew that from my job as a general practitioner in Waihi. My older patients would limp into my consultation room with their aching arthritic hips and and they would all say the same thing: "Don't get old, Doc."

Forty five seemed to be the cut-off, the age after which things started going wrong. In my time as a doctor I had seen thousands of patients and it was a definite pattern. It was as if people contained an internal hourglass – more a '45 yearglass' – which simply ran out of sand one day. From that point on it was all downhill. If you had been a caveman in prehistory, forty five would have been very old. It was old for modern man too – yes, we had medicines and vaccines and surgery now, but the human body was still the same apparatus. A sobering thought, especially as the aforementioned age came ever closer. At least I still had four 'good' years left.

"Forget changing the bait, son," Rennie said to Manu. "Fish out on the other side of the boat. It worked for the apostles. That's from Mark, Chapter…"

"… Seventeen, verse 10," I said, finishing the sentence for him.

After listening to Rennie's daily snippets for so many years, I knew Mark's gospel practically off by heart.

Manu didn't move but he didn't change his bait either.

Rennie turned to me. "Do you see that, John? They don't listen anymore…"

Manu waved at the water in exasperation. "Come on, Pa. That was the Sea of Galilee; this is the Pacific."

"He's got a point, Pa," Kahu said. "My guess is that those apostles were probably using the wrong bait too."

Rennie shook his head. "… Not to a word I say."

A silence fell over our party.

"Well, I'll try…" I said, trying to cheer my friend up a little.

Winding my line all the way in, I went over to the other side of the boat, replaced the bait on my hook – a new shrimp – and cast it back into the waters. I let the line play all the way out until I felt the tackle bump onto the sea bed.

No sooner had I set the lock than there was a sharp tug, then another, and then a whole succession as the rod became alive with the struggling fish, jerking the line in a series of desperate manoeuvres to escape the hook.

I jammed my feet against the gunnels and gripped tightly as the rod arched.

"I've got one!"

The rod might break or the line might snap, but there was no way the fish was going to get off the hook. It was a piece of steel two inches long and I had removed it from a hapless fisherman's leg in my surgery the day before. Like Rennie, the fisherman had miscast spectacularly, only he had managed to embed the hook into his ankle nearly as far as the bone. I had used a scalpel to get it out, and put in four catgut stitches. As part payment, he had given me his hook and now it was doing its work on some unknown creature in the depths.

With a hunter's grin, I started to wind the fish in.

Rennie had dropped his mess of a line and was hovering in my peripheral vision, waving the net around excitedly.

"Goodness me, John, the good Lord has blessed you this time."

"It's a big one... Kingfish I reckon," Kahu said.

"It has to be a Kingfish," I heard his brother say in agreement.

Though I couldn't see the boys because my attention was fully on the rod, I could tell from the tone of their voices that Kahu was admiring the drama, whereas Manu was full of envy, regretting not having heeded his father's advice.

Rennie scooped the fish into the boat and we all crowded round to see a prehistoric looking spike-finned specimen flapping around limply on the deck.

It wasn't a Kingfish.

Manu nudged it gently with his foot. "What on earth is that?"

"That, boys," I said, "is a John Dory. A rare fish indeed."

I looked up at Rennie, wondering if he had remembered.

"Also known as the St. Peter fish," he said, smiling for the first time that evening.

In 1900, when Rennie and I had arrived in Australia, we had walked past a fishmonger's stall in Fremantle and seen a John Dory on display. Rennie had said that the black mark on the side of the fish was St Peter's actual thumb-print and I had argued for it being an evolutionary adaptation instead. Although always good natured, our argument still wasn't over; occasionally one of us would inch towards the other's position before veering away again. I was his long-term conversion project. As for my 'converting' Rennie, I knew he was never going to change his mind and leave his God for my world of modern scientific logic. For him, the dinosaurs had walked the earth six thousand years before, and there was nothing I could say to convince him otherwise. It didn't bother me much anymore – he was still my best friend – and to tell the truth, I half-believed there was *something* special underneath all the mess. Science was good for explaining some things but not others. There had been times in my life when I had seen it reduced to a meek pupil in the presence of a greater schoolmaster.

Using a towel to protect his hands from the spikes, Kahu carefully picked up the still flapping John Dory and put it into the bucket to join his two snapper. Manu meanwhile, couldn't hide the disappointment on his face.

"Son, I know how you feel," Rennie said, patting Manu on the back. "Back in England when I was your age I fished all day with my father and didn't catch anything either."

"You don't catch anything now, Pa, let alone when you were young."

"All day I had waited," Rennie said, ignoring his son, "and afterwards I was sulking about it, just like you. Then my father told me a story. Do you want to hear it?"

Manu hunched his shoulders. Rennie took this as his cue to keep talking.

"Good… A fisherman dies and wakes up on a grassy bank next to a roaring river. The river has rapids and pools and is set against a magnificent mountain vista, a veritable fisherman's paradise. There's even a cabin stocked with the finest fishing gear. Then a stranger appears. 'This is all for you' he says to the fisherman, '… fish it to your heart's content. The only condition is that you stick to your allotted part of the river'. The stranger points out a stretch several hundred yards long with two large trees marking the limits… Delighted, the fisherman casts and immediately lands a large salmon. All day long, he keeps catching big fish. Steadily, he wades downstream until he reaches the tree marking the far boundary. Beyond it, the rapids are even more dramatic.

'Can I?' he says, looking at the new area. The stranger shakes his head.

'Sorry… you have to stick to your stretch.'

'Let me get this right,' the fisherman says, 'I can only fish this stretch?'

'Correct.'

'And each time I cast, I catch the perfect fish?'

'Correct again – all day long, every day, forever.' The stranger notices the fisherman frowning. 'You seem disappointed,' he says.

The fisherman nods. 'I just thought heaven might be better than this.'

On hearing the fisherman's last remark, the stranger smiles. 'Who said this was heaven?'"

Manu laughed and clapped his father on the back, and I could see that Kahu was smiling too.

Who had or hadn't caught the fish seemed irrelevant now.

Rennie and I had watched the boys grow up whilst fishing in this old boat; listening to their chit chat, their problems and worries, telling jokes and cheering them up with tales when the need arose. We had witnessed their catches and the ones that had got away, the successes and failures. It seemed that all of life's lessons could be taught in a fishing boat. Though neither of us ever said it out loud, we were there for the boys, and not really for the fishing, there to gently mould their characters – Rennie as their father and myself as godfather – and I liked to think we had done a reasonable job.

Deciding we had caught enough to eat, Rennie drove the boat to shore, steering onto a wave so that the hull rode right up onto the sand of Orokawa beach.

While the boys set about making a fire under the bough of one of the Pohutakawas, Rennie wandered a little way off, and sat down close to the water's edge. I went over to join him.

He had that troubled look again and I started whistling the tune to *I saw three ships* as a way of letting him know I was there and that he could talk about it if he wanted to. But he just kept staring out to sea.

Every few seconds the surf thumped against the steep shelf of sand and washed up to our feet before retreating, while overhead an indigo blue sky was replacing the orange after-glow of sunset.

An island sat squat and dark on the horizon. Captain Cook had seen fit to name it Mayor Island in 1769, when charting these waters aboard the Endeavour, for no other reason than it had happened to be Lord Mayor's Day back in London that week. The Maoris called it *Tuhua*, the word for black obsidian to be found there – the ancient volcanic lava from which they had once made their skull crunching weapons. White Europeans had blundered their way into other cultures, imposing their values and naming bits of land after grandees from their mother countries. I had seen it in Australia and I had seen it here.

Here in New Zealand, there was a different dynamic between the Europeans and the native inhabitants. The Maoris had a word for the white man – the *Pakeha*. *Pakeha* was not a term of derision, just a description, and was used as much by white men of themselves. It simply spoke of the reality as it stood: us and them. The *Pakeha* and the Maori had achieved an uneasy integration, not helped by wars from the last century, but somehow, at least on the surface, it seemed to be working. Better than in Australia, anyway.

"What is it, Sean?"

He took a deep breath and let it out slowly.

"The other day Materoa told me the boys have been making noises about joining up."

"They can't do that," I said straight off, before the impact of what he'd said had fully sunk in. I counted out the reasons on my fingers: "Number one, they don't have to… there's no conscription for Maori; number two, they are only fifteen… way too young; number three, they'll be in harm's way; number four, you won't ever let them…"

The first three facts were undeniably true.

So far conscription was only for *Pakeha*, that is to say, New Zealanders of European descent. The Military Service Act of 1916 had come into effect just a few months before – conscription for all men aged twenty to forty five. Interestingly, the authorities had made the age cut off the same as that of my medical observations in my practice. Somehow, they had known that the human body would perform less efficiently after forty five. I had guessed conscription might come; there had been dwindling numbers of volunteers for the last year or so, ever since the newspapers had detailed the carnage going on out in Gallipoli and the Somme.

The propaganda posters had started to sound desperate. One in particular from the year before had stuck in my mind:

'GET INTO KHAKI.
YOUR COMRADES AT GALLIPOLI ARE CALLING YOU.
THIS IS NOT THE TIME FOR FOOTBALL
AND TENNIS MATCHES.
IT IS SERIOUS.
SHOW THAT YOU REALISE THIS BY ENLISTING AT ONCE.'

This is what they were trying to say:

'COME AND DIE.
YOUR COMRADES AT GALLIPOLI ARE DYING.
THIS IS THE TIME FOR DYING.
WE ARE DESPERATE.
SHOW THAT YOU WANT TO DIE BY ENLISTING
AT ONCE.'

I hadn't been interested.

That summer, right in the middle of the town, a woman had given me a white feather. "You go on ahead if you want to," I had said to her, "I'm staying here." I made a writing quill out of the feather and used it at work.

But the Military Service Act had changed all that and now there was no hiding from it. If you didn't sign up, you went to gaol.

On 15th September 1916, I had to enrol as a reservist in the 'First Division' which meant single men without dependants. With what I thought was a nice trace of irony, I had signed the page using the quill pen. Monthly conscription ballots had followed: or the 'lottery of death' as it was more commonly called. In the December ballot I finally received my call-up. It was the NZ Medical Corps for me – Field Ambulance. Front line – right in the thick of it, apparently. Maybe the recruitment officer had seen my white feather pen and found me the most dangerous doctoring job he could think of.

I hadn't yet had the heart to tell Rennie I was leaving in a fortnight's time. I had tried to pretend it wasn't happening and, since receiving the letter, had been making excuses to myself about the time not being quite right to mention it. Anyway, now was definitely not the right time.

Rennie let out another deep sigh and cupped his face with his hands. This muffled his voice so that it sounded as if he was in another room.

I had to strain to hear what he was saying.

"The age limit's loose," he said. "Only the other day I was reading about a Maori from the Arawa tribe. He enlisted with the first Maori contingent and fought at Gallipoli. He was invalided home, married an Arawa girl and then volunteered for further service. That was when his new wife stepped in and told the authorities he was only seventeen. I have a bad feeling about this, John, and it's a feeling I can't shake. The boys keep talking about a new unit – an all Maori battalion called the Pioneers. At dinner the other night they said they want to make *mana* for themselves."

Mana was Maori for 'honour'. Mana in battle was seen as the highest virtue among the Maori, at least in the old days it had been, when fighting was a way of life.

From the way he was talking, it sounded as if he had already given in to the boys' wishes. As if he had some kind of healthy respect for the concept of mana.

"And where did all that mana get the Maori, Sean?"

He lifted his head out of his hands. "Meaning what?"

"Well… you know the history. All that inter-tribal fighting. At least before us *Pakeha* there was some kind of equilibrium. Once there were muskets it was total carnage."

"That wasn't just from fighting. It was from disease too."

"True. But they died of disease because they spent all their time growing flax in the swampy lowlands to sell to the Europeans… in exchange for guns."

"They stopped in the end," Rennie said.

"Yes… just in time, before they wiped themselves out. They could see what was happening and how mana and these new weapons did not mix. They questioned the use of fighting for revenge and converted to Christianity instead."

"Yes," Rennie said, agreeing with me now. "It was the better way."

"Well yes, better than genocide. It's not just the Maori, Sean, there's mana everywhere. An American once told me that the most admirable characteristic of the English was the way they honoured their treaties and how a handshake from an Englishman was worth more than a written contract from any other country."

"I remember. Hoover wasn't it? That mining engineer in Kalgoorlie?"

I nodded.

"Can't you see what's happening, Sean?" I said. "Honouring treaties is why the world is in the mess it is now. Do the men on the Somme really care if Serbia wants independence from the Austro-Hungarian Empire? What does that have to do with us? The armies of Europe have plunged headlong into their own version of the Musket Wars between the Maori tribes, and for exactly the same reason as the Maoris did a hundred years ago: Mana. Anyway, where's the honour when you fight for generals who sit twenty miles behind the front lines in their Châteaux? You've read the papers… the Somme… twenty thousand dead on the first day. Is that what your boys want? Where's the bloody mana in that? It makes Bloemfontein look like a Sunday school picnic, and that was bad enough."

Rennie stared out at the breaking surf for a long time. Then he started sifting sand through his fingers.

"I've said all this," he said. "The boys don't hear it."

I looked up at the sky in exasperation – all the colours had gone and it was dark now.

At school we had read *Henry IV Part One* and I remembered what Falstaff had said – about honour being just a word – a piece of air. How it had no skill in surgery. His words made perfect sense from my perspective as a medic: 'Can honour set a broken leg? No. Or an arm? No. Can it make a wound stop hurting?'

But no-one cared about speeches from old plays. When I had signed up in the enrolment office it was under the imperious gaze of Lord Kitchener, pointing from a poster tacked onto the wall: 'YOUR

COUNTRY NEEDS YOU' he was saying. It may as well have been a sign on an abattoir door encouraging cattle to go inside.

Once again, my fate was being steered by the British Army. As a young volunteer medic in the Boer War, I had seen war close-up and personal and the end result had been the death of my brother. Now the tentacles of England's misplaced honour were reaching right around the planet to her Southern Hemisphere dominions, to the small gold town of Waihi and our quiet lives. Once again, a war was impinging on people I cared about, even all the way out here to a sandy beach under the Pohutakawa trees – a place which up until now I had assumed to be out of reach.

"Materoa accepts it," Rennie said, pinching the bridge of his nose with his eyes closed. "She says she understands about their wanting *mana…*"

I shook my head in disbelief.

"Listen," I said, trying to keep calm, "there was once a good reason for the Maori to fight – they were trying to defend their homeland back then, trying to survive… but all that belongs to the history books."

"Yes, yes, I know all of that. But this concept of bravery is at the core of the Maori people, John, as you well know from the history lesson you've just chosen to deliver."

I looked at Rennie, trying to work out if he was being sarcastic or not. So far I hadn't been much of a listening post to my friend's deepest concerns.

His comment made me feel remorseful.

"All I know is what I've picked up from Materoa over the years. I'm sorry, Sean. You know all this already."

He reached out and touched my shoulder, instantly forgiving me.

"John," he said, "I knew all this would happen when I fell in love with her, when we got married and had children. I knew I had to accept everything about her background, just as she put up with my bible thumping. You've seen the Moko tattoos the boys have had done. They feel their ancestors calling out to them and there's not a damn thing I can do about it."

If it wasn't about mana, it was about the ancestors, and in that respect the Maori were a lot like the Australian Aboriginals.

When I had arrived at Waihi and offered to be the doctor for the locals, the Maori had thrown a *Powhiri* welcome for me at their main meeting lodge – the *Marai*. I had walked slowly across a lawn to an ornately carved wooden entrance where three women were singing a high-pitched and mournful song, more like a funeral than a welcome. The chief had given a speech and told me, "Talk of your *whakapapa*." When I hadn't understood, he had drawn a picture of a family tree on some paper. "Whakapapa," he'd repeated, tapping his drawing. So I had talked about my parents and then their parents, as far back as I could go, which was only a few generations. Even though it was a short story, the assembled company had listened intently – it was how they understood the person standing in front of them.

Rennie's voice was quiet now, no more than a whisper.

"You know the hardest thing about having children?"

"What?"

"Letting them go. It seems like yesterday I was carrying them around on my shoulders. Before you know it they're not yours anymore. They never really were."

"Come on, old men," Manu said from further up the beach. "Dinner time."

I stood up and held my hand out to Rennie, which he accepted. I leant back and hauled him up off the sand.

"They're still boys," I said. "Don't worry, Sean; Materoa will help them see straight."

I tried to sound strong and sincere, using my best doctor's voice, but in my heart I knew a course of events had already begun – a change in the way things were, like the first crack of an avalanche ringing out around the mountains.

"So," Rennie said to his sons, in between mouthfuls of fish, "since we're talking of good fishermen, I assume you've heard of who caught the biggest ever."

The boys exchanged blank looks.

"Your mother hasn't told you about Maui yet? My God – this is part of your heritage, my boys."

"Tell us, Pa," Manu said.

Kahu put his food down on his lap. "Yes, Pa, tell us. We want to know."

Rennie grinned with all the attention. "Well," he said, "…once there was a demigod called Maui who had magical powers, but his older brothers were suspicious of his powers and didn't want him on their fishing trip. So Maui hid under the floorboards of their canoe the night before, only coming out the next day when they were already well out to sea. He persuaded his brothers to row out into the deepest part of the ocean and, using blood from his nose as bait, cast a fishhook made from his grandmother's jawbone. It sank below the waves and hooked the underwater house of Tonganui, the grandson of Tongaroa, the god of the sea. Using all his strength, Maui hauled his catch above the water. What he had caught was *Te Ika a Maui* – 'the fish of Maui' and this became the land that is now called the North Island of New Zealand. The South Island is Maui's canoe - *Te Waka a Maui*. Having done all this, Maui knew he had to appease the god of the sea and went off to find a priest, telling his brothers not to cut up the fish until he got back. But they didn't wait and started carving out the pieces to get their share. Immediately the fish started to writhe in agony, causing it to break into mountains, cliffs and valleys. If his brothers had been patient the island would have been a level plain and people would have been able to travel easily over its surface."

Rennie drew the outline of the North Island onto the sand with a stick.

"Now some say that the fish was a stingray," he said, pointing out the features. "The head of the fish is in the south where Wellington is now and the tail way up here in the north. The Coromandel peninsula, where we are sitting right now, is the barb at the base of the tail."

Rennie threw the stick into the fire and started to eat his fish again.

"Well, what do you think of that?" he said, chewing.

Manu and Kahu stared open-mouthed at their father.

I think they weren't as much surprised by the story as they were to hear him talk so animatedly about Maori legend and not the New Testament apostles.

"Your mother tells beautiful stories," Rennie said in a quiet voice, as if reading their thoughts.

In that moment I saw just how much my friend loved Materoa.

Once the meal was over, the others got back into the boat and I pushed them off. They were going to row around the headland back to the settlement of Waihi Beach, where we owned a cabin, or *bach* as the locals called them. We had built it in 1911, after they had put in a road to the beach from the main town eight miles away.

After work, I often rode my bicycle out to Waihi Beach, ran to Orokawa and back for sport, and then spent the night in the bach before cycling back to work the next morning. Some weeks I stayed more nights there than I did in my own house in Waihi.

To clear my head of all the war talk, I wanted to walk back to the bach alone – a good half hour's march along the track. I hoped that by then I might have thought of something to say to make Rennie feel better.

I climbed the steep path up from the beach, eventually emerging from the bush onto a narrow path which clung to the cliff edge. By then I was breathing heavily. Depending on fitness levels, I had walked or run this track a thousand times over the years and I knew every gradient, every turn, and every drooping palm frond. I knew how, in the dark, you could follow the way by the silver light shining out from the underside of the ferns lining the track.

At the highest point was a wooden seat set against the rock face, positioned at a bend so that you had a panoramic view of the Bay of Plenty; northwards to Orokawa and the Coromandel peninsula, southwards to the five mile long strip of sand that made up Waihi beach, and in between these points, a great swathe of ocean.

I stopped to rest at the bench and wiped the sweat from my face with my hand.

In the twilight, I could see a string of lights flickering from the windows of the inhabited baches on Waihi Beach. Beyond that was the darkly forested strip of Matakana Island which divided the ocean from a large estuary called Tauranga harbour. Matakana stretched out all the way to the city of Tauranga thirty miles distant, visible as a dim yellow glow on the dark horizon. Over the ocean to the north east, a thin steam plume rose into the sky, white in the moonlight. Though I couldn't see the origin, I knew this was the active volcano of White Island.

Far below I heard the clunk of the oars in the rollocks and the sound of voices.

I yelled out into the dark.

"Helloooo…"

One of the boys called back, "Race you," but instead I lingered on the bench until the sounds from the boat had faded. They must have rounded the cliff and were now aiming for home.

I set off again along the cliff path, trying to focus on the simple rhythm of the march and my breathing patterns. For a hundred yards or so, the plan to clear my head seemed to be working, but then without warning, photographic stills started lighting up in my mind's eye – things I hadn't thought about for many years. Things I hadn't *wanted* to see again. The memories appeared clear and crisp, as though they had been carefully dusted off for this new viewing; hundreds of black, disease-ridden flies in a tent hospital in South Africa, crawling all over the faces of sick soldiers, a moving mass of the little bastards. After returning from the Boer War, the fly-covered men dying of typhoid fever had given me sleepless nights for a month. Strong young men we were talking about, not the frail and elderly. Life was so fragile. That's what had hit me.

War was coming my way; a fact as inescapable as the rip tides menacing this part of the coast. Already I could see how it would be. In Europe there were going to be more terrible events for me to see, more bad memories to forge. Fewer flies than in South Africa perhaps, but more mud and a lot more men. It seemed like a whole generation was being erased in this war.

God, I had got myself into a real state now. I wished I had gone back in the boat with the others; being on my own hadn't helped at all.

As I entered a forested ravine, the temperature dropped unexpectedly, and it made me shiver.

Perhaps it was a combination of the war memories, the cold and the darkness, but a terrible sensation hit me at that moment, another old fear from those days which I had kept suppressed for years.

The Grey Lady was back; at least it felt that way. Sudden cold was her calling card. When the Grey Lady was around, death followed close behind.

I sensed her presence on the Orokawa track with almost as much certainty as the pull of the John Dory on my line earlier that evening. I had only ever seen her once, but that had been enough to set off a cavalcade of terrors and nightmares. That day turned out to be the worst of my life.

In May 1900, after being invalided out of South Africa with typhoid fever, my brother Freddie and I had ended up at the huge Royal Victoria Military Hospital on Southampton Water. We were on a ward in C block, the part of the hospital for officers; being brothers, they put us into neighbouring beds. After all that had happened, we couldn't get to sleep, and so after 'lights out' we would sneak out to the hospital pier. It ran a hundred yards out from the shore and had benches at the far end. Sitting out there, smoking rolled cigarettes and being surrounded by water on all sides had kept us sane.

One night we had gone and sat out in a light rain. Freddie had developed a cough that day, and was coughing out on the pier, but joking around too, and I hadn't thought it all that serious; only when the rain became heavier had we returned to the hospital ward.

Later, I had woken with a start, the way you sometimes do before quickly drifting off back to sleep again. In that small window of time, three distinct impressions registered: one was of being cold and seeing my own breath in the air, despite it being the English summer; the second was of the faintest smell of lavender in the ward; and the last impression was of a monochrome figure of a nurse in the shadows, at the foot of my brother's bed. As I say, this all happened quickly and I was soon asleep again. It was only in retrospect that the episode took on a profound and sinister significance.

The next morning, Freddie was dead.

He must have died in the small hours – perhaps even at the moment I had woken.

Through my raw disbelief I asked the day staff if the night nurse had noticed any deterioration when checking up on him. They had looked uneasily at one another before saying no nurses had been on duty in the night, only male orderlies, and that I was mistaken. Later on, however, an older nurse took me aside and told me the story of the Grey Lady ghost; how she always turned the room cold, how she wore lavender perfume, how the patient she attended always died the next day – *always*. It hadn't taken me long to accept that's what I had seen. Everything made sense when the nurse explained to me what I had unknowingly witnessed.

If there was anything pertinent to take away from that terrible night it was this: there are some things in life cannot be explained, phenomena that don't fit with a logical scientific worldview. Not only that, *death* is an entity; a cold, black, insidious, palpable, silent force. It has no malice – or none that I felt, but it has no empathy either; it's just an icy, unfeeling vacuum with a job to do. Death was in the ward alongside the Grey Lady, right there at the end of my brother's bed. Though too drowsy with sleep to fully appreciate it at the time, I later worked out that death had come for my brother. I hadn't actually seen it, not like I had seen the Grey Lady ghost, but I had *felt* it alright, that waiting presence. My God, the realisation had really given me *the fear*. It's there death is, around the corner, in the next room, ready to take you God knows where, but away from this place anyway. I thought the Grey Lady might come for me too and it drove me half mad, that combination of grief and fear. It changed me, turned me into a lonely, spooked neurotic for a while, truth be told.

Later, when I had been out in the desolation of Western Australia, the fear had finally left me. But even then, I still wasn't quite the old John Hunston. When you've seen a ghost and sensed death in the room you're never the same again. And the fear had stayed away all these years, well, at least until now.

Frightened, I started to run, and when the coldness stayed with me I ran faster. I couldn't escape it though. Death was right with me, easily keeping pace, pestering me – as if it was trying to tell me something. Then, in mid flight, I had a vision – the dark Orokawa track became a desolate landscape of mud and shell craters full of brackish water. Bodies, dozens of them, lay scattered – all still in uniform – shredded soldiers with half their heads missing and their limbs twisted in agonised contortions. 'Here's a sneak preview of what is going to happen out on the Front,' death seemed to be saying. 'Just wanted to let you know… I'll see you there soon.'

I shouted out loud to make it go away.

As my yell echoed around the ravine, a startled bird beat its wings and shrieked loudly, a noise which brought me back into the world, as if a hypnotist had clapped his hands and awoken me from a trance.

At last I sprinted out of the forest and onto the sand of the beach, collapsing to my knees in exhaustion. For a full minute I stayed hunched over, panting heavily and with my eyes shut tight, not wanting to open them in case the ghastly vision returned. When I did look up, it was because of the sound of familiar voices; Rennie and the boys pulling the boat up the beach.

"Hey, John," Manu said on seeing me. "You beat us."

Heart pounding, I acknowledged him with a wave and wondered if he could see my hand shaking.

****

"Wake up," the voice said again.

I opened my eyes to see an orderly standing over me. His breath smelt of tobacco and he had a small scar on his chin – a pale island amongst the surrounding sea of stubble. With a sinking feeling, I realised I was back in D Block.

A feeble milky light was seeping into the ward through the windows.

"Didn't you hear the bell?" the orderly said, his voice hard and uncaring. He didn't wait for an answer because he knew by now that none would be forthcoming, not even a shake of the head. I was the 'Quiet man'.

"You've slept in."

He kicked the side of the bed for extra effect: "Breakfast."

I sat up to show him I had heard and he moved off in that easy, slow walk they all had, one which gave you the impression they weren't in any great hurry to move onto their next task. Intermittent shrieks and yells and banging could be heard coming from somewhere in the building; another patient no doubt, another poor sod to talk down, or coax out from under a bed. I could well empathise with the slothful demeanour of the orderlies – why hurry? We were all so far gone that their attendance made little difference anyway. They would have worked that out on their first week in the job.

In the patients' canteen everybody else was already seated at a long table in the centre of the room and they were all eating their breakfast, heads bowed low over their bowls.

I accepted a ladle full of the grey porridge from the unsmiling cook and took my place at the table. Looking down at the gruel made me think back to a time when breakfasts had been better than this.

Chapter Three

"Mussel fritters please, Frank… and one of your strong coffees."

The chef sitting behind the counter of the empty Mohuku café glanced up from his newspaper.

"Sure, Doc."

He got to his feet, folded the paper and put on a band that swept his long black hair away from his face.

After emigrating from Spain at the turn of the century it hadn't taken Francesco long to anglicise his name to Frank. Nor had it taken long to discover that cooking was a far better way to earn a living than hacking away at a rock face all day with the other miners. Frank had married a woman called Mohuku who was from Niue, a tiny Pacific Island. Mohuku meant 'fern' in Niuean, though everyone called her Mo. She was front of house, the owner of a beaming smile that kept the satisfied customers coming back for more. Frank was usually hidden away in the back kitchen, chopping vegetables, filleting fish, or bent over pans of the steaming seafood chowder for which he was renowned.

"Where's Mo?"

"Still getting her beauty sleep… one Amaretto too many," Frank said.

I was a little disappointed that Mo wasn't there to greet me and Frank must have noticed.

"I'm afraid I'm in charge this morning, Doc, and I realise I'm not as pretty to look at as Mo, but it'll taste the same. Go and take a seat, I'll bring it all out."

I half turned from the counter, then turned back.

"Happy New Year, Frank."

He was already cracking eggs into a bowl with his left hand and stirring vigorously with the right. He looked up again, grinned, and then focused back on the mixing bowl.

"Nine - teen sev - en - teen," he said, breaking up the date into one syllable chunks, talking more to himself than to me.

Outside the immediacy of the kitchen, everything ran to a different beat in this place. There was no rush, no imperative to hurry your drink or meal. The ethos mirrored the laid-back manner of its owners. On Frank's forearm was a tattoo of a Spanish phrase which could be roughly translated as: 'don't over-do it'.

Frank had an inventive way of preparing food.

Kahu's two snapper had been ample at the Orakawa Christmas barbeque and my John Dory had been left over, so I had taken it to Frank early on Boxing Day. He had filleted the fish and put the raw steaks in lemon juice. By the next morning the citric acid had turned the meat white. Rennie and I had eaten it at the café for lunch on the 27th – cold with hot potatoes.

Frank's seafood chowder was delicious, but the mussel fritters were my favourite. He would take raw green-lipped mussels, gathered from the rocks down at the beach, and then add parsley, onion, an egg and some flour to make patties. "Until it's a holding together consistency," he had explained to me once, while rolling them in his hands.

Those fritters and a coffee would be as good a New Year's celebration as any I might have missed.

For as long as I could remember I had worked the New Year's Eve shift, notorious because the miners got into even more fights than usual. But I was happy to miss the party atmosphere and suture up their lacerations instead. I enjoyed the chat in the otherwise quiet, sterile theatre at the hospital. By the time I was suturing, the miners would be calm and sober, the fight and the reason for it a distant memory. They would be lying alongside their adversaries of half an hour before and chatting amicably. Being busy all night made the prospect of the mussel fritters all the more tantalising. Frank and I were probably the only adults in town without hangovers, except for perhaps Rennie and Materoa.

I sat out in the café garden under the shade of a fern whose spiralling fronds were just beginning to unroll in the morning sun.

At the top of Haszard Street the tallest building in town stood silent.

For a decade the thumping engines of the Cornish Pump House had been heard all over town, coping with increasing quantities of groundwater as the mine workings probed ever deeper. In all, seven vertical shafts had been sunk into the bedrock, at least one of them going more than four hundred yards straight down. A network of tunnels on fifteen different levels radiated out from the shafts like a lattice.

Then in 1913 the power source for the pumps changed – coming all the way from a hydroelectric dam on the Waikato River fifty miles away. Electricity came to town, carried along drooping wires held up by steel towers, assemblies like giant metallic beings from another world bestriding the pristine forest of the Kaimai Range. It was an ugly sight.

Now that electric pumps did the job, the pump house was just a silent relic.

The water extracted from the mine shafts ran down the deep gutters of Haszard Street and made a pleasant trickling sound, similar to a country brook. Some of the water was used to fill the public swimming baths, the rest drained straight into the Ohinemuri River and out to sea.

Even though four years had passed since the arrival of electricity, the miners still didn't totally trust this new-fangled power source and the equipment in the pump house was kept in working order 'just in case'. From time to time they would do a test run and the familiar sound would pulsate around the town, a reminder to everyone that, at a moment's notice, they were ready to bring back the old ways.

As a young man I had seen how the pursuit of gold had ruined large tracts of Western Australia. The same thing had happened here too. Rough, dirty mining towns had sprung up in the wilderness – places of disease and poverty – where the poor toiled for the mega rich. Profit, shares, stocks and bonds – these were the words you saw banded about by the newspaper reports on the mining industry. When I had been in Australia, an Aboriginal friend called Eugene had observed how Europeans lived in a make-believe world of numbers, a construction which didn't physically exist in nature. He had been right. We only understood the world in distinct units of currency, time, temperature, height, weight, electric power, air pressure and speed.

Even the newspaper articles on the war focused on the numbers of men killed – twenty thousand on that day, five thousand on another – bare units, not in any way an adequate description of the destruction they represented. If you wanted to get a real idea of the war you would need to have kiosks selling chunks of stinking, rotting, bloody meat rather than news headlines. Each would be wrapped in paper with the words: *THIS IS A PIECE OF SOMEONE YOU KNEW.*

No numbers, no heroic descriptions – just the nauseating, gut-wrenching truth.

It wasn't just quiet because of the redundant pump-house. At one time hordes of men in black woollen vests would have been crowded into the Mohuku café, out from their nightshift and wanting their fill of mussel fritters.

Before the war, the Waihi Gold Mining Company had employed fifteen hundred men, but over the past three years most of them had joined the NZ tunnelling company and gone off to Europe. With both sides trying to tunnel under one another's lines to lay explosives, miners' skills were at a premium. Men had swapped the Number 5 shaft of the Martha Mine for the chalk under the Western Front near Arras. The word was that NZ tunnellers could dig three times faster than the Germans and I could believe it. Having sutured them for as many years as I could remember, I knew how hard these men were; often refusing local anaesthetic during my repairs. A miner had once come into my surgery with a hole in his lower lip, so big he could poke his tongue through it. 'Just a scratch, Doc,' he had said.

Reports from the Front said the NZ tunnellers 'did not take kindly to drill', meaning – I imagined – that they were much happier swinging a heavy pick instead, and getting up a proper sweat.

Frank brought out my breakfast and his newspaper.

"Last week's I'm afraid," he said. "The paper, I mean…"

"It's fine, Frank."

I let the fritters cool down a little, and leafed through the Christmas edition of the *New Zealand Observer*.

On the second page was a cartoon of a Maori solider charging two Ottoman Turk soldiers with his bayonet, the ghost of a Maori warrior behind him. The cartoon was called 'Spirit of his fathers' – they were using *'Tu mata uenga'*, the spirit of the Maori god of war to get Maori youth enlisting. This was the sort of thing Manu and Kahu would be reading. If the cartoon wasn't a mana magnet for impressionable lads, I didn't know what was.

In one respect, I was surprised the boys wanted to go; the Maori princess Te Puea was a staunch opponent of conscription for the Waikato Maori. She had come to town a few months before and given a speech outside the pump house, quoting her grandfather King Tawhiao. After making peace with the English in 1881, he had forbidden the Waikato to ever take up arms again:

'Listen, listen, the sky above, the earth below, and all the people assembled here. The killing of men must stop; the destruction of land must stop. I shall bury my patu in the earth and it shall not rise again… Waikato, lie down. Do not allow blood to flow from this time on.'

The *patu* was a club-like weapon designed to bash in the skull of your enemy. Materoa had a greenstone patu displayed on her mantelpiece, one which had been handed down through the generations. It signified great mana and was on show next to the tooth of a sperm whale; again, an heirloom from her forebears. The tooth – several inches of curved ivory – was pierced at each end and threaded through with brown twine which widened into a rope necklace. Sometimes one of the boys would wear it and strut about the house and the other would pick up the patu and chase him. When you took into account their Moko tattoos and their brawn, it didn't need a great leap of the imagination to see how frightening the Maori must have looked to the British in the series of battles fought from 1845 to 1872.

Rennie came into the courtyard and sat down opposite me.

"Ah, Sean," I said. "Good to see you… and a happy New Year."

He did not smile.

"When were you going to tell me?"

"Tell you what?"

"That you're going off to war."

I shifted uncomfortably in my chair.

"How did you find out?"

"I'm the town minister. People talk."

He was right about that. People told Rennie everything, even more than they told me in the surgery.

I leant forward and tried to sound reassuring.

"I'm not going to fight, Sean. I'm going to be a doctor out there; it's different."

"You're still going though, right?"

I sat back and threw my hands up in the air.

"You think I want to? You think I want a ring-side seat to watch as half of civilisation tries to destroy itself?"

"Certainly not, but you're going all the same," he said again, pulling my plate of mussel fritters over to his side of the table.

"I can't duck out of this conscription thing, Sean."

He ignored me and started forking my breakfast into his mouth.

"Help yourself," I said.

My sarcasm went straight over his head.

"The boys will want to follow you," he said with his mouth full. "You going will be the last straw. Have you forgotten our little chat on the beach last week? All they keep talking about is the Maori Pioneer Battalion. I thought you might talk some sense into them; say something to put them off. That won't work now."

"And I thought you had resigned yourself to them going, Sean. At the beach you seemed very fatalistic about the whole thing."

"I was telling you my *fears*, John. That doesn't mean I want them to go. Why do you think I've not been myself all these weeks? I've been worried sick. I was hoping you were going to do something to help persuade them to stay. Your going off to war is not the kind of example I had in mind."

I held up the 'Spirit of our fathers' cartoon for Rennie to see.

"This is the kind of stuff that's dragging them in, not me."

He glanced up at the newspaper, snorted, and went back to eating my fritters.

I moved my chair closer to him.

"I'll still talk to the boys," I said.

"Don't bother. They're not stupid. It will smack of hypocrisy."

His words cut deep and I flushed with embarrassment.

"Is that what you think I am? A hypocrite?"

"You hated the war in South Africa… hated it. Remember when I first met you – how bitter you were? That war as good as killed your brother. And now, here you are about to put on another uniform and go through it all again."

"Well, what do you bloody well suggest I do?"

The mention of my brother had got me agitated. I hardly ever swore in front of Rennie.

"Tell them you're a conscientious objector."

"What? And get sent to gaol like that politician?"

A few weeks before, a minister from the Labour party had been charged with sedition for trying to repeal the Military Service Act; he'd said that New Zealand workers had no quarrel with German workers.

"Gaol would be better than dying."

"People spit at you in the street," I said. "They give you white feathers and call you a coward."

Rennie took a swig of my coffee.

"So? Laugh it off. You used to."

I shook my head.

"I can't anymore. I'm tired of fighting against it. It feels like giant cogwheels are turning and they're too big to stop."

"Giant cogwheels? Is that fate you're talking about?"

"I don't know."

It was exactly what I was talking about.

Rennie rubbed his hands together and went slightly cross-eyed, the way he did when he was excited. He was warming himself up for a talk on the divine. I could tell our seventeen year argument was about to resume its course.

"You think that *God* is making all this happen?" he said.

I took my coffee back and swirled the dregs around in the mug. Rennie had drunk the bloody lot.

"I don't know, Sean... but sometimes I feel I'm being steered by something. It's as if someone's saying; 'don't fight this... don't fight my plan, because the harder you fight it, the harder I will make life for you'."

"Is that *God* you're quoting?"

I felt my cheeks go warm.

"No."

Rennie chuckled. He pulled out his small black bible theatrically and started thumbing through its tissue thin pages.

"Hmmm... 'Don't fight my plan'," he said. "I know it's in here somewhere..."

To try and ignore him, I pulled a frond off the fern and studied its silver underside. The Maori called the spiral shape of the young fronds *koru*. Always the English word and then the Maori – I thought this way automatically now. If you didn't know both languages then you didn't understand New Zealand properly.

I put the fern onto the table.

"Maybe someday it will all make sense," I said.

Rennie stared down at the fern as he ate my last Mussel fritter and then looked up at me questioningly.

"Oh? How so?"

"You might be right, Sean. I don't know about thumb-prints on the sides of fish, but sometimes it does feel as if there's a steersman out there."

"So it *was* God you were quoting," he said, a big smile creasing his face. He obviously felt he was making some progress with his long-term conversion project this morning. 1917 was already looking up for him.

"I don't know about God. I'm just trying to tell you how I feel."

Rennie kept smiling, although now it looked like one of pity.

"So many 'I don't knows', my poor agnostic friend."

"I might get to see Freddie again if I died," I said, my voice husky and quiet.

He sat back, closed his eyes and started to nod his head gently.

Seconds passed.

"I'm going, Sean," I said, "so you might as well get used to it."

I turned my face up to the blue sky and the warm sun. Perhaps he had heard the catch in my voice, because in the corner of my vision I saw him hold up his hands in surrender, as if to say, 'I'm not going to argue anymore'.

From my inside pocket I pulled out my silver flask of cognac. Swigging from a flask was a bad habit I had picked up from an Australian back in Kalgoorlie – you could pick up all manner of bad habits from Australians. My old friend Dudley's poison had been rum; mine was brandy, aged in oak-casks in dusty, cool French cellars. From a town called Segonzac. It cost an arm and a leg and I had to get it through a specialist importer in Auckland, but who cared? I was a lonely bachelor with some money to spend.

I drank some of the brandy and felt the warmth sink down slowly through my chest.

Then I held out the flask to Rennie.

"I need your blessing on this, Sean. I'll feel jinxed otherwise. I can't go off to war knowing you're at odds with me."

Rennie hardly ever drank and certainly not from a flask in public places, but this time he took it and tilted it back against his lips.

"To you getting through it," he said, thumping his chest as the burn hit home.

After that we sat together quietly for an hour or so, the way we had always done.

Rennie opened up his bible again and started preparing his next sermon.

I day-dreamt, watching my thoughts come and go.

My mention of the steersman had been a surprise to me and not just my God-fearing friend. I hadn't realised I had fully-formed notions like that in my head, but from what I had just come out with, it seemed I may have been skirting on the edges of belief for some considerable time. I couldn't be sure though. How could anyone be so bloody sure?

I looked at my friend, absorbed in the good book.

He was sure, so certain of the existence of the steersman. I envied him that certainty, I really did.

I closed my eyes and day-dreamt vividly.

I floated away from myself and from Rennie at the table in the courtyard, climbing ever higher, so that soon the whole country could be seen below, the enormity of the Pacific Ocean rendering the New Zealand landmass insignificant. Finally, I was so far up that when I looked down I could see our whole pale blue planet against the backdrop of space.

My daydreams often followed this pattern of floating away. Oddly, I found it comforting out there. The feeling was hard to describe, but it was almost like hearing a sound – albeit a very faint one – like the quiet ocean roar you hear when putting a spiral sea shell up to your ear.

From my high point in the heavens I gazed around at the distant stars and tried to tune in to this elemental sound of the Universe, the mysterious tonic note that seemed to pervade everything. Space didn't feel like a complete void. It really felt as though *something* was there, sharing in my thoughts and keeping me company. Was it the 'Word' which Rennie often talked about? Even though it wasn't from Mark it was one of his favourite lines: 'In the beginning was the Word, and the Word was with God, and the Word was God.'

If it *was* God I was sensing, then this way you didn't need a bible, and you didn't have to be on your knees in the darkness of a church. I found myself hoping these space flights might be my way of communing with the Almighty.

Knowing versus hoping – that was the difference between Rennie and me.

****

Royal Victoria Military Hospital, November 10th 1918

I opened my eyes.

I was outside on the patio behind D-block, seated at a table with three other men and we were all basket weaving. For some reason, this activity had been deemed to be of therapeutic value. Some men at the other table were even doing embroidery.

At the far end of the lawn, a gardener was burning leaves. He would rake the leaves into a pile then bend down and pick up as many as he could. The more he threw onto the fire, the more the fire would smoke, billowing around the gardener so that he disappeared in and out of sight.

The earthy smell drifted over to me and my fellows.

While the others coughed and spluttered I inhaled as deeply as I could because it helped me escape once more to another time.

Chapter Four

New Zealand, January 1917

Materoa Rennie was having a *hangi* and a cloud of earthy smoke hung low over the garden, like a morning mist.

Earlier, she had heated rocks in a fire pit and covered the rocks with cabbage leaves. These were there to stop the food burning as it cooked. Next, she had lowered down a basket of fish, chicken and sweet potato - *kumara*, and then covered it all over with a wet cloth and a few shovelfuls of earth.

So far, the food had been 'in the oven' for three hours.

She stood fifteen yards away with her hands on her hips looking over to where Rennie and I were drinking tea under the shade of a pine tree.

"You just sit there, you great lump," she said to her husband from across the garden, more Gallic than Kiwi, with her sensual frown and pouting lips.

Materoa is still a beauty. That's what I was thinking as I watched her tending to the cooking and admonishing her husband for being of no use whatsoever. Blue Moko covered her lips and chin in the traditional Maori way – she had two lines over the upper lip, three on the lower lip and a pattern on the chin – but she also wore a simple blouse and skirt in the European style. It wasn't just her looks that shone. At thirty-six Materoa's character was intensifying like the oak-aged cognac that I carried in my flask. Rennie was a lucky man.

She had been young when they married – only twenty – but she had been right to trust her instincts at the time, because it was clear she still loved him. Even as she scolded my friend now, it was with a sparkle in her eye, a smile and a tone in her voice that belied all she was saying. If I ever ended up marrying someone, I would want to use these two as a blueprint. From what I had seen over the years, the secret was the freedom they allowed each other. No jealousy, just trust.

"Go fishing with your friend," Materoa would say to him. "Talk to him, John," she would say to me, when she felt her husband needed to hear another voice. She would let him go and I would see how it meant she truly loved *him*, not some ideal that she wanted him to be. This liberty had to work both ways though; it was what Rennie had meant on Orokawa beach when he'd told me about accepting Mataroa's Maori background – the mana, the Moko, the ancestors. He knew if he ever interfered with this part of Materoa or tried to control it, then she would wither like a plant being deprived of water. This was not to say they were the same people they had been sixteen years before. Everyone changes, but that was the other secret about their relationship – they had changed together.

"My darling," Rennie said, "you know how much of a pig's ear I would make of things if I tried to help."

"A pig's ear?"

"Yes, a pig's ear, my sweetheart."

He winked at me and lifted his cup to his lips.

I decided not to play along – it was best to keep out of this. The only person who could tease Materoa and get away with it was Rennie.

She was smouldering again, but still with the twinkle in her eye.

Being a bystander during their amorous squabbles always made me feel a little awkward. It also brought home the fact that I had no wife of my own to squabble with.

Self-consciously I stirred the leaves in the old jade teapot which we always used. As well as being an object of beauty, this pot was useful – unlike my friend, who in the eyes of his wife was neither.

The inside had a tannin-stained patina from our years of tea drinking, but the outside had kept its original lustre. I had bought it from a Chinese trader as a belated wedding present for Rennie and Materoa. The Chinaman told me it was hand-carved from a single piece of jade, a mineral highly prized by Maoris, and this made it a real collector's item. The pot had cost me the fist-sized nugget of gold I had kept hidden in my luggage since leaving Australia, a gift from Eugene, my Aboriginal friend. Although I was no expert, the nugget had been worth many thousands, but the price was neither here nor there; the important thing was that Materoa and Rennie loved the jade teapot and used it every day. That was what made it priceless.

I dropped the lid back onto the pot and it made a high-pitched clink. The noise skirted the edge of their silent stand-off and let them both know I was still there and feeling awkward.

"A pig's ear…" Materoa said. "What strange *Pakeha* English is that?"

"It means I would ruin things, my dearest."

Materoa frowned for a moment before bursting out laughing.

Rennie was temporarily bemused by her reaction.

"What's got you so merry?"

"I remember you trying to dance at our wedding. You kept stepping on my feet all the time. You made a pig's ear out of that too."

"But you love me still?"

She walked over and bent forward, putting her face very close to Rennie's until their foreheads and noses were touching.

"Yes," she said.

I had never quite become used to these public displays of affection between my best friend and his wife. It was so un-English. I looked down at my feet and pretended to scrub off some dirt from my shoe.

"You are embarrassing John, my dear," Rennie said.

Materoa stepped back and put her hands on her hips.

"So, John… when are you going to find a nice girl whose feet you can step on?"

I crossed my arms defensively.

The Materoa marriage chat happened every time I came to dinner. Sometimes it lasted a few minutes, sometimes half an hour, but it always happened.

"I have absolutely no idea."

"Sweetheart, leave the poor man alone," Rennie said.

I held up my hand. "It's all right, Sean." I looked from him to Materoa. "I really don't know, Matty. They just seem to drift away."

"You know why?"

Here we go, I thought. "Why?"

She tapped the heel of her hand over her heart. "It's because you don't let them in… here."

I heard Rennie half choke on his mouthful of tea. "My darling, please…"

"It's true," Materoa said. "You're a closed book, John. All those girlfriends you've had over the years. They see you won't let them in and they all give up in the end. What happened to that nice nurse? I liked her. Where did she go?"

"She ran off with the doctor from Thames…"

"What? The fat one?"

I nodded.

Materoa was obviously finding this hard to take in: "…The one who kept talking about himself and didn't listen to a word anyone else was saying?"

"That's him" I said.

The man she was referring to had attended the opening ceremony of a new ward at Waihi Hospital a few months before.

"One of your Type 2s," Rennie said, giving me a friendly punch on the arm.

I couldn't help but smile at his comment. Rennie was referring to a coded system I often used to classify people. It had originally come from my father, who had once told me there were three kinds of people in the world:

Type 1 – those who never think about or question anything.

Type 2 – those who know all the answers and are comfortable with it all.

Type 3 – those who ask themselves what it is all about.

The Type 3s might be restless worriers, but at least they weren't complacent, "and complacency is a bad thing," my father said.

For a long time, I hadn't really understood what my father had meant. As a young doctor I thought I knew it all – I was a classic Type

2, no doubt about it. The Boer War had changed all that. In the tent hospital outside Bloemfontein – knee deep in flies and typhoid fever cases – I saw how miserable life could really be. That was when all I thought I knew, and all I had been taught about life up to that point, struck me as one big lie. There on the Veldt, in amongst the stench and the fatigue, I had started to convert to a Type 3. The clear apparition of the Grey Lady on the night of my brother's death completed the metamorphosis. Facing the possibility of other worlds turned me into a half neurotic Type 3 – I didn't know the answers to anything anymore. And I continually asked myself what it was all about.

I was beginning to realise that too many years had passed since this change, and the more time had elapsed, the more my logic had consigned the Grey Lady to the status of a 'vivid dream'. I felt ashamed to say that I had slowly drifted towards a Type 1 – not bothering to think much about it at all.

Anyway, the corpulent doctor from Thames was a classic Type 2 – and he had moved in on my girl like I didn't even exist. She had luxuriated in this new and different personality, enjoying all the attention he gave her. He was smooth and slick, and of course I could see he only wanted one thing, the oily cad. But women can be blind to the cad part if the bastard is smooth and slick enough. There had been a dreadful inevitability about the whole thing. I couldn't blame her really, for being sick of me I mean – half the time I was sick of me. Restless worrying could be very wearisome, both to the owner and those around. And my encroaching Type 1 traits hadn't helped either – the habit of 'not thinking' about anything. When it came to intimacy I was still an ice man – frozen high on a mountain, cold and distant. In seventeen years I still hadn't thawed out.

Simply put, I had been gazing at my own damn navel for too long. Not cherished her. Not committed. What happened at the hospital party was the logical ending in a long line of small missed chances in our relationship. By God, a few minutes of standing on the edge of their increasingly flirtatious conversation and I had become completely invisible. Seeing it play out made me want to change, try and improve, thaw myself out and learn to love, but the body language told me I was already too late.

Materoa came and perched herself on the arm of Rennie's chair and leant forward to speak to me. She had an arm around Rennie and one hand on her knee. It looked as though they were both ganging up on me.

"Why did she leave you? You're not fat, you don't talk about yourself and you do listen to other people."

I was getting dejected now.

"Maybe she liked what he had to say."

It might be true – the Type 2s had a certain confidence that was attractive in many ways. Rennie, for instance – essentially a Type 2 – had that confidence and enthusiasm which drew you in.

"No. That's not why. It's because you don't let them in, John," she said again, tapping her left chest. "Here."

Rennie looked away. By now he'd given up defending me because he knew it was true.

There was a reason I didn't let anyone in of course – it was because I didn't *dare* to love anymore. I knew how it felt to have it all snatched away. Losing my brother had been a huge body blow and I didn't want to risk experiencing that feeling again. Perhaps the worst aspect was that I only realised how special things had been once they were gone. And so I had a distorted version of reality now – in the form of two distinct sections of my life – my own personal version of the BC/AD split in human history. There was the time before Freddie had died, bright and colourful, and there was the time afterwards, dull and sad in comparison. It shouldn't have become like that, but that's what had happened; a bloody great wedge being driven down the middle of everything. In a way, I had been two different people in my life – the 'old' John Hunston, and the one after. The Type 2 and then the Type 3.

I was so used to the sorrow I had started to feel comfortable wallowing in it, scared of changing and moving on. Freddie's death had been festering for years, like a scar that had never quite healed. I knew it was an unhealthy state of mind, but it was what it was. Except for

Rennie and his family, I had no close friends. I was used to being a man frozen in ice.

"Maybe it can't always be magical," I said, "like it is for you two."

Materoa reached across and put her hand on my cheek.

"It can be, John," she said, "if you open up a little."

She let her hand drop back onto her lap.

It had felt good to be touched.

"How did you know, Matty?" I said, pointing at Rennie as if he was an inanimate waxwork. "How did you know he was the one?"

She hunched her shoulders. "I just… knew."

"You just knew… well, that's just great." My tone had more sarcasm than I had intended. "Sorry, Matty. I didn't mean it like that."

She smiled, but sat back, hurt.

"She's right, John," Rennie said, coming to her defence. "You do just know and there's no mistaking it. No doubts whatsoever. Remember what I told you once… that there is a plan. It will happen for you one day. I've prayed for it."

"You hear that, John?" Materoa said. "One day all that cast-iron casing surrounding your heart will break off."

She prodded me in the chest firmly. "It'll be like being hit by a patu."

The way they said all of this, with such conviction, actually made me begin to believe it.

Maybe there was a woman out there who would understand me, someone who would put up with me the same way Materoa put up with Rennie. Maybe there was someone who, despite all my foibles, would love me no matter what.

"Ah… there it is," Materoa said. "That's the smile they'll want to see."

Tousling my hair affectionately, she turned and walked back across the garden to look after the hangi.

The fact that Rennie and Materoa wished me to experience the same spell that had been cast upon them pleased me greatly – it meant they wished all the world's treasures upon me, in terms of love and not money. It was the best thing that they could think of. Perhaps they were right and I just hadn't had the chance to find out yet.

The best thing I had ever felt was hope. I found it right at the bottom of Pandora's Box when I had been out in the desert of Western Australia. But like all experiences, it had faded in my memory and was impossible to recapture.

Try to change, I said to myself, *try to leave it behind*.

By sheer force of will, I turned my attention back onto my friends there in the garden, rather than dwelling on sad things.

"Tell me how you two met again," I said to them, looking forward to the retelling of the tale once more.

I had never tired of hearing about Rennie's first meeting Materoa and how it had been love at first sight.

Before his arrival in New Zealand in early 1901, it had been a rough few months for Rennie. He had caught typhoid fever in Western Australia and for a week his brow had burned at temperatures conducive to strange hallucinations, 'of the type that would cause a man to write Revelations,' he would later reflect. As soon as he was out of danger, he'd been moved to a Wesleyan Convalescent Home overlooking Cottesloe beach in the suburbs of Perth. During his recovery, he had received orders to take up a new position in New Zealand, something he had initially thought of as a demotion. But it would turn out the Wesleyan hierarchy were not going soft on their charge – the Waihi and Karangahake circuit on the North Island of New Zealand was as tough as anything Australia had to offer.

Materoa had been one of the three women singing at his welcome at the town Marai. Still weak, Rennie had walked slowly up the path towards the entrance where they were singing for him. On the approach, he had wondered if attending such a native ceremony would draw frowns from his Church superiors, but decided then and there that the Maoris needed to hear God's word as much as the *Pakeha*. After that he was able to relax and look about him.

He hadn't noticed Materoa at first because she had been shielded by the other two plump Maori women. It was only after the speeches, when everyone lined up for the *hongi*, that he first saw her. The hongi involved pressing your nose and forehead against everyone else's – the Maori equivalent of a hand-shake. It had felt a lot more intimate than that. When Rennie had pressed his face against the young Maori woman's with the strange tattoo, something significant had happened; he'd described it to me as if a current of electricity had relayed back from the connection points where their skin was touching and then sparked off in an unknown and – up to that moment – an unused corner of his brain. The French have a saying for what had happened to him; *coup de foudre,* which means 'struck by lightning'.

Later that same day, as they drank tea and ate cake together, Materoa had told Rennie how the Maori believed that during the hongi the two individuals share the breath of life, a breath coming directly from the gods.

This 'holy spirit' explanation had struck a chord with Rennie. "The breath of life," he had said, "…just like in Genesis 2:7 – 'and the Lord God formed man of the dust of the ground, and breathed into his nostrils the breath of life; and man became a living soul'."

Another lightning strike; it had been as if God was telling Rennie in no uncertain terms: 'THIS IS THE ONE'.

Materoa's family had liked this eccentric Wesleyan from the start, not minding that he was *Pakeha*. A force came out of Rennie – even after the ravages of the typhoid fever – that same positive energy which had attracted me aboard our ship out to Australia when we had first met. This vigour was the reason we had become friends, despite our disagreements on matters pertaining to God and Science. You simply felt better when he was around.

Rennie marrying Materoa within three months of his arrival had been no great surprise, not if you knew him well. Spontaneity was one of his main character traits, stemming – I suspect – from his belief that he was backed up by the Almighty.

The reason for the *hangi* was to celebrate Kahu and Manu's team winning the regional rugby tournament that day.

It had been a home game between Waihi schoolboys and a team from Katikati, a town fifteen miles to the east. Katikati was steeped in rugby legend: the All-black player Dave Gallaher had grown up there and he had been the captain of the 1905 'Originals', a team beating everyone in Europe. In these parts, saying you were from the same town as Dave Gallaher was roughly equivalent to a Scandinavian hailing from the same town as Thor.

I had never really known rugby, but that had all changed in recent years. Now I must have seen more than a hundred hours of it, watching my godsons rampaging around the pitches of the Coromandel at weekends. There was no doubt that New Zealand was a rugby nation – the game seemed to glue its inhabitants together into a united front. One of the war recruitment posters in town was of an All-black player with protective headgear, his foot atop a rugby ball-shaped world, issuing the challenge: 'Let 'em all come'.

Katikati were the reigning champions and, as their supporters saw it, reclaiming the cup was going to be a formality; they had packed the visitors' stand before the game and started the chant: 'EASY… EASY… EASY…' Real sporting buffs would have known competition within the arena is no respecter of past glories and that someone determined enough can upset everything in a second, which is of course what happened. The fastest Katikati player was making another of his spearhead runs. He had already scored a try and was heading for his next, travelling at full pace with the Waihi players trailing in his wake.

Then he had run into Kahu.

The stopping distance had been virtually zero – the player might as well have run into a rhinoceros. The slap of the impact had reverberated around the ground to a resounding 'Oohh' from the crowd. Kahu had managed to get back up on his legs within seconds and limp back towards the rest of his forwards, but the Katikati man had stayed down, bringing proceedings to a temporary halt. As the local doctor, I was called on to check on the winded lad. Holding up two fingers, I asked him how many he could see. When the reply had been 'four', he was led off the field to gather his senses. He didn't come back on. The sheer physicality of Kahu's tackle had thrown the rest of the Katikati team. They had played on in fear of the next big hit, with the timidity of a group of gazelles who have just seen a lion maul one of their own. Taking full advantage of their psychological edge from that moment on, the ragtag Waihi team had gone on to secure a historic victory.

Kahu and Manu wandered out into the garden and put their kit-bags down on the grass. The bags were hand-woven with flax, the same type Materoa had used to hold the food in the *hangi* and which she also took with her whenever she went gathering green-lipped mussels from the beach.

"Ah… finally," Materoa said from over by the fire pit.

Manu's face was scuffed and rubbed from all the mauling and scrimmaging of the game.

"Sorry we're late, Ma," he said. "There was a celebration in the clubhouse."

Materoa then talked in Maori to Manu and he went over to the *hangi*. She handed him a spade and looked up at the sun, trying to judge how long the food had been in the oven.

Kahu limped over to where Rennie and I were sitting.

I got to my feet.

"Congratulations," I said, patting Kahu on the back.

Rennie pulled himself up off his chair and bear-hugged his son.

"Quite some game, son" he said, "quite some game."

"Thanks, Pa."

I noticed him wince slightly under his father's grip. "Hurt?"

"Just a knock," he said with a shrug.

Manu came over from the *hangi*, still holding the shovel.

"That Katikati lad didn't know what day it was," he said. "Kahu's tackle won us the match – their number ten was their best player up to that point… running circles round us."

From the bottom of the garden, Materoa called out, "Kahu can you bring the plates out of the kitchen? We'll eat in the garden. It's such a nice evening."

"Yes, Ma," he said, obediently limping off into the house.

"Manu… What are you doing over there?"

"Coming, Ma."

He went back over to the *hangi* and started to shovel away the layer of earth above the pit so rapidly that it only took him a few moments to reach the food.

I had read that the Maori pioneer unit could disappear completely below ground level in the space of an hour. More than six feet. They were already called the 'digging battalion' or 'diggers' and now the whole of the Anzac forces had picked up the nickname. This skill was nothing new – Materoa liked to tell of how in 1864 her ancestors had dug an elaborate system of trenches while fighting the British for the Upper Waikato, completely bamboozling the general in charge.

The smell of *hangi* food reminded me of burnt earth.

In Western Australia, Eugene – the same man who had given me the gold nugget – had also cooked me a kangaroo in a fire pit covered over with dirt. The ancestors, the cooking – these were the similarities between the two indigenous peoples. The one big difference was how the Aboriginals and the Maoris mixed with the Europeans. You could analyse it a hundred different ways. For me, I suspected that the 'world of numbers' had been too alien a concept for the Aboriginals to get their heads round; and they had not quite grasped the fact that, from the white man's perspective, there had to be winners and losers. On the other hand, before the arrival of Europeans, the Maori had been used to fighting neighbouring tribes. They knew exactly what it meant to win and lose and this aggression had earned them a treaty in 1840 with the British. Though the Maori Wars continued for another thirty years, a mutual respect between the two peoples had been forged. Of the two neighbouring countries, New Zealand seemed to be the one which had gone forward; the treaty agreeing that all should live and work together as one nation. As far as I could make out, Australia had gone down a different path.

The celebration of the big win was the official reason for the *hangi* that night – but there was another reason Rennie had gathered us together. The time had come to break the news to the boys about my imminent departure to Europe.

I picked at the chicken on my plate and watched the family I knew so well, chatting and eating their meals happily. Despite the fact that these four were the only people in the world who cared whether I went to war or not, more than ever before I realised that I was just an add-on to the Rennie family. When it came down to it I had nobody; no children to worry about, no wife, no living relatives. No God. I was a so-called 'First Division enroller' – a single man with no dependants.

It struck me I had nothing to lose at all and I actually felt relief. I wasn't frightened of dying anymore. The Grey Lady could come for me if she wanted. I felt ready now.

When we had finished eating, Rennie put his plate down on the ground and cleared his throat, the same way he did when he was about to give a sermon. He caught Materoa's eye and she gave a small nod. I had been dreading this moment all day and tried to sink lower into my chair.

"Boys, John has something to tell you…"

The noise of the cutlery on the plates stopped and Rennie's sons both looked up at me. They were sitting cross-legged on the lawn.

Kahu's features were filled with concern because he had heard the trepidation in his father's voice.

"What's happened?"

"He's joined up, bru," Manu said.

It was an easy enough guess to make I suppose. I thought about saying something, but changed my mind and just nodded back at them to confirm it.

For a long time there was just silence in the garden. A Tui bird started up and a gentle whistle came out from the trees.

It was Manu who spoke again. "Aren't you too old?"

I shrugged. "Apparently not."

His question reminded me of the time I told my colleagues in Harley Street that I was going off to the Boer War and asked if they were interested in going too. "Good God, JH," the senior partner had said, "middle age men going off to war? What a vulgar notion!"

"This is weird," Kahu said.

"I'm not fighting, boys. I'm going as a doctor; so you don't have to worry. I'll be safe."

"I've read about the medical teams," Manu said. "Their field ambulance units are right up near the front lines."

I noticed that they both had expressions approaching awe. Materoa had seen it too. Abruptly, she stood up and took her plate into the kitchen. Rennie watched her go and shook his head.

"Not like the soldiers, boys. He'll be behind all that."

"Uncle John," Kahu said, "I thought you didn't want to go. I remember that lady in the street giving you a white feather and you laughing about it."

The boys often referred to me as 'uncle', probably because their father and I were like brothers.

I thought about what he had said for a moment, trying to get it straight in my head how I would reply.

"You're right, Kahu. To tell you the truth I don't really want to go. I've been in a war before and it isn't all it's cracked up to be. But now they've told me I have to go; it's either that or get sent to gaol. So that's it."

"I've heard the Germans have 'In Treue fest' written on their belt buckles," Manu said, from out of nowhere.

Now it was Rennie's turn to look concerned.

"It's German for 'in true faith'," Manu said, thinking his father did not know.

Rennie already knew what it meant, and it wasn't the reason he was frowning. Sure enough, the question he must have been anticipating followed on.

"Who's right, Pa?" Manu said. "Whose side is God on? Why would God even pick sides?"

On hearing this, I decided to look up at the sky and pretend I wasn't there.

"I have absolutely no idea, son," I heard Rennie say. "But I know Jesus said how nation would rise against nation and kingdom against kingdom… all sorts of terrible things would happen… that even children would rise up against their parents, and cause them to be put to death."

He opened up his bible.

"'*But in those days, after that tribulation, the sun shall be darkened, and the moon shall not give her light. And the stars of heaven shall fall, and the powers that are in heaven shall be shaken.*'"

"Sounds grim," Manu said.

"Yes," Rennie said. "But at the end of the passage Jesus said that he would come again."

He quickly found the place he was looking for.

"'*…and then shall they see the Son of Man coming in the clouds with great power and glory. And then shall he send his angels, and shall gather together his elect from the four winds, from the uttermost part of the earth to the uttermost part of heaven.*' It won't matter if they are from Germany or New Zealand boys."

I was still gazing up at the sky, watching the clouds and I opened my mouth before thinking.

"A man coming through clouds… you really believe that?"

"He'll come back one day, John."

"Well, if he ever does, I'll be the first to apologise for having had '*nicht in treue fest*' carved onto my heart for so long."

I could almost feel Rennie's reaction to my blasphemy and the torment it caused him. "God is with you, John. Always has been."

I shook my head. "I'm not like you, my friend. You are what they call a doer of the Word. I just hear it and make fun of it."

On hearing this, Rennie stood up and took his plate inside, leaving the boys and me sitting in silence. I felt a burning shame for having upset my closest two friends.

Damn it. I had spoilt everything.

****

Royal Victoria Military Hospital, November 10th 1918

'Be ye doers of the word, not hearers only'.

That was the advice carved into the mahogany pulpit of the hospital chapel.

I stared at the words as the sermon washed over me; the chaplain's voice an indistinct echoing drawl.

Back in 1900 my brother and I had sat on these pews and read that very same inscription. On the day Freddie had been decorated – his South Africa medal being pinned to his lapel by Queen Victoria herself – we had visited this chapel. It was a quiet place which, much like the pier, gave us space to think. There, sitting in a pew near the pulpit, Freddie had talked to me of the war; how he had shared his chocolate with an Indian stretcher bearer after the battle of Spion Kop, how he had encountered a group of Australian soldiers in Cape Town and what it had felt like to be shot.

As the congregation bowed their heads for the Lord's Prayer I tried to say it too, but the words were not there. I was still mute.

God still wasn't helping me. Perhaps it was because I had made fun of his words for so long.

Afterwards, the D-block men and I walked over to the hospital cemetery to attend the burial. We had been sitting through a funeral service, you see. The week before, a D-block patient had thrown himself over the upstairs bannister rail and landed on his head on the stone floor below. At least he was out of his misery.

Standing back a little way from the crowd, I turned and looked over to the Boer War section where Freddie was buried. Seeing the grave didn't stir up much of a reaction; my mind was too numb. Instead I remembered how he had once lived in the forests of New Zealand before becoming a soldier. The trees in the wood beyond the graveyard were spindly and short, nothing like the giants in New Zealand.

What had those trees been called?

No matter how hard I tried, I couldn't remember the name – patients from D-block were liable to forget a lot of things in their mind fog – but at least I could remember climbing the mountain where the giants grew.

Chapter Five

I leant against a rock and examined my forearms, clammy with sweat and covered in criss-cross scratches from the gorse bushes lining the mountain track. There wasn't much room to move around up here on the summit ledge, it was just a small space with steep drops on all sides. A warm wind was blowing against the side of the mountain and making strange whistling sounds as it found small gaps within the rock face. At two and a half thousand feet, I could see the whole Coromandel Peninsula – the barb on the mythological sting ray of the North Island, as Rennie had described in his story of Maui. To the north was Mount Moehau, to the south Mount Te Aroha – all in a sixty mile sweep.

I took a swig from my drinking can – it had been a three hour climb under a strong sun and I had been perspiring heavily, my hair sticking to my head and my shirt to my back. The sweat stung the scratches on my arms and so I doused them in water from the can too. It had once belonged to a man who had fought for the Boers and whom I had later treated in Kalgoorlie. Most things I owned seemed to be mementos from another era, as if part of me wanted to live back in that time.

I watched as the drops of water evaporated on the ground by my foot. 'Rhyolite' – that's what they called the rock in these parts – formed by volcanos millions of years before; Maui's brothers dividing up the giant stingray. The sun was drying the cleaned cuts on my forearms too, my skin tightening like a drum.

"Bloody gorse" I said out loud.

The damn stuff had been introduced to the country by well-meaning Scottish immigrants around a hundred years ago, and in some places it had completely taken over – finding a foothold with ease, since none of its natural competitors were out here. Once this place would have been much more barren, with just a few grasses and ferns that could tolerate the altitude. The gorse and the cuts and the sweat were all just minor hardships, the real reason I was cursing an innocent plant was because I could not find what I had come up here to see.

Ever since arriving in New Zealand I had meant to climb the 'Pinnacles'. But I had let things drift; life had always got in the way and years had passed. It was only now I was about to leave the country, that I realised there might not be another time. Though there wasn't much positive to say about my conscription, at least it had injected some urgency into my life. This climb was a pilgrimage of sorts, re-tracing Freddie's footsteps to the place where he had carved his name into a rock. Except it wasn't there.

A small lizard appeared by my boot.

"Hello" I said.

It took one look at me and scurried up a rock, disappearing under an overhanging fern which had taken root in a crevice. I pulled away the leaves to see it hiding there, frozen and presumably hoping its natural camouflage was good enough. That was the moment I saw the graffiti – angular and evenly chiseled into the granite like surface. The lizard darted off as I moved forward to get a better look:

A.H. 1/1/97

My brother – Alfred Hunston – had made it. Though his letter had said it would be here, finding it still sent tingles down my spine. I traced out the indents in the stone with my finger and my hand trembled as I did so. Freddie was close by, like a figure behind a misted window, as if I was at a place where the worlds of the living and the dead almost touched. Rennie might have said it differently perhaps, maybe called it a 'holy place', but either way you looked at it, I was sure Freddie was there with me, gazing out on the same vista – sitting where he had felt able to talk to God without shame.

That morning I had woken at dawn and wheeled my old Raleigh bicycle down to the train station.

Near Karangahake, the East Coast Main Trunk line ran down the Ohinemuri gorge, entering a tunnel which ran straight through the belly of a mountain. They had finished digging it out in 1905 and the day before it opened, Rennie and I had walked through. Half way, at around a quarter of a mile in, it was so dark you couldn't see your hand in front of your face. We just kept aiming for the dot of light in the distance, stumbling over the tracks like blind men. Water dripping from the brick lined ceiling had tapped at my shoulder and made me quicken my pace. Knowing a million tonnes of rock lay directly above my head wasn't the only reason I had hurried – I had also thought maybe Rennie and I had got the opening day wrong and that a train was going to come through at any minute, hurtling towards us with no escape route available.

At Paeroa I changed train and headed north towards the large town of Thames, twenty miles away across the Hauraki plains. The flat, green landscape reminded me of the English Weald, although towards the end of the journey the mountains of the Coromandel reared up to the right of the carriage and then it was not like Southern England at all. From Thames, I cycled up the valley road into the mountains; when the track became too steep, I leant the bicycle up against a tree and continued onwards by foot.

Two-thirds of the way up the mountain, I found a derelict logger's shed, half hidden by bush growth. There was a wooden sign-post bearing the words 'HYDRO CAMP' lying on the ground, confirming it was the place where Freddie had lived briefly back in the 1890s.

Several of the wall panels were broken and cracked, and parts of the roof had fallen in. Inside the shell of the building some of the wooden bunk frames were still there, although ferns were growing out from the dirt floor into the gaps where the mattresses had once been. A wide stone fireplace and corrugated iron chimney were undamaged. Some carbonised logs from the last fire lay scattered around the hearth.

To one side of the ruin was a rusty metal tub set up off the ground at each end by piles of rocks and half full of stinking rain water. Beyond the camp, the mountain dropped away steeply and on the other side of the valley was a curious outcrop of rock, shaped like a giant egg – an old volcano which seemed to have turned to stone just as the magma bubbled out.

I sat down on a tree stump and rummaged around in my rucksack, feeling the ghosts of the loggers at my shoulder. Now I had made it this far, I wanted to read Freddie's letter again. I opened the old Boer War chocolate tin which had once belonged to him and took out its precious contents; his letters, which had replaced tobacco, which had in turn replaced the original chocolate. Rifling through them I found the one I was after, written almost twenty years ago to the day.

New Zealand, Jan 1897
Dear John,

I arrived in this country a few months ago and for the last few weeks have lived in the mountains of the Kauaeranga River Valley near to the town of Thames, my temporary abode an old loggers hut called the 'Hydro Camp'.

Let me tell you something of my adventures:

In November I climbed a volcano called Mount Ngauruhoe further south of here – it just had to be climbed… the perfect symmetrical cone. As I stood there at the crater's edge on the summit, its neighbour not three miles away erupted spectacularly. A great smokestack of ash climbed into the sky and the noise – it was something indescribable. By God, brother, though it had taken me two hours to get to the top, I sprinted down that black scree in twenty minutes flat and didn't stop running for at least five miles!

Enough drama – let me explain how I came to live in a cabin all on my own. I had been asking around in the hotels in town for cheap accommodation since my resources are next to nil. Someone overheard and told me of a place where I could live for free if I didn't mind walking a few miles. He wore a black woollen vest and had arms like a circus strongman – said he'd once stayed there until a man from his logging crew got the sack and set fire to the forest in 1888. The whole operation was abandoned, he said, but the hut was still there and unused.

So I bought some supplies and hiked up into the mountains until I found the place. The fire didn't get to it – and it was less derelict than I had feared it might be. The paling walls and shingled roof are still intact, as are the bunks inside. There's even a small fireplace with an iron pot for me to cook. When I arrived I had to clear out the old ash from the woodsmen's fires of years ago.

Outside, there's a galvanised tub and once a week I have a bath in it – carrying several buckets of water from the nearby stream and then lighting a fire underneath to heat the water. As I soak in complete luxury I watch the massive dome of Tauranikau to the north, glowing in the setting sun. It is the oddest mountain I have ever seen; a domed volcanic plug petrified in some ancient eruption as if witnessed by the Medusa herself. I smoke my tobacco in that bath and stare at the volcano and, you know what, brother? I am happy. In the evenings I read by lamplight and play patience… I've made a diary of my thoughts… and even drawn a few sketches in it.

This is the beauty of travelling alone; you and you alone make the decisions. Though I could have done with some company for the first few days, I was very content in the hydro camp – finally 'living' after the monotonous security of school life. I don't regret what happened. Being away has helped me grow up a lot and I'm positively trying to learn something from everything I do.

There's been some re-growth of the flora and fauna since the fire of '88, but even so, it is a great shame most of the Kauri trees have been logged, as it must have been quite something when they were here. Those still standing have a 'pre-historic' look about them.

There was evidence of the mass destruction at the camp when I arrived here - a rusty crosscut saw – a tool eight feet long – still leaning against the hut, as if the loggers might decide to come back here one day and cut the rest down. No wonder the logger back in town was so muscular – I could hardly lift the saw myself.

Only a few stands of Kauri are left now, in the hard-to-get-to steeper sections of forest near the Billygoat waterfalls – specimens the loggers couldn't reach and which the fire didn't consume. I feel insignificant among these wonders of nature which have been standing since the time of the pyramids, an interloper in another world where lifespans are measured in eons and not decades. There are stumps in the forest measuring 19 feet up there. The man in town talked of a tree called 'The Great Ghost' which was thirty feet across, alas consumed by the forest fire. He told another story of a botanist working further up the peninsula counting the rings of one stump and estimating it to be more than 4000 years old.

Less than a decade ago, logs were being pushed down the mountainside by torrents of water from tripped dams, thundering on down towards the main Kauaeranga River and onwards to the salt water of the Firth of Thames, from where the tugs used to tow them across to Auckland.

There were times when I was almost convinced I could hear the slow groan of the Kauri as they fell to the ground, their eon of existence wiped out in moments.

On New Year's Day I walked from the camp to the summit of the mountain – steep drops on all sides – a wild place serrated with volcanic lava stacks and aptly named 'the Pinnacles'.

I hope you might get to see it someday, John, because being up there makes you think differently about the world. You can see the entire peninsula – a volcanic ridge running north-south. I am not ashamed to tell you that I shed tears up there on that summit. At last I felt that I had found a sanctuary where the hypocrisy of the world counts for nothing, a place where you can talk aloud to God and not feel stupid. I felt so inspired I even carved my name on the rock.

I am <u>really living</u>!

Life is all about the moments when you REALLY FEEL ALIVE, when everything feels right. And how many of those moments do most people get in one single day? Perhaps one or two, perhaps none at all. Out there in the forest I swear I was living each moment. The way I see it, my being out there a fortnight was the equivalent of someone else's sixty years.

In the end, late one afternoon, I left the camp and the forest and came back to town as darkness fell… And the reason for my change of heart? Simply that I was missing human company after all.

I'm in the 'Brian Boru' hotel spending the last of my savings on a decent bed and proper food. There's a young lady here who seems to like me after my stay in the woods; calls me a modern day 'Thoreau' and I feel pleased to have impressed her, for as you well know 'Walden' was one of my favourites. When I quoted back at her that 'I wanted to live deep and suck out the marrow of life' – well I think she fell for me right there and then.

My plan is to head to the Americas on the next ship – perhaps make my way to the Yukon and the Klondike gold rush, though even as I write I am thinking I may stay here a while longer and try get to know this girl a little better… More soon.

Your loving brother,

Freddie

I folded the faded pages of Freddie's letter and carefully tucked them back into the tin. His story was one of the reasons I had chosen New Zealand after leaving Western Australia in early 1901. At the port of Esperance I had been presented with the option of going east or west – one ship was going back to England and another was leaving for New Zealand. I had chosen east; taking passage on a ship named: 'The Long White Cloud'. Yes, Rennie having gone to New Zealand was a reason too, but Freddie's letter was the deciding factor.

That evening I sat at the bar of the crowded *Brian Boru* saloon – perhaps at the very spot where Freddie had written his missive all those years ago.

The barmaid had recommended a particular brand of beer, and the way she had said it, with the sincere cheerfulness typical of New Zealanders, made me smile and accept her word unquestioningly. "Oh, you'll like Monteith's," she'd said, pulling the drink and handing it across the bar to me.

She was right – the beer was good, although at that moment anything cold would have been well received. The day's trek had taken more out of me than I had expected. From the Pinnacles summit, there had been a two hour return journey to the valley floor where I had left my bicycle, and then an hour's ride back into Thames. My legs were really feeling it now.

Even so, I was in an optimistic frame of mind and it wasn't just the Monteith's.

The higher I had climbed the mountain, from Freddie's hydro camp, the more I sensed the threads of our lives reconnecting. Seeing the graffiti carved into the rock, probably for all time, had been the perfect conclusion to my quest.

I sipped the beer and closed my eyes.

Though Freddie was always in my thoughts, time had worn away at the memories, rubbing holes in them like the ones in the elbows of my old sports jacket. There were just snapshots now, disconnected and out of order. Sometimes I could hardly picture what he looked like; but at other times an image would flash into my mind's eye, crystal clear and perfect. There was one image that I wanted to forget but couldn't – Freddie's motionless body in his hospital bed that awful morning, his mouth slightly open and the tips of his teeth showing.

I had spent hours constructing worlds in which he hadn't died; fantasising how, if this or that hadn't happened, then everything might have turned out differently. That had got me nowhere.

It wasn't only his face that had faded; his voice had become indistinct too, drowned out with static like a song on a worn gramophone record.

There was a time when I had heard him clearly enough; in Australia, several months after he had died. I had been crossing the Nullarbor Plain on bicycle – a wilderness which must rank as one of the most barren on earth – and I had been close to death myself. Out of water, resigned to my fate, and too exhausted to care, I had decided to lie down on the dirt and go to sleep forever.

What happened next made no real sense; Freddie had spoken to me.

"Get up!" his voice had said. "Get up, John, and get back on the bike."

I had obeyed the command without question and roused myself from the desert floor.

For half an hour or more he had nagged and encouraged me to keep on riding and it had only been when a farmstead had appeared on the horizon that I realised he had gone. I never heard his voice again.

I had spent years trying to work out what had happened that day. The rational explanation was that the febrile machinations of my own brain were trying to save my life with a last throw of the dice by summoning up Freddie from my memory banks. Or had it somehow been *him*? Perhaps our two worlds had come within touching distance in that ethereal hour, even more so than on the Pinnacles summit, enough for me to be able to actually *hear* him speaking. At the time, the episode had given me great hope in what Rennie often referred to as 'the plan', but with the passage of time what had happened had been dulled and put to the back of my mind.

I held up my empty glass and, with my free hand, tapped the Monteith's handle.

"Please," I said, catching the barmaid's attention.

After having been alone in the mountains on my own all day, caught between 1897 and 1917, it felt strange to be talking again. Monosyllables were the best I could manage.

At a guess the barmaid was about the same age as me; good looking, in an azure blue dress with a striking red shawl – more a Spanish señorita than a Kiwi girl from Thames.

As she pulled the drink she stared at me like I was a difficult clue on a crossword puzzle. "You remind me of someone," she said.

"Is that so?"

"You don't have a brother do you?"

There was something about the way she said the word 'brother' that caught me off guard. It was fairly specific; the way she'd said it in the singular.

Whenever someone asked me if I had any kin my standard response was to say that I didn't – flat out deny it. It always made me feel like a traitor, and I could almost hear the cock crow whenever I said it, but I just didn't want to get into it; telling people was always a conversation stopper and the looks of pity made me feel foul.

"No, just me," I said, looking down at my dirty boots in embarrassment.

"Oh. It's none of my business…of course…"

I looked up again.

"Not at all, miss. The fact is I have no family at all."

A voice cut in, "Doctor Hunston? Is that you over there?"

The atmosphere in the pub instantly changed; it was as if the swing doors at the far end of the saloon had been blasted open by a chill wind from the Antarctic.

An overweight middle-aged man was approaching the bar and grinning at me in a self-satisfied way.

It was bloody Westbourne, the man who'd stolen my girl.

I caught sight of my own reflection in the mirror behind the bar – the colour had drained from my face, but the pretty barmaid looked even paler, so maybe it was just the light.

In a half-hearted attempt at keeping up the pretence of civility, I extricated myself from the barstool to go and shake Westbourne's hand.

"Please excuse me," I said to the barmaid.

She nodded without smiling, no longer the cheerful person of a moment before. *An odd reaction*, I thought for a fleeting moment.

"Hello, Westbourne," I said, walking over to him.

He was wearing a wide pinstriped suit and his hair was oiled back neatly so that he looked more like a swanky businessman than a doctor. Begrudgingly, I had to concede he was handsome, even if he was corpulent. He was from a wealthy family who had made their money from logging and mining interests on the Coromandel.

Jennifer, my former sweetheart, was crossing the room towards us.

When she saw me she slowed her approach. I thought I could detect a slight blush. Possibly one of embarrassment at this uncomfortable meeting, or did she still harbour feelings for me?

"Darling you're late," Westbourne said, looking first at her, and then down at his watch.

I had to watch him peck each of her cheeks lightly with a welcome kiss.

"I'm sorry," she said, glancing at me nervously.

I felt a pain in my chest; a nagging ache in my sternum where an old scar bothered me whenever I became agitated.

Just hearing the way he spoke to her made my bile rise.

"Of course you know this young lady, don't you, Hunston?" Westbourne said.

"Yes."

"My fiancée, I am pleased to announce."

The imperious bastard had the look of the all-conquering victor. "Ah…"

"Hello, John," Jennifer said quietly.

"Hello, Jennifer." I shook her outstretched hand limply. "Congratulations."

I had once held that hand as we walked on Orokawa beach, barefoot in the sand. But I had never fully *committed*. She had ended our courtship the day after meeting Westbourne, citing my coldness as the reason. Materoa had been spot on.

Standing there, shaking her hand and knowing she was with someone else made me realise I had loved her, and also that I had missed my chance. Protecting myself had taken priority.

YOU BLOODY IDIOT.

Silently, I was shouting at this self-protective, selfish part of my mind, the part that wanted to avoid emotional anguish at all costs, the part that had assumed control when Freddie had died. It had been a necessary move for survival at the time, as the rest of my mind had slowly picked up the pieces from the trauma. But it had become a despot, not knowing when to relinquish control so I could get on with living again. For all these years, I had been guided by this cold, calculating compulsion which always had the final say in decisions of the heart. When Jennifer had wanted more, this homunculus had hammered down its decree like a court judge. 'Remember what happened after Freddie?' it had said. 'Could you take that hurt again?' So I had stepped back.

IDIOT.

The pain in my chest intensified, but it wasn't the scar anymore; it was heartache, pure and simple. I damn well felt like crying. Jennifer couldn't possibly marry this fool. I started rubbing my face vigorously with both hands as if to try and wipe away the scene. It was like being trapped in a bad dream.

Westbourne waded back into my misery.

"And what were you talking about with that nice barmaid that's made you so sullen?"

He said it jovially, as if it was very pleasing to him that I appeared to be unhappy.

"The war," I said, making up an answer on the spot.

Westbourne started nodding with a mock solemn look on his face. "Yes, well… I'm too old to go, in case that's what you're thinking," he said. "A fat lot of good a forty-seven year old duffer like me would be out there. It's a rum thing."

"A rum thing indeed," I said, repeating his phrase and catching Jennifer's eye at the same time.

She looked down and became intensely focused on a knot of wood on the table top.

An awkward silence ensued, at least it was an awkward one between Jennifer and me; I doubted whether Westbourne was a man who let any such subtleties impact on his outer shell. As I have already mentioned, he was a classic Type 2.

Surprisingly it was Jennifer who came back into the conversation. She was addressing me.

"Sometimes I feel as if I should do something," she said, "maybe volunteer as a nurse."

"Good God, darling – I just wouldn't allow it," Westbourne said. "It's no place for a woman."

As I watched her flush from the humiliation of being put down by her beau in front of me, I clenched my right fist impotently and started an internal debate as to whether or not I should just get it over with and deck the man. This was all vanity on my part of course; I had lost my chance with Jennifer, but it was galling to know she had chosen an idiot like Westbourne who would only ever make her unhappy. 'Wouldn't allow it?' There was her future right there. Not a good one. He wasn't going to be taking any tips from the Rennie and Materoa rule-book of marriage, that was for sure.

"What about you, Hunston? You're more junior than me… You going?"

He couldn't just say 'you look younger' of course, it had to be the word 'junior'. Another put down, in its own fashion.

The question was asked in good humour, but imbued with the sort of accusatory tone that made me feel as if I might be handed another white feather. For once it felt good be able to reply in the affirmative.

"Training starts next week as it happens."

Jennifer continued to be fascinated by the table top, but now she was even more agitated, alternating her attention between the knot of wood and me.

"Army Medical Corps," I said, by way of explanation.

"Is that so?"

Westbourne sounded a shade more respectful than he had done a few moments before. "I sincerely wish you well. Bit envious, if you want to know the truth…"

He put his hand on my shoulder as if we were now the best of friends.

"Excuse me, will you Hunston?" he said. "Got to visit the men's room. Now don't you go running off with my girl while I'm gone… *Ha Ha Ha.*"

That's exactly what I'm going to try and do, you bastard, I thought as I watched him blunder off through the crowded bar. Some wit had hung a sign with the word 'LOGGERS' on the door of the WC.

It had been hard to look directly at Jennifer when Westbourne had been there, but now I couldn't help myself.

She was still focused on the table, picking away at it. At the rate she was going all the varnish would soon be scraped off.

I wasn't used to seeing her with her hair pinned up. With me, she would let it down when we were alone. I had always been fascinated by her brown hair, the way it hung over her shoulders, smooth as silk. Whenever she moved it swung around like a loose curtain in the wind. She was so pretty that you had to look twice. Everyone looked at her twice the first time. Initially, just a brief glance, then as her beauty slowly registered and you fell under the spell, you had to look again. Even Rennie had done this when he had first met her. At least he had been honest about it. "Goodness me, you're rather lovely," he had said, drawing an eye-roll from Materoa. Smiling, she had rolled her eyes at Jennifer again and made her laugh.

Jennifer partially hid her looks behind a pair of spectacles, as if unconsciously she had realised the need to wear a disguise or face never getting more than ten yards without being stopped by another gawping male. But in my eyes, doing that had only made her more attractive.

Had I been blind to this? What in God's name had I been thinking when I let her go? *YOU ARE A TOTAL BLOODY IDIOT, HUNSTON*, my mind kept saying.

I wanted to reach out and touch her.

"He's not too bad a fellow," I said, trying to sound like I meant it.

My words hung in the air, their insincerity palpable.

"Jen, you were right about me shutting you out, and I'm sorry... I can see why you left me. I want to change, Jen. I can change. I want to say..."

She cut me off mid-sentence.

"Don't say anymore, please..." she said, holding her hand up and looking at me properly for the first time.

A tear ran down her cheek and I couldn't help myself from reaching over and brushing it away. Then I couldn't help myself from leaning over and kissing that part of her cheek very quickly. She let me do it too.

We stared at one another for several seconds.

"I made a mistake leaving you and I'll wait for you to come back," she said.

Just at that moment Westbourne re-emerged, oblivious to everything.

"Christ is that the time?" he said, checking his watch. "We should be going, my dear. The show begins in five minutes."

He had a bone crusher handshake, like all Type 2 men, sure of themselves and of the workings of the world.

"Look after yourself, Hunston."

"I'll try," I said, massaging my hand back to life after he released it. My mind was still reeling.

Had Jennifer really said that? Had I heard her right?

She was already halfway to the door, trailing behind Westbourne.

"Jen..." I said, raising my voice to be heard above the din of the saloon.

She waved back at me, visibly flustered.

I watched them disappear out into the street and returned to my barstool, completely confused. Should I be chasing outside after her? I decided that I would have to trust her and wait. I didn't dare assume anything, but hoped she would be calling off their engagement right then and there, telling him where to shove his dictatorial opinions. She might be back inside in a minute, holding my hand. I convinced myself that it was going to happen.

Ten minutes later, she still hadn't come back.

****

Waihi, 5 days later

I sat in my consultation room with my legs up on the desk, staring out of the window at the Kaimai Mountains.

My imminent departure made everything seem different; the mountains more majestic, the colours brighter, the scents of the bush stronger. Now that it was too late, I was really appreciating it all.

Manu had been right – there was a good chance that my field ambulance unit was going to be near the front line. I had read how both sides pounded away at one another's lines with heavy shelling before the pitched battles were even fought. The year before, on the opening day of the Battle of Verdun, the Germans had fired two million shells along an eight mile piece of front. *Two million*. The estimates of French and German casualties from that battle numbered three quarters of a million. You didn't need a mathematics degree to work out the odds were not good for surviving a war involving these kinds of numbers.

In my head I had already left New Zealand and a part of me had come to accept the fact that I was already dead. Somehow, by assuming that, the fear went away.

I wondered what would happen after the shell landed, or the bullet or shrapnel hit home.

Going to heaven, as Rennie believed?

Freddie standing there and waiting for me on the other side, a smile on his face and a cigarette between his lips, ready to pick up from where we had left off?

Maybe there would just be nothing at all.

The knocking had been growing louder and at last it punctured the bubble of my daydreaming.

"Come in," I said, swinging my feet off the desk onto the floor.

Dobbs, the town photographer, walked in and I sighed with relief.

General practice worked this way – each patient took a chunk of the doctor's energy; sometimes a large chunk, sometimes a small one, but they invariably took, and by the end of the day your energy was utterly spent. Every night I would replenish my reserves; be it with a beer in the *Rob Roy*, a rejuvenating walk along the Orakawa track, or dinner with the Rennie family at the Manse. Then I would go back to work the next day and have it all drained out of me again. As the years passed I had grown to accept the never ending cycle – it was the way things must be – and though it left me with a constant weariness, I was used to it. With experience, you became more adept at parcelling out your energy, a necessity, since getting older meant you had less of it to spare.

I had seen thousands of patients over the years, but could only name a handful like Dobbs. He actually gave me energy back.

"Dobbs… good to see you. Nothing wrong I hope?"

"No Doc, everything's fine actually – I just came to say goodbye."

"You didn't have to book an appointment. You could have come round to the house; we could have gone for a drink."

"I wanted to make your last slot an easy one, Doc. Don't want you all stressed before you go off to war."

We both laughed.

From the way he was talking, with such finality, I had the distinct impression that it wasn't just me who thought I wouldn't be coming back.

"So… I've brought you a small present," he said, passing over an envelope.

I reached inside and pulled out a photograph.

"Oh? What's all this then?"

It had been taken at the town Marai soon after my arrival in New Zealand. In the picture was my younger self standing next to Rennie and Materoa.

In the bottom right hand corner someone – I presume Dobbs – had scrawled in longhand: *May 1901, Powphiri for new town doctor.*

"Ah… I remember this one. It was in the newspaper, wasn't it?"

Dobbs nodded. "That's right, Doc; my first published photograph. Found it in my archives."

I continued staring at the image, lost in the past. "I don't know what to say."

Most of the other people in the shot were blurred; either too far back from the point of focus or having moved at the moment the picture had been taken. Only Rennie, Materoa and I were completely clear. Materoa's dark eyes burned into the camera lens and, though she wasn't scowling, she certainly wasn't smiling. She held her stomach with both hands, instinctively protecting her growing twin sons. It looked as if Rennie and I had been talking about something profound just the moment before, because our expressions were serious too. How confident we looked, so sure of ourselves.

"We look so bloody young."

"You and the Rev really livened up the place," he said.

"I'm not dead yet, Dobbs."

"Sorry… of course not, Doc."

I held up the photograph with one hand and shook his hand with the other.

"I'll take it with me to Europe."

"I hope it brings you luck," he said.

After Dobbs had left the room, I looked at the picture for a while longer, then put it down and started to tidy up my desk.

A myriad of memories flashed through my mind as I packed away other old photographs from my bookshelf – the opening of the town hospital in 1903 which I had helped build; groups of typhoid fever patients I had looked after; me on the first day I had set up my general practice in the one storey building near the town school and opposite Rennie's church. In the picture I was standing under the large palm tree out front, next to my sign: 'Dr John Hunston DM'. Rennie had taken that photograph. Manu and Kahu were both sitting on the grass in front of the sign – no more than five years old. The time had gone quickly. The years had raced by.

There wasn't much to clear away; stethoscope, otoscope, thermometer. I stuffed them all into my Gladstone, tattered and worn, but still functional. For my whole career I had used that bag; in Harley Street in London, during my first year as a general practitioner, and afterwards in Australia in 1900. I almost lost it then, such were the harried circumstances of my departure from the St. John of God hospital in Kalgoorlie. Quitting town with the bare minimum of luggage, I had left it there, assuming another doctor would use the bag and my medical instruments. Instead, loyal to the last, my rum-drinking friend Dudley had sent it out to me here in Waihi. The bag was how the locals saw me: 'Here's Gladstone' they would say, thinking it perfectly fine to substitute the object for my name.

There was a human skull on the desk which I used as a paperweight, acquired back in my Medical School days. My father had sent it out to New Zealand when it became apparent I wasn't coming home. The skull had a removable top part – what was known as a calvarium – you could take it off by unhooking it and peer inside at all the white ridges and bony lumps. Once I had known all the names.

"Goodbye old friend," I said, carefully placing the boney head into a cardboard box. Saying this made me sorry for myself; you knew you were lonely when you counted a skull as a friend, let alone talked to it.

"Hello? Doctor Hunston? Am I disturbing you?" a woman's voice called out from behind the door, still slightly ajar after Dobbs' departure.

"Can I help? My surgery is over, I'm afraid…"

The door opened to reveal a striking woman wearing a black dress. She was familiar, though I could not readily place her.

"I'm not here for a consultation," she said. "But I do need to speak to you."

I stood up. "Do I know you?"

"I work at the Brian Boru Hotel in Thames," she said. "Behind the bar… We talked last week."

"Ah…yes. Of course, I remember now. You're a long way from Thames, Mrs…?"

"Miss Kate Ingram."

"Oh… Miss Ingram."

She looked down at her black attire and then back up at me.

"I've just been at a funeral in Karangahake… a soldier's memorial service more like – the body is buried in France. He was one of my son's former school friends."

"I'm very sorry to hear that, Miss Ingram."

"Please, call me Kate. Miss Ingram makes me feel old."

I nodded: "Of course. You are not unwell, I hope?"

"No… I'm in good health."

"Have a seat," I said, pointing to the chair opposite mine.

This all felt very odd indeed. She sat down and I followed suit. "So, Miss… um…Kate… What brings you here?"

"I'm not sure how to say it" she said, her voice nervous, "The man in the bar the other night called you Doctor Hunston – I asked around and found out you worked in this town."

"I see. Go on…Kate."

"It's a personal matter…" Her voice broke off.

I could see that she was uneasy – perched on the edge of the chair like a worried patient about to divulge a list of dire symptoms.

"As I hope you know, Kate, everything is confidential in this room."

"Yes, yes. Of course it is…"

I waited patiently for her to carry on but the silence continued.

"Kate?"

She started. Hearing her name spoken seemed to rouse her into talking again.

"Well… I'm afraid I haven't been able to sleep very well since meeting you in Thames the other day."

For a second, in vanity, I wondered if she was about to make a pass at me.

"You remind me very much of someone, you see," she said quickly, as if reading my thoughts. "I think I mentioned it last week when we met."

"Yes, I recall you did say that" I said, completely at sea now.

Kate Ingram looked directly at me. "Doctor Hunston, when you said you had no brother, you weren't telling me the truth, were you?"

Something strange was going on here. In my confusion, I toyed with the idea of denying Freddie again before banishing the thought.

"No," I said.

I took down the last framed photograph from the shelf above my desk, and handed it over to her.

It was of Freddie and me sitting on the pier in the hospital grounds, both wearing our blue pyjama-like uniforms, nick-named the 'hospital undress'. Freddie was smoking. His crutch was leaning against the rail behind the bench and his trouser leg was tied in a knot at the knee because of an amputation.

"That's my brother and me in England after the Boer War."

Her response was little louder than a whisper. "Freddie," she said.

"Pardon me?"

Kate Ingram tapped at the glass in the frame with her fingernail. Her expression was deadly serious. "I know him," she said. "I know your brother."

For a few seconds I had the sensation of falling uncontrollably as if in a dream.

"How?" I managed to say.

"We met in the *Brian Boru*, back in the January of '97… We had a… a thing; a very special thing… He left for the Yukon but promised he would come back for me one day. He wrote for a while, but then the letters stopped and I never heard from him again. Is he back in England? Did he ever get married?"

I scratched my head, and at the same time felt my heart sink, knowing I was about to ruin her day. This woman was talking as if he was still alive: she didn't know.

"I'm very sorry to have to tell you this Kate, but my brother died in 1900."

My revelation was delivered in a quiet voice, with a tone of finality and solemnity that told her it was indeed the painful truth. It was the way I told patients they were going to die, gently but simply, without trying to sugar coat it. Her reaction was immediate and raw; she lifted her hands to her mouth, her eyes filling with tears and then the tears running down her cheeks. I could see it draining away; the hope she must have had all these years that he might one day turn up out of the blue.

Instinctively, I dug around in my pocket, found a handkerchief and handed it over.

I put my hand on her shoulder as she wept quietly and, for a long minute, we sat there together. It was difficult for me to imagine what she must be feeling – only hearing the news now, after all this time. To see such an acute reaction made it feel as if the intervening seventeen years had been distilled into a few seconds.

"It was a long time ago," I said, choosing my words carefully. "I'm sorry you never knew Kate."

"I loved him," she said through her tears. "I got to know him for a few weeks and for one night I loved him, and I've loved him ever since."

I nodded slowly, piecing it together from his letter.

"You met him in town? When he returned from the forest?"

"Yes" she said. "He told you?"

A girl in New Zealand…in the letter yes, he had alluded to a fledgling affair, but now I came to think of it, he had also spoken of her.

He had come to see me in Oxford – a reunion after his returning from five years of travels. Now through the mists of time, his words drifted through: 'Met a girl in New Zealand' he had told me in the college quadrangle. And then later that same evening in my room, he had looked at the map on my wall marked with all the places he had visited, pointed to New Zealand and said: '…the woman I was telling you about lived there…her name's Katherine.' At the time I hadn't really listened because he had also told me he had joined the army and

I was more concerned about his going to war and being shot at by Boers than hearing about love affairs.

"He did" I said, "He told me your name… He also mentioned the *Brian Boru* in one of his letters. That's why I went in there the other evening."

I found the old chocolate tin in my drawer and pulled out the letter, exchanging it for the framed photograph which Kate Ingram was still holding.

As she read it, I watched her and struggled to cope with my own emotions. To meet someone else who cared for Freddie made me feel elated in a way. After my father had died, I had assumed I was the only person left in the world who thought of Freddie at all, but now this woman was crying over my brother and telling me she loved him.

When she finished reading, she looked up at me. She was crying again, but quietly now.

"It's very touching that you still remember him," I said.

"Freddie was different to the other men who came to the bar" she said, "there was his youth and his English accent, but he also seemed so *independent*… so much his own person and happy in his own company. Anyway, we couldn't take our eyes off each other. He was my first love…"

"Kate, if it's too painful, you don't have to tell me all this."

She looked down, stopped in her tracks by my comment, and I regretted my words immediately. I was trying to save her more torment from going on, but I was also trying to save myself more torment too. It was that self-protective mechanism kicking into action once more. *STOP PAIN AT ALL COSTS* it was saying. I felt selfish and guilty.

"I'm sorry, Kate. I stopped you abruptly just then. Please go on…"

She lifted her head and spoke to me again.

"I *want* to talk about him. I need to… It's why I came today. After we had been together he told me he loved me and that he wanted to take me away and show me a better life. He was such a…"

"…An idealist?"

She managed a small smile through her veil of tears. "I was going to say dreamer."

I smiled back at her. "Yes, a dreamer," I said. "That was Freddie all right."

"Being the realist I said we would need some money if we were going to live out his dream. He was fiercely opposed to asking his father – your father – in England for any funds. He wanted to be self-sufficient. You know what he said to me? He said he would go and make something of himself and then come back for me… and I never stopped waiting."

As I listened to this, a big thought sank down through my mind like a heavy depth charge, landing with a soft thud and then exploding. I saw it all now, my whole life so far, how cause and effect had shaped it.

I recalled Freddie's reasons for joining the army – how he was tired of being a 'nobody', never having any money, needing respect, how he could thrive in the Middlesex Regiment. Unwittingly, to prove himself, he had started off down a path that would eventually lead to his own destruction. I even remembered him saying it out on the pier on the last day of his life: how he wanted to be able to look after her properly. I had put it out of my mind all this time.

I had gone to the war in South Africa because of Freddie, to look out for him, and then I had gone out to Western Australia because of him too, to complete the adventure he hadn't had the chance to begin. I had even come out to New Zealand because of his letter. And all of it, literally all of it, had been because of the woman sitting in front of me right now.

Vaguely, through this fog, I heard Kate talking again.

"So what happened to him?"

I exhaled slowly, only then realising that I had been holding my breath.

"He told me everything when we were together" she said, "How he had walked out of that fancy school of yours and gone travelling. After he left I received the occasional letter and telegram from far flung places – of his time in the Yukon, during the gold rush, and how he didn't strike it rich there. I know he went overland to New York. The last I heard he was about to board a ship for England. After that though, nothing… I assumed he must have forgotten about me… or found some other woman perhaps…"

"No Kate, it wasn't like that at all."

She looked over at the framed photograph which I had placed on my desk.

"You said that was taken after the Boer War…Freddie was a soldier?"

I nodded and sighed at the same time, knowing I was going to have to re-tell the whole sorry tale.

"He came to visit me at University in the summer of '98. It was the first time I had seen him in five years. He was in a uniform - he had joined the Army – the Middlesex Regiment. It was for you, Kate. He wanted to earn your respect… I remember him telling me about you. It was practically the first thing he did. He was quite emotional about it all. I couldn't believe my dreamer of a brother had joined up. I ended up becoming an Army Medic so I could go and look out for him."

Kate Ingram frowned.

"Why did he stop writing to me? Why didn't he tell me?"

I thought about that. I knew nothing about Freddie's correspondences with Kate, or lack of them, and he had never mentioned any reasons for not writing. I put myself in his shoes to try and understand why.

"I don't know for sure. My guess is that he didn't want you worrying about the fact he was going off to fight the Boers."

She looked at me doubtfully.

"It fits with the brother I knew," I said, old memories being triggered.

"What makes you say that?"

"As schoolboys we rowed together for years, just the two of us in the boat. Sometimes, in the winter months we would catch colds. When I had one I would moan about it and not want to practice. But when Freddie had a cold, he never said a thing and you hardly knew; he hid it and trained just the same as usual. When I asked him why he said: 'why make it 'a thing', when it doesn't need to be? 'A thing' affects the morale of the team, and that might make the difference between winning and losing.'"

In response, she gave the slightest of nods.

"That's the way he thought, Kate. It sounds mundane, but it's essentially the same psychology as not telling you he had committed himself to the Boer War. He hid it from you to protect you. Because he loved you, I imagine…"

Now she had started to weep again. "Yes, I suppose he did," she said, pressing the handkerchief to her eyes. "I feel terrible. All he wanted to do was prove himself to me. I should have just accepted him for what he was at the time. Things would have been fine and he wouldn't have left New Zealand."

From experience I knew you could drive yourself half mad mulling on the 'what ifs', so I didn't linger on the matter and indulge her speculations.

"Anyway," I said, continuing with the story, "the next time I saw him was in a hospital ship – a shadow of his former physical self, with typhoid fever and his right leg amputated, but still the same old Freddie. We were both invalided back to a hospital in the South of England."

I picked up the framed photograph and handed it back to her again. "That place."

"My God" she said. "Poor Freddie."

"He talked about you at the hospital Kate. He was worried you might think less of him because of the amputation… that you might reject him. Of course I told him that if you were the right woman it wouldn't matter."

The tears continued to come, running down her cheeks and being wiped away by my already sodden handkerchief.

My voice had a wobble in it now. I wasn't used to giving this account out loud.

"Anyway… a week after that photograph was taken, he caught double pneumonia and died."

"You were with him?"

I nodded back at her. "In the next bed on the ward. He just slipped away one night… hell of a thing. Just about broke me, truth be told."

"Oh… I am so sorry."

This suddenly felt like confessional hour, but I decided to keep talking.

"I had a fancy job back in Harley Street waiting for me, but after Freddie died I lost interest in my old life... lost interest in everything. I didn't want to know anymore; couldn't stand it. Wanted to get as far away as possible. Just before he died, Freddie had been talking about coming out to the gold rush in Australia. It was his next hare-brained scheme to make his fortune and prove himself to you I suppose. Because of that, I decided to work out in Australia, to honour his last wish in a way. On the journey, I befriended a Minister who helped to slowly pull me back into the world. Reverend Rennie..."

"Reverend Rennie?"

"That's right."

"He gave the funeral service today."

"Yes, that makes sense. He covers Karangahake as well as Waihi."

"So you both came out to New Zealand after Australia?"

"That's right. He was transferred out here in late 1900 and I followed a few months later. Freddie's time here was a part of why I came too. That letter... It was a connection to him. Can you understand that?"

Kate's eyes locked onto mine, as sincere a look as I had ever seen.

"Yes, yes I can, Dr Hunston," she said.

"Please, call me John..."

"John" she said, with a small smile.

"So that's my story Kate... I've been here ever since."

She gave me the pier photograph and I put it back onto my desk. Then she reached into her purse, pulled out another photograph and held it out for me to see.

A man in an army uniform.

"My God!" I said. "Freddie..."

At least in my makeshift memory it was Freddie, but only at first glance – the more I looked at the picture, the more differences I could see. Subtle ones.

"Not Freddie... my son, Harry."

I had not worked it out yet. There it was, right in front of my eyes, and I still couldn't see it.

She spoke again. "Freddie's son."

The words did not register properly at first.

"Can I offer you a drink Miss…Kate?'

I stood up and looked over to my small stand in the corner where a bottle of Segonzac stood tall next to two brandy balloons.

She sat back, surprised. "All right, yes… thank you…"

I went over and poured us each a glass.

"It's very good cognac. It really is," I said, handing hers over and then sitting back down in my consultation chair.

She took a sip and smiled weakly. It looked as though she was feeling sorry for me.

"John, did you hear what I said before… about the man in the photograph?"

I stared at her and drained my brandy down in one go. Then I put the glass down on my desk and picked up the photograph again.

Freddie's son.

"Did you hear me, John?"

"Yes, I did," I was finally able to say.

When someone is told shocking news, their mind becomes like a medieval castle – the drawbridge is rapidly drawn up and they peer from the crenelated turrets out across the moat where the words still wait in attack formation. Words such as these herald news which will change the listener's life irrevocably. Usually it is bad news; the sort of thing a doctor has to tell a patient who does not have long to live. I had seen the reactions dozens of times over the course of my career. People hearing what was being said but at the same time not really listening. Sometimes the news would be completely ignored, and they would resume the conversation with mundane questions. I would have to repeat it again, and then again; like a trebuchet flinging great missiles at the resistant stone walls. Finally there is a direct hit and the castle crumbles. That is the worst time of all, to witness what happens when someone's entire framework collapses and everything they have taken for granted up until that moment is dismantled. To see them bewildered and frightened amongst the billowing dust of their ruins is a sorry sight indeed. When Freddie died I hadn't really believed it for several hours; I had withdrawn into the innermost chamber of my keep and occupied a twilight world of denial. It is a strange dreamy sensation to deny reality, yet easy to do it. Part of you knows the truth, but another part of you desperately attempts to cover it up. And remarkably, at least for a while, this cover-up persona manages to do a reasonable job of it. The protective survival instinct built into the human mind is an astounding and powerful force.

What I am getting around to saying, in a meandering way, is that the same mechanism sometimes kicks into operation with shockingly good news – seemingly too good to be true, and this was what was happening with me right now.

I peered out from a slit in the drawbridge I had just involuntarily raised.

"Can you say it again for me please?"

"Harry is Freddie's son… your nephew," Kate said, this time more loudly, "born in October 1897. Nineteen years old."

I slowly lowered the drawbridge and ventured out tentatively. I stared at the proof in my trembling hands – the almost carbon copy of my brother in the photograph.

"My God" I said, "and Freddie never knew."

She shook her head.

"No. For my whole pregnancy he was an elusive shadow in the Americas – always transitory. Always saying how he was heading on to the next place. And then – like I have already said – nothing…"

My thoughts were in turmoil.

Would it have helped – his knowing? Would it have changed things? Might he somehow have lived out a long and happy life?

I rubbed my eyes with the fingers of both hands. Now here I was contemplating the 'what ifs'. I knew this kind of thinking was a miserable game to play and best left well alone. I had to try to consign it to the bulging file of 'what may have beens' I had stored in my memory banks.

I looked from the photograph to Kate. "And you're a 'Miss' – you never married?"

She shook her head. "No. I always thought Freddie would come back. Even when the letters stopped coming, I still hoped. Having

Harry was like having him back in a way. I brought him up the best I could. He's a good boy."

"He looks like a fine young man," I said. "Raising him on your own must have been tough."

"Yes, it was."

She didn't elaborate; instead, she bit her lower lip and took another sip of the cognac.

Earlier, on her looks alone, I had seen why any man would have fallen for her. What I found most beguiling though, was how she hadn't been hardened. A barmaid, living through the stigma of being an unmarried mother for the last twenty years, and yet there wasn't a single trace of bitterness that I could detect. This tenderness of spirit would have been there when Freddie had met her and I knew it would have been this quality that had drawn him in, much more than her good looks.

"Freddie would be so proud," I said. I stopped to find the right words. "This news… well, it means the world to me. It means I have a family, Kate."

She smiled. "I suspected it as soon as I saw you in the bar the other night," she said. "You look a lot like him."

"Yes, even though Freddie and I were non-identical twins we looked a lot like each other. I was five minutes older."

"When I saw you the other evening, I wondered if it could be possible. When that man called you Hunston I knew it to be true."

Now I recalled how pale she had become when Westbourne had called over to me.

"It all fitted into place," she said. "That's why I haven't been able to sleep. That's why I came here today."

"Does Harry know who his father is?"

"Yes, he knows everything except the surname… I didn't want Harry to go looking for him, or anything foolhardy like that. I was afraid of what he might find out."

I studied the photograph again.

Harry Ingram was wearing the crown of his felt hat creased 'fore-and-aft' rather than in regulation 'lemon squeezer' style; a rebel just like his father had been. I shook my head in disbelief again – the resemblance to Freddie was uncanny. On the upper arm was a single chevron – a Lance Corporal, and above the chevron a black triangle. A badge with the black lettering 'NZRB' was on the shoulder strap.

"The shoulder flash is the 3rd Rifle battalion," Kate said, seeing me staring. "He's in the New Zealand Rifle Brigade. The Earl of Liverpool's own, nicknamed The Dinks."

More similarities – Freddie's Middlesex Regiment had also been called the Duke of Cambridge's own, nicknamed The Diehards.

"Every time I look at him, I think of Freddie," she said, "and I always will. I'll never forget your brother, John. I knew there had to have been a good reason why he didn't come back to me… Of course part of me knew he might have died, but I didn't really want to go there. I was too scared to find out the truth. So I just kept waiting and hoping, though as the years passed, my hope dwindled to just a tiny flame. And then you walked into the saloon and… and…"

She started to cry again, prompting me to reach to my pocket for a handkerchief, but it wasn't there; she already had it scrunched up in her hand.

"I should have run off with him when he asked me to."

Her face had gone red and blotchy and, seeing it like that, made me want to hug her. I reached over and held her hand instead.

"I came to ask you a favour," she said, in between sobs.

"Name it."

"Will you look out for my boy? I heard what you said to that man in the pub the other night, how you were heading off to Europe."

I didn't even need to think. My answer came straight out. "Yes, Kate," I said, "I'll find him, and I'll do all I can to get him back to you alive. You two are the only family I have left."

After she had gone, I sat in my chair for a long time, staring out of the window at the Kaimai Mountain range.

I tried to remember the feeling I had been enjoying earlier, the fearless state in which I cared not about living or dying. That feeling was gone now, and in its place were the worries of my new mission – to prevent the destruction of my brother's son. I had tried doing the same with Freddie in South Africa and had ultimately failed. I didn't want to fail again. I never felt more determined in my life, but having something to live for had made me feel afraid again.

"Bloody hell, Freddie," I said out loud, rapping my knuckles on the desk and thcn laughing.

Chapter Six

Royal Victoria Military Hospital, 10th November 1918

I heard the doctors approaching the ward long before I saw them. They sounded confident and loud; more so than usual. I wondered what they were doing here in the middle of the afternoon, since the ward round was always in the morning.

As they got closer I noticed a new voice, one with gravitas. Whenever this newcomer said something, the others kept quiet and as soon as he'd finished speaking there would follow either hearty laughter or respectful mumblings of agreement.

I guessed that someone important had come. At medical school I'd seen the same sycophantic palaver which accompanied the professors on rounds. It usually went one of two ways – either the professors assumed themselves to be minor deities or their posse of students did, fawning around them and asking questions to which they already knew the answers.

It turned out the high-ranking man was on D-block specifically for me.

The group breezed into the ward, the white coats of the MOs billowing out like the topsails of a man-o-war. There was no film camera today.

The new man wore a dark suit and his hair was jet black. He looked a lot younger than his voice had sounded out in the corridor.

They bypassed all the other beds before halting at the end of mine.

"This is the intractable case we need your help with, Professor," one of the MOs said. "Hysterical mutism and dysgraphia; in fact the first time we tried to get him to write, he became so frustrated that he snapped the pencil in half."

"Did he indeed?" the professor said, staring at me and not the MO.

He sat down on the bed and studied me more closely, his face expressionless.

"Yes, Professor… I'm afraid to report that after this incident he refused to co-operate with us further… Been in his own world for nearly a year. He is almost inaccessible and frequently makes grimaces as though he is afraid of something."

I watched as the professor removed his black rimmed spectacles and started polishing them with his handkerchief. He breathed warm air onto the lenses and polished them a little more. As far as I could make out, the professor's eyes were black too. He finished cleaning his glasses and put them back on.

"Refused to co-operate," he said, smiling now and watching me like a leering bird of prey. "Go on," he said to the MO.

"He won't even acknowledge us with a nod or a shake of his head. We've tried everything, Professor."

"Where was he picked up?"

"What do you mean?"

"I mean from which part of the front?"

The MO rifled through the notes and found the brown field medical card; a record initiated at the time I was first assessed, and which had accompanied me throughout my evacuation from the front lines.

"Let me see… he was found near Passchendaele, in the Ypres Salient."

The professor held out his hand to the MO, but didn't take his gaze off me.

"May I?"

"Of course, Professor."

The professor started to read it to himself, every few seconds glancing up at me before reading on. The card was no more than a short summary of my stops at medical facilities down the chain. When the professor finished, he handed back the field medical card the same way he had asked for it, with his eyes trained on mine and his arm outstretched to the MO.

"His card, gentlemen," the professor said, "starts on October 13th at a Dressing Station just outside Ypres."

Both MOs studied the relevant entry which had been scrawled in longhand by the duty doctor.

"Unknown British Soldier NYDN," one of them said, reading it out loud. "And what do you deduce from that, Professor?"

"Well, I deduce that the event which resulted in this man's mental injury probably occurred a day or two before he was brought in."

"But Third Ypres was a battle which lasted over three months, Professor."

"Yes, yes, yes… but there were battles within the battle, Doctor. It can be narrowed down. There was an attack on the 12th October at one of the ridges leading up to Passchendaele – at a place called Bellevue Spur, if my memory serves me correctly. I read about it in the papers. 'New Zealand's blackest day' was the headline used."

My hands started to tremble.

"Gentlemen, I wonder if we might in fact be dealing with a New Zealander and not a Brit at all."

The MO scoured the field medical card.

"He was found with no ID tags or recognisable uniform. For all we know he could be a Fritz, Professor."

The professor smiled and held my quivering hand in both of his. His hands were warm. He leant forward.

"Bist du Deutscher?"

Almost imperceptibly, I shook my head.

"Ah… You see, gentlemen? Already we are making progress… He is not a Fritz!"

Both MOs flushed crimson with embarrassment and I drew some satisfaction from their reaction. In two minutes this professor had made more progress with my case than they had managed in a year. They still had no clue why I had been conducting my own silent vendetta against them in all that time. It wasn't *what* they had done to me; it was *the way* they had done it.

The two D block doctors had failed at the first hurdle; they had given nothing of *themselves* and had kept me at arm's length. To treat someone properly, you had to transmit something of yourself, some part of your energy. Twenty years of general practice had taught me that fundamental law. It was more important than the drugs. For a patient, there had to be this perceived transmission of commitment – the sense that the doctor *actually cared*. I had not felt anything from the MOs, except for an aloofness bordering on derision. The way I saw it, these doctors only cared about their gilt-edged reputations and research publications, not my well-being. The two of them may as well have been a pair of automatons. They were never going to become exhausted by the job because they weren't expending any genuine emotion. I felt nothing from them. My subconscious dictated that if the doctors looking after me weren't going to *really* try, then neither was I.

"Why, that's astounding, Professor. Nothing we've done has elicited the slightest reaction – not even electricity. We tried it soon after he was admitted to D-block."

"You weren't doing it properly then," the professor said, with a bluntness that made the MOs stare down at their shoes in an awkward silence.

I was aware that the professor was still holding my hand in his; giving me his commitment, winning my trust.

"So… you're not a German. A New Zealander perhaps?"

Slowly I nodded.

"Very good," the Professor said, smiling. "You're already making excellent progress."

He turned his attention to the two doctors standing there with their mouths wide open in astonishment.

"Are you taking this down, *Boswell?*" he said in a disparaging tone to the MO holding the notes.

I smiled inwardly. More sweet revenge. The flustered MO started scrabbling around in the pockets of his white coat for something to write with.

"Oh God," the Professor said, barely able to contain his impatience. "Here, use mine."

He held out an ink pen. Black ink no doubt, I thought to myself, to go with his black eyes and his black hair and suit. On the side of the pen I could make out part of an inscription: *'Professor S'*, but was unable to make out the surname. I would think of him as that then: an initial.

"Now take this down," Professor S said, starting to dictate. "Patient X is a New Zealander and has started to communicate using nods and shakes of the head. Have you got that?"

"Yes, Professor."

"It's the tenth of November 1918. This man was admitted here on October twenty-third 1917, more than a year ago. Why didn't you call me down sooner?"

"Well, Professor," the MO with the notes said, glancing sideways at his colleague for back-up. "We assumed if the electricity didn't work straight away then it wasn't going to at all. We didn't want to bother you."

"Yes, that's what happened," the other MO said. "Electricity was a non-starter."

The professor raised his voice a notch.

"Not true. It always works in the hands of a skilled operator."

"Yes, of course. I'm sorry, Professor. Of course we should have contacted you. It's our mistake entirely."

I was actually beginning to feel sorry for Tweedledum and Tweedledee. No-one wanted to watch too much humiliation. The apology had been made, and even though it hadn't been made directly to me, I knew my vendetta was over.

"Not to mind," the professor said. "It's not too late."

I noticed he wasn't holding my hand any longer.

"Now you listen to me, New Zealander," he said, his tone somewhat stern with me now too. "I work in a laboratory, not the test tubes and Bunsen burner type of laboratory mind you, but the type of laboratory geared to dealing with patients like you; men who have come back damaged from the war. Where I work at the National Hospital in Queen Square, I see men like you all the time. For the last two years, it's all I've done. Do you understand me?"

I nodded my head slowly, more uncertain now. The ground seemed to be shifting under me.

My hand was trembling again and this time the professor did not hold it.

"Before the war I worked with epileptics," he said. "Now you may not know this but epilepsy is a circuit phenomenon. Do you understand what I mean by that?"

I didn't and shook my head.

"Well, let me explain it more simply. Your brain in there," the Professor said, tapping his finger on my forehead, "is nothing more than a complicated circuit, like the electrical circuit in a house. Now, somewhere in that mess of wires you've shorted out and a light has gone off. It's happened somewhere in the connectors to your larynx… here…" The professor gripped my throat gently but firmly and kept his hand there.

"It's probably due to a chemical disruption. These two doctors have called me all the way down here from London especially to see you. We need to repair your wiring. Do you understand that? Nod if you do."

I obeyed: moving my head was uncomfortable under the pressure of his grip.

The professor smiled at me and squeezed slightly harder on my throat. I swallowed and felt my cartilaginous larynx move up and down within his fingers.

His voice was almost a whisper now.

"Soon I will start my treatment and I am sure that your voice will be restored before the night is out. My success rate is very high. I am *the* authority on this treatment. I do not tolerate failure, you see."

The professor took his hand off my neck and stood up from the bed, rubbing his hands.

"Where is the electrical laboratory?" he said.

A wooden chair occupied the centre of the room, its four sturdy legs screwed down to metal plates set into the floorboards. The presence of thick adjustable leather straps on the arm rests and on the front legs made it look even more ominous. I had heard they executed prisoners in America in contraptions like these.

Seeing me looking at it, Professor S put a consoling hand on my shoulder. "Don't trouble yourself too much," he said. "We might not need to resort to that.'

The only light was from a single bare light bulb hanging from the ceiling. There were no blinds at the windows and outside it was already dark. Though the window panes simply reflected the room's interior, I knew we were on the side of the building facing out to the woods, beyond which lay the military cemetery, the final resting place of my brother.

It was cold in the room, so cold I could see my own breath.

Apart from the chair, the only other piece of furniture was a single table. Placed in the middle of it was a large rectangular box. I presumed it was a battery of some kind because two brown wires snaked out from it, each ending with different pieces of equipment – one a square metal pad, the other a long metallic probe. Some spare probes lay nearby. A jug of water and a glass were set down on a tray on the table. That was it. That was the entirety of the 'electrical laboratory'.

I shivered.

I found the starkness of the room vaguely familiar and I wandered down an old corridor of associative memory, an attempt to deflect my attention from what was about to befall me in this sinister chamber. Strange what the mind will do to soften anticipated blows. The electrical laboratory reminded me of my study at boarding school – another cold and barren place, and one imbued with the same feeling of impending doom. There might not have been electric shocks, but the assorted tortures on the menu had been just as inventive and painful. I would be in the middle of prep and some bastard prefect twice my size would suddenly walk in and, without warning:

a) whip me across the back of the legs with a rolled-up wet towel;

b) seize my forearm and twist the skin in opposite directions – the so-called 'Chinese burn';

c) put his hand down the back of my trousers, grab a hold of the waist of my underpants and yank upwards as hard as possible, so that it felt like I was being split in two – the so-called 'wedgie'.

I was probably going to be electrocuted in a few minutes, but at least with Professor S it was for a *reason* – he was trying to help me speak again. In boarding school the violence had always been random and unjustified. These prefects would go on trampling through their entire lives, dishing out punishment – that was how the Empire was run.

The professor took off his jacket, laid it across the table and started rolling up his sleeves, his look one of grim resignation, as if he knew how much he was about to hurt me, but had to go through with it anyway.

"Know why they called me?"

I shook my head.

"It's because I'm the best. I'll get you talking sure enough. Together, we will not leave this room until you are cured. I'm in this too now. I care. Now, are you ready to be helped?"

At first I stared ahead, trying to avoid his eyes, but it was too late for any denial now.

I nodded at him.

As if reading my thoughts he simply said, "In a way, you belong to me now. You have signed yourself over to me."

From his trouser pocket he took out a packet of Wrigley's pepsin gum and unwrapped three sticks, slowly placing each of them into his mouth, one at a time. For a minute or so he chewed and I watched, wondering what on earth was about to follow.

"It's good," he said at last, smiling at the taste.

When he moved again I thought that he might be about to offer me a piece of the gum, but instead he pulled out a wooden tongue depressor from his pocket.

"Now, open up and let's have a look inside," he said.

I opened my mouth wide and he inserted the depressor. It was right the way in, nudging the back of my throat. Slightly uncomfortable, but not too bad.

"Hmm…" he said, retracting it again. "Just as I thought; your gag reflex is significantly diminished, virtually absent. Your ninth and tenth cranial nerves are fast asleep. There's a break in the motor pathways…"

Unknown to Professor S, I was familiar with the nerves to which he was referring – the 'glossopharyngeal' and the 'vagus'.

"Try to say ahhhh," he said.

I strained hard, but nothing. No great surprise there.

He poured out a glass of water and handed it to me.

"Take a mouthful and try to gargle."

I did so, but it was a poor effort, half of the water going down my windpipe and the other half coughed up over the professor.

With a slow, almost exaggerated calmness, he took the glass back and put it on the table. Then he pulled out a handkerchief from the breast pocket of his jacket and dried his spectacles and dabbed at his face. He didn't appear at all bothered by what I had done to him.

"I'm afraid," he said, still focusing on the drying, "that we're not making any headway. Your case is going to require Faradism. It's going to be a lot easier if you're in the chair. Can you take off your shirt?"

I hesitated, looking over at the chair and then back at Professor S, frightened for the first time.

"Listen," he said. "Things are going to get tough. In fact it's going to seem as if *I* am being tough… I won't lie to you, perhaps *too* tough. But you need to remember, it's so that I can cure you. I'm going to get your speech working again. All right?"

I held his stare and could see the truth there. This man really believed in himself.

I removed my shirt. I was shivering more now, and could see that my arms were covered in goosebumps.

"Good, New Zealander. I think you're beginning to realise how much you need my help. Now sit down."

Nervously, I did as he said, my movements as wooden and stiff as the chair.

"I think we'll only need these for now," he said, securing the arm straps. "I'll leave your legs free and see how we go.'

He picked up the pad-shaped electrode and from his mouth pulled out the large wad of gum and stuck it onto the base of the electrode. Then he reached behind and placed the electrode against my lower back. The gum was holding it securely in place, I supposed to 'earth' me.

I watched on in horror – he flipped a switch down on the battery. Three small lights came on and a gentle hum started up. He adjusted a dial on the side.

Then he held up the long probe.

"I am going to put it into your throat. I'm going to stimulate your pharynx with it. All right?'

"Not all right," my eyes were saying.

I nodded again, despite myself. Instinct told me to obey, that if I resisted it would only make things worse.

"Now open your mouth, please."

I closed my eyes and opened up.

Again there wasn't a normal gag reflex – all I could feel was a weak current being applied intermittently as he moved the probe on and off the back of my throat – just a tickling and fizzing sensation.

"Nod to me when you are ready to attempt to speak."

I nodded.

"Do you wish to be cured?"

I gave another quick nod in his direction, more frantic than the one preceding.

"Good. Remember I am not leaving this room until you are cured. Know that I am investing myself in your cure. I'm committed. Are you?"

I continued to stare at him, wide-eyed with fear, but also perversely pleased that this doctor was giving me so much of his undivided attention. I really did want to get better. I nodded at him again, fully throwing myself into the process.

Half an hour later, though utterly spent, came a moment of progress: I opened my lips and a hoarse whisper was released.

"Ahhh…"

It was strange to hear my voice after all this time; in fact, at first I thought Professor S might be saying it just to make me feel better.

The effort to achieve that small breakthrough had involved several dozen shocks of increasing intensity, the dial slowly creeping round to the higher numbers. All the while Professor S was continuing with his strict instructions: "Come on, you've got to put some effort into this. You think I'm going to do all the work? If you do, you are very much mistaken. You need to play your part…"

He was like my old rowing coach, encouraging me to expend ever greater effort in pulling my oar through the water.

Hearing my own voice – albeit that first faint syllable – had come as a big surprise, just as I had been surprised at what I could really do in a boat on the river when I really committed to pushing through the pain barrier. In those instances, you started to trust the coach and that is what was happening now. I was starting to believe in Professor S. He knew what the limits were, and just what he could get from me. I found myself wanting to get better, not just for me but for him too, I wanted to make him proud.

Despite my growing confidence, my progress seemed to stall over the following hour. A series of croaks: 'Aaah… aaah… aaah…" and nothing else.

Professor S hit the table in frustration with the palm of his hand and the sudden noise made me jump in shock, ironically with more violence than any of the electrical shocks I had received so far.

"Damnation," he said under his breath. "Damn and blast it all to hell."

From his pocket he pulled out a piece of paper and started to write vigorously. A minute later he held it up for me to see:

> *Nov 10 1918.*
>
> *This is to certify that I, the NZ patient with mutism treated by Professor S on this day, have decided to discharge myself from D-block (Royal Victoria Military Hospital) because I am afraid to undergo treatment which has proved beneficial to me so far. I take full responsibility for what may happen to me after I leave D-block.*
>
> *Signed,*

"Go on then," he said, holding out his pen. "Mark an X at the bottom and it's over. You can give up now. Perhaps you're not the man I thought you were. Make it easy on yourself. Go on, give up and make your mark of surrender."

I shook my head.

"N… N… N…"

I wasn't giving up: his letter had a ring of truth – the treatment *had* proved beneficial so far. After all, he had managed to get me making sounds.

"Well, for Christ's sake then!" he said, his face red with anger. "ARE YOU GOING TO COMMIT TO THIS PROCESS, OR NOT?"

To punctuate his sentence he smashed his hand down onto the table again.

"YAAAGHHH," I managed to say in response, more loudly than before, gurgling in the saliva which had collected in the back of my throat.

His head jerked back in surprise at my new volume.

"Good… Excellent. Now that is much better."

He balled up the letter in his fist and threw it into the corner of the room.

"It seems you are finally willing to meet me halfway. I think you are now ready for the next stage of the treatment. This will consist of stronger shocks to the outside of your neck; these will be transmitted to your voice box and you will soon be able to speak."

He turned off the battery and changed the attachment at the end to another paddle shaped electrode.

"This is going to hurt I'm afraid," he said. "I'm going to tie your legs down now."

He did this, and then turned up the dial again so that the machine started humming intensely.

When he placed the paddle against my neck I immediately felt the effect of the stronger current; it made my neck seize up and tears flow down my face involuntarily.

"Let's work on single syllables… no harder than a walk in the park."

The professor applied the electrode quickly each time and with each shock, told me what to say:

"Say Aah"

Bzzzz...

"Aah!"

"Say Bah!"

Bzzzz...

"Bah!"

"Say Cah!"

Bzzzz.

No response. The professor turned the dial up another notch.

"I said say Cah."

Bzzzz...

"CAH... CAH... CAH!"

He smiled.

"Excellent. You are doing splendidly, and I know you are now determined to talk. I am very pleased with you, New Zealander... In fact, I am proud of you."

I smiled, pleased to have pleased him. All of this was madness, undeniably, but it was nowhere near the madness of the war.

The next set of shocks didn't work. Another barrier to be scaled within my stubborn mind. Another half hour passed.

Instead of thumping the table in anger, Professor S leant forward with his face just inches away. His forehead was glistening with perspiration. I certainly couldn't fault him on the effort he was putting into this. I was sweating too, the cold and the shivering a distant memory.

"Is there nobody you want to get better for? No-one at all? You must have someone you care about. You need to pull yourself together and get better for them."

His breath smelt of stale spearmint.

What he said – about there being no-one to get better for – struck a nerve, and I flared with anger.

I struggled under my ties and tried to shout.

"Fah!"

"We've already done Fah… This isn't what I would call progress."

He glanced at his wristwatch.

"It's getting late. I'm going to have to make it more painful for you."

He put the paddle down and changed back to the long probe again.

The dial had been turned all the way round to its extreme limit.

I spat at him, the gobbet landing on his chin.

He came close again, wiping it away with his handkerchief.

"Good… good. Let it out. Anger is good."

I had had enough of his method now. Maybe this was how Dr Kauffmann's 'Surprise Method' worked – it got you so angry that the nerve connections sparked up to life from their hibernation state. There was no way he was going to stick that bloody thing down my gullet again.

"Fu… Fu…"

"Yes, New Zealander. Go on and bloody well say it!"

"Fu… fuck… Yu…Yu…YOU! FUCK YOU!"

The professor clapped his hands.

"Yes, Yes. That's it man!"

Through my rage it hit me that I had actually spoken and my eyes opened wide with astonishment.

"Come on," he said, discarding the probe. "Speak to me… tell me the names of the people you want to live for."

"J… J… Jennifer."

"Who is she?"

"The… the… wo-man I want… to… to… mar-ry."

"That's good. Anyone else?"

"Rennie," I said, without any stutter. "My best friend…"

I saw pure delight in the man's eyes. I had known all along that he really did care. I had witnessed how much energy he had invested into my case – I had even seen his sweat. It didn't matter to me that some of the energy he had used happened to involve electrocution.

"And you? What is your name, New Zealander?"

"John Hunston."

When I said that, he undid the straps which had held me down.

"Welcome back, John… I told you we would do it, didn't I?"

He wiped the sweat from his brow and looked at his watch.

"Seven hours," he said. "I think that's a record. You were a hard nut to crack."

I started to laugh.

After this point, it was as if a dam had burst, and my voice came flooding back.

Full sentences were a bit tricky at first, accompanied by a considerable stammer, but after another half hour of gentle conversation, even this problem resolved itself.

We sat next to each other on the floor, leaning back against the wall of the electrical room. The professor reached to one side and turned the radiator tap two revolutions and a tricking sound started up as hot water filled the pipes.

"You're a bloody doctor?" he said, after I had told him who I was.

He had turned slightly pale.

"Christ Almighty. I'm sorry to have put you through that. It's the quickest way though. There are only two options available. You could go up to Craiglockhart Hospital in Scotland and have 'the talking cure', or you can have Faradism from me. Shock treatment is the only way I know. If I came across as a bit harsh, it was when I saw you were going backwards and I was beginning to lose you."

The torture session had been eclipsed by the results it had achieved, but I was still finding it hard to believe that I could speak.

"How… does it… work? Is it really all about circuits?"

"It's based on a simple premise," he said, using hand signals in the air to help explain. "A disorder originating in suggestion should yield to counter-suggestion. The precise method of counter-suggestion is really immaterial, so long as it is strong enough. It could be hypnotism; it could be the 'talking cure'. But I've found that the Faradic battery does the job best. Only in the right hands, mind you. I've been doing it for two years. I read your notes. What those two monkeys tried with cigarettes on your tongue was pure barbarism…"

"They knew no better," I said, surprising myself that I was defending them.

The professor still seemed appalled at what they had done.

"Cigarettes though… my God," he said, shaking his head. "Talking of which, shall we have a smoke?"

"Yes, why not?"

He got up and went over to his jacket and brought it over. He took a packet of cigarettes from one of the pockets and draped his jacket over my bare shoulders. I appreciated the gesture – the room was a bit warmer now and I couldn't see my own breath anymore – but his doing that made me feel human again.

"Listen," he said, glancing at his watch, "it's two o'clock in the morning. I won't be able to sleep now. Not after all that." He pointed towards the battery and the chair as if I might have forgotten what he had just put me through. "And I doubt you'll be able to sleep much either. How about you tell me what the hell happened to you out in Ypres?"

"My disorder originated in suggestion," I said, smiling ruefully as I used his line. "And you want to know what suggested it?'

The professor laughed. He was back to being Mr Hyde now; Dr Jekyll was long gone.

"God I hate that bare light," he said, going over and switching it off. The only light in the room now was coming from the resistance bulbs of the battery. It definitely made the place seem a little more, well… homely.

"Yes," he said, resuming his place next to me on the floor. "What led to the suggestion?"

"You… you might want to keep the door locked," I said.

"Why?"

"Because… I'm not sure I want to tell it."

He brought out the key and gave it to me.

"I'll let you decide," he said. "You're not my patient anymore. You can leave if you want to."

I thought for a few moments before making up my mind and handing him back the key.

"You kept your word and made me talk again; I suppose I owe you something."

He smiled at that and proceeded to light two cigarettes.
As we both smoked in the dark, I finally started to talk.

Chapter Seven

"I'm not sure where to start."

I was staring at the glow of my cigarette, imagining I was high up on a rocky promontory in one of the glow worm lit Waitomo grottos back home, looking down into a whirlpool of my war memories.

It was daunting to know I had to re-enter those waters – I had become very comfortable living on my quiet rock ledge sanctuary, shut off from the world, and now I was reluctant to leave.

"Why don't you start from when you shipped out," the professor said.

I thought about that, and one of the memories made me laugh out loud. The professor was looking at me and probably wondering if he'd applied too much electricity.

"What's so funny?"

"Our troopship, the one we sailed in from New Zealand to Europe – my friend thought it looked like a zebra. He's perfectly sane by the way… It *did* look like a zebra."

"Hmm… Go on."

Hesitantly, I took one more look down at the swirling current below and leapt from my rock ledge.

****

Lt. John Hunston, NZMC
Awapuni training camp
Palmerston
February 1917

Dear Sean,
I hope this finds you and Matty both well.

I arrived at the camp a month ago and I haven't written before because I've been busy with exams and tests all this time. Training is certainly harder than it was when I joined the RAMC for the Boer War – there they just threw you onto the boat for South Africa. This has been a different experience altogether. That, in turn, has told me this war is a different one altogether.

The camp is on a racecourse. It takes me back to my days in London when I worked at the Manor practice in Harley Street. There we covered the courses of Ascot and Sandown and the feel is similar – an enormous grass expanse covered in large tents. It's easy to imagine the thunder of hooves on the course, especially since we are sleeping on the seats of the grandstand, which are only partly closed off from the elements with canvas screens – I have a view of the start from my bunk.

Palmerston is a couple of miles down the road and I have gone into town a couple of times, but mainly I am focused on my studies. Along with a group of eleven other MOs, I have been undergoing an intensive instruction course.

I have specifically asked to serve with the 3rd Field Ambulance, since it is attached to the Rifles – and that is Harry Ingram's brigade. I assumed it would be the best way of finding him over in Europe. So far though, I haven't been told anything.

The Senior MOs at the camp were impressed that I had served in the RAMC in the Boer War and promised they would try their best to grant my request, although they did express some caution saying: 'things were largely out of their hands'.

The routine is as follows: 9 to 9.30 am squad drill; 10 to 12, lectures; at 1 o'clock, lunch; lectures from 2pm to 4; and dinner at 6.

The instructors make no bones about the task ahead. They have given us a fair idea of the obstacles we'll be facing as doctors. The damage done from German bullets and shells is just the start; there is phosgene gas, wound sepsis, venereal disease, lice, scabies, trench foot, trench fever and trench nephritis to be dealing with. One morning we were made to wear box respirators and walk through a room filled with wood-smoke. It was claustrophobic, chaotic and frightening.

The most controversial condition, by far, is 'shell shock'. At the time of the Boer War, my brother and I saw one or two patients through the gates of D-block – although back then the condition was more loosely referred to as 'disordered action of the heart'. They were soldiers who had been caught up in Spion Kop and other major battles – but on the whole the condition was a rarity. This war, however, is throwing up a multitude of cases.

The term shell shock has become 'a can of worms'. Not my words – that's what our instructor told us.

Basically, it's costing too much. Let me explain – up until recently, it was possible to classify shell shock as a wound – something the MO could mark on the ticket as a 'W'. This not only gave a soldier the right to a wound stripe on his arm, but also a possible disability war pension later on if he didn't recover. The problem is one of sheer volume – after the Somme offensive – between July and December last year – 16,000 cases were classified as 'shell shock W' and were repatriated back to special centres in Britain. This evacuation and specialised treatment is too expensive for the government and so is the impending pension bill. It's also a manpower issue: prolonged absence from the ranks hinders the war effort.

During the class, the instructor picked up a piece of chalk, wrote a big letter W on the blackboard and then drew a line through it.

"Field MOs" he said, "are NOT to label any Tom, Dick or Harry who comes in with a nervous disorder as 'shell shock W'. If you do decide the case is genuine, then you will write 'neurasthenia S' on the Field Medical Card."

He rubbed out the W and wrote a large letter S instead.

"…S denoting sickness."

As you might have guessed by now, S classified soldiers are NOT entitled to a wound-stripes or pensions.

The instructor said most cases are simply suffering from strain and exhaustion, which can be fixed with a few days away and a decent rum ration. This will happen in a centre near the front. The aim is to get as many of these men back fighting as soon as possible – "ASAP," was the way the instructor said it, "To get them operational again."

The Army likes to use longer words than necessary. 'Operational' is my particular favourite.

Using five syllables where one would suffice (the word 'fit' for example) tells you something about the mentality – as does form-filling in triplicate, making your bed and using a ruler to measure the exact amount of sheet folded over. They make us learn a certain way of turning around when marching – your feet making a 'T', an 'L' and a 'V' – before marching off again on the parade square. I had two days confined to barracks for going on parade without an overcoat.

'DO NOT QUESTION THE SYSTEM' is what the course is drilling into our heads.

You are familiar with my classification system aren't you? Well, the Army is trying to turn us into Type 1 automatons.

We are just units in a great machine: unquestioning, obedient, expendable.

Twenty years ago, after a training session when my University rowing coach hadn't been pleased with my form (I must have looked unconcerned, as my Type 2 overconfidence would have dictated), he told me something I have never forgotten: "Hunston," he said, "to me you are just a piece of meat. If you cannot do the job properly I will just get another piece of meat to replace you."

That's what we are in the Army too – Type 1 pieces of meat.

Having said all this, the course instructors are decent enough fellows, most having taken part in earlier campaigns. One was wounded at Gallipoli – he blinks a lot and, whenever he writes on the blackboard, his hand trembles as if he has Parkinson's. We pretend not to notice and do our best to decipher what he's trying to tell us.

I find myself trying to please these veteran instructors, to cheer them up in some way. I recognise the look in their eyes; the haunted, blank, vacuous stare which tells me they have seen the worst. I'm sure that in quiet moments,

they question the very system they teach. I strongly suspect they are Type 3s,
being forced to teach a world view in which they no longer believe. Anyway,
I feel we have a shared camaraderie of sorts and that is why I have thrown
myself into the course and shelved my cynicism. They deserve the best from
me, these men.

By the way, although I have always teased you about being a Type 2
because of your unshakable belief in God, please know that you NEVER
come across as complacent. You certainly don't have the arrogance I had
when once upon a time I thought I knew it all.

Your friend as always,
John
P.S. We are due to ship out from Wellington in less than a fortnight
aboard troopship 'Navua'. Please write to me here before I leave.

By Valentine's Day we were stationed in Wellington ready for departure.

In the afternoon I caught the cable car up to Kelburn Park and wandered through the Botanical gardens.

Near the Hector Observatory I sat down at the foot of a very old Pohutakawa tree, its trunk like thick pieces of shipping rope twisted together. The roots made a mesh above ground and formed a natural armchair through which you could see daylight, but which was strong enough to take my weight. There I made myself comfortable and daydreamt.

They were using the observatory to monitor seismological activity, not the stars. There was a radical new theory called 'Continental drift' which essentially said that New Zealand was at the boundary of two great continents under the oceans; the Australian continent and the Pacific, and that the edges were rubbing against one another, setting off earthquakes all the time. The man behind the theory – a German – had proposed that 'the continents are moving' and that at one stage in the dim and distant past, they had all been merged in one supercontinent called 'Pangaea', before splitting apart. It made sense to me – when you looked at a world map, it was obvious that some of the landmasses seemed to fit together like pieces of a puzzle. At school Freddie had once asked in a Geography lesson why the eastern edge of South America seemed to fit so well with the western edge of Africa: "Do you think they were joined at one time, sir?" The teacher had scolded Freddie and given him one hundred lines as a punishment: 'I must not make wild and erratic claims about things which just happen to look a certain way'. It made me smile now, to know that a scientist had come up with the very same idea and that there was some credible proof for the theory.

The entire country was unstable. You didn't need to be a scientist to know that. Three years ago, there had been an earthquake near Waihi. It had happened on a Sunday evening while Rennie was in the middle of a service. Several ladies in the congregation had fainted and I was called upon to administer basic first aid.

The strange thing is that he had been speaking about earthquakes in his sermon, about the 'signs' of the end times, including 'earthquakes in divers places'; the same passage he had used when saying whose side God was on in this war, about 'Nation rising against nation…'

So there I was, sitting under a solitary Pohutakawa tree and looking at the volcanic rim of mountains surrounding the city and thinking about Continental drift and earthquakes. It was a clear day and, across the choppy waters of the Cook Straight, I could see the snow-capped mountains of the Kaikura ranges on the South Island. Nearer, in Wellington harbour was Somes Island where they were holding anyone with German connections. It's where they would have locked up my German colleague if he had still been around. Klaus and I had got along well enough when we had worked together three years before. He was a lot more practical than me, always ready with good advice and with a dry sense of humour. Once, when I had been on-call during New Year's Eve, there had been so many fights that I had soon used up all the suturing equipment stitching the miners' faces back together. At a loss and too exhausted to think straight, I had telephoned Klaus to ask if he knew where any spares might be. He questioned why I wasn't re-using them.

"Because they're dirty," I had said.

I would never forget his strong accent down the telephone, presumably accompanied by his sardonic grin: "Well zen, Hunston… put zem in ze autoclave…"

"But I don't know how it works."

"Why, you read ze instructions… and do it yourself… zis is not Buckingham Palace…you are not ze King, ja?"

From my viewpoint I could just make out the collection of buildings and tents for the internees, but I knew Klaus was not one of them; he had left six months before the war to return to his homeland in Bavaria. I had never heard from Klaus again, though I supposed he must have joined the German war effort and was on the front somewhere.

I certainly didn't wish him any ill-will, as he had been a nice enough chap and a fellow scientific thinker. I had heard rumours that conditions in the island camp were harsh, in any event, and that the camp commandant had sanctioned regular beatings, poor rationing and ritual humiliation. I was glad Klaus wasn't there.

"They said you'd be up here somewhere," said a voice from behind, scattering my thoughts like papers in the wind.

I spun round in amazement.

It was Rennie, wearing an army uniform complete with a dog collar. He was holding his cap nervously and his hair was all matted at the sides from where the rim had been pressing down. I sprang up, not quite believing what I was seeing.

"Sean!"

"That's Padre Rennie to you. Chaplain to the Forces."

"Your uniform looks real," I said, still thinking it might be a joke.

"It *is* real. I'm in the Army."

I saw from his face that he wasn't joking.

"What happened?"

"The boys joined the Pioneer battalion. They did it the day after you left… planned it down to the last detail too. Told me they were going to stay over at the bach and fish off the rocks for the weekend. When they didn't come home, I went over there and found a letter on the table. It said, by the time I was reading it, they would be in their camp at Narrow Neck in Auckland. They said I would've only tried to stop them if they had asked for permission to go. So I left it alone. I bit my lip and didn't get them... their troopship left a month ago..."

"Christ..."

I didn't know what else to say, except to blaspheme in front of my God-fearing friend. It wasn't the biggest surprise I suppose – all the signs had been there – but hearing that they had actually gone ahead with it was still shocking.

"And as soon as their ship sailed, I knew I had to go too. So I joined up as a Padre, Chaplain to the Forces."

Rennie took a seat amongst the twisted roots, leant back against the gnarled trunk of the Pohutakawa and gazed out over Wellington harbour.

I resumed my seat in silence.

Picturing the boys in uniform, digging trenches on the Western Front was hard. But it was harder to picture Materoa alone in the family home – Rennie, Manu and Kahu were her world.

At last I managed to steel myself to say something.

"How's Matty?"

"She's a mess, completely devastated... All her tough talk about Maoris fighting for mana seems to count for nothing now."

Poor Rennie sounded as if he might cry.

"You know what she said? She said that if the boys are killed I am to bring their Mokomokai back to New Zealand."

Mokomokai was the name for a dried head. It was an old Maori tradition to keep the embalmed heads of loved ones in baskets scented with oil, to be brought out from time to time to mourn over. The heads would be decorated with feathers and kept in the house. Enemies as well as loved ones could be preserved – though typically in the past the enemies were displayed on stakes by their vanquishers.

Rennie closed his eyes and started shaking his head slowly, as if he was reliving I could only guess what... perhaps the sight of her reading their sons' goodbye letter, or the look in her eyes when he had said goodbye, or her asking him to bring back their heads if the worst happened. His eyes were still closed when he started speaking again.

"She looked so small when she came to see me off at the train station this morning; small, timid and helpless. Can you imagine that, John? My Materoa?"

"No," I said, "I can't."

I didn't want to either. Materoa represented the best of New Zealand to me – the level-headed wisdom, robust health and inner strength; all the good sides of life.

Rennie took a deep breath and, on letting it out, made such a sad sigh that I thought it best to give him a few moments alone.

I walked off a few yards and stared out at Somes Island. "Put zem in ze autoclave…" I said absentmindedly.

"What's that, John?"

"Nothing," I said. I hadn't been thinking when I had said it but there was something very apt about the German's words now. Those boys were heading to the autoclave – about to be tested in the furnace of the Western Front.

Rennie came and stood beside me.

He was patting his various pockets looking for something.

"Before I forget," he said. "Your old girlfriend was looking for you."

"Jennifer?"

He nodded. "She came round to the Manse a week ago. When I told her I was going to be joining you, she wrote you a letter right there and then for me to pass on. Now, which pocket did I put it in? Confounded jacket… Ah, here it is…"

He pulled out a crumpled letter from his breast pocket and handed it over. It was unopened, still sealed with a blob of wax imprinted with Rennie's seal, a simple cross.

"Go ahead and read it now if you want. I don't mind."

"Thanks," I said, too excited to even sound sarcastic about his giving me permission.

I peeled open the envelope, my heart thumping up around my ears.

Her writing was instantly familiar – rounded and neat. I remembered seeing it for the first time when she had written in the observation charts at Waihi Hospital. It hadn't taken long for us to get together. One night in the mess we were having coffee and I was chatting away when she just reached across the table and took my hand in hers. We didn't say anything – just held hands for several minutes, staring at one another intently. That was when I risked letting her into my lonely heart. For a few months I opened up to her, a feeling quite wonderful and new. But then the sheer intensity of love frightened me so much that I started shutting down again, pulling up all the barriers around my heart, breaking hers and pushing her away into the arms of that sleaze Westbourne.

The letterhead was Rennie's: *Reverend S. Rennie, The Manse, Haszard Street, Waihi.*

I hardly dared continue.

> *John,*
>
> *I am writing this letter in your friend's study, so please excuse all the emotion within – there's no time to re-read and re-write, and pare it down of all the initial off-the-cuff feelings. Perhaps it is better this way. I should have thrown a dozen away and you would have a watered down version if I had been given more time.*
>
> *I haven't been able to stop thinking about you.*
>
> *Seeing you that night in the bar in Thames had a profound effect on me I could not have predicted. Everything suddenly became clear. I was heading for the biggest mistake of my life and not doing a thing about it. Perhaps I didn't need to see you to know it, but our encounter was the catalyst I needed to act. I called off my engagement – did so as soon as I left you, right there in the street outside. I couldn't live the lie for a second longer. Of course he took it badly and I doubt I shall ever see him again. He wasn't too bad a fellow really – but he wasn't you…*
>
> *Afterwards I couldn't come back to find you. I was far too upset about everything. I needed to be alone for a while. I hope you can understand that.*
>
> *You going off to Europe after everything you'd previously said about the war inspired me and I resolved to join the NZ Army Nursing Service, with no-one telling me what I could or could not do. In fact I went to the*

recruitment office in town the following morning. I'll be leaving soon. Nurses are at a premium – arguably more so than doctors, dare I say it.

Please thank your friend Reverend Rennie and his wife for being so friendly. They gave me a cup of tea when they saw how upset I was at having missed you. I think Mrs Rennie likes me – she was very pleased when I intimated how special you are to me. They tried to explain why you are the way you are, John. Rennie told me that just before he first met you, your brother died and he said you were still damaged in a way, still grieving.

John – it's so hard for me to find the right words. I realise I can't replace your brother, but I want to take you closely in my arms and give you all my love and strength.

I pray that we shall meet again and that you, Rennie, and his sons all remain safe.

Jennifer

As I read her letter I felt warmth radiating from deep in my core. It was as if a piece of coal had been sitting in my chest where my heart was supposed to be – for years black and cold – and now it was glowing brightly again. The ice man was beginning to thaw.

I carefully folded the letter and put it away. I would never lose it; it would always stay with me, to re-read and fan those embers whenever I wanted.

"What did she say?"

"She said she loves me," I said, unable to help myself from smiling.

He reached over and patted me on the back.

"I guessed she might – I'm happy for you, John – you deserve it."

"Thank you for looking after her."

"Made Materoa's day, I can tell you," he said. "She won't be bothering you anymore about women."

I laughed. "No, perhaps not."

"She'll find a new way of embarrassing you though. Questions about when a baby is on the way, probably."

We both laughed after he said this.

I was happy that his mood had lifted; pleased Jennifer's letter had distracted him from the pain he had been feeling.

I thought about Manu and Kahu again.

"We'll track the boys down somehow, Sean."

The optimism in my voice came from Jenny's letter, not from the belief that we could actually do anything to help. Deep down I already knew you couldn't really look out for anybody in a war – not Freddie, not Harry Ingram and not Manu and Kahu. It was down to fate in the end. But that didn't mean you couldn't at least try.

"Perhaps," he said, "but even then I won't be able to stop them. They would never have spoken to me again if I had them sent home for being underage. They've chosen their paths, John. I need to see them face to face, and then attempt to persuade them to go back home… I tried writing to them of course, but sometimes the power of the word alone is not enough…"

Rennie was right.

Essentially he agreed with my private conclusions. People made their own decisions and anyone else was just a bystander and a bit player in the grand show. If we were lucky and providence was smiling on us, we might find the boys. We might, by some miracle, change their minds or get them reassigned to safer duties or even sent home. But the ideal scenario rarely happened in life. You couldn't control anyone. Trying to do so only made matters worse.

"Anyhow, I couldn't live with myself knowing they were gone and that I was still there in town. Materoa understood. So I talked to a few people and signed the papers. I mentioned your name and they assigned me to your transport – simple as that."

"Simple? How on earth did you swing it?"

"I called in some favours."

"What favours?"

"Remember that old boy network from England? Well, the church has an old boy network of its own and a pretty powerful one at that."

I laughed again. "Astounding… You have no fear. Only you would have the gall to gate-crash a war."

"A war," he said. "By God."

There was a dark look on his face, as if he was hearing for the first time what it was he was actually doing.

"Listen, Sean. None of us will actually be fighting. I'm a medic, you're a padre and the boys are trench diggers. Chances are, we'll all be back here within the year, in the boat fishing, looking at volcanoes and telling the boys old Maori legends. Materoa will be back in charge and things will be the way they were again."

Rennie wasn't smiling.

He shook his head, like a Greek Titan about to set a decree that he knew wasn't going to sit well with the mortals.

"I've got a bad feeling about all this, John. Remember that fear you had when we first met? Kept you awake at nights, didn't it? Well, I have it now. I feel like I'm in the garden of Gethsemane."

For my friend to talk this way was alarming, because he hardly ever had bad feelings about anything. He was the one with the thick skin who had always steam-rolled through life without worrying.

I couldn't let him see my concern though. I had to be strong for the both of us. He had kept me going all these years – dragging me out of my lows with his optimism, so it only seemed right that it was my turn to raise his spirits now.

"Gethsemane?" I said, indicating the surroundings. "Not this little hill, Sean. Besides, Gethsemane had olive trees, not Pohutakawas."

Rennie kept staring straight ahead, not in the least cheered up by my weak joke.

"The last letter the boys sent to me was describing the view from their camp – how it looked over the Hauraki Gulf to Rangitoto Island."

"Yes, I remember seeing that place."

It was a perfectly symmetrical volcanic island with shallow slopes, covered in Pohutakawa trees, just off the Devonport beaches in north Auckland.

"You know what Rangitoto means in Maori?" Rennie said, with a haunted look.

I glanced at him. "No."

"Materoa told me. It means: Bloody sky."

"Why is it called that?"

"Once upon a time, a Maori chief was seriously injured in a battle there… not a good omen."

I nearly asked him why he had started to believe in omens that weren't from the Bible, but something in the way he was looking and sounding made me hold my tongue.

Next day I stood on the dock with the other men from the Field Ambulance waiting to board. The white kitbags were slung over our shoulders and made us all look as if we were carrying out the laundry.

Being a man of the cloth, Rennie won an instant respect from the other MOs, something which had taken me weeks to establish. They all saluted him and said, "Morning, Padre."

For now he seemed to be his old self again, the enthusiasm back.

"What on earth is that?" he said, gawping at our troop ship. "It looks like a zebra."

Our transport was called the Navua and there was the most curious black and white striped pattern painted onto the hull. We had been taught about this on the Awapuni course.

"It's dazzle camouflage," I said. "It's there to make everything look a bit wonky, so we don't get sunk by a torpedo."

"Good God. Are you serious? It makes the ship look more noticeable, not less so."

"Imagine you're a boxer in the ring – you can't make yourself invisible so what do you do?"

"You knock the other man out."

Rennie made an uppercut as he said this which drew laughter from the other men.

"Yes, but what if you can't punch?" I said. "Look at our ship – you see any guns? No. So what do you do to protect yourself?"

"I don't know. Make it harder for him to hit you I suppose."

"Exactly... You're a German U-Boat commander, peering through your periscope at our ship against the horizon, perhaps from a mile away, perhaps at twilight. Screw up your eyes and you'll get some idea."

"I can still see the ship," he said, squinting.

"Right, but remember those torpedoes are being fired from a long way off. You'll have to aim well ahead of the target if you're going to score a hit. So you've got to know the ship's course and speed. Now anything disguising that, anything causing even the slightest error in those calculations, can make you miss. Look closely – can you see the illusion, as if there's more than one hull? That section has been painted to look as if the ship could be coming towards you and there's even a fake bow-wave on the stern to make it seem as if the ship is moving in the other direction."

Rennie was peering through the circular periscope he'd made with his fingers.

"They tested it on toy models," I said, "and asked submarine captains to look at them through optical range finders. Some of their calculations were off by fifty-five degrees. It only needs to be off by eight degrees for a torpedo to miss a ship. It's all about perception. The world is whatever we construct it to be. The dazzle camouflage changes our constructions."

I could tell he was still doubtful. "Even Mary Magdalen mistook Jesus for the gardener," I said.

The biblical footnote struck the chord I hoped it would. It wasn't in Mark and I could tell he was impressed.

"Hmm… I suppose so," Rennie said, looking at me now. "If you were a long way away and the light wasn't good, I suppose it might look confusing. Sometimes when I see the boys with their striped Moko tattoos, it's hard to tell them apart."

For the first half of the journey I slept well – it was a good chance to catch up on all the missed sleep from years of on-calls.

We stopped off at Hobart and then crossed the Great Australian Bight. It felt as if my life was reversing – going back the way I had come in early 1901 and then the journey before that, in 1900.

The closer we got to Europe, the more jittery I became. In the early hours I would wake up in a sweat with my heart thumping hard and, as I lay there in the bunk, my old coach's words would come rattling back from the past: "You're just a piece of meat… just a piece of meat," over and over again.

Chapter Eight

We reached England on the clear morning of 26th April 1917.

From the deck of the troopship I could just make out the hills beyond Devonport. It was all immediately familiar, despite having been away for so long. I certainly hadn't expected to feel such a sense of belonging, but seeing the land of my birth made me feel like I had come home. A new order was forming in my affairs – New Zealand had been consigned to history and England was going to be the dominant force in my life once again. I remembered leaving in 1900 and being desperate to get away – to forget Harley Street and the London cliques, to put Freddie's death right out of my mind. But here it was again and I found myself almost pleased to be back, even if it was for another war.

I think that all this time I had been blaming the country for allowing Freddie to die here. It is strange, blaming the place, as if the very soil itself was culpable. In the Australian outback my Aboriginal friend Eugene made me rub the dirt from the desert floor onto my skin and then throw it back down on the ground. "Now the land knows your smell," he had said. "Now the ancestral spirits know you are travelling over their land. They will protect you."

Perhaps that is why I held England accountable – because its ancestral spirits hadn't been able to keep Freddie alive.

We berthed next to a minelayer, its hull painted in diamond chequers like a harlequin's costume. Dazzle camouflage had clearly become an art form in its own right.

You knew at once that the biggest war in the history of mankind was raging just across the water. For a start, every man I saw was in uniform. Cranes were lifting pallets of crates onto a dozen waiting ships: heavy guns, ammunition, food and medical supplies. 'FRAY BENTOS CORNED BEEF' read the lettering on one set of crates. Horses were going up gangplanks; some happy to be led, but others having to be pushed up by the grooms, two or three men leaning their shoulders against the horses' behinds like a mixed species rugby scrum.

Departing soldiers already aboard their transports were waving down at sad families on the quayside. Somewhere in the hubbub, a band was playing a marching tune.

Most of the soldiers on board *Navua* were going off to Sling camp on the Salisbury Plain for further training, but the Medical Corps were heading further east to a small village called Ewshot in Hampshire, where the NZMC camp was based.

Rennie was straight off to France, heading for Etaples and then inland. He had received a telegram that morning and had been reading it to himself again and again, as if it was a crossword clue and the more times that he said it, the more likely the moment would come when the answer presented itself.

"What is it, Sean?" I had said to him, pointing at the telegram.

"My orders, I think – but I can't make head or tail of them."

He handed me the piece of paper:

PADRE RENNIE. PROCEED STRAIGHT TO TOC H, POP, YPRES SECTOR. PADRE MONEY, CF, NZEF

"Proceed straight to Toc H, Pop," I said, repeating the orders like Rennie had been doing. He looked at me as if I might understand the clue now. "Well… I think it's definitely an Army order – who else would use the word 'proceed' when you could just use 'go'?"

I handed back the telegram. "You know this Money?"

"Yes, at least I think I do, if it's the one I'm thinking of. Reverend Humphrey Money. A good man… met him once or twice over the years at national Wesleyan meetings. He worked in Christchurch before the war."

A few hours later we parted at the dockside, Rennie boarding the next ship going over the Channel and I on a train east to Hampshire. After a brief handshake and a few 'good lucks', both of us were off to war.

****

Lt John Hunston, NZMC
Ewshot Camp
Hampshire
May 18th 1917

Dear Sean

The camp is a nice enough place, surrounded by pine trees. Coincidentally, it's not a million miles from Witworth Park; Egremont's place, my old employer. It's where he lived before he hit financial ruin. Remember the papers in 1904? How he did himself in during his corruption trial – swallowing a cyanide pill at the Royal Courts of Justice after being given seven years. Anyway, when I went to Witworth Park to interview for my Australia job I suspected then he was crooked. If memory serves, you quoted Proverbs to me - 'Pride goeth before destruction and a haughty spirit before the fall.' It turned out to be true! He was the archetypal Type 2 alright.

I sometimes try to imagine how it would have turned out if I had never gone to Australia – I would probably still be at the Manor Practice in Harley Street – fat, rich, jaded and none the wiser, married to some socialite and miserable as sin. Instead of the way I am now – thin, poor and jaded, unmarried and miserable as sin!

So to bring you up to date – we've been going over a lot of the same ground that we covered back in Awapuni. There's been plenty of repetition and revision, but my CO McKenzie keeps saying: 'to fail to prepare is to prepare to fail', and so we keep at it.

On arrival at the camp I was classified 'A' which meant more training. The other category – 'B' - was farmed off to man New Zealand Hospitals in England and various Hospital ships. Captain McKenzie knew I was keen to be stationed at the Front and that is why I have been blindly obeying everything he orders me to do, anything to get me assigned to a Field Ambulance so that I can find Harry Ingram. Simply being stationed in some English Base Hospital would be a disaster – wouldn't be able to do a damn thing to try and save him. Nothing fills me with more dread than my promise to his mother becoming an empty one. So I've been passing my exams with top marks as though Harry's life depends on it. I'm turning into 'a half-decent bloody medic' as McKenzie grudgingly admits.

I have even had a taste of working in 'dug-out' conditions. They have an Advanced Dressing Station – an 'ADS' – built into a trench system here and we have spent whole days and nights down there, working with gas masks and bandaging. Makes you feel like you're already on the front, although I realise things will be a lot worse in Belgium, where it will be raining shells, and then when autumn comes – assuming we get through that far – there will be the mud and the cold. Here in our camp we have large plunge baths with hot running water. There, we'll be soaking wet and struggling to prevent trench foot.

Gruesome stories are doing the rounds; tales of self-inflicted wounds or 'SIWs' which we talk about in low voices. Such an act is a capital offence: we have been told to suspect wounds to the hands and feet. Knowing which type of bullet has made the wound is crucial, and so we've also been taught some ballistics: how the British Lee Enfield rifles fire .303 calibre bullets, compared with the .323 calibre of the German Mausers. Woe betides the soldier whose wound is discovered to have come from his own bullet.

Some soldiers are going beyond an SIW and choosing suicide; the usual method is to remove the boot and sock from one foot, place the muzzle of the Lee-Enfield rifle in the mouth and then press the trigger with the big toe. I can't understand why they don't all choose the simpler way: standing on the trench fire-step and receiving a head shot from a German sniper.

I already know something about the measures men resort to in desperation. In South Africa we used a surgical instrument called 'the coin catcher' on soldiers who had swallowed penny pieces to escape the firing line.

*And it doesn't have to be war, does it? Remember the Waihi Gold-
mining museum where the pickled thumbs of old-time miners were kept on
the shelf, bottled in that straw coloured formalin? How in the early years there
had been no pensions and the only way to get compensation after a lifetime's
hard graft was to be declared unfit – so they would hack off their own thumbs?
The boys used to like seeing them – it makes me smile to think of their wide
eyes staring at the objects in the jars and then at their own thumbs.*

*You say you have been given a weekend's leave – that is perfect timing.
Our unit is due to leave for France that same weekend. As it transpires, there
will be a few hours to kill in Southampton… and that got me thinking: could
you come back across the Channel and meet me there? I want to show you
where my brother is buried. The place is only a few miles from the city. I'm
sure you will be able to ride with us back over to France. Would you do that?
It would mean a great deal to me.*

*We had an exam today: chlorination of water, defensive measures against
gas, early treatment of gassed cases. My God, Sean, what have we got
ourselves into?*

Your friend,
John

****

Royal Victoria Military Hospital, 11th November 1918

Professor S was standing at the window in the electrical laboratory,
staring out at the grey pre-dawn light. I was still sitting on the floor.

"Your brother's buried out there?" he said.

"Yes, in the military cemetery on the other side of those woods."

"So you were here in 1900 as well as now…"

"Yes," I said. "The damn place is like a second home."

It was quiet in the electrical room, just our hushed voices. Outside,
there was no noise at all, not even birdsong.

"Did Rennie make it over, as you had asked in your letter?"

"He did. You would've laughed if you had read his reply – full of his
usual bombast."

I imitated Rennie: "'Good God, John! You don't even have to ask. Of course we're going… After all your stories I feel I know the lad – it's like he was my own brother too.'"

Professor S smiled.

"Anyway," I said, "he pulled some strings and managed to meet me in Southampton."

"He's a good friend to you, this Rennie fellow."

"The very best."

Professor S came and sat back down. He reached over to the packet and lighter on the floor between us.

"Cigarette, John?"

A small pile of stubs lay on the floor.

"Please."

For the first time I noticed the make.

"They're Player's Navy Cut."

"Does that mean something to you?"

"Just that they remind me of visiting the cemetery that day."

We each lit up.

Professor S exhaled slowly. "I'm all ears" he said.

****

Royal Victoria Military Hospital, May 27th 1917

We met up on the station platform at Southampton and boarded a train taking injured soldiers the three miles to Netley along the branch line. The carriages were filled to the gunnels with stretcher cases from the front and at first it seemed as though there would be no room for us, but after seeing the silver ferns on our collars the driver let us ride in his cab with no questions asked and we soon found out the reason why.

"Once played your lot at rugby," he said "Devon against New Zealand – first match of their 1905 tour."

The train driver certainly looked the part – cauliflower ears and crooked nose. He was a thick set man – that Anglo-Saxon type who, in days gone by, would have been one of King Harold's Housecarls at

Hastings, those bodyguards swinging the biggest two-handed battle axes in the entire Army.

"Fifty-five points to bloody four they beat us by, and we were the favourites mind… felt like we was run over by a steamroller. Should've known they meant business when they did their war dance before the match. Asked one of them afterwards what their secret was. Gallaher his name was – their captain; quiet fellow, modest. Know what he told me? Said they used the 'Sandow developer' on the ship on the way over to build up their muscles. You know it? That spring contraption that you stretch… tell you what though, the hiding we took made me go out and buy one the very next day, and blow me down if my game didn't improve. Anyhow, it was after that game that our local newspaper – the Express and Echo – first called them the 'All Blacks'."

Rennie humoured the driver by listening to his old stories, saying 'is that so?' and 'my goodness' at various points. He was very good at this – I suppose it was no different to visiting parishioners back home when he would have to sip tea and socialise. Rennie excelled at making people feel important, because to him they were. Perhaps it was because he believed that his earthly conduct would be judged one day: 'inasmuch as ye have done it unto one of the least of these my brethren, ye have done it unto me.' He was always saying that.

I just stared out of the window, still hypnotised by the England I had almost forgotten, details that I had never really noticed. Oak trees for instance. As a child and young man, they had been the green backdrop to my observable world. Now it felt as if I was really seeing them for the first time, like a girl you have known for years who you suddenly realise is truly beautiful.

A bugle call announced our train's arrival at the hospital.

The driver told us he would be returning to the docks at noon and that we were welcome to ride back with him.

We stepped out onto a platform packed with soldiers. Some were in uniform with kitbags at their feet, returning to duty, others were propped up on crutches, arms in slings or legs missing; men who had been discharged home to an uncertain future. 'God only knows what's in store for me now' their expressions seemed to be saying. And the faces of the soldiers heading back to the front weren't much different.

On the station wall was a poster of a soldier in 'hospital undress' – the distinctive blue suit and red tie. He was in a wheelchair and a nurse was attending him. Unlike those on the platform, the characters in the poster seemed inordinately happy, the caption reading:

'ARE WE DOWNHEARTED? NO! NOT AT NETLEY.'

Right behind the station was the chapel and beyond that the main hospital building. On the third floor, I could see a nurse leaning out of a window, watching the new arrivals with interest, perhaps triaging them in her mind to work out who among the gathering would be going to her ward. For some reason I felt compelled to wave up at her. She smiled and waved back. It was only a fleeting connection but it went straight to the heart; one of those rare moments Freddie had described as 'really' living. The sociable train driver had been friendly and generous enough, but this small gesture meant more to me and made visiting Freddie's grave feel a lot less daunting.

The cemetery was a good half mile from the hospital, at the end of a forest track.

On the left, just visible through the woods, was the asylum – 'D block' – which I could vaguely recall from my time at the hospital complex in 1900, though we had never gone too close to it then.

Somewhere in the trees a wood pigeon was cooing. It was always the sounds of the birds that I found most evocative of a place. Arriving in Australia, hearing the shrieks of the multi-coloured parrots and the cackling laughs of the Kookaburra had made me realise what an alien place it was. And then the call of the Tui bird in New Zealand, with a peculiar sound all of its own… The green of the oak trees and the coo of the pigeon were having the same effect now.

Even though I thought of Freddie most days, and he was always there in the background of my mind, it would still be strange to see his headstone again after all this time.

I started feeling uneasy.

Rennie and I walked in silence. No bible quotes now – he knew the significance of this pilgrimage and was being respectful of my feelings. He was good that way, with enough empathy to read a situation and decide when it was best to say nothing. A lot smarter in fact, than he sometimes made himself out to be. I was certainly glad of his company. As my best friend – practically a brother himself – I had always wanted him to see the place where my real brother was buried.

In the cemetery were two freshly dug graves, with the earth piled onto flat wooden boards beside them. Two gravediggers were standing to one side of the holes, leaning on their shovels and smoking. The scene pierced into my memory painfully. At Freddie's funeral, it had been almost the same layout, though with just one grave, one flat board of dirt and one gravedigger smoking.

It was a warm day now, like it had been when Freddie was buried.

The grave-diggers' shirtsleeves were rolled up and their jackets were hanging over the fence. I thought of Manu and Kahu and wondered if this is how they would appear on the front, digging trenches and smoking cigarettes with their new army friends, perhaps even preparing graves for other fallen soldiers.

Rennie and I walked over to another part of the cemetery – the Boer War section. It seemed paltry and half-forgotten compared to the neat lines of wooden crosses from the current war, but at least the old graves had proper headstones.

There it was, lonely and forgotten with no fresh flowers.

My father had died in 1912 and I suppose the grave had not been visited by anyone since. My mother had died bringing Freddie and I into the world. Apart from me, no-one else knew he was buried here. Not even the only other living beings connected to Freddie – Kate and Harry Ingram – knew this place existed.

Freddie's headstone was covered in a thin film of green and yellow lichen and the words were all but illegible. I unfolded my pocketknife and, like an archaeologist deciphering hieroglyphics on some ancient tomb, I started scratching out the lichen from the grooves of the lettering. It came away easily, revealing the inscription:

ALFRED HUNSTON
MIDDLESEX REGIMENT
DIED JUNE 1, 1900
FROM FEVER CONTRACTED IN SOUTH AFRICA,
AGE 25.
'MEMENTO MORI'

There was a mound of composted clippings and discarded flowers in the corner of the cemetery and, while I was busy with the knife, Rennie picked through the pile, coming back with a forlorn looking bunch of daffodils and setting them down carefully at the base of Freddie's plinth.

He knelt down and pointed at the epitaph.

"What does this mean – *Memento Mori?*"

"Remember you will die," I said. "It was one of his favourite expressions. He said it reminded him to live fully, not to waste a moment."

"I do like that… I like that a lot. Do you mind if I make a note of that, John – for my sermons I mean?"

I glanced at him, smiling. "I don't mind at all, Sean."

He took his bible from a pocket, bound with a rubber band which also held a pen. Removing the lid, he licked at the nib to get the ink running. It was a compliment – his wanting to record the words – because Rennie's black book was his most precious possession and whatever was written in the margins had to be deemed especially worthy.

As he scribbled, I stood there at Freddie's graveside feeling nothing much. It was hard to be sad. The acute grief from long ago had morphed itself into a kind of weary acceptance. So much time had passed. Besides, Freddie – or his 'figment', or whatever it was – had been with me all these years. He certainly wasn't here. This was just a stone marking the place where his bones were buried.

"Do you really think that he's… well… that he's *somewhere?*" I said.

Rennie had finished writing. Still crouching, he put his hand on the headstone, looked up at me and nodded.

"Yes."

Memento Mori – remember you will die. To my shame I had forgotten this. Now the pain started to come but it wasn't sorrow – it was regret. Somewhere along the line, I had stopped living and become afraid. Materoa knew it – she had seen how I had closed myself off. Jennifer had known it too. The feeling of remorse – of not having done Freddie's memory justice – threatened to overwhelm me. I had been wallowing in grief when I should have been focusing on living.

"SEVENTEEN YEARS," my brother was shouting at me. "THAT'S HOW MUCH BLOODY TIME YOU'VE WASTED, YOU MISERABLE OLD BUGGER. I COULD HAVE LIVED A HUNDRED LIFETIMES IN SEVENTEEN YEARS."

I shook my head as I acknowledged this truth. "I've been wasting my life, haven't I, Sean?"

Rennie stood up and put his hand on my shoulder.

"No, John. I don't think so… not at all. And don't ask me to judge you. I can't even begin to comprehend what you must have been through."

He gave a small smile.

"You didn't waste it" he said again.

It was unlike Rennie to be so, well… 'normal' I suppose. Not coming at me with bible quotes here on the hallowed ground, making everything solvable with some lines from one of the gospels. We stood there in silence for perhaps another minute or so, looking at the headstone together. 1900 – My God. It was another era entirely. So much had happened since, and so much was going to happen, and then there was Freddie, consigned for all time to his allotted 1875 – 1900 span. Just a memory from another era, unless you happened to believe there was another place. Here in the cemetery though, where everything felt so bloody final and dead, it was hard to believe.

I stepped back, not taking my eyes off the grave.

"You know, Sean," I said, "It's the strangest thing. You don't ever get over loss, but in time, your grief becomes a friend. You get used to it. Even get to *depend* on it."

I didn't believe Rennie's reassurance that I hadn't been wasting my time and the weight of my remorse hung heavy. Walking back down the tree-lined avenue towards the hospital I had a newfound feeling of resolve – not to waste another second. To live the way Freddie had once advised – moment to moment. It was time to wake up.

We were diverted by a funeral taking place on a patch of lawn just out of sight of the hospital. It was a Hindu burial with a funeral pyre which had already been lit. Standing in solemn attendance was a crowd of men in turbans, sheltered by a tall open-air structure with a canvas roof. A shallow trench had been dug under the burning pyre and two young men were steadily pouring water from a gallon drum into the far end of the trench so that it flowed down, under the pyre and then into a natural stream and out towards Southampton Water.

"Why have they done that?" I said to Rennie.

"In India, cremations are always carried out by a sacred river – preferably the Ganges. It looks like they've decided to make one of their own. Perhaps in a few years some of the dead man's molecules will have reached the Ganges thousands of miles away, and what are a few years in the time-span of eternity?"

"And why the tent? It's a nice summer's day. They don't need it."

"It's the 1902 Cremation Act," Rennie said in a whisper. "As long as it's in an enclosed building a cremation is allowed."

I looked at the temporary-looking shelter – a fairly loose interpretation of a building.

One of the Hindu men was saying a prayer and his voice carried over to where we were standing.

"O Supreme light, lead us from untruth to truth, from darkness to light and from death to immortality."

Rennie got out his Bible again and started to write.

"I think I'll visit the chapel," Rennie said, as we approached the main hospital building.

I was enjoying the sun on my face and didn't want to sit inside in the dark.

"Fine" I said, "I'll be out on the pier. Come and find me when you're done."

Determined not to lose my sense of purpose, I walked around to the front of the hospital which faced Southampton Water.

A group of convalescents were on the lawn having their photograph taken. The men in the front row were either sitting or lying on the grass, their crutches and canes nearby, all wearing the blue 'hospital undress'. In the second row were a few red-caped nurses and two men in basket stretchers. At the foot end of one of the stretchers was a small boy, sitting on the quilt covering the man I presumed to be his injured father. The boy was looking as sombre as possible and the photographer kept lifting his head away from the eyepiece of his camera and shouting over, "Come on now, young laddy, give us a smile."

Just then the boy noticed me standing there. Without thinking, I pulled a funny face and poked out my tongue and he started to laugh.

The pier hadn't changed and neither had the sound the boards made under my footfall – they still rumbled in their steel frame like a giant wooden xylophone.

I walked to the end and sat on the bench where Freddie and I had spent his final days, making plans and smoking roll ups.

Someone else was there. A man was sitting at the edge of the pier just a few yards away, his feet dangling over the side. He was in 'hospital undress' and mumbling to himself and I didn't know whether or not he had heard me arrive. I leant forward and listened closely; it wasn't English – he was speaking Latin.

"Dulce et decorum est pro patria mori," he kept saying repetitively, rocking slightly in rhythm to the words.

I recognised the "Dulce et decorum est," from school. Crosbie – our old Latin teacher – had made each one of us stand at the front of the class and recite it.

"The Odes of Horace," I said out loud.

The man stopped talking to himself and turned round to look at me, and when I saw his sad hollow face, I immediately recognised it as the frontage of a mind loaded with bad memories. In his case, they were undoubtedly memories from the war. He had long fair hair, swept right back, except for a few rebellious strands which had sprung forward and were hanging over his forehead, like the fronds of a fern. Despite being young, he looked absolutely worn out.

"It is sweet and fitting to die for your country," I said. "From Horace, correct?"

He didn't say anything.

"Two thousand years old – it's an ancient saying."

Still no reply.

Perhaps he could see I was new, that I hadn't been marked by the horrors of this war.

I didn't know if it was my clean uniform that gave me away or the fact that I must have just looked like a novice, my fresh features as yet untroubled by the sights from the Front. Despite the fact I was twice as old as him, it seemed as if he were the older man.

"I'm just visiting here" I said, "I leave for France this afternoon."

The man continued to stare at me.

"My brother's buried here," I said.

The soldier didn't seem to take in the words. He just turned back round to stare out across the blue waters to the New Forest on the other side.

"He died a long time ago," I said, continuing on, despite his apparent lack of interest. "Not in this war, in the Boer War. We used to sit here on this pier and smoke together; used to leave our ward in the night and smoke out here in the dark"

God, I was gabbling.

The man stayed silent and I kept up the one way conversation. Strangely I found it quite comforting.

I decided to have one more go at engaging him.

"How are you finding the place?"

Instead of replying directly, he started to mumble more obscure Latin phrases to himself again and rock back and forth.

I looked out across the water, in the same direction as his stare.

On the other side, the New Forest hugged the shoreline. The trees came right down to the shingle and made it look like a wild, unexplored land in a remote part of the world.

He was praying now – the Lord's Prayer, again in Latin:

"Pater noster
qui es in coelis...
sanctificatur nomen tuum…
adveniat regnum tuum….
fiat voluntus tua…"

As he chanted his way through it, I let myself go back to the trees across the water.

I wondered what we might look like from over there, two small figures on the pier with the giant building behind us. My intention on coming out here had been to reflect on the past and fine tune my new philosophy of living, but that plan had been ambushed. Now I wanted to be over on that far shore, enjoying the peace and quiet, and not here, listening to this damaged soldier. From over the water he would just look like a man sitting on the pier, not the shell-shocked husk that seemed to have resorted to mouthing anything Latin that entered his head.

He finished the prayer and then started it again, as if the more he recited it, the more likely it was that God might intervene and make everything better in his mind.

After the third time the soldier said a final, "Amen," and slowly stood up to leave, shaking his head, possibly in disappointment that the Almighty had not responded. As he passed the bench I was on, he reached down and gave me his Player's Navy Cut and a box of matches.

"To help you remember your brother," he said, with unexpected tenderness. He then walked away down the pier. I called out my thanks and he just raised his hand without looking back.

I struck a match and lit one of the cigarettes. The man was right – the tobacco smoke did bring back memories of Freddie, far more than the trip to the graveyard had done. It was the smell of it. I could swear that smell was the most nostalgic of all the senses, with a line direct to 'memory central'. It was as if I had been transported back in a time machine.

When I heard footsteps I thought the man might have changed his mind about the cigarettes, but it was Rennie. He plonked himself down heavily on the bench.

"I've never seen you smoke."

"Well you have now."

"Can I try one?"

It wasn't really a question; he had already taken one from the packet.

I watched him struggling to light the cigarette, before taking a deep draw. Rather amateurish.

"This'll be interesting," I said.

Rennie proceeded to cough for an entire minute. Just when I thought the spasms were over, another set began again.

It should have been funny but the coughing reminded me too much of Freddie's pneumonia on the night he had died. With considerable effort, I pushed the association to the back of my mind.

Memento Mori - I remembered that I had resolved to start living for a change, to make connections and accumulate moments. *Remember you will die,* and my addendum; *so you should get on with some living.* It would be my new credo.

You had to laugh at the timing though; just as we were going off to war. Thinking this made me smile and Rennie wrongly assumed it was amusement at his botched attempt at smoking.

"Confounded thing… You could have told me how to do it properly."

He threw the burning cigarette over the side and into the water.

"At least you've given it a proper Hindu funeral," I said.

I went over and leant against the railing, smoking the rest of my cigarette and gazing out at the far shore.

Chapter Nine

There I was, aboard ship, leaning on another handrail, smoking another cigarette.

Since meeting the man on the hospital pier earlier that day I had smoked all his Navy Cut, bought myself a thirty packet carton from a tobacconist at Southampton docks and was into my next packet already.

For the last ten minutes I had been standing on the deck of the troopship, watching the coastline of Northern France getting closer. I was thinking, not unreasonably, that it might be the last time I ever saw the sea. I wondered what would happen if I decided to jump overboard and start swimming back to England. Would they turn the ship around? Would they shoot me? Or would they just let me go, leaving me to the waiting depths. I couldn't see the coastline of England anymore, but swimming back was tempting. It wasn't an impossible feat. There were a couple of people who had done it before, though I doubted I would last much longer than an hour.

"Hunston, stop your bloody daydreaming," a voice said. It was Captain McKenzie, my CO. I threw the cigarette over the side, turned around and saluted him.

He thrust a piece of paper into my hand.

"Read it" he said.

HQ RAMC, Number 13 General Hospital, the Casino, Boulogne-Sur-Mer

"What's this, sir?"

"What does it look like? It's a bloody address."

McKenzie liked to swear a lot. He swore even more than the Australians I had once known and that was saying something. Rennie – thank God – had gone to work on a sermon in the lounge and was not around to hear my CO's colourful language. I'm not sure McKenzie would have toned it down even he had been standing right next to me. Not out of disrespect, mind you, but because swearing was just an innate part of his speech pattern, as if a genetic mutation had affected the Broca's area of his brain in some way, and was therefore something he couldn't control.

I was fairly certain McKenzie wasn't actually angry, that it was just his way. He certainly thought a lot of himself, I could see that. It was Type 2 confidence. McKenzie had trained as a general surgeon, so even before he'd joined the army and had been made captain he would already have thought he was pretty special. It was just the two of us standing there, but it felt as if we were on a big ward round and it was my turn to be humiliated. It didn't get to me at all though – I was too old to care. I was good at taking whatever it was he wanted to dish out.

"What I meant, sir, is why are you giving it to me?"

"I want you to bloody well go there."

"Go there, sir?"

"Yes. As soon as we disembark. You're to report to Colonel Wright."

"Colonel Wright, sir?"

I was wondering if it was the same Wright I had once known.

"Christ almighty, Hunston – what's got into you today? Are you going to parrot everything I bloody well say back to me? Have you turned into a bloody parrot, Hunston?"

"No, sir."

"Do I look like a bloody idiot, Hunston?"

He did a little.

"No, sir."

"Find out the latest information on treating field wounds. Wright has set up an entire laboratory devoted solely to wound sepsis."

"Right, sir."

"Can I trust you to do that, Hunston?"

"Yes, sir."

"I don't want us arriving at the front and poring through medical manuals like a bunch of bloody idiots. I want us to be fully operational, Hunston. I want us to be the most effective Field Ambulance in the whole bloody NZEF."

"Yes, sir, operational, sir."

"Good. You have two hours before we move out towards the front."

I looked at the address again.

"The Casino... Are you sure about that, sir?"

"Yes I'm bloody sure, Hunston. It says so on that bloody bit of paper, doesn't it?"

"Yes, sir – it does."

"You think I'm wrong, Hunston. Is that it?"

"No, sir."

I saluted him again and trotted off like an obedient dog.

The one thing McKenzie had going for himself was that, in his own unique way, he actually did care.

Yes sir, no sir, three bags bloody full, sir – it was all a game and I was happy to play along if it meant fewer men dying.

I found the Casino on the seafront, where any decent Casino should be.

To the side of the building under a veranda lay a line of men on stretchers, all wrapped up in woollen blankets and wearing caps. Down on the beach a group of soldiers were having a kick about with a football – Australians against English from what I could make out from the accents. "Call that a tackle, ya pommie bastard..."

"Let's put these criminals back on the transports boys..."

Whoever had carried the stretcher cases out, had unthinkingly laid them down facing the sandbags of the Casino wall and not out towards the beach. A few were craning their necks to try and see the match, but most just lay still, staring up at the canopy and listening to the competitive shouts among the players.

"I'm Lieutenant Hunston, here to see Colonel Wright" I said.

The Royal Army Medical Corps orderly at the front desk saw the cherry-red band on my lemon-squeezer hat.

"You the N Zedder?"

"That's right."

"One moment, sir."

As he picked up the telephone on his desk I studied his uniform, familiar because I had once worn the very same. The button holding down his shoulder strap had the rod of Asclepius – the snake winding around the staff – and the brass title 'RAMC' was clearly visible. My shoulder strap had the same cherry red trim as his and the same button. The only difference was that my brass title spelt out 'NZMC'.

Behind the orderly, the door to the baccarat room was ajar and I could see it was full of beds, lined up end to end, each occupied by a patient. Jam packed. So far in Boulogne I had seen more injured men than healthy ones.

"Colonel, I have an ANZAC MO to see you… Lieutenant Hunston… Yes, sir."

The orderly replaced the receiver and pointed to the stairs.

"Top floor, sir… end of the corridor. The lab is in the fencing school. The sign above the door says 'Salle d'Escrime'."

"Can I just enquire; is the Colonel's full name Almroth Wright?"

"Yes sir, it certainly is – Sir Almroth Edward Wright."

So it was the same man I had once met.

No doubt the lab would be all men – Wright being a Victorian male-chauvinist dinosaur. Not only did he forbid females to work in his laboratories but he also opposed their entering medicine at all, famously stating as far back as 1895 that, "Women are by nature unfitted for the pursuit and practice of the medical profession." More recently, he had been outspoken in his opposition to women's suffrage; in a letter to *The Times* in 1912 he had claimed that the window breaking protests and agitation of the suffragettes was due to their 'physiology' and their being unmarried.

Materoa would have made mincemeat of him.

That was the negative side of the man. Paradoxically it was this bull-headed, opinionated personality that had helped him rise to the top of his specialism. He pursued pathology with a pathological zeal and was legendary in his field; when developing his typhoid inoculation, he had injected himself first with doses of the dead bacteria.

I had met him in June 1900 when I had been convalescing at the Royal Victoria Military Hospital after returning from the Boer War. At that time he had been Professor of Pathology for the Royal Army Medical College with laboratories occupying a whole floor of 'C block'.

My clearest memory of that visit was the rattling sound of glass vials in a test-tube stand after he had thumped the lab bench in anger. He had done it because of his frustration at the men running the War Office, and how they had been swayed by a statistician's opinion that the typhoid inoculation data showed no significant benefit to the patient. As a result, inoculations were suspended, a catastrophic decision leading to thousands of British soldiers dying in the Bloemfontein typhoid epidemic, far more than those killed at the hands of the Boers. I had seen the disaster unfold in the field, and then experienced it first-hand after contracting the disease myself in April 1900.

Wright had sworn to me that he would be perfecting the inoculation for the next war and history had proved him to be as good as his word. Over the years, I had kept tabs on him. Resigning his post at Netley in disgust, he had gone to work at St Mary's in London. Fourteen years were to pass before his chance at redemption had come in the form of another war. By then he had prepared ten million doses of vaccine. I had read about it in a frayed and yellowing copy of *The Times* which somehow had pitched up in my surgery waiting room in New Zealand during the winter of 1914. The newspaper contained an article by Wright, which was essentially a direct appeal to the War Office, drawing attention to the risk of typhoid among the troops fighting in Northern France.

This time the Army had listened – Kitchener ordered a mandatory inoculation programme for all troops serving abroad and the incidence of typhoid on the Western Front had been negligible.

It was with bitter retrospect that I wished the decision makers in 1900 had listened to Wright; if they had heeded his recommendations, then the lives of thousands, Freddie's and mine included, would have turned out very differently.

But typhoid was yesterday's news; the major issue for the medical services in France was wound sepsis. That's why McKenzie had sent me here; to glean something of value, anything that might help our cause and give us the edge. And if the advice was coming from the mouth of Professor Almroth Wright himself, then I was only too happy to listen.

The door to the 'Salle d'Escrime' was wide open. The large room – which pre-war had been graced by men in white battling each other with swords – was now a working bacteriological laboratory where men in white coats battled against microbes. It was a make-do affair: wood-panelled walls, some scrounged benches and chairs, methylated spirit burners instead of Bunsen's, presumably because there was no gas supply, and oil heaters for incubators. A roulette table – its grooves filled with test tubes – had been wired up to a motor and was spinning around like a centrifuge. There was a stove standing to one side, the chimney pipe going up through the ceiling, but it wasn't very large, and I imagined that in winter, conditions here would be bitterly cold.

Almroth Wright was sitting with a colleague at a green felt table which had once been used for blackjack. I approached them both and saluted.

"Colonel."

He hadn't changed much – a little greyer at the temples perhaps, the moustache bushier – but his penetrating gaze told me his intellect was still razor sharp. He made a vague attempt at a salute which didn't surprise me. After his past experience of the Army I was surprised he bothered to salute at all.

"Ah, Lieutenant Hunston," he said, "your CO called ahead and told me you would be visiting. Welcome to the war." He pointed to the man sitting next to him. "This is my colleague, Doctor Fleming."

Fleming was in a clean white lab coat, but his eyes were dark and in shadow, like those of a chronic insomniac. He nodded at me.

"And over there," Wright said, indicating a man leaning over the tubes at the Roulette table, "is my able assistant, Sergeant Clayden."

I saluted the assistant and he saluted back.

"Sit," Wright said, waving at me to take an empty chair at their blackjack table, like a high rolling gambler being dealt in.

An uncomfortable silence passed. Lab scientists were always so bloody awkward. I was just about to say something when Wright finally spoke.

"Alex here found the cure for syphilis," he said, breaking the ice.

"Oh, Salvarsan. Yes, I've used it." I said.

The two English scientists glanced at one another momentarily, eyebrows raised.

"On patients, I mean."

Wright leant his head back and looked up at the ceiling. Was that a smile I could see?

"Doctor Hunston here worked for the RAMC in the Boer War, Alex."

I was stunned by Wright's memory – I had doubted he would even remember me.

He kept talking to his colleague Fleming.

"Do you know Alex, that on one troopship, all my boxes of typhoid inoculation serum were thrown into the Southampton Water before it had even set sail for South Africa? That's how stupid the Army brass was at the time."

Fleming looked at me, his expression unchanging.

Wright started to laugh to himself and talked on.

"There was a lot of misunderstanding about the inoculation... once I received a rather stuck up message requesting a dose of typhoid vaccine 'suitable for the Marquis of X'. Know what I did?"

Fleming shook his head.

"I sent it by special messenger with a covering note: 'Enclosed please find a dose of vaccine suitable for the Marquis of X' – and then, in brackets I added: 'SAME DOSE AS FOR COMMON SOLDIER…'"

I smiled at the anecdote, but Fleming didn't – it was as if the story had been told in a foreign language.

"So you never married?" Wright said, noting the absence of a wedding ring on my finger.

"No, not yet."

I looked around the room out of embarrassment, avoiding his eye.

"Don't expect to find any women in here," Wright said, mis-reading my action. "I don't have them in the laboratory. If they are ugly they annoy me, and if they are pretty they trouble me."

Wright checked himself.

"Anyhow," he said, coming back to the point, "as I recall, you came back to Netley riddled with typhoid fever… both you and your brother, wasn't it?"

"That's right."

"How's he doing?"

"He didn't make it, sir."

"Oh dear, forgive me. I'd forgotten that."

Even Wright's memory was fallible then.

"Not at all," I said without emotion. "It was a long time ago."

"I had a crippled son who lived in constant pain," he said. "Four years ago he shot himself in the chest because he couldn't stand it anymore. I was at his bedside when he died."

In 1900 Wright had reminded me of my own father, the same serious stare and the same handlebar moustache. Seeing him now, with the hurt in his face as he talked of his dead son, brought back a vivid memory of my father after Freddie had died. There are no words to describe what I had seen in my father's face. A part of him had broken beyond repair. He did not speak for the entire day of the funeral – not one word. It had been terrible, truly terrible to see him that way – perhaps even worse than seeing Freddie in his coffin. As a brother I had suffered, but I could not even begin to imagine the pain of losing a child. I suddenly felt very sorry for poor old Wright.

He appeared to gather himself and he moved the conversation along, addressing me again.

"Alex here was in South Africa too? Isn't that right, Alex?"

Fleming nodded. "London Scottish," he said.

"You will observe that my colleague is a man of few words," Wright said, "but don't take it personally, Hunston. It's modesty, not rudeness."

Another silence ensued. Fleming seemed like a man more comfortable staring down the lens of a microscope than conducting human discourse. The conversation was going along like a motor vehicle which kept breaking down just as it got up to speed.

Across the room, the lab assistant had switched off the roulette motor and was removing the test tubes, one at a time, and putting them into wooden test tube holders.

Wright pointed at my uniform.

"So... New Zealand, eh? The last time I saw you, you were thinking about going to Australia, weren't you? What happened?"

"Correct again, Colonel. Your recall is formidable. I did indeed work in Australia for a time but I finally ended up crossing the Tasman. Gold rush towns seem to be my chosen domain. Anyway, before I knew it, I'd clocked up seventeen years."

Wright made a snorting sound that I took to be mirth of some kind.

"Then came conscription," I said. "And here I am, in the Field Ambulance, and off to the front."

"The story of my life by Lieutenant Hunston," Wright said, I think in an attempt to make a joke, though it came across as slightly mean. I could see he was becoming impatient – a man used to hearing his own voice rather than that of others.

Wright started drumming his fingers on the table, as if he was asking the blackjack dealer for another card. "What are you doing here Hunston?"

I tried to say my speech the way I had practised it on the walk to the Casino.

"My CO wants our unit to hit the ground running when we go up the line. He's a surgeon by training and he's keen to get the latest advice on wound care. Any tips would be useful."

Wright twirled the ends of his moustache thoughtfully.

"Tips?"

"Um…yes. I've seen what happens when people ignore what you have to say, Professor; seen it up close and personal as you have just recalled. I realise that the typhoid fever angle has now been covered, of course."

The edges of Wright's eyes creased and he almost grinned.

"Yes, it has, hasn't it? In South Africa there were over 57,000 cases, with 9000 deaths, in an army of two hundred thousand. Here, there are around two million men… bear in mind the conditions here are much more suited to typhoid fever. I estimate there would be around 125,000 typhoid fever deaths had my inoculation not been made mandatory; as it is there have only been around 1,000. So yes, that angle, as you so eloquently say, has been covered."

He looked to Fleming.

"Anything to offer our friend here, Alex? Young Hunston here is searching for *tips*…"

Fleming furrowed his brow for a moment.

"Your CO is right; wounds will be your big problem," he said.

"I've seen battlefield wounds before," I said, "in South Africa, I mean."

Fleming shook his head as if I didn't understand.

"Shrapnel wounds from the Western Front make the Mauser wounds from the Boer war look like pin pricks in comparison."

Despite all the bullying and the swearing, McKenzie assumed that I was the battalion authority on this kind of thing because I had been in the Boer War. For that, I had his begrudging respect and I am sure that is why he had given me this job. Now it turned out I actually knew nothing.

Seeing my uncertainty, Fleming tried to explain: "In South Africa, the Veldt was bare and dry and contained next to no pathogens. Projectile wounds were mainly from bullets fired from a distance, often passing through limbs and healing quickly and without complication. Flanders fields are cultivated, fertilised with manure for hundreds of years. There are thousands of horses out there now. The Germans have even started pointing their outflow pipes towards our lines. The mud is full of faecal bacteria and spores. A soldier will come to you with severe lacerations, his soft tissues crushed and devitalised. Deep in the wounds will be fragments of shell or bomb and pieces of clothing, mud, and bacteria, carried in by the missile."

Wright chipped in at this point: "We are wont to classify the patients in our military hospitals as sick or wounded – 'S' or 'W'. In reality, all, or nearly all, are suffering from bacterial infections."

"So we should be writing 'B' on their medical cards" I said, thinking myself quite the wit.

The two of them looked at me without expression, not a trace of humour on their faces.

Bloody pathologists, I thought.

Fleming reached across to a pile of journals on the green baize and passed the uppermost to me.

"*The Lancet* 1915 – it's all there in black and white."

The title of the paper read: '*On the bacteriology of septic wounds*'.

He jabbed his finger onto a table buried amongst the text.

"This shows the timelines for the bugs – when their numbers peak after a wound. In a new wound you not only have your anaerobes – your clostridium tetani and your bacillus aerogenes capsulatus – but also your staphylococci and streptococci. And then there are all the faecal pathogens – the coliforms – from all the excrement."

Fleming looked at me to check if I was keeping up.

Discussing microbes had turned him into a chatterbox. He talked about these things as if they were neighbours living down the street; the Smiths, the Turners, the Joneses.

"Coliforms," I said, nodding vigorously, "from the sewage."

I was trying to recall what they had taught me in the School of Pathology as an eighteen year old student. It wasn't much – in fact on a particularly hot summer's day I had been so bored that I had climbed out of an open window when the lecturer's back was turned and headed down to the river to row.

"Luckily we have the anti-tetanus serum, so that's one anaerobe taken care of" Fleming said. "It's the other anaerobe that'll be your biggest nightmare – bacillus aerogenes capsulatus. It causes gas gangrene and it's in 80% of wounds from days 1 to 9 after the injury. Gas gangrene is a disaster. It only takes eight hours for a man wounded in the leg to be gangrenous up to the level of the umbilicus. A man lying around injured all day in no man's land is as good as dead."

Fleming was starting to scare me.

"Put simply," he said, "you need to tell your CO that the faster the men can be operated on, the less chance they have of getting gangrene. Antiseptic is about as much use as spitting into the wind… does more harm than good as a matter of fact. It kills the body's natural defences and actually encourages the growth of the anaerobes. Do NOT use it. Cleaning the wound with a simple 5% hypertonic saline solution is what works best; it promotes the flow of lymph which contains the phagocytes."

I had pulled out my notebook by now and was jotting it all down.

"Five percent saline," I said out loud.

Wright looked at me.

"Unfortunately, Hunston," he said, "our opinions on antiseptics and their general uselessness has caused a rumpus with the esteemed Sir William Cheyne, President of the Royal College of Surgeons. Politics always gets in the way of what's right. You won't be surprised to learn that some rather vitriolic exchanges between Cheyne and I have been aired in the journals these last few years. So far our recommendations haven't been taken up by the army medical services – they're still favouring strong antiseptic."

"So antiseptics should be avoided?"

This was counter to what I had been taught at Awapuni and Ewshot. Half my medical bag was filled with bottles of 2 % creosol.

"Indeed they should," Wright said. "I'm afraid Sir William has been making his judgements within a committee, and as we all know, committees don't get anything practical done at all. He has not seen for himself the wounds inflicted by high explosives out here. He and his committee of acolytes do not seriously consider the possibility that microbes might be embedded in the tissues. There's no evidence that antiseptics will kill microbes deeper deeper than a surface scratch…

and I'm afraid that we're dealing with slightly more than scratches in this war. There are men downstairs whose wounds have gone right down to the bone."

Wright sighed before adding:

"My esteemed surgical colleague is more soothsayer than scientist. He says that in disinfecting a wound – and I quote – 'the surgeon must *believe* that such disinfection is possible'. I'm afraid that's the sort of hocus pocus we've been up against."

"I can assure you that I will act on your advice, gentlemen, and so will my CO… even if he is a surgeon."

"Good," Fleming said, smiling and taking up the reins once more. "When a patient presents to your RAP, just whack on a field dressing, give him his anti-tetanus serum and some morphia and get him back to the CCS straightaway."

"Fast treatment in the Regimental Aid Post then off to the Casualty Clearing Station," I said, trying to show I was paying attention, and that I had remembered the acronyms for all these places.

"Yes, because the CCS is where the most important procedure will occur – the operation to remove the debris from the wounds and to debride the dead tissue. If this happens early enough, the patient stands a good chance. If not, then the gas gangrene will kill him in a matter of days. If that doesn't, then the pus-forming bacteria in the wound will finish the job later on." Fleming pointed at the figures again. "See how the staph and strep numbers in the wound spike after twenty days."

"I must say, it's demoralising stuff."

"You're right about that, Hunston. The wounds will be more ghastly than anything you've ever seen or smelt. I'm still working on an antibacterial…" Fleming's voice trailed away and he had a far-off look in his eyes, as if he was staring down a very long straight road, along which he was going to have to travel many miles.

"Fast access to surgery," I said, writing it down and trying to bring him back from his daydream.

"Yes, that's right."

He numbered off the points on his fingers.

"Number one: anti tetanus serum; number two: fast surgery. All dead and devitalised tissues to be removed surgically from the wounds A.S.A.P. Number three: thoroughly irrigate the wound with hypertonic saline. Don't use antiseptics. That's it in a nutshell."

Fleming held up the journal and threw it back onto the pile.

"This is all just academic," he said. "You don't need a degree in pathology, what you need is muscle; stretcher bearers who will carry men back to the CCS."

The lab assistant was hovering at Fleming's shoulder.

"I'm sorry to disturb you, Doctor Fleming," he said in a whisper, "but it has happened again, I'm afraid."

"Oh, I'd better have a look at my samples," Fleming said, as if he was a parent going to check on the children. He stood up to go. "If you'll please excuse me. God speed to you, Doctor."

I got up from my chair and shook his hand. "Of course. Your advice is much appreciated. Good luck with your research."

I watched him scurry over and peer at the opaque contents of the test tubes.

"Anything else?" I said to Wright.

He frowned briefly.

"No, Hunston. We've given you the facts, we can't give you the brains."

"Fair enough," I said, taking the jibe well. McKenzie had dished out a lot worse than that.

"I must say, Hunston," Wright said in a low voice, standing up to join me, "I've never heard Fleming in such an expansive mood. Consider yourself lucky. He's one of the most driven people I've ever met, absolutely obsessed with finding something effective to stamp out these microbes. He doesn't usually say much to humans, just mutters to the bacteria in their petri dishes."

Across the room, Fleming was shaking his head and putting each of the tubes back onto the roulette wheel for more centrifuging.

Wright paused for a moment and tried to press down a small tear in the green baize.

"He's right you know," he said.

"Oh? About what?"

"That what you will see on the Western Front will be worse than anything you have ever seen as a doctor; be it the typhoid epidemic in Bloemfontein or Western Australia."

I already knew this, but Wright saying it gave it more immediacy and filled me with trepidation.

"It's the sheer numbers that will overwhelm you," he said. "Sixty thousand British casualties in a single day on the Somme, twenty thousand of them dead. Unbelievable until you actually see it for yourself."

"I appreciate your honesty."

"We might not be shooting at the Boche, Hunston, but you can be assured that Fleming and I will be doing all we can."

Such was the scowl of determination on Wright's face, I almost felt sorry for the pathogens. He pulled out a grubby card from his lab coat pocket and handed it over.

"Give this to your CO. If he wants to know anything else, tell him to get in touch."

I stared at the dog-eared card, worn and smudged with God knows what.

"And tell him you dirtied it," he said.

Pathologists were oddballs, but you couldn't deny the raw facts – these oddballs had saved hundreds of thousands of lives with their anti-tetanus and typhoid inoculations alone. In their own fashion they were keeping the Grey Lady away.

Chapter Ten

Several moss green ambulances were waiting at the dock when I returned from the Casino, their sides marked with large red crosses. Fern leaves on the cab doors indicated that these were the property of the NZ Medical Corps.

Two young ladies were sitting in the front.

"Excuse me, miss?" I said to the one in the driver's seat.

"Yes, sir?"

"When are the ambulance drivers arriving?"

"We are the drivers, sir."

"Oh… right… I see."

Rennie waded in, not in the least put out.

"Can you drop me off at Toc H?" he said.

"No problem at all, Padre. We can drive you there after dropping the Medical Corps at Hazebrouck. It's not too much further on."

I rode in the back of the vehicle with Rennie and a group of ten men.

Toc H was still an enigma. I only knew its location from addressing my letters to Rennie – it was in the town of Poperinghe, just over the Belgian border. All of Rennie's correspondence had been about his heartache for the boys and biblical references. He wrote letters as if they were sermons, with no mention of his day-to-day life. For him, events were inextricably linked to some kind of grand scheme – with Eternity, Heaven and Hell the stage settings, and God, the Devil, angels and demons as the major players. The letters read more like the book of Revelation than war gossip. Although he had mentioned his efforts in trying to track down his sons – so far fruitless – as to his lodgings and his war-time role, he hadn't bothered to elaborate.

I looked at my friend.

"What is this place you've been assigned to? You never say much about it."

"It's a kind of gentlemen's club. Poperinghe is the garrison town near the front."

"A gentlemen's club? What on earth is it doing there?"

"Ahhh," he said, with a broad smile. "Now that would be telling."

Rennie was enjoying his little air of mystery, and I let him have his moment. I knew he would spill the beans in the end. He just liked to surprise people – I think it added a bit of biblical drama to life for him. A minute went by with no explanation. He wasn't ready to tell me yet.

I leant forward and put my hands on the back of the passenger seat.

"Do you know this Toc H?" I said to the woman in front of me.

"Erm… yes, sir," she said, catching Rennie's eye in the rear view mirror. "It's as your friend said, a kind of gentleman's club."

"Why, you're more enigmatic than the Mona Lisa."

I looked from her to Rennie and back again.

"What is this? Piggy in the middle?"

She laughed and I sat back, none the wiser.

"What the hell is this place, Sean?"

Now he was laughing too.

"You'll understand when you visit," he said. "I want it to be a surprise."

The Field Ambulance was not a vehicle; it was a mobile front line medical unit consisting of ten officers and over two hundred men. It was a team.

This is how it worked:

Each Field Ambulance was responsible for a brigade, around three thousand men. Usually, there were three brigades to a division, but since that February, the one NZ Division had been bolstered to four brigades, necessitating a fourth Field Ambulance. The mission of each was to establish a number of points along the casualty evacuation chain for its brigade, including one advanced dressing station – ADS – and the necessary Regimental Aid Posts – RAPs – even closer to the front.

We were the new recruits, brought in to fill in the gaps where they arose, and as yet we did not know which Field Ambulance we would be joining.

Before leaving Boulogne, McKenzie had told us the provisional plan – we were going to a large hospital at Hazebrouck, further back from the front than the Casualty Clearing Stations. There, we would await our orders. As soon as these were issued, we would be moving up the line to help set up the evacuation chain.

On the drive, my thoughts were on our destination of Hazebrouck, where the NZ Stationary Hospital was based. Even though it was called the Stationary Hospital, it had been 'moved' from Amiens on May 31st – just days before. The hospital followed the Division, as the fighting shifted to different areas.

The journey from Boulogne was slow and tedious because we were in a traffic jam the whole way. Giant Howitzers, towed by caterpillar tractors, were moving up to the front, and whenever we overtook one, another would be there, fifty yards in front of us. For four hours we trailed behind these iron monsters, all the way across the Pas de Calais, enveloped in a cloud of dust and gasoline fumes.

Eventually we entered hop country, the vines already half way up the poles. But alongside the hop fields were crops of a completely different nature – plantations of soldiers with their packs and Lee Enfield rifles. Tents – hundreds of them – covered acres of ground. It was a military build-up on a massive scale.

Silhouetting the eastern skyline was a low wooded hill, the only discernible feature on an otherwise bleak and flat horizon. I could see a building of some sort poking out from among the trees on the top.

"What's up on that elevation?" I said to the ambulance driver.

That's what the military was doing to me – getting me to say 'elevation' instead of 'hill'.

"It's part of a Trappist Monastery, sir."

"Oh?"

"Called 'Mont des Cats'. They say the monks brew their own beer up there."

The way she said 'up there' made it sound as if you might need a rope and crampons if you ever dared ascend, though the ridge was more of a pimple on the landscape than a 'mont'. Like other flat places in the world, insignificant rises in the land seemed to take on an enormous importance. The deserts of Western Australia had been the same, with every hillock named by some explorer as if it were Mount Everest. I wondered how Nepali soldiers in the British Expeditionary Force reacted to the piddling topographical features out here in Flanders, when the mighty snow-capped peaks from home were still fresh in their memories.

Rennie stared at the distant monastery.

"Did you say beer-drinking monks?"

"Yes, Padre," she said.

He shook his head in surprise. "Good gracious. I don't know what the world's coming to. Whatever next?"

"How about army Padres running gentlemen's clubs," I said, nudging him in the ribs.

O'Neill, the Lieutenant Colonel who ran the Stationary Hospital, had grey hair which looked incongruous with his young face; so strange it made me think the change in colour had happened recently, and possibly overnight.

The NZMC had taken over a girls' boarding school called College St Francois. The children had simply been moved to another part of the building, and as O'Neill led us down the corridors you could hear the pupils singing or chanting their prayers from the nearby classrooms.

The hospital had three hundred beds, spread over three floors, with space for fifty extra stretchers if needed. On the ground floor was an operating room with two tables. An additional operating theatre had just been fitted out with an adjoining X-ray room. You had the sense that capacity was being ratcheted up; O'Neill said they would be specialising in head injuries when the next big intake came.

We were sitting in the mess on the top floor, drinking tea, when the bell rang for the end of classes. From the window I watched the children filing out of the building into the yard, stepping carefully over stretcher cases waiting to be processed. I could just hear their small voices, shrill and excited; the way all children's voices are after school, chatting away, ignoring the injured soldiers, as if it was the most normal thing in the world to have bleeding and bandaged men lying in their playground.

No orders came.

The next day McKenzie had us all doing odd jobs around the hospital to keep us occupied.

I was loading some theatre supplies when a voice from the new X-ray room stopped me dead in my tracks. The accent was American with a deep nasal resonance, and immediately familiar.

What I could hear was the one-sided conversation of a telephone call:

"This is Captain Poyntz at the NZ Stationary Hospital in Hazebrouck… I'm doing well thank you, Major. I wonder if you can tell me the best magnet for foreign body removal which can be run on a one hundred and ten volt current?"

I poked my head around the doorway.

Poyntz's voice was exactly the same – he had always sounded as if he was suffering from a heavy cold – even the dry air of the Australian desert had failed to clear his chronic rhinitis. If anything, he sounded more congested now.

His general appearance hadn't changed much either. Tall and thin with the same crew cut, his face was lit up starkly by an X-ray light box, making the childhood acne scars pitting his face look like craters on the moon.

The X-ray showed fragments of metal, possibly bullets, lodged into the soft tissue of someone's neck. Poyntz was peering at it while speaking.

"Yes, that's the voltage we have here… What's that, sir? Oh, some poor stretcher bearer from near Hill 63. Shrapnel missed his internal carotid by a Gnat's cock… I know, a lucky fellow sir… All right, yes… What's that? Right, sir, I'll use that one."

He replaced the receiver and ran his hand through his short hair. Then he took another look at the X-ray.

"Goddamn," he said.

He still hadn't noticed me.

The last time I had seen Poyntz was New Year's Eve, 1900 in Kalgoorlie, Western Australia. For four months we had worked together at the St John of God Hospital in that dust ridden metropolis.

When I said, "Hello, Poyntz," he did not turn around straight away.

Instead, for several seconds, he stayed frozen in the same position, processing my voice and sifting it through his memory banks. Then his shoulders relaxed and he started to laugh.

"What the hell?" he said, slowly turning around. "Jack Hunston? Is that really you?"

He strode over to me, gripping my shoulders and studying my face with the same intensity he had been giving the X-ray, before deciding it really was Jack Hunston and clasping me in a bear hug.

I couldn't stop smiling. Poyntz was the only person I had ever known who called me Jack.

"It's really me, Poyntz," I said.

He noticed the silver fern on my collar.

"Goddamn… What's this? New Zealand?"

"Yes."

"So that's where you ended up…" he said, more to himself than to me. "We never heard from you again, Jack… Didn't know what the hell had happened for a while."

He sounded a little hurt now.

I shrugged. "I'm sorry, Poyntz. That bloody town… it nearly killed me."

He put his hand on my shoulder.

"I know, I know. In the end Dudley filled us in…"

He shook his head as if he had already had enough of telling me off and smiled again.

"Goddamn… this calls for a celebration."

Poyntz's quarters were a bell tent in the school field.

He had lined up three ration boxes to make a desk, each crate stencilled with the words 'Simcoe Pork & Beans, Plain Sauce' on one side and 'Dominion Canners Limited, Pure Food Products' on the other.

On the desk was a Gray's Anatomy, open at a page detailing the arteries of the neck. In the drawing they looked like a bundle of long worms. Poyntz's scribbled annotations covered the margins of the page, much like Rennie's notes in his Bible.

He picked up a rum jar, uncorked it and filled two tumblers. He saw me looking at the letters 'SRD' marked on the rim of the jar.

"It stands for Supply Ration Depot, though the Tommies prefer 'Soon Runs Dry'."

I laughed.

"Jack Hunston," he said, handing me my glass and lifting his up. "I still can't quite believe it's you; like a goddamn ghost."

We clinked glasses and drank. The rum tasted like Trinders cough mixture and I wondered if I should get out my cognac instead. I had my flask stashed away in a pocket.

"What's it been?" he said. "Fifteen years?"

"Seventeen."

"We should set it up," Poyntz said, pointing to a chessboard on his desk.

The chessmen were in an upturned helmet on the floor.

Chess had been our way of whiling away the hot days in the St John of God Hospital mess. For weeks we had sat opposite one another, huddled over the board, sweltering and playing games in between ward rounds.

"Allow me," I said, picking up the helmet and emptying out the pieces onto the board.

I looked at the helmet again.

"Is this German?"

"Yep, an M16. See the bullet hole?"

There was a small circular hole on the side, through which he pushed his pen.

"Sometimes I get to fix Germans. This one had a penetrating skull injury. He was still conscious, you know… kept saying 'Mercy Kamerad,' to me. Was still saying it as we put him under anaesthetic. Anyway, I saved his life and he gave me his helmet as a memento."

Poyntz sat down on a collapsible canvas chair and motioned for me to take a seat on his cot, on the other side of the boxes.

Silently, we lined up our pieces and started to play. The loose canvas flap at the tent's entrance moved to and fro in the wind and made a repetitive snapping sound. Seeing Poyntz again had stirred up old memories of Kalgoorlie and I was finding it hard to concentrate. Within a minute he had taken two of my pawns.

"Is your favourite piece still the knight, Jack?"

The fact that he remembered made me smile.

"I suppose so. I haven't played in a long time."

Poyntz took one of my knights and held it up in front of me.

"That's gotta hurt," he said, laughing.

I looked around his digs, my mind not on the game at all.

A rat-eared book was lying face down on his pillow.

"What are you reading?"

"*The Red Badge of Courage*," he said. "It's about the American civil war. I wanted to try and get into the mind-set of a soldier. Turns out the author never even saw a gun fired in anger. Just used his imagination."

I picked up the book and read from the page Poyntz was on:

'At times he regarded the wounded soldiers in an envious way. He conceived persons with torn bodies to be peculiarly happy.'

It was hard to imagine being happy to have a wound. I put the book back down.

A framed wedding photograph was hanging from a nail in the pole by the head of his cot. I unhooked it and looked closely at the picture. It was of Poyntz and Sister B, the nurse we had both adored from the St. John of God Hospital.

"I see that you took my advice and asked her to marry you."

Poyntz smiled.

"That I did, my friend, that I did."

"Is she well?"

I tried to sound as cool as possible. Seeing B again had made my heart do a small somersault. I returned the picture to its place.

He pulled out another photograph from his breast pocket.

"Yup. Here's the latest."

The picture was of B sitting on a lawn, looking right at the camera and laughing. *God almighty,* I thought, *she is still beautiful.* I felt a vestige of the old spell she had once cast over me.

"You're bloody lucky, Poyntz."

"I know it," he said.

There were skyscrapers in the backdrop of the photograph.

"New York?"

He nodded. "Home."

"Any small Poyntzes?"

"Yup. Five – three girls and two boys."

"Five… Good God."

Poyntz laughed. "If you recall, Jack, you were the only non-Catholic member on the staff at the St John of God…"

The Egremont mining company, my employer, had made a deal with the Catholic Hospital in Kalgoorlie; appropriating one of the wards for its own workers for an undisclosed sum of money. The Catholics were happy – the money went to the general upkeep of the place. Sister Bernadette – Sister 'B' as she liked to be called – had been a nursing nun on the wards. Fortunately for Poyntz she was still a postulant, meaning she had not yet taken her vows.

Although every man in the hospital was in love with her, Poyntz had won her heart long before I had shown up on the scene. Sometimes, when we were together in the mess, they let the pretence of being work colleagues drop. Seeing them hold hands or B resting her head against Poyntz's shoulder as we played chess had been bitter sweet.

Poyntz took my queen.

"I still remember what you said to me; that I had better go ahead and marry her before you did. You remember that, Jack?"

"I didn't mean it like that. I just wanted you to get a move on before she became a bride of Christ."

I had meant it like that though – I would have married B in a second, if she had ever expressed an interest, which she never did.

"I know, I know. Anyway, I listened to you, Jack. I needed that kick up the butt. So, I suppose I should thank you."

He put the photograph back in his pocket and looked at me.

"You married?"

"No."

My answer was swallowed up by the enclosed space of the tent. The same question Professor Almroth Wright had asked at the Casino. I was getting sick of everyone asking.

Poyntz leant forward.

"I can see that old look of yours, Jack."

"What look?"

I moved my knight in a vain attempt to prevent Poyntz's invading army overwhelming mine.

"You remember what I once told you about those Cheyenne Indians?"

"Those Contraries you mean?"

"That's it. You do remember. You still a Contrary, Jack?"

I ignored him and concentrated on the board, my chessmen in disarray.

When Poyntz first told me I reminded him of a Cheyenne 'Contrary', it had got right under my skin and I had drunk so much whisky that I had finished up in the deep end of the empty Kalgoorlie swimming baths, drowning in regrets and memories. Later that same night I had paid a visit to a prostitute and that hadn't gone well either – which only served to prove that Poyntz's insight was correct. I was indeed a 'contrary', in matters of physical intimacy as well as in everything else.

A 'Contrary', you see, was a Red Indian who acted by opposites. If they wanted to say 'Yes', they said 'No'. If you asked a Contrary to go away, he came nearer. If invited, he left. When bathing, he washed in the sand and dried off in the river. Somehow, by living this reverse life, the Contraries were purifying themselves into the ultimate warriors; the only time they did things the right way round was in battle.

"Jack? You hear me?"

I sighed. Already, Poyntz had cut me down to the quick. It was as if we had never stopped our games.

"You still think I might be like that?"

"Well, you still got that crazy look."

Poyntz and Materoa – they could both see it as clear as day, as if it was tattooed on my face like a Moko.

A peal of thunder sounded off in the distance and I started.

"Sounds like a storm's coming."

"It's not thunder, Jack – that's shelling at the front."

The noise became a continual rumble.

"You know how someone became a Contrary, Jack?"

I let out another sigh.

"No," I said. "You never told me that part."

Poyntz pointed up.

"Thunder… you had to be afraid of thunder. So a Contrary would go around carrying a sacred spear called the 'thunder-bow' which contained the thunder's… well, its power."

"Like Thor's hammer."

"You got it. This bow was around eight feet long, with a sharp flint at one end, like a lance… and always strung tight. With that in his hand, the contrary wasn't afraid of anything. Not thunder or lightning or battle. In fact, he would lead the charge alone and the other warriors would only follow when he gave the signal."

I imagined riding headlong against a tribe of screaming, bloodthirsty enemy and not being frightened. It would require a complete re-wiring of my brain to be like that. No wonder they had to do everything back to front. It was the best way to get rid of all the normal human instincts, the ones which told you to run away from danger and not towards it.

"You know what, Jack? A man could be a Contrary for a very long time, and the only way he could relinquish his role was if someone else in the tribe had a dream about the thunder-bow or thunder spirits. Then they could ask a Contrary for his lance. So if no-one asked, he had to keep it."

I looked up from the board.

"A man could be a Contrary for a very long time," he said again.

"What are you trying to say Poyntz? That I've been one for all these years?"

He held up his hands defensively.

"All I'm saying is that you still remind me of one. Most Contraries were unmarried, like you. And even if they were married, they spoke to their wives in inverted speech. If the Contrary said to his woman, 'Do not bring any more wood, we have plenty', she knew that the wood had run out, and that more should be brought."

I thought of the time when Rennie and I had been lounging in the garden watching Materoa cooking and she had shouted over at him, "You just sit there you great lump," when she had actually wanted him to help. Wives used inverted speech with their husbands all the time.

"Maybe you're right, Poyntz, maybe I am a bloody Contrary."

I was riled again; just like I had been in Kalgoorlie when he had said it for the first time. Poyntz knew what was going on in my head, and it still grated.

Seeing my dark expression he softened his tone.

"Hey Jack, I'm just talking about similarities... a real Contrary's home, and most of his possessions, were painted red. He was in a crowd only during a fight, when all were charging. In the camp he was always alone, often on a distant hill by himself. I know that's not you at all."

His last comment made me think of the Orokawa cliff path back in New Zealand and the bench where I would often go and sit on my own. I was *exactly* like that.

Seeing Poyntz's photograph of B – a beautiful laughing woman looking into the camera lens made me vow to myself, there and then, that I ever got out of this mess, I would go and find Jennifer. We would go for long walks and I would make her laugh. I would make her laugh so much her face muscles would ache. And I would carry a photograph of her in my breast pocket all the time.

Poyntz had just moved into a check-mate position and was sitting back and nodding admiringly at his devastating attack.

I dragged my wandering mind back to the present.

"Damn, you've improved… or I've got worse."

"Probably a bit of both," he said.

He was serious all of a sudden.

"Jack, I always wanted to thank you. Dudley told me what Cowdray had wanted to do."

Involuntarily, I touched the thin scar on my left cheek, the place where the blade had cut me on the night I had last seen Poyntz.

Cowdray was a mine manager back in Kalgoorlie who had threatened to kill Poyntz over some gold. It was me who knew where it was hidden, but it was Poyntz he had wanted to harm – Cowdray had seen I didn't care about living, but he was smart enough to realise I still cared about my friends. I had given up the secret without hesitation.

"It was an easy decision," I said.

"I heard he eventually tracked you down in the Nullarbor… and that the Aboriginal saved you."

It sounded like a boy's own adventure story now, but the scar on my cheek was real enough, as was the larger pale scar which ran four inches down my sternum – something else Cowdray had done with his knife after catching up with me.

My memories of the events in the desert were vague – how my gaping chest wound had been virtually healed in a single night, for instance. There was a lot about what happened in the Nullarbor desert that still didn't make any sense in 20th Century scientific terms.

"Cowdray," I said, "he… well…"

"You don't have to say it, Jack. Like I said earlier, Dudley told me and B everything, everything the Aboriginal had witnessed.

An image of my old friend Dudley, the Australian Boer war veteran – with his eye-patch and his tanned crinkled face – flashed into my thoughts. Whenever I swigged from my flask I remembered him, which was fairly often.

"Are you still in touch with Dudley?" I said.

Poyntz shook his head. "Saw him from time to time while we were there. He's probably still sitting in that pub with his friend…what was that damn place called?"

"The British Arms" I said.

"That's it... the British Arms... anyway, how about you, Jack? You two were good pals weren't ya?"

"You know how these things go... every now and then I get a letter... a few lines. He became the Mayor in '07."

"Wow," Poyntz said. "Good old Dudley... he really loved the place, didn't he?"

"He did. Had the support of the Aboriginals too... worked hard to improve relations, which weren't very good."

"We could learn from Dudley – on how to treat our indigenous people, I mean."

I refrained from judging something I knew nothing about. But I could see that it was a disarmingly honest comment by Poyntz – if he was going to cite Cheyenne traditions all the time, he needed to deal with what had happened in his home country too.

He decided to probe again.

"What the hell happened out there in the Nullarbor? After Cowdray had died? That's one hell of a bike ride you went on..."

I decided to skip to the end and miss out the middle part.

"Once I reached the coast, I took a passage straight to New Zealand and met up with Rennie again."

Poyntz laughed and clapped his hands together at hearing my mention of another familiar name from the past.

"Ah yes, Rennie! A very fine fellow. I remember him well. How's he doing?"

"I was with him yesterday as a matter of fact. He's an army Padre, stationed in a place called Toc H."

"Toc H you say, Jack? Why that's perfect. I'm off there tonight – to play in a chess tournament. We'll go together and see him then."

"That's quite some coincidence," I said.

"Not really. Everyone goes to Toc H – and I mean *everyone* – if there's one place in the Ypres sector where you might bump into someone you know by accident, Toc H would be it."

"He was ordered to go there when we arrived from overseas, to replace another Padre for a while. What is it? Some kind of religious social club?"

Poyntz grinned.

"Kind of. There's a small chapel there where they hold regular services. The place would suit him down to the ground. How is the old bible thumper anyhow? He ever get married?"

"He did. She's called Materoa – a Maori woman – and they have twin fifteen year old sons, both of whom joined a battalion called the Maori Pioneers. Underage and in danger – that's why Rennie came out here. Truth be told, he's been in a right state about it."

"Jeez," Poyntz said, seeing all the implications and understanding at once.

"The only comfort is that they're not soldiers, so at least they don't have to go over the top. Mostly, the Pioneers dig trenches and carry stretchers… that kind of thing."

I remembered the X-ray from the light box earlier – that was from a stretcher bearer. Poyntz stayed quiet. Maybe he was thinking the same thing.

"How about you, Poyntz? I heard from Dudley that they made you the boss of the St John of God."

"Yup. That's what happened. Then B and I married, summer of 1901. The next year the water pipe finally opened and pretty soon after that there was no more typhoid fever. So, I went back to America, back to Johns Hopkins where I'd trained in the first place. Took up surgery and specialised in head trauma."

As he said this he took the German helmet and wiggled his little finger through the bullet hole.

"Then in 1910 we moved up to New York. I work in a hospital called St Vincent's and we live in an apartment off Central Park. Every day after work, B and I take the kids there to play."

Poyntz tapped at the chessboard detailing my recent annihilation.

"Sometimes I take this very board down and teach them the moves."

"How come you're out here, Poyntz? This is a dangerous place for a family man."

"Well, yes. But we doughboys are in the war now, Jack. I promised B I would go no closer to the front than a CCS. One of my old mentors from Johns Hopkins asked me to join a group of American surgeons on secondment to the British Expeditionary Force. I was speaking to him on the telephone when you walked in on me. Major Cushing – he's been using electro-magnets to remove shrapnel from brains."

He put the German helmet on.

"That's how I saved this Fritz – with a magnet."

It sounded dramatic, but this was the medical world, always changing and striving for improvement. It was the surgical equivalent to Wright and Fleming's bacterial work. I reached over for the rum ration.

"May I?"

"Knock yourself out."

Knock yourself out. Now I remembered why I had liked Poyntz so much in Australia. The funny way the Americans talked – with their eternal optimism and their quirky phrases. It had really cheered me up.

I took a swig and held up the rum bottle for Poyntz.

"Better not," he said, checking his watch, "still have one more case to do."

I re-corked the rum and set it down again on the ground.

"Then let me assist," I said. "That way you can finish up earlier and we can play another game; practice for tonight's tournament at Toc H."

Ponytz grinned at me.

"All right," he said.

"What have you got?"

"It's the case I was on the phone about. Head and neck shrapnel… shouldn't be more than thirty minutes. You sure about this, Jack?"

I stood up.

"Let's go."

Poyntz and I scrubbed using bowls of clean water in a pre-op room next to theatre two.

It had been quite a while since I had assisted in an operation and I was beginning to feel a little nervous.

In theatre an orderly was lathering and shaving blood-clotted hair from the patient's scalp where pieces of shrapnel were embedded. I had to swallow back my rising bile. The queasiness had started out in the corridor when I had seen the stretcher bearer's haversack lying open, everything inside spattered with blood – dressings, candle lantern, water bottle and a forlorn medical dictionary, its cover torn and muddied.

The anaesthetist stepped up and put the patient under with 'rag and bottle' anaesthesia – ether and chloroform.

When I saw the mashed neck of the patient close up, it was not clean and ordered like the picture in Gray's atlas – the whole area was blackened and messy – and I had no idea how Poyntz knew which vessel was which.

I did what he told me, holding open the wounds with the retractors and giving him the best view possible, hoping the whole time I would not faint on the job. The cloying smell of the blood – that warm, metallic tang – reminded me why I had not chosen surgery as a career. At one point in the procedure, Poyntz looked up and, even though his mouth was covered by the green surgical face mask, the creasing around his eyes showed he was smiling.

"Can you stick it, Jack?"

"I'm fine," I said, lying.

After a while though, I was fine, and by the time Poyntz was pulling out fragments of metal with the magnet, I felt I could watch anything.

Chapter Eleven

After assisting in the magnet operation, I lost again at chess.

I wasn't just rusty; Poyntz had got a lot better. In fact it transpired that he was the best player in the US Medical Corps. It was funny to think that in the old days I had held the upper hand in our games. All the neighbouring units were sending their champions to that evening's tournament at Toc H and Poyntz had even been allocated a staff car for the occasion – a grimy Daimler which came with a chauffeur.

It was only a twelve mile journey to Poperinghe, just across the border. Even so, we were caught behind a single file of ammunition and supply trucks and barely made it in time for the start of the tournament. On the outskirts of the original town was a new 'suburb' of tents, marquees and huts of all sizes, intersected by new roads and light railways. Everywhere was activity.

The car pulled up outside an unremarkable building in one of the central streets of Poperinghe. "Here we are, sir," the chauffeur announced.

Hanging out front, like an English pub sign, was a large wooden notice:

TALBOT
HOUSE
1915 - ?
EVERY-MAN'S
CLUB

"Welcome to Toc H," Poyntz said.

"Toc H? It says Talbot House on the sign."

"Toc is British Army signalese for the letter T."

"What about the H part? Is that signalese too?"

"No, the H stands for house."

"What's signalese for the letter H?"

"Harry."

"So why don't they call it Toc Harry?"

"Hell, I don't know, Jack. Toc H is quicker to say, I guess."

Poyntz punched me on the arm.

"What was that for?"

"That was for being such a damn Contrary."

He opened the car door.

"Come on, Jack. Do you want to see inside, or do you want to stay here arguing all night?"

We pulled a lever and the doorbell rang.

It was Rennie himself who answered.

"John! What a surprise. Welcome, welcome… and you've brought a friend. Poyntz! Good gracious. Is that you? How good it is to see you. Come in, come in."

We stepped through into a large, marble-floored hallway.

Somewhere at the back of the house, someone was playing *Pack up your troubles* on a piano, accompanied by several singers.

Rennie shook Poyntz's hand vigorously and talked at nineteen to the dozen.

"And how's the lovely B? Well, I hope. Did you marry her? Why Poyntz, you haven't changed since I last saw you in Kalgoorlie. Are you stationed nearby?"

The American did his best to pepper back the answers to Rennie's questions.

"Um… ah, yes, we married, she's very well. That's right, a brain surgeon, stationed at Hazebrouck at the moment, that's where I bumped into this fella. You're the same too. It's swell to see you too, Reverend."

Poyntz checked his watch.

"At the risk of sounding rude, I'd better get upstairs. I'm in the tournament."

"Absolutely," Rennie said. "The chess competition. In all the excitement I've forgotten about it. Go right on up, Poyntz. They're all up there already, in the Canadian room."

"Excuse me then, gents. Catch me up, Jack."

Rennie put one hand on my shoulder and waved Poyntz away with the other.

"I'll look after him," he said to Poyntz. "You go on ahead."

As soon as Poyntz had gone, the door bell sounded.

"Oh, more guests," Rennie said. "There's no let up."

"You look like you've got your hands full."

"All demanding my attention. I'm sorry, John, I'll explain when I get a free moment. Be sure to take a look around before you go and see Poyntz's match. My batman will show you the sights. Pettifer? Would you be kind enough to give my friend here the tour?"

Rennie went over to the door and welcomed another group of soldiers with the same zeal as he had greeted us.

A uniformed man who had been hovering nearby approached.

"I'm Pettifer, sir."

"Hello," I said, still surprised and distracted by Rennie's cheerful mood. It was certainly good to see him charged up and back to his bombastic self. During the ship's passage from New Zealand, my friend had been quiet and withdrawn, immersed in his Bible even more than usual and silent for whole days at a time. I knew the boys were on his mind – how could they not be? Diplomatically, I had steered away from discussing it, as there was nothing either of us could do.

Now though, he was a changed man – you could almost see the energy crackling off him like mini bolts of lightning. His spirit was back; that evangelical get-up-and-go that had oozed out of the Rennie of old – Toc H seemed to have cured him of his malaise.

Pettifer pointed at a tatty map on the wall entitled 'HAZEBROUCK', covering something like a 30 mile radius around the town. The map was lined with deep, well-worn creases, which suggested it had been folded up in a soldier's pocket for a time before being pinned up here.

"Let's get the geography lesson out of the way, shall we? I always find it helps to know the lie of the land, makes you feel a little more at home, rather than all at sea."

I looked at him in surprise. The confident way he spoke made the layout of this part of the front seem like the most natural subject to be discussing.

"A geography lesson?" I said. "All right then."

Pettifer ploughed onwards, moving his hand over different parts of the map in a deliberate and precise manner. "The landscape of Flanders is dominated by an ancient ridge to the east of Ypres, a natural obstacle in an otherwise flat region; a strategic obstacle."

When he said the word 'strategic' he looked at me solemnly, as though he was a distinguished professor who had used a very clever word.

I stared back at him, wondering if he was joking or not.

"For two thousand years, men having been fighting over this piece of high ground. They say that Julius Caesar even mentioned it in his campaign notes."

Pettifer gave me another serious look, one which demanded some kind of a response to confirm his undoubted genius.

"How interesting," I said, hoping that might suffice.

He puffed out his chest with pride.

"In 1914 the German invasion came to a standstill at the ridge and it has remained a stalemate ever since. The Germans call it the Ypernbogen; the British, the Ypres Salient. I want you to picture the salient as a bow, drawn back by some titanic archer before the arrow is sped…"

He drew a large curve on the eastern edge of the map with his finger, around Ypres to mark out the bow. Then he pointed to Poperinghe in the west.

"Pop here is the feather of the arrow; the seven mile road leading to Ypres is the shaft, and Ypres itself is the barb."

He was in full flow now. I imagined he gave the same spiel to every newcomer because the map was smudged brown in these areas by greasy fingerprints.

"In the last three years, a million or more men have passed along that shaft, from feather to barb, men destined to hold the salient itself or to be flung into that sea of mud in the desperate effort to drive the enemy from their hill top. They say Ypres was a pretty town before the war…"

I nodded in agreement. "Yes it was," I said, "… a very pretty place."

Pettifer didn't pick up on my remark, because he was, in fact, not a genius. If he had been listening as well as he was talking he would have stopped and asked what I meant. Instead, he just assumed I was agreeing with him and continued on with his lesson.

Hazy memories floated past my mind's eye, like flotsam on the tide.

I had been to Ypres before, in another life. That's why I knew what it had been like before the war.

In 1890, as fifteen year olds, Freddie and I were sent to stay with a family in Ypres. Our father was a big believer in this kind of broadening of one's horizons. I can't recall exactly how he found this family – although I think it was to do with a Belgian surgical connection of his. Part of the old boy's network. My father had hoped the visit would improve our French. As it happened, the father of the family spoke Flemish, though the mother was French speaking, and they alternated between the two languages as if one or the other might wither away and become a lost tongue if they didn't.

We had stayed in a house on the edge of town for three consecutive summers; a fortnight each time. There had been a son and a daughter and we would spend all our time together, the four of us, speaking pigeon English or pigeon French, or a mix of the two. The only Flemish we picked up on was the swearword: 'Godverdomme', which the father would sometimes mutter if he was cross or bemused. It was the Flemish equivalent of Poyntz's 'Goddamn'.

Sometimes we would cycle down the canal for a picnic, and other times ride into town and drink hot chocolate in the shade of the giant Cloth Hall. By the time of our last visit, we were like family; the parents always laughing and happy to see us, the son a great friend, and the beautiful daughter someone Freddie and I both adored, always vying for her attention.

I couldn't for the life of me remember the surname: 'Van' something. It had been nearly thirty years ago. Like my chess skills, my powers of recall were fading too.

As I watched Pettifer's mouth moving, I wondered what had happened to my old Belgian friends and if the house itself was still standing.

The door bell sounded again. Since Rennie was still occupied with the previous arrivals, Pettifer excused himself to answer the door and left me on my own.

Saved by the bell!

I slunk away, deciding to explore the place and avoid more of Pettifer's lecturing. Off the main entrance to the left was a lounge which led into a narrow billiards room with open doorways at both ends. The billiards table barely fitted into the space and the cues had a way of pushing their butt ends through the open doors and into the crowded traffic of officers and privates jostling together.

Tacked to the walls were glass-framed signs with pithy sayings. 'Beware of half-truths, yours may be the wrong half', one declared. 'Don't lose your temper, no-one else wants it', proclaimed another. In the bottom right hand corner were the initials PBC.

Beyond the billiard room was a large conservatory, with tall windows running all along one side, allowing good views out to the garden. The group of singing soldiers, whom I had heard on my arrival – a dozen or so of them – were all crowded round the piano and still in full flow:

'…Pack up your troubles in your old kit bag and smile, smile, smile. While you've a lucifer to light your fag, smile boys, that's the style. What's the use in worrying?
It was never worthwhile, so pack up your troubles in your old kit bag and smile, smile, smile…'

On the opposite side of the main hallway, was a kitchen where a giant vat of tea was being siphoned continuously by a line of uniformed men holding tin cups.

It was about as different as you could get from my old club 'The Blue Boar' in London's Pall Mall. That institution had been virtually silent – reserved exclusively for the so-called elite. The pictures on the wall had been Spy Cartoons of the great and the good and the atmosphere was church-like, with shards of sunlight revealing floating dust particles within the quiet gloom. To give the club its due, it had been the perfect place for me to brood undisturbed. If there was one thing the English did well, it was allowing someone their privacy.

The only use I had for my old club tie these days was in the garden; it was presently lashing the flimsy trunk of a young lemon tree to its stake and slowly mouldering away in the rain, wind and sunshine, as the tree grew ever stronger.

Back in the main hall was a notice which read: *'THIS SPACE IS RESERVED FOR FRIENDSHIP'* and beneath this, a board with dozens of small notes shoved into horizontal slits, like a tennis club ladder:

– *Captain Y, Your brother Charlie is now with his unit at 'D' Camp…*
– *Lt. so and so would like to meet his old friend…*
– *Colonel X has been transferred to the 5th Hospital…*

Without hesitating, I picked up one of the blank cards stacked on the table and scribbled out a note:

– *Lt. John Hunston, NZ Field Ambulance, c/o NZ Stationary Hospital, would like to meet Lance Cpl Harry Ingram, 3rd Battalion, NZ Rifle Bde. An important family matter.*

Rennie appeared at my shoulder.
"Ah… I see you've found Friendship's Corner," he said.
He read my card.

"That's a good idea. I'm certain he'll find it, John. In fact I'm hoping the boys might show up soon. I've no idea where they are, but pretty much everyone seems to pass through here."

For a second I saw his pain again under the cheery exterior.

"What exactly is this place, Sean? Who is Talbot?"

"Was," Rennie said, correcting me. "He died in action in July 1915. His older brother is a senior chaplain in the Sixth Army and he wanted somewhere to be set up in his brother's name, basically to act as a rest house for troops. This building was vacated by a wealthy brewer after being hit by shelling and the Army rent it from him for 150 francs a month. The Royal Engineers have fixed it up nicely – even converted the hop loft into a chapel, believe it or not."

"And where do you fit in?"

"The reverend who runs it is on sick leave. Phillip Byard Clayton – you've probably seen his initials on the signs on the walls. He's fairly famous around these parts by all accounts – the men call him 'Tubby' Clayton. Anyhow, when he went on sick leave he called in an old acquaintance to hold the fort."

"Reverend Money?"

"Yes… and now Money has been called away unexpectedly. He found out I was coming and drafted me in."

"Substitute of the substitute," I said.

"That's one way of saying it." Rennie waved his hand around him excitedly. "It's a place where you can get it all off your mind, without having to do so in a debauched way, as they tend to do in the other establishments around town."

"Get what off your mind?"

"Why, the war of course, John. We cater to various interests; on this floor there's a canteen, billiards table and a rest room with a piano; upstairs, my digs, the warden's office – where I can host guests, offer them some spiritual refreshment. On the second floor there's a writing room, and a library; and at the top of the house, in the 'upper room', the chapel. If you don't want any of that, you can just sit in the back garden and forget for a while. This man Clayton has given the place a certain… atmosphere, shall we say. Rank is left at the door. Why, just this afternoon I had a tea party with a general, a staff captain, a second lieutenant and a Canadian private. Why not? In a trench crisis, a life and death emergency, every man is judged by his character, not his rank. It's all written there on the Toc H creed…"

Rennie pointed out a notice on the opposite wall to the map.

'This house aims at reminding you just a little bit of your ain folk. Hence pictures, flowers and freedom. Down, therefore with all Teuton conduct: be friendly and of a club-able spirit.'

"I like it already," I said with a smile, secretly amused at the thought of such a notice being pinned to the oak doors of the Blue Boar club. Their creed would have been: 'This place aims at reminding you that you are better than others, that we are an exclusive group with the God-given right to lord it over others. Forget this at your peril.'

Fourteen chess games were being played in the 'Canadian lounge' upstairs on the first floor. The lounge was directly above the piano room and the kitchen and appeared to have been built as a rather makeshift extension to the house, because to get to it you had to climb up a few steps and out through a window.

It was packed to the gunnels, but a British officer kindly made space for me to step through the window and squeeze in amongst the spectators.

"I say, budge up, old chap," he said to the person next to him.

Tentatively, I pushed my way in.

"Are you sure there's enough room?"

"Oh, don't worry, New Zealand," he said to me, seeing my uniform. "This place can hold some seventy men, as long as they are inured to spatial propinquity. What!"

It sounded like part of a line I would have been given at school as a punishment: *I must not shove my fellows in class, since they are not inured to spatial propinquity.*

I looked at the officer. He wasn't joking – he had really meant to use the phrase. I liked the fact that he had called me a country and before

I knew it I was mimicking him – not mockingly, but as a form of flattery. In a single moment I had been thrown back into my old English skin.

"Seventy! Well, if you say so, England."

I still couldn't see Poyntz very well and tapped the officer on the shoulder.

"I say, could I push past so I can see my friend's match."

"Blaze away, old boy."

Poyntz was playing a private and was in a winning position. As the poor private tried to think of escape routes, he kept scratching his head, causing bits of dirt and dandruff to fall softly down onto the board. Some of the fallout was moving.

"Mate," Poyntz soon said sitting right back in his chair, in an attempt to avoid picking up any of the lice.

He turned round to me. "Grab a seat, Jack. You're giving me a damn neck ache."

I took the chair the vanquished private had just vacated, brushing away the debris that had fallen from his filthy hair.

Poyntz rubbed at his crew cut, as if he had already been infected.

"Sorry about leaving you back there," he said.

"No problem. Rennie's batman told me all about the Salient."

"Let me guess… the giant bow and arrow? Goddamn… Pettifer tells everyone that story. I'll tell ya what you really need to know."

He cleared the pieces and thumped a rook down on one side of the board.

"Ypres…"

Then he laid out a line of pawns to the right of the rook.

"The front line… a couple of miles to the east of Ypres."

I felt as if I had been put into the remedial class.

"You payin' attention, Jack?"

"Yes, Captain," I said, with unveiled sarcasm.

He tapped his fingernail in the space between the pawns and the rook.

"The Regimental Aid Posts are all up there… less than a mile behind the front. Now there's a canal that runs north-south through Ypres, and the Advanced Dressing Stations are strung out along it."

I didn't say anything. Didn't mention I had once known the canal well.

He put another rook behind the one representing Ypres.

"Pop… to the west," he said.

"I'm with you."

He put down some bishops around the rook of Pop. To the onlookers, it must have seemed like a chess game was going on between two lunatics.

"These are the CCSs," he said. "Divisional level hospitals around ten miles behind the front; these are where the soldiers will get the knife, fork and spoon ops – amputations and the like. 'Dosinghem', 'Mendinghem', 'Bandagehem' – you've just gotta love the Tommies' sense of humour."

He grabbed one of the knights and put it just beyond the board.

"And here's the NZ Stationary Hospital, another step back, where I've been doing head ops. Now, what you have to bear in mind, is that in all of these places, the Germans have the capability to take out the pieces, should they so wish. A mass resignation, you could say…"

Poyntz swept his hand across the board and knocked everything over with a clatter.

"Oh, by the way, did I mention the generals…"

He placed the king on the table right away from the board at arm's length. "They're sitting pretty over here."

Lesson over, he started to line up the pieces properly and grinned at me.

"Welcome to the war, bud."

When Poyntz started his next game I left to explore the upper floors of Toc H.

Rennie's office was just off the Canadian room on the first floor. The phrase, 'All rank abandon ye who enter here' was written on the doorframe. It could have been a sitting room in an English country cottage, not an office in a war zone: flowery wallpaper, a stove with an enamel kettle perched on top, a phonograph still turning and crackling. A fat cat was occupying prime position on a bed in the corner. On the desk was an 'Underwood' typewriter, an upturned copy of Hans Andersen's Fairy Tales and a beaker containing a spoon and a fork.

The library on the second floor was unmanned. A pile of caps lay on the floor amongst the bookshelves.

"A cap for a book," Rennie said, catching up with me again. "It's the system here. No-one can report for duty without their cap, so that means the books come back."

To get to the 'upper room' we mounted a set of steep stairs, almost a ladder, to enter a peaceful, carpeted chapel framed by rafters; the former hop loft.

We sat down together on one of the pews and I took it all in.

Waist high, arched semi-circular windows were letting in the last of the evening sun. A worn old carpenter's bench served as the altar. The faintest smell of hops and the ladder entrance made me feel as if I was in some kind of illicit church where, instead of praying quietly with their eyes closed, the worshippers drank beer and toasted God.

"Toc H's foundations are in the roof," Rennie said. "There's a spirit here – a collective spirit that seems immune to the horrors going on ten miles away. A brotherhood of man. Can you feel it?"

"Yes, I can actually."

I meant it too, the spirit was palpable, even to a struggling agnostic like me.

"This place has given me hope, John."

"I'm glad to hear it. I'm happy you've been posted here."

"And Poyntz – how strange to see him again after all this time," Rennie said.

"I know. I could hardly believe it when I came across him, Sean. It really threw me. Funny, isn't it? All of us being together again in one place. It makes you wonder."

"Wonder? Wonder about what?"

"Oh, I don't know. I suppose about that plan of yours that you're always talking about."

"I'm glad it makes you wonder, John. Me? I feel I know. I know things are going to a plan."

I looked at him. If it had been anyone else in the world saying what he had just said – with that Type 2 certainty – I would have been angry, but not with my friend, I couldn't be.

"Bully for you," I said.

"Talking of plans – do you have your orders yet?"

"No… we should hear tomorrow. I'm hoping to get assigned to the 3rd Field Ambulance – the one affiliated to the Rifle Brigade. I might find Harry Ingram that way… in case he doesn't find the message in Friendship's Corner."

Rennie stared ahead at the rough wooden altar, nodding.

"There's something else…" I said.

"What?"

"The 3rd Field Ambulance look after the Pioneer battalion… I might get to keep an eye on the boys… in case they don't pass by here either."

Rennie bowed his head.

"Sean? Did you hear what I said?"

"Yes, I heard you."

"So what do you think? Why have you gone quiet?"

"I'm praying."

"Praying for what?"

"I'm praying you get the 3rd Field Ambulance."

"Won't that be in the plan?"

"I'm just reminding Him," Rennie said, his eyes closed and a smile appearing across his face.

Later that evening, a very strange thing happened.

Just as the final round of matches began, a middle-aged gunner came into the Canadian room and started up a quiet conversation with Rennie.

"I hear you've got some chessmen," he said.

"Yes, no less than fourteen boards, though all of them are in use for the time being. But if you wait you'll get a game."

"Can you arrange this for me? I should be glad to play the winners."

"What do you mean? It's 7.30 and the house closes at 9. Even supposing that they are all winning now, it would take you all night to play the lot."

"No, I don't mean that at all, I want to play the fourteen games at once."

This statement started a low murmur amongst the crowd of spectators.

"All right… Why not?" Rennie said, picking up on the air of excitement.

As soon as the existing matches had been played, the winners stayed on and set up the boards again. They all sat on the same side and the man proceeded to walk up and down the table; playing fourteen games simultaneously. Within thirty minutes, he had won twelve and drawn two, Poyntz being one of those who had managed to force a draw.

Then the man said 'goodnight' and left the room.

No-one even knew his name.

Chapter Twelve

5th June 1917

"Hunston?"

I looked up to see McKenzie striding across the hospital mess towards me.

Poyntz and I had been playing chess in between operations and the games hadn't been going my way, so to tell the truth McKenzie's arrival was a welcome distraction.

"Morning, sir," I said, standing up smartly.

Poyntz stood too, but in a somewhat more leisurely manner.

"Cap'n," he said with his nasal American drawl and the most half-hearted salute I had ever seen.

"Captain Poyntz," McKenzie said, saluting back. They had been introduced to one another the day before. He looked at Poyntz as if he was another species – the unruly lackadaisical American who answered to no-one.

Then he turned to me.

"Pack your gear, Lieutenant. We're going south to Messines."

"What… today, sir?"

"Yes, right now… today."

"It's all a bit sudden isn't it, sir?"

"Oh, is the timing all right with you, Hunston?" he said, feigning concern. "Or do you want me to call General Haig and ask for an extension? Tell him we haven't settled in yet. Shall I go and do that?"

Sometimes he seemed so tightly wound up that I thought he might explode. Perhaps it would be a good idea to stop playing the dumb subordinate – a role I excelled at – for his health's sake. I had been enjoying it though. Seeing McKenzie's blood pressure going up was reassuring in its predictability. I decided to keep it going for a little while longer.

"No, sir, of course not, sir."

McKenzie forced a grin so hard I could see his back teeth.

"By the way," he said, "today isn't the 5th of June anymore. The Army have renamed it 'X' day. Yesterday was 'W' day. Do you know what day it is tomorrow, Hunston?"

"Y day?"

"The man's a bloody genius," he said, looking to Poyntz.

"And then 'Z' day, sir?"

"Christ Almighty, Hunston, you could've been a surgeon."

"Not a brain surgeon though," Poyntz said, leaning down and moving a piece on the board. He straightened back up and smiled at the both of us. "Check mate."

"It sounds as if we're building up to something, sir," I said, looking from the chessboard to McKenzie.

"You're spot on, Hunston. The big attack is due to take place on 'Z' day at 'Zero' hour. Assemble in the courtyard in thirty minutes. We're moving out."

"Yes, sir."

After McKenzie had left, Poyntz sat back down.

He rubbed his head and then started pushing pieces around the board.

"What are you doing?" I said, taking my seat opposite him. "You've already beaten me."

"Messines... Messines... Messines," he said, mumbling to himself.

"What about it?"

"It's a small village on the southern portion of the salient," he said, "perched up on the so-called 'high ground' of the ridge. It's not much of a rise but round here any height advantage is a real ball breaker... It gives the Bosch views over Ypres, not only for shelling, but for observation."

"And?"

"Well, I think I can see where this is all going."

"What are you thinking, Poyntz? Spit it out."

He stared hard at the board.

"This is like a chess game, Jack… a massive chess game, of which the push to capture Messines is just one move. If I was in charge, I would want to straighten up that part of the line too. That way the German pieces are pushed back and they won't be able to see my build up for the end game – the check mate move. Surprise, Jack. Finish things fast – rip out their heart. With the Germans blind to our troop movements, I would want to punch through their lines east of Ypres."

He rapped on one of the squares on the chess board with his knuckles.

"Up onto the Passchendaele plateau, and then swing round for the coast; neutralise the U-Boat ports in Zeebrugge and Ostend. Check mate."

"Sounds easy enough," I said.

"Yeah… too damn easy. If I can work it out in two minutes, I suspect the German High Command might have worked it out too."

When we pulled out of the Stationary Hospital in ambulance trucks thirty minutes later, Poyntz watched us go, standing with his hands on his hips in the courtyard. Behind him a gang of engineers were putting up Nissen huts in the school field – arch shaped constructions of corrugated iron. The capacity of the Stationary Hospital was being increased to one thousand; in two days' time – on Z day – all the head cases from the front would be coming here.

Poyntz was in his surgical greens, about to operate again I guessed. The baggy clothing made him look skinny, and for the first time, I noticed that he had aged. *Old Poyntz,* I thought to myself. It was his posture – his shoulders and upper back were rounded, taking an inch or so off his height. Up close I had only been able to see his ageless face, but from thirty yards away he looked like an old man.

We had said our goodbyes in the X-ray room. "I'll keep the chessboard ready for when you get back," he had said. "Just make sure you get some practice in, or it's going to be embarrassing."

I was feeling very sorry for myself as we drove south. Anxious thoughts flew around in my head like black crows. I wondered if I would ever see Poyntz again, regretting the limited time we had just spent together. Then my mind was on Jennifer and Rennie, but it was too painful to even contemplate not seeing them again so I shifted to another face; Harry Ingram. Would I ever be able to locate him in this giant engine of a war machine? Kate Ingram was pinning her hopes on me to find her boy. And although Rennie and Materoa hadn't said anything, I still felt the pressure to do something about the twins. It was fast becoming obvious that I had over-reached myself. I cursed at having had the audacity to think I could save anyone, let alone promise it.

The section of front held by the New Zealand division lay in a wedge of land between two roads which converged on Messines; the Wulverghem road from the west and the Ploegsteert – or 'Plug Street' – road running straight up from the south.

Near each road, Advanced Dressing Stations had been set up; one at Kandahar Farm and the other at Underhill Farm. We were driven to Underhill Farm, near the wooded elevation of 'Hill 63'. To our south was Plug Street Wood, a large forest already dotted with small stands of graves from earlier battles in the war.

'X' was a fine, bright day.

It was hard to believe that two huge armies were facing off one another across the flat river plain in front of the Messines Ridge. What with the summer weather and the surrounding woodland, it felt like we were going for a picnic. Then I remembered the stretcher bearer with the shrapnel in his neck had been in the vicinity of Hill 63. As if to reinforce the fact it was a dangerous place, just after we had turned left at a crossroads called 'Hyde Park Corner', a shell landed a mere fifty yards away. Every man in the truck flinched. When I looked back, a cloud of black smoke was billowing around a stand of newly defoliated trees and torn branches.

Being on the lee side of Hill 63, the Underhill Farm ADS could not be seen by the Germans, but that did not mean we were safe; the whole area was subject to regular heavy bombardments since our own artillery positions were in the same location.

Underhill ADS was so well sandbagged that it had so far withstood near direct hits from even the biggest shells. Beams the size of railway sleepers lined the corridors, sucking up all the sound and creating a tomb-like atmosphere. Even in the day, the interior was dark and had to be lit by acetylene lamps.

In the main treatment room, a doctor and an orderly were busy sorting supplies in an effort to be ready for the expected influx. Blankets, shell dressings, and dozens of splints were stacked up against one wall. A pair of trestles stood on the floor, five feet apart, waiting for the first stretcher case to be laid down across them. The two men were chatting away cheerfully, as if they didn't know what was coming. Oddly, it reminded me of a nativity scene – the same cheery optimism, a manger with Gold, Frankinsense and Myrhh, a happy Mary and Joseph. That story wasn't going to end well either. I felt the same weary inevitability about this place as I did at Christmas time.

Somewhere in the shelter I could hear the clatter of a typewriter, but even then my feelings of portent continued: 'you're being sent to your deaths' the keys were saying in their staccato beat. The last letter in the alphabet was coming up fast – 'Z' day. God I was feeling maudlin, totally listless in the face of the approaching doom. I wasn't the only one realising I wasn't in the best frame of mind.

"Lieutenant Hunston," McKenzie said, suddenly appearing alongside me, "what's got you looking so bloody constipated?"

I didn't want to tell him about my existential concerns so gave him another truth instead.

"Actually, sir, that's an accurate diagnosis…" I rubbed at my stomach. "I think it's something I ate at the Stationary Hospital Mess."

It was worth it just to watch his jaw drop. For once I had rendered him temporarily speechless.

"You don't have any syrup of figs do you, sir?" I said as a follow up. "I suppose that might help shift things a bit."

"Jesus Christ, Hunston… no I bloody well don't. Now you listen and you listen well… I want you to be on top of your game in twenty four hours, you hear? Not crying off with belly ache." I turned to leave. "Where the hell do you think you're going?"

"Very sorry, sir, I was going to the men's room. Permission to go and sort out my bowels, sir, as instructed."

"Oh," he said, wrong-footed, "well in that case, permission bloody granted."

On the wall of the latrine was a picture of Ludendorff, decorated with a pair of devil's horns. There were dozens of tiny holes pitting his face, reaching such a density in the centre that they blacked out his nose entirely; clearly a popular place for a game of darts when defecating.

It was the first communal toilet I had seen since boarding school, although this one was of a more basic construction – a long bench with several holes, side by side, resting over a pit. A bucket of sawdust sat nearby – the 'flush' – and for toilet paper you pulled off small square sheets of newspaper which were strung together and hanging from a nail on the wall.

Afterwards, I found a bunk in the dorm. It had a sheepskin draped over the covers for extra warmth and comfort and I spent most of the afternoon lying there in a more focused frame of mind, wondering how I was ever going to beat Poyntz at chess. I was way out of practice. I played a series of gambits in my head, but after three moves I would forget my place. Losing my mind to chess was the only way of staving off the panic attacks which had been happening with increasing frequency since leaving Hazebrouck that morning – searing bouts of chest pain with my heart thumping and my hands tingling, followed by a wave of nausea. Bloody hell, it hadn't been as bad as this since Freddie had died.

I was woken in the night by a sudden and strange noise: *Phtt Phtt Phtt* "Gas! Gas!"

It was McKenzie who was shouting, half falling out of his bunk as he did so.

For the first time since playing around in the smoke room at Ewshot, I donned my small box respirator, flailing around with the straps and the tubing like the novice I was. As I fidgeted with my mask, making sure the rubber seal was good, I glanced over at McKenzie. A giant fly, that's what he looked like, with bug eyes and a proboscis, in the form of the tubing connecting to the box filter. I knew I must have appeared the same to him.

Facts I had learnt in training sprang into my head – first, it was probably phosgene – a potent killing agent, even more so than chlorine. Second, if it was phosgene, it would be difficult to detect as it was colourless, although it was said to smell of mouldy hay. Third, it had a delayed effect – sometimes taking 24 hours before inflicting its terrible form of suffering. By then it was too late to do anything about it. The gas reacted with the water in the lungs to form hydrochloric acid, which in turn caused fluid accumulation in the air spaces – pulmonary oedema. You drowned from within. The certainty of this delayed death was the most terrifying aspect of all.

Masked up, we tore down the corridor and ran into the large assembly room. The old guard – men who had been stationed here long before we had arrived – were all sitting around and smoking cigarettes. None of them were wearing their masks. When McKenzie and I burst in, they started to laugh.

Gas shells *had* landed – that part was real, but it turned out that Underhill was gas proof; the doors constantly sprayed with an anti-gas solution so that the staff could work inside without the encumbrance of the respirators.

Despite this all being explained through the laughter, I didn't trust the spray and as soon as my mask was off I was sure that I could smell mouldy hay. I kept thinking about the skull and crossbones sign marked on the hydrochloric acid bottle in my chemistry class at school and slept the rest of the night with my gas mask on.

On the morning of 'Y' day McKenzie found me on my bunk – I was spooning up meat from a tin of 'Fray Bentos' and reading an old copy of the *Wipers Times* I had found lying around. A spoof advertisement was making me smile:

FOR SALE
THE SALIENT ESTATE
INTENDING PURCHASERS WILL BE SHOWN
ROUND ANY TIME DAY OR NIGHT
UNDERGROUND RESIDENCES READY FOR
HABITATION
Splendid motoring estate! Shooting perfect!!
DO FOR HOME FOR INEBRIATES OR OTHER
CHARITABLE INSTITUTION
Delay is dangerous! You might miss it!!
Apply for particulars, etc., to:
Thomas, Atkins, Sapper & Co., Zillebeke and Hooge

"Hunston?"

McKenzie's face was unreadable, the way a doctor can often appear, whether or not the news he is about to impart is good or bad.

Still holding my food and reading material, I swung my legs off the bunk and stood up slowly.

"More gas, sir?"

He winced a little at the memory of the previous evening's embarrassment, but there was a sparkle in his eyes which told me he could at least take the joke.

"As much as it pains me to say it, Hunston, you seem to have the most common sense and resilience out of our Ewshot Group."

"Thank you, sir."

"So that's why I'm taking you with me to man the RAP at the front. Staff asked for volunteers and I volunteered us. We'll be right in the thick of things up there."

I looked down at the mashed up meat in my tin.

"Yes… well… thank you, sir… for thinking of me."

This bugger is going to get us both killed, I thought.

"Don't mention it," he said.

I could see from his face that the man had no fear, none whatsoever. He was either incredibly brave, or a very good actor.

"I suppose it's quite an honour, sir," I said, determined not to let him know I was terrified.

"Yes, I'm glad you think so. We are to be the vanguard of the 3rd Field Ambulance."

"Did you say the 3rd Ambulance, sir?"

"That's right. We've been brought in as reinforcements."

Now I had heard this, I knew that Harry Ingram and the twins were close. Rennie's prayer had bloody well worked and, for a split second, I felt happiness and relief flood over me.

"How are your bowels?"

"Much better, thank you for asking, sir."

He nodded to himself thoughtfully.

"I just have two things to say to you, Hunston."

"Yes sir?"

"Don't bloody let me down, and don't bloody die."

For once he sounded concerned.

McKenzie was being deadly serious now and, for the first time, I could tell he actually liked me, despite himself.

He was holding out a package wrapped in brown paper.

"Here's something to help prevent the latter."

It was a 'Dayfield' body shield to wear under my tunic – a vest with metal plates sewn in.

"Resists bayonet, sword or lance thrusts," he said, reading from the bold lettering on the label.

I continued for him, "… Also spent bullets and shell fragments."

This part was written in a smaller font, which made it look as if the manufacturers were a little less confident about that claim.

McKenzie slapped a map onto the body armour.

"When you've finished breakfast, Hunston, you can lead the way."

We were heading for the RAP at 'Spring Street' which lay further across the Douve Valley towards the Messines Ridge. Poyntz had been right when he had talked about the ridge – it was nothing really – a low scarp, perhaps no more than one hundred feet high. From our viewpoint it looked a lot less than that. In peacetime it would have been utterly insignificant. Now though, it was the focus of the entire Allied forces.

Our team numbered twelve in all – mainly regimental stretcher bearers and orderlies – and we probably could have reached the RAP in short order since there was a trench tramway running directly to the front, built by the Maori Pioneers to evacuate the expected 'lying down cases' in battle. However, due to repeated shelling of that route, I chose a smaller parallel track, opting to listen to my own instinct.

Beyond Hill 63, we came into the viewfinders of the German spotters on the ridge, and because of that, the track I had chosen became a sandbagged communications trench some eight feet deep. This had pros and cons – the Germans couldn't see us, but I was unable to see any landmarks. We zigzagged back and forth through the trench network like rats in a maze.

'Y' day was even warmer than 'X' had been – oppressively so – and the extra layer of the Dayfield vest was making me perspire freely. Between us we were lugging six great canvas duffel bags containing all manner of supplies we had cadged from Underhill: blankets, stretchers, shell dressings, triangular bandages, roller bandages, arm splints, leg splints, Thomas and Liston splints, petrol tins of chlorinated water as well as food. But it wasn't just the heat and hard work that had caused my uniform to be drenched in sweat. Map reading had never been my strong point and now I had got us all lost. At forks in the trench, there were signposts pointing in different directions; 'King Edward's trench', 'Medicine Hat trail', 'Currie Avenue', but these didn't help. They might have been written on the chart, but my concentration had gone. I repeatedly wiped the sweat away from my eyes as I examined the trench markings on the map, hoping no-one realised that it had become just a hodgepodge of different coloured lines.

I wanted to impress McKenzie, or at least not let him down – one of the two cardinal rules he had given me, but already I was breaking the first in a spectacular fashion.

We came to a bearer relay post at the remains of 'Ration Farm' – nothing more than a sandbagged dugout next to a pile of bricks of a ruined building. In the battle, the men here would be taking over from my ambulance bearers as they arrived from the Spring Street RAP with the wounded on stretchers, like fresh horses in the Pony Express.

The men were smoking when we came through, but as we approached they all saluted, as if anyone walking towards the Germans deserved an extra dose of respect.

We were following what I thought was 'Medicine Hat trail', though the signs had petered out some way back and I hadn't expected to come upon this post.

I checked my trench map again, rapidly correcting my position and pointing east.

"Spring Street?" I said to one of the relay bearers.

"That's it. Keep going, sir. On down Currie Avenue. You're only a few hundred yards away."

"I thought as much," I said, in the manner of a Type 2, loudly and with swagger.

As long as I sounded confident I knew I would inspire confidence. I needed to make decisions fast, and in one sense it didn't matter if they were the right or wrong ones, so long as I made them. Men could spot weakness in a millisecond. Boarding school had been a cauldron of bully-boys spotting weaknesses and other boys trying to avoid having their weaknesses spotted. You soon learned to grow a thick skin. My strategy of false confidence was working now; as I bluffed my way through the directions, our lads were blagging cigarettes off the relay bearers and sharing jokes. I glanced at McKenzie – even he looked fooled, though you never quite knew with him.

'Spring Street' Regimental Aid Post was a dugout in a communications trench, a hundred yards or so behind the front line. We joined the survivors of the RAP team from the day before, the lucky few not killed or injured in the previous evening's shelling. There were only three of them left.

Very soon after our arrival there was a short-lived, but torrential, thunderstorm which all but obscured the Messines Ridge. We huddled together in the shelter; squatting on sandbags as we arranged the gear. It wasn't enough rain to turn the trench into a quagmire and the ground was soon dry again after the storm. The downpour proved to be a blessing; the earlier sultry heat had gone and the late afternoon was cooler.

As the evening wore on, we brewed up some cocoa on a primus stove under the light of a full moon and kept quiet, with just the sound of the roaring gas flame in the RAP. Biscuits were passed around, but I wasn't hungry and instead of eating I re-read Jennifer's letter by candlelight: *I haven't been able to stop thinking about you… I want to take you closely in my arms and give you all my love and strength…*

Reading the words I could picture her in front of me, and imagine a future together. It was up to me to go to her and make it happen. For now they just remained words. All the same, it was strange how powerful they were on their own, reading them there in that trench. I pulled out Dobb's photograph of Rennie, Materoa and me when we were young. We looked so different, Rennie and I, our faces without creases and our hair without any hint of grey. Even then, we had been older than most of the soldiers out here. Only Materoa looked unchanged. I wondered how she was looking right at this moment with all her men gone.

At 9pm there was another heavy gas bombardment, but we were too close to the front to be in the impact zone. The shells flew over our heads and landed on Hill 63 and further back, but we still put on our respirators in case the wind blew north. At midnight the shelling stopped.

Sometime later, troops from the 3rd Brigade passed by the RAP silently, heading for the assembly trench. Hundreds of them. Some had the black triangle on their shoulders signifying the 3rd Rifle Battalion, just like Harry Ingram's uniform in the photograph Kate had shown me. There was no way I was going to spot him in the moonlight with his gas mask on; all I could see was a series of black and white men with insect heads walking to battle.

Zero hour was set for 03.10.

McKenzie said that mines had been laid all along the ridge, the explosive packed into underground galleries dug right under the German lines. They were all set to blow at zero hour.

I couldn't sleep and kept looking at my wrist watch as the hour approached. The small second hand dial in the middle of the watch face seemed to pause and stretch out each moment. More than once I held it to my ear to check if it was still ticking.

At 3.00 am we got out of the RAP and lay down on the ground behind the front trench. Out to the north I could hear nightingales.

McKenzie turned to me and spoke in a hushed voice.

"Know what they're saying to the soldiers, Hunston… those birds?"

"What?"

"'Brother, brother, if this be the last song you shall sing, sing well for you may not sing another; brother sing.'"

"Never had you down as the poetical type, sir."

"It's Julian Grenfell," McKenzie said.

Grenfell had been one of the war's prominent casualties – he had died in 1915. On the same day his death was announced *The Times* had published his poem *Into Battle*.

"You know, sir, I met his father once – William Grenfell, now Lord Desborough – at a dinner party… Quite a sportsman, a formidable man… and his wife too. A fine woman, sir… razor sharp wit."

McKenzie looked impressed.

"Is that so, Hunston? You move in some bloody high circles."

"It was a long time ago. My circles have since lowered… no offence intended, sir."

"None bloody taken," he said. "You have to bloody feel for them both though… Losing a son, I mean."

Absentmindedly, I scooped up a clod of mud and rubbed it into my hands.

"They lost another son too, sir. Julian's younger brother Billy, just two months after."

"Christ," McKenzie said, frowning and shaking his head as he absorbed the full magnitude of the Grenfell family's losses. "I'm just glad my boy is too young to be caught up in this mess."

McKenzie was really opening up. Maybe he was scared.

"You have any sons, Hunston?"

"No, sir, but out here somewhere, I've a nephew and two godsons."

A gentle tinkling noise interrupted our conversation.

"They're fixing bayonets," McKenzie said.

I checked my watch again. Eight minutes past three.

"'The thundering line of battle stands, and in the air Death moans and sings, but Day shall clasp him with strong hands, and Night shall fold him in soft wings.' That's how it ends."

"Sounds comforting," I said.

"Except when you realise that the poor bugger who wrote it stopped a shell splinter with his head. Not so bloody comforting when you think of it like that."

"No," I said, "perhaps not."

It was hard for me to picture Lord Desborough as a broken man. He had been an indomitable Type 2 character; certain of his place in the world and his dominion over it; in fact the most confident and self-assured man I had ever met. He had practically broken my arm in a demonstration of his fighting skills. I had been hugely impressed by him at the time – it was hard not to be – and I had liked him, despite his Type 2 bearing. Even at the age of 50 he had been fit enough to win international medals in fencing.

Nine minutes past. I looked out to the trenches of our front. The mist was clearing and the visibility was now around one hundred yards.

The image of my father at Freddie's funeral swirled into my mind's eye, and when it did, I suddenly found it easy to picture even a man like Desborough as someone who could be broken. I watched the seconds approach zero hour on my watch – five, four, three, two, one…

At 3.10 am precisely I saw, heard and felt something that I will never forget.

To either side of us and all along the Messines Ridge, a series of detonations erupted savagely as more than 400 tonnes of high explosive sent 10,000 Germans and their positions to kingdom come. Red sheets of flame shot up into the skies and the ground around us shook, heaving and rocking like a ship on heavy seas.

Strangely, the noise of the blasts at zero hour seemed to come from somewhere behind us rather than in front; the sound of Death moaning and singing – to use Julian Grenfell's words – had the quality of a ventriloquist.

Living men appeared to be growing from the ground: our troops were swarming out of the trenches and crossing no man's land. A shock wave moved through the low lying mist across the grass like an ocean swell, with enough force to knock over the men already in the open.

Then clods of earth, some the size of carts and weighing several tonnes, started to rain down all around us, making sickening thuds as they hit the ground. For several bone-shuddering seconds, we simply curled up with our hands on our heads.

When I dared to look up again I saw the debris and dust spewed up along the Messines Ridge was shining white. Lit by the moon above and the white flares beneath and in front, it looked like a long white cloud, an 'Aotearoa' of the Western front.

Then our heavy guns started up on the German positions, so that from the cloud you could see the flashes of shell detonations and then hear the deafening cracks of sound a few seconds later. It had the appearance of lightning in a storm cloud and such was the intensity of the barrage that a constant orange glow settled over the ridge.

The Tommies had a good phrase for this kind of thing – they called it 'the hate'.

We didn't know it then, but the detonations were even heard in London over one hundred and thirty miles away. When you added them together as one, it was the biggest man-made explosion in history.

Chapter Thirteen

As the last of NZ 3ʳᵈ Brigade left the trenches, McKenzie grabbed my shoulder and handed me a bag of gear.

"I want you to advance the RAP," he said. "Head over the top for Ulcer trench. It's marked on the map as the German front line. But it's not anymore. When you're done, send a runner back so we know exactly where you are."

He gave me four stretcher bearers, an orderly, a water duty man, and the runner.

Five minutes after zero hour, the German artillery opened up on our old front line, but they were too late – the trenches were already empty of infantry. Only McKenzie and his team were there, sheltering in the RAP dugout as the shells hit.

Our advance across no man's land was dictated by the speed of the 'creeping barrage', a moving curtain of death which came from our own guns and obliterated everything in its path. It was leading the first wave of NZ soldiers who were already half-way up the ridge. I estimated the creep to be about three hundred feet a minute – a reasonable pace – like factory workers leaving at the end of the day. The forward trajectory of the shells meant the shrapnel was also thrown forwards, away from our advancing soldiers. Even so, it was astonishing just how close our men could get to the barrage and not be blown to smithereens – no more than fifty feet in places.

We reached Ulcer trench without sustaining any casualties. At least it had been a trench once. Now the sides were caved in and it was a churned up mess, the wooden supporting posts scattered about like matchsticks. In amongst all this lay Germans, some contorted like rag-dolls in their death rictus, others barely recognisable as human beings. One concrete pillbox had been blasted from the earth and was lying upside down; the clearest indication I had seen so far of the sheer energy the explosions had carried.

I chose a shell crater nearby for our new RAP, reasoning that the chances of another shell landing in the exact same spot was nigh on zero. I knew enough mathematics to understand the probability of sustaining a hit was no better and no worse in the crater than anywhere else, but in my gut I felt it would be safer. I gave the order and we dug in, deepening the crater so that soon we could fully stand and yet still remain below ground level.

The runner was dispatched.

Soldiers started to arrive in ones and twos. It was like the end of some kind of ghoulish summer ball; they were staggering slightly as if already drunk, but instead of champagne bottles they held Lee-Enfield rifles and instead of black tie they were dressed in drab uniforms smeared with blood and dust.

We pointed the walking wounded back in the direction of McKenzie at Spring Street. The word was that our 3rd Brigade was already in Messines village.

Mark IV tanks lumbered past our position heading towards Messines; giant three-dimensional steel parallelograms squeaking and clanking their way to the action. I counted twelve of these slow moving monsters spread out over the plain, their tell-tale dust trails white in the pre-dawn light like miniature versions of the massive long white cloud which had earlier hung over the ridge.

Two NZ soldiers approached the RAP. They looked like a pair of scarecrows, their steel helmets camouflaged with sacking, and they were still wearing gas masks. One was being held up by his fellow – limping badly with an arm hanging loosely by his side.

Both men fell down into the crater, exhausted.

The injured one ripped off his mask, choking and trying to get his breath.

"Ah shit, Doc… I feel like I'm bloody drowning."

I listened to his chest with my stethoscope, an act about as futile as that of the boy who put his finger into the Dutch dyke.

"If you can talk, you can breathe. You'll live," I said with certainty, not at all certain that he would. Placebo words were all I had.

The other soldier had pushed himself up into a sitting position and was leaning back against the side of the crater watching me work on his friend.

He pulled his mask up onto his forehead.

"Fucking phosgene," he said.

He had a wide streak of blood running down the left side of his face and his uniform was decorated with hundreds of small red spots. What wasn't spattered in blood was covered in dirt. He looked as if he had been born out of the ground.

In a clipped New Zealand accent, this soldier spoke again, pointing to his friend. "Put on his respirator late, the bloody idiot."

"How come?"

"He was too busy being the bloody hero, Doc. Two machine gun posts at the edge of town slowed our advance. Destroying us, they were. This mad bugger decides to charge them – runs straight through our own barrage and destroys both Maxims, and their crews… with grenades. Never seen anything like it… it's the bloody VC for you, Fricks."

"Stop blowing sunshine up my arse, Mad Dog," the wounded man said. "You were there too."

"Yeah, I followed, you deaf bastard… yelling at you to put your bloody mask on as you went on your charge. Jesus… you were faster than a fat kid running to a sweet shop." The two soldiers started laughing.

Then the injured man, Fricks, winced and I had to give him a shot of morphine. Carefully, I marked an 'M' on his wrist with a blue skin pencil, so the medics down the line would know and not overdose him later. While I was at it, I gave him an anti-tetanus jab and marked his forehead with an 'AT'. My orderly put on field dressings to his bloodied arm and hip.

"Lieutenant!"

The shout came from one of the stretcher bearers in our RAP. He was pointing up at the lip of the crater and calling out to me.

Two German soldiers were standing there, instantly recognisable because of the shape of their helmets.

They were holding their weapons.

It was hard to tell if they were just bewildered or intent on a killing spree of revenge. Their eyes certainly looked wild.

The soldier called Mad Dog was on his feet in a second and aiming his rifle up at them.

"Kap-it-ul-at-ion," he said, breaking the word up slowly into its syllables.

He didn't have to shout. His poor German pronunciation of the word dripped with intent, although the raised Lee-Enfield was warning enough. I deduced 'kapitulation' meant 'surrender'. With the story I had heard of their exploits in Messines, combined with the blood spattered uniform and his fierce stare – it didn't take much of an imagination to see why this soldier had earned his nickname.

The Germans suddenly woke from their torpor. When they looked down at their hands and saw they were still holding their rifles, they threw them away in horror and held their hands up high.

"Mercy, Kamerad," one said, his eyes wide open in desperation.

A rattle of gunfire sounded off in the distance.

It sounded like a woodpecker in a forest. Knock… knock… knock… knock… knock… knock.

Then it was quiet in the RAP.

Slowly, Mad Dog lowered his rifle and turned back to his friend.

"I've been babysitting you long enough, Fricks," he said. "I'd better get back to the boys."

Fricks nodded.

"Make sure you get to the blue line beyond the village. Remember, at seven the 1st Brigade will be coming through. I don't want anyone saying our brigade has gone soft."

Mad Dog appeared to take this in, and then turned his attention back to the Germans. They were sitting on the edge of the crater now and surveying the scene.

"You two can carry him back," he said to them, making actions like a game of charades.

They started talking to each other in rapid German.

"Tragen… ja?" one said. He slid down into the crater and picked up one of the free stretchers. "Tragen… ja?" he said again.

Mad Dog nodded.

I supervised the Germans lifting Fricks onto the stretcher. They both smelt strongly of stale coffee.

Once Fricks had been successfully moved, one of the Germans lit a cigarette and held it out as a peace offering. From his place on the stretcher, Fricks took it and inhaled deeply.

"Danke," he said.

The German soldier smiled.

"Bitte, Kamerad."

I looked at Mad Dog and pointed at the blood on his uniform.

"Are you sure you've not been hit?"

"No… that's someone else's. I think I bayonetted an artery."

He reached over and took the cigarette out of Frick's hand.

The two of them exchanged a quick glance.

"Blue line," Fricks said again.

"Blue line… We'll get there."

As he turned to leave, Mad Dog patted me on the shoulder as a gesture of thanks. Then he climbed out of the crater and was gone.

"Bugger stole my cigarette," Fricks said.

I pulled out a packet of my Navy Cut, lit one, and took a drag before giving it to him.

As I tilted my head back to exhale, I noticed Z day had dawned bright and clear.

I threw the packet to the men who passed it around. When it reached the Germans they hesitated, but I waved them on and they each took one. I had plenty of packets back at Hazebrouck, left with Poyntz for safe-keeping.

"I feel pretty good now, thanks Doc," Fricks said.

"That's the morphine."

He looked at the M on his wrist as if it was some undecipherable symbol, his pupils just small dots from the opiate.

"Oh, right…"

"What's Fricks short for?"

"Frickleton, Doc. Name's Samuel Frickleton… Lance Corporal, 3rd Rifle Battalion."

It was only then that I saw the black triangle on his sleeve.

"Did you say 3rd Rifle Battalion?"

"That's right… The Dinks."

"You don't know a Harry Ingram do you?"

"Course I bloody do… He was the bugger who just walked off with my smoke."

I looked at Fricks in surprise, then scrambled up the side of the RAP and scanned the ridge.

No-one.

I called out:

"Harry! Harry Ingram… Mad Dog!"

Nothing.

Freddie's dirt-covered, blood-spattered son was gone, back into the battle for Messines.

I realised now that there had been a small clue to his identity; a simple action, just the way he had shrugged his shoulders and made a face when I had asked him if he was injured. Freddie used to do the exact same thing whenever the teachers at school chastised him about his effort in class.

"You know him, Doc?"

It was Frickleton calling up to me from his stretcher. Now he was the one who looked surprised.

"He's my nephew."

"Really? He didn't even bloody recognise you."

"No… It's the first time I've ever met him."

I had let him go. Damn. If the Germans didn't do it then Kate Ingram was going to kill me.

Fricks must have seen the worry written all over my face.

"Oh, listen… don't worry, Doc. He'll be fine. I'm sure of it. We've been through some scrapes together, I can tell you… Flers… Morval… Thiepval Ridge…"

I looked at the injured Frickleton on the stretcher, bandaged and dopey, with his pin point pupils and a grin on his face. He listed off the names like someone remembering places they had visited on holiday.

"You're not together now though," I said.

"You're right, Doc, we're not… But you misunderstand. It's not me who's been doing the protecting; it's been the other way round."

"What do you mean?"

Frickleton looked at me, then up at the Germans and sighed.

"You get a sense of these things… especially out here. You get, well…superstitious, I suppose. Some people just don't get hurt, Doc. Some people are good luck. Anyway… you want to hang around them; hope some of their luck might rub off on you. It was only because he was with me today that I did what I did up there in the village. I knew I wouldn't die, you see. I was certain of it… because I was with him. That bugger's got more lives than a bloody cat. You might think I'm crazy, but I swear he's got a guardian angel, that lad."

I stood there smoking as I listened to Frickleton. When he had finished speaking the German stretcher bearers sensed that it was time to leave.

"A guardian angel," he said again, as they carried him away.

I watched them pick their way through the battle-field, heading to Spring Street.

A guardian angel.

I remembered Freddie's voice in the Australian desert. How it had spoken to me – woken me from my death sleep and encouraged me to get up and keep going.

"That's my brother," I said in a whisper.

Ten minutes later, at five-thirty, an enemy barrage started up again. Shelling at close quarters is indescribable; the terror replaced by a nervous awe, a feeling of exhilaration. The same type of feeling as being caught in a sudden hailstorm, but greatly magnified. I wanted to laugh out loud at the intense force the explosions carried, an elemental power which made the world I had been living in up to that point seem dilute and feeble by comparison.

A squad of bearers made it through at six and cleared two more stretcher cases which had come in. One of the bearers had a note for me from McKenzie:

Well done Lt - we received Frickleton safe and sound from the Germans. Good improvisation. One thing – get your RAP out of the open you bloody idiot. Find a Pillbox and send back the new co-ordinates. Concrete is better protection than air. Capt. McKenzie.

At seven-thirty, as the enemy guns fell silent again, soldiers of the NZ 1st Brigade moved past our position towards Messines, just as Frickleton had said they would.

I did as I was told; relocating the RAP a hundred yards further forward, to a concrete pillbox still within the Ulcer trench system. The roof was covered in netting, presumably to camouflage it from spotter planes, and a wooden sign hung above the entrance: *RATTE KELLAR* it said.

Rat cellar – the German sense of humour reminded me of my old colleague Klaus.

There wasn't anything to laugh about here anymore, though. Dead men lay sprawled outside, shot down as they had tried to flee.

In the blind side sap next to the pillbox was a warm Maxim MG 08/15, its former operators curled up at the bottom of the trench in twisted positions, bodies and heads riddled with bullet holes.

There had been no mercy in this place, not from either side; two soldiers of the NZ 3rd Rifle battalion lay dead, yards away, felled during a direct charge.

Three German dead had been bayonetted near the entrance and half a dozen others were inside the pillbox. From the lingering wisps of smoke hanging there in the gloom and the butchers' display of human meat, I guessed that grenades had been posted through the firing slit during the attack.

I found a box with word 'Verbandkasten' written on the lid and a Red Cross sign. It was a German medical examination kit containing salve and bandages, as well as a steel case holding ampoules of morphine and hypodermic syringes – a treasure trove for our small band. There was also a white cotton case with five separate pockets containing a thermometer, some tweezers, a metal spatula and two probes. Through the darkness of the interior I now noticed that the dead man nearest the box had a Red Cross armband. He was my counterpart – a German medic.

We were now on the lower slopes of the Messines Ridge, as far as I could work out the most advanced RAP in the whole southern NZ sector. Apart from the whine of the Royal Flying Corps planes circling over the German lines like birds of prey, it was eerily quiet in the aftermath of the shelling.

I was helping clear out the German dead from the Pillbox when I heard a yell.

"Uncle John!"

It was the twins, approaching with a group of thirty or so other Maori Pioneers, all carrying shovels and wearing the characteristic small box respirator haversacks strapped to the front of their chests. The blue shirts of their uniform had short white collars, which made them look like a troop of vicars on a walking tour. All the Pioneers had rolled up their sleeves, revealing the thick muscles of their tattooed forearms. Muscular vicars.

I had never been so pleased to see them.

"Manu… Kahu…"

When we exchanged the hongi their small box respirators bumped against mine.

"Thank God you're both safe," I said, realising the absurdity of my statement, standing as we were on the Messines Ridge on 'Z' day. "Your father's looking for you…"

Manu's smile turned to a frown of confusion.

"He joined up after you did," I said. "The chaplain's forces. We shipped out together."

The rest of the Pioneers were standing around us now and so were my men.

The Maori were all large, like Manu and Kahu, and a few of them had Moko tattoos on their faces. As a collective they looked frightening – frightening, not frightened. The officer spoke to the boys in Maori and they nodded.

"Sorry, John," Kahu said. "We've got to go. We're digging communications trenches to the new front line."

"He's working at Poperinghe in a place called Toc H," I said. "Make sure you get there, boys."

They were already jogging off to join their comrades who were moving on up the ridge.

"Toc H," I said again, more loudly this time, although I couldn't say for certain if they heard me.

After the Pioneer Company were out of sight, I had trouble convincing myself that I had just seen the boys at all. It had been so fleeting and unexpected a reunion that it didn't seem real. Maybe we were all dead and this was the afterlife. Maybe a big shell had exploded right next to me and I had been shunted to the next place, where all my dead friends were. Assuming I was wrong, I used the skin pencil to write it down on a piece of paper: 'Sean, saw Kahu and Manu with group of Pioneers. Day Z. Both safe and well. John.' I folded the piece of paper into four, wrote: 'Padre Sean Rennie, Toc H' on one side and stowed it into my pocket. My belly ache was back. I decided I would go and deal with that and check my pocket when I got back. If the note was still there, then I was still alive and had indeed seen the boys. If it wasn't then I would know I was in some nebulous dreamworld where things came and went and where nothing mattered any more, because I was dead.

I wandered across the ridge to a quiet field in order to relieve myself in privacy. I hadn't been since the Ludendorff latrine at Underhill Farm on X day. Bloody McKenzie never had furnished me with any syrup of figs.

I stood next to a battered hedgerow and was just about to unbuckle my belt and squat down when I sensed something was wrong.

A figure on the skyline was watching me – still as a statue. It was a soldier on horseback. He had his rifle strapped to his back, and was holding a lance in his right hand, held forward at an angle of forty five degrees. Where his face should have been was a gas-mask, the distinctive German type – the so-called 'gummimaske'. The can-like snout differed to the hose-like protrusion of the British mask and made him look like a pig instead of a giant insect.

He raised his lance and charged.

The noise of galloping hooves enveloped me and I was so frozen with fear that I didn't even put up my hands. I simply closed my eyes.

This is it… a strangely dissociated part of myself was shouting, like a commentary. *This is bloody well it…* at least I knew for certain that I hadn't died earlier, because now it was about to really happen.

Then I heard the horse's hooves thump to a halt and I opened my eyes again.

The German was staring at me; at least I assumed he was – the reflective oval glass eyepieces of his gas-mask gave nothing away.

"Mercy Kamerad," I said.

The soldier removed his helmet and pulled up his gas mask. He was smiling.

"Sanitater," he said, jabbing his lance in my direction.

Before I could comprehend his meaning, a shot rang out and the side of his head exploded into a fine red mist. His body jerked and he rolled off his saddle onto the ground, though his right boot was caught up in the stirrup and he remained joined to his horse.

The animal hadn't even startled.

One of the bushes from the hedge bordering the field started moving towards me. It was a soldier, camouflaged with twigs and leaves, and wearing the British small box respirator. When he lifted his mask I saw that his face was daubed black.

He knelt down at the dead man's side and started going through the pockets.

"Uhlan," he said. "From Prussia."

The soldier's accent was Australian.

He found some food: a hunk of dark bread and a sausage wrapped in a Frankfurt newspaper. Taking a large bite, he held a piece out to me and spoke with his mouth full.

"Want some sausage?"

"No thanks. I've lost my appetite."

"Suit yourself, mate."

I gazed down at the dead man and the fearsome hole in his head.

"Why didn't he kill me?"

The soldier stood up and pointed to my Red Cross armband.

"Didn't you hear what he said? Even I heard it… Sanitater… He didn't kill you because you're a medic."

"So why did you kill him?"

"Do I look like the fucking Red Cross, mate? Fritz here killed two of my men an hour ago. He had it coming to him."

The Australian unsheathed a knife from his belt and started carving a notch on his rifle butt. There were a dozen there already. He carved the mark crudely, just like Robinson Crusoe making notches on his walking stick for the number of days he had spent on his Island.

The Uhlan's lance was lying next to my feet in the long grass. When he had been shot, his right arm had reflexively released it in my direction. I picked it up and weighed it in my hand. It was heavy, ten feet long and made of rolled steel plate. Both ends were pointed.

The Australian sniper had finished making his notch and was looking at me.

I held out the lance but he shook his head.

"Keep it," he said.

He unhooked the lancer's boot from the stirrup, grabbed the reins and started leading the horse away towards the hedgerow. Half a dozen camouflaged soldiers stepped out of the undergrowth.

"I advise you take a shit somewhere else, Doc," the Australian said. "It's a dangerous place to be out with your trousers round your ankles."

The whole unit started laughing at me.

When I got back to the RAP, I sent a runner to let McKenzie know our new position and also gave him the note to get to Rennie. Moments later, enemy artillery started pounding the area. The shells seemed to be honing in right on the zone between our pillbox and Spring Street – the exact area the runner had gone into. We cowered in the building, smoking and worrying about him as the hate rained down.

That day we received mainly Australian wounded. Their entire 4th Division had moved in to secure the final objective line – the 'Oosttaverne line' – a mile to the east of Messines. A furious battle could be heard raging until early evening.

I became expert on the sounds of shells as I worked; the injured soldiers I was treating would say: "Hear that 'woof woof' sound, Doc? That's the medium-range trench mortars – the 'minenwerfer' – being shot out, make no noise once they're in the air though."; "That's the 'whiz-bang' of the mixed shrapnel and high explosive shells."; "That one's a 'Jack Johnson', after the American boxing Champion… It packs the biggest punch and gives off black smoke."

One injured soldier told me he had seen a Maori company take just one hour to dig a trench seven feet deep. They had continued to dig it right through an enemy barrage, yards away from exploding shells. Some had died. I had no way of knowing if this had been the boys' company and I could only hope that Rennie's prayers were working, because the fate of those lads was completely out of my hands, just as it was for Harry Ingram. Part of me regretted having sent the note saying that they were alright, because it might be out of date by the time he received it, and that would be a cruel blow indeed.

No NZ bearer parties came from the rear.

Either the runner hadn't made it, or no support could get through the barrage to reach us.

The pillbox filled with stretcher cases and the extra casualties had to be laid out in the surrounding trenches. My three remaining bearers went on scouting sorties to help bring in the wounded, leaving the orderly and me with the field dressings, the anti-tetanus and the morphine. Our water man managed to find a supply pipe near the pillbox. Because of the delay in evacuation we had plenty of time, and I irrigated the wounds thoroughly before bandaging, to try and clear out as many of Wright and Fleming's pathogens as possible.

At last, towards 9pm, a group of Australian bearer teams arrived on their way through to set up advanced posts in Messines. They cleared the RAP, taking the injured back to Spring Street with instructions to tell McKenzie our position in case the message hadn't got through.

I worked more or less continuously for the next thirty-six hours, sleeping only in snatches due to the influx of cases and the lack of manpower to deal with it all. Dying soldiers called out for three things: home, their mothers, or a last puff on a cigarette.

Right at the end the fear left their eyes and they seemed to accept the way things were, watching me and smiling. "It's beautiful, Doc," one of them even said, his eyes dreamy.

Finally, on the third morning – 9th June – McKenzie made it through, bringing with him several bearer squads. He surveyed the scene, and then saluted me.

"You've done well," he said. "You're being relieved now."

I could tell that McKenzie was clinically assessing my sanity. He must have wondered if I had become deranged since last seeing him, dehumanised like some of the shell-shocked German soldiers I had met. Their hollowed-out stares were hard to get out of your mind. When they had staggered out of the Messines smoke cloud towards us, their expressions told you all you needed to know about the frailty of man.

I wasn't wearing a shirt at all, my trousers were stained red from all the blood and the wall of the pillbox at the entrance was red from bloody handprints too. I had replaced the *Ratte Kellar* sign above the doorway with the Uhlan's lance.

I really had become one of Poyntz's 'Contraries'; on my own away from the main body of the tribe, my clothes and house red. I had even taken possession of my own thunder bow. According to Poyntz, once you were in possession of the lance you should not be afraid. But I was. Every time I closed my eyes, all I could see was the Uhlan's skull shattering into a fine red mist. I was afraid that the same kind of barbarity would be meted out to Harry Ingram and the twins, and that their lives would be obliterated in an instant.

Chapter Fourteen

Early morning light was streaming into the electrical room.

I checked my watch – seven o'clock.

I was going to be all right; I could feel it. Despite everything that had happened, I was optimistic about the world today.

Although I didn't know, this was a momentous day. In four hours' time the Armistice would take effect and the war would be over.

A pile of cigarette butts lay scattered on the floor around our feet and the place had the smoky ambience of a jazz club after an all-night session.

It was hard to believe I had been mute for a year after the monologue I had just delivered, but I suppose the words had been collecting in my brain for months, like water behind a dam. The professor had simply opened the floodgates and the torrent had poured forth. I had talked the whole night through and by now it felt as if I had known the professor all my life; he knew more about my war than my dearest friends. God, none of them even knew if I was alive, and they had not known for over a year. The realisation filled me with horror – what pain they must have gone through after I had been declared: 'missing, presumed dead'. I was probably listed in a cemetery somewhere; my true grave 'known only unto God.'

The professor was fixing me with his analytical stare.

"So…?" I could tell he was trying to be tactful, trying to choose his words as carefully as possible. "Did you end up here because one of those boys died? Or was it your nephew… that Mad Dog fellow?"

He was perceptive, the professor; you didn't get a job at an establishment like Queen Square if you weren't smart, but this time he was wrong.

"No," I said. "It wasn't because of the boys. They made it. And it wasn't because of Mad Dog either, although I'm fairly sure he's dead. As I far as I know virtually everyone in his unit was annihilated on October 12ᵗʰ 1917. No, Professor, the reason I ended up here was because of something I saw."

He nodded, more to himself than to me, as if it was something he had been pondering for some time. It made sense if you thought about it – as a physician he was a diagnostician – he pieced the clues together and came up with the answer. For his own intellectual satisfaction he would want to know what had broken me.

"Not your experience of Messines?"

I took a deep breath.

"No."

"So a later battle?"

"Yes, Professor, in fact – the battle you alluded to yesterday. Bellevue Spur… It took place on October 12ᵗʰ 1917."

"So on the same day Mad Dog was killed?"

I hesitated because I didn't want to say it, didn't want to kill Harry Ingram off for good, but I had to face the cruel truth.

"Yes," I said.

"What was worse about Bellevue Spur compared to what you saw at Messines?"

I laughed at his naïve question.

"Messines was a strategic triumph. Casualties yes, but a swift victory all the same. From zero hour and the explosions, the Germans were on the back foot and it was a crushing defeat for them. But they got back up off the canvas and came back at us hard. Poyntz was right, you know – the generals wanted those ports on the Belgian coast, and the only way through was across the Passchendaele plateau. You just needed a chess brain to work it out. By the time Third Ypres started, they were ready for us all right."

"I've read about it in the newspapers," the professor said. "The conditions described are hard for me to imagine."

I thought about what I had experienced, how to sum it up best in a nice neat package for the professor's smart mind.

"Passchendaele," I said. "It was as if the devil himself had sat down and really put his mind to it, thought long and hard about the best way of replicating hell on earth. Clever, the devil is – I always thought hell would be hot. But instead there was nothing for miles around except a cold sea of mud and desolation… plenty of death, you know that too of course. Remember the poem, Professor? *'And in the air, Death moans and sings…'* Not like Messines. Slaughter on an industrial scale, like the Somme… but in the rain this time. What went on near Passchendaele were the sorts of events that rock a nation's psyche permanently. People will still be speaking of it in one hundred years."

For once, the professor had no quick response.

"You know what bothers me the most?" I said.

He shook his head.

"The fact that it didn't have to happen… two Germans carried Frickleton back to Spring Street, for Christ's sake. Human beings just like us. They liked a smoke, they had empathy, they had fear, and they understood us. Even the Uhlan had a human touch. He wouldn't have killed me… I know that for sure. The last thing he ever did was smile at me. These bloody wars of nations… the Boer War, this war, the people at the top almost *want* them to happen. They think it's going to be like a playground fight. They're desperate to prove themselves, to prove their honour. I hold every leader to account – the big tough chess players, playing their big games to make themselves feel important. I hope Rennie is right, about judgement day, I mean. I hope that one day they'll be made to face up to what they've done."

"I didn't think you had religious leanings," the professor said. "From what I've heard tonight, you and your friend Rennie appear to have been fighting each other on that matter for years."

I laughed.

"Yes, I was unsure, but not anymore, not after what I saw out there."

Saying this made goose bumps run down my back at the memory.

"Really?" the professor said, genuinely curious. "What did you see? God?"

"No – I saw Death."

"Yes, you've just said you saw a lot of people dying."

"No, Professor. You don't understand. I saw the entity called Death, with a capital bloody D. I had glimpsed it before, on the night my brother died – as a ghostly nurse and a darkness which had accompanied her – but I had eventually managed to dismiss it as a bad dream. After what happened at Bellevue Spur though, I no longer have any doubt. The Grim Reaper is real. And if it's real, then I'm sure there's a God too."

Professor S was looking over at the electrical apparatus, possibly contemplating another dose of voltage to get rid of this superstitious claptrap from my brain. Then he looked at me again and appeared to change his mind.

Instead of picking up the probe, he lit us another two cigarettes.

"I'm not mad, Professor, don't worry. I never have been. A switch was turned off, that's all… and you've managed to switch it back on again. I'll tell you everything. But you'll have to keep that scientific mind of yours open. If you do that, then when I'm finished, maybe you'll believe it too."

I took a long drag on the cigarette and waited on his verdict.

"I'm listening," he said, after a while.

"Good. First let me ask you this, Professor. During your medical career, inexplicable events will have happened, am I right? Rumours and stories and gossip on the wards, perhaps rooms associated with bad luck? Every hospital I've ever worked in has these places."

Professor S nodded almost imperceptibly and I saw a look of recognition in his eyes.

"Hold that thought," I said. "Hold that figment of the unknown for a while longer. It'll help you keep an open mind for what I have to tell you."

"Go on…" he said.

NZ Stationary Hospital, Wisques, 28th September 1917

Captain McKenzie was eyeballing me at close range. We were alone.

Outside it was raining again and the rain beat against the windows, disturbing the silence. All it ever seemed to do was bloody rain. It had rained pretty much every day in August, and looked to be doing the same for September too.

We were in the billiards room of the YMCA hut – part of the new NZ Stationary Hospital at Wisques near St Omer, relocated after Hazebrouck was shelled at the end of July. More than 600 patients had been evacuated the day afterwards, and within 6 weeks the new Stationary Hospital was up and running.

McKenzie stood just inches away, right in my space.

When he had entered the room I had been slowly pacing the floor, my mind somewhere else.

I had just read a letter from Jennifer which had found its way to me that morning. She was at the NZ No.1 General Hospital in England now, at Brockenhurst in the New Forest, just across Southampton water from the Royal Victoria Military Hospital. The NZ Medical Corps had been allotted the Balmer Lawn Hotel, and her quarters were in a small room in the roof eaves which had been the maid's quarters before the war.

After the action the NZ division had seen at Messines, Jennifer had been busy. By the sounds of it, she was doing more than I was; being 'worked to the bone' by an authoritative Matron called Fanny Wilson: *'She never stops talking, John; barely draws breath – orders, telling offs, the way she wants things to be. If it's not us, she's talking to the patients, or the doctors. Our nickname for her is 'Transmit'. It actually makes me rather nervous. Even when I'm in bed at night, her voice is still echoing in my head and sometimes even my dreams. The only time she's quiet is when the Colonel-in-charge of the hospital comes around. He is about sixty years old and wears a 'pea jacket' even on warm days. He has a flat cap and shiny black boots up to his knees and he hardly ever smiles. The other staff nurses and I think Transmit has a thing for him because, when he speaks to her, she turns as scarlet as her cape and goes quiet – a quick reply, nothing more. None of us can work out if he's married or not because his hands are always in the pockets of his great big coat – oh dear… It's the one time I feel sorry for her… poor Matron…'*

Jennifer's writing style was chatty, almost cheerful, as if she was talking to a close confidant. This made me very happy. Then I had found something to make me even happier; a pressed flower tucked into the letter, a bluebell. It was a fragile, beautiful thing which told me more than she could have written in fifty pages. She was still my girl.

Smiling, I had held it in my palm for a while before putting it carefully back between the pages.

The bluebell reminded me of the times my father had taken Freddie and me out into the woods near our childhood home. Every spring we would go there, forging small tracks in the carpet of flowers and looking for suitable pieces of wood to use as pretend weapons – spears, bows and arrows, swords. Rifles too. For two small boys, the bluebells had just been the background to our war play, but even so, I remembered them clearly.

At the moment McKenzie entered the billiards hut I was imagining walking in bluebell woods with Jennifer, holding her hand and laughing as our children ran around us.

As soon as I saw McKenzie on his determined approach, my dream world vaporised and I stuffed the letter down the waist of my trousers.

He hadn't said anything yet; not 'hello' or 'how are you doing', he was just silently staring.

A lot of surgeons had a strange mentality; a sort of idiosyncratic behaviour that came from getting to play God so often. They were the sorts who looked confused in interviews when asked if they had any weaknesses, because it was something they had never bothered to consider. Almost anyone who thought they were a 'big shot' had it to a certain degree.

'Big shot' was a favourite expression of Poyntz's; he said it all the time.

When we had still been in Hazebrouck, a general had come to the Stationary Hospital and glided round the wards with his gaggle of sycophants, handing out MCs to the bandaged men in their beds. The general had been nice enough, but you still had the feeling when he talked to you that you were a creature near the bottom of the food chain, and that he was most certainly at the top of it. Whenever he said anything his junior officers smiled and nodded in agreement. Anything – even if it was something mundane, such as 'it's still raining'. You would think he had just invented time travel, judging by the looks of awe on their faces. After the procession had moved on, Poyntz nudged me and said: "Who does that guy think he is? I'll tell you – some kind of goddamn big shot, that's who."

They were Type 2's, if you used my father's classification system. Poyntz's 'big shot' appellation was just an American way of saying the same thing.

These people thought the normal rules somehow didn't apply to them because they were special. So they seemed cold and aloof – almost inhuman. They can't have always been like that though, they must have become that way somewhere along the line. For me, that was the saddest part, for there to have been a time when they had been normal and humble.

Sometimes I felt like a biologist, classifying animals and birds into different categories – kingdom, phylum and genus – only I seemed to do it with humans; type 1, type 3, type 3. I was too judgmental, I knew it. But it wasn't reserved for other people exclusively – I judged myself too, and in my simple categorising system I had failed to live up to my own expectations just as much as everyone else.

No matter how hard I tried I would never succeed – I would never get to those remote, stand-offish realms where the Type 2s lived, that proud place of no doubts, no worries and no fear. It would be good to live without fear.

If I was honest with myself, painfully honest, there was one reason why.

At the back of my head, like a small beating metronome, there was a constant guilt ticking, quiet but always there. It was a voice which had been talking ever since Freddie had died. Sometimes it was loud, sometimes you could hardly hear it, but it was always there. For nearly twenty years the pendulum had been swinging back and forth: *it should have been me… it should have been me… it should have been me…*

McKenzie's long stare was right at the edge of the oddness spectrum, but I had seen it all before – dealt with people far more unpredictable, more dangerous, and a hell of a lot more unlikeable than him.

I could handle McKenzie. He was good at heart; I knew that from what I had seen, and I think deep down he knew he wasn't a 'big shot' too. He must have picked up this macho act from other macho surgeons in order to survive in their competitive macho world. There must have been a time when he had just been himself, way back at the beginning of medical school, before the 'gods' had warped his character to mimic theirs and before the army had finished the transformation. That was the McKenzie I liked, the original McKenzie, the one beneath all the layers of crud he had accumulated to protect himself. I could see him trying to be tough and at the same time glimpse the real him beneath those layers – a poignant thing to witness.

His eyes weren't giving much away though. McKenzie would have made a fine poker player. I knew exactly what he was doing – he was looking deep into my soul to see if anything was wrong.

He wouldn't work it out though; he was only a surgeon, not a soothsayer.

This was one little battle I would win. I might have lost it a bit at Messines, I admit that, but no more than any other man would have done in the same set of circumstances. And I hadn't turned into a jabbering nervous wreck like some of the shell-shocked soldiers. I had done my job. I hadn't let McKenzie down.

The moment dragged on – five seconds… ten seconds… twenty.

It felt like waiting for zero hour to arrive.

I was feeling uncomfortable, but was determined McKenzie would be the first to break. I couldn't let him see any weakness, not this time, not like he had observed at Messines, when I had been half-crazed with fatigue.

If asked about my weaknesses in a job interview I would have happily said: "It's a long list, where do you want me to start?" But something told me to hide them from McKenzie today. It might affect his judgment about my fitness for service, and in a warped way, I actually did care what he thought of me. He was a wiser man than I had given him credit for. The real McKenzie was all right.

When he had found me at the pillbox, McKenzie had seen something in my demeanour that had troubled him. Though he never said it outright, he must have thought I had shot my bolt. Perhaps it was the spear hanging above the door that had made him suspicious, that and the fact I had insisted on taking it back to the Underhill ADS with me. *Bloody hell, you can't leave a thunder-bow just hanging around on the battlefield. The Uhlan has passed it on to me: I am the chosen Contrary.* Of course I hadn't been so stupid as to say this out loud to McKenzie. I just told him it was a souvenir. But even so, he had sniffed out something was wrong about me that day and made a decision. It was the way he had spoken to me that had given away his thoughts – he talked in the same way you would do if you were trying to talk down a man standing on the top of a tall building. He didn't even know the craziest part – my confusion over whether I was alive or dead and of how I had put a note in my pocket to try and work out which it was.

He assigned me to work with Poyntz, knowing us to be old friends. It was some kind of sabbatical as far as I could tell. While McKenzie stayed at Underhill with the rest of the 3rd Ambulance, for nearly two months I worked as Poyntz's surgical assistant in the theatre back at Hazebrouck – holding the retractors and the like. You didn't have to be a surgeon to do that, even medical students could assist. As long as you had a strong stomach and a steady hand and you did exactly what the surgeon asked you to do, it was fairly simple. I became used to the top of people's heads being removed under anaesthesia, and Poyntz delicately peeling through their brain matter to get at damaged areas, or extracting shrapnel with his magnet. You didn't have to know all the names of the muscles, nerves and blood vessels – that was Poyntz's job. It was quite relaxing actually, being there for hours at a time, locked in quiet concentration with my friend on the other side of the table – a bit like our games of chess.

I suppose McKenzie hoped I would lose the wild look in my eye, and return to normal under Poyntz's steadying influence.

Sometimes, during the night, I would dream of the mounted German Lancer – pointing at me and smiling, and then his head shattering. It took a month for me to start feeling better – until one morning I realised the nightmares had stopped. Soon I began to think clearly again, more clearly than before Messines. I even started beating Poyntz at chess like in the old days. Together we established a workable equilibrium; in theatre he was the boss and on the chess board it was me.

Only Poyntz understood the significance of the lance which lay on the floor of my bell tent at Hazebrouck. The weapon would be right there as we played our chess games. Occasionally, he would lift it up above his head and say: "The thunder bow of the Contrary's wigwam." Though I would smile, underneath I didn't find it funny at all – the lance was deadly serious. To me, being a Contrary was real and frightening.

In between moves, we would talk about his wife in New York and laugh about how Bernadette's beauty had hypnotised us all in Western Australia. He listened to my tales of Messines and in turn I listened to his descriptions of head injuries, and the new surgical techniques being pioneered to extract bullets from various parts of a soldier's brain.

During our games there would be the constant pitter-patter of rain on the tent. Like I already said, the rain never seemed to let up.

'Third Ypres' had started on 31st July after a two week bombardment of over four million shells. That was the day Hazebrouck was bombed too. In August there were only three rainless days, the rainfall being twice the usual average for the month. With all the shelling and rain, the whole of Flanders turned into a quagmire.

We heard the stories coming back from the front, how soldiers were slipping off the duckboards and drowning in the mud, how it needed six or even eight stretcher bearers to carry just one injured man back. How wounded men would crawl into a shell hole as cover, only to drown in the rising rainwater.

When the hospital moved out of Hazebrouck, Poyntz and I were split up. He was transferred to a neurosurgical unit at a Casualty Clearing Station called 'Mendinghem' to work alongside his boss, Major Cushing. I remained with the NZ Stationary, helping to set up the new hospital at Wisques. At the entrance they put up a carved wooden gateway in the Maori style, depicting mythical figures with their tongues sticking out. I wondered if one of them might be the demigod Maui.

Despite being on a hill, the ground was marshy and, until Nissen huts were erected, we were all under canvas. Duckboards above the sludge connected the various tents but even with those in place and our supposedly waterproofed boots, trench foot was common. I had spent most of September drying my sodden footwear by the stove in the games hut.

In fact I was barefoot now while waiting for my boots to dry. McKenzie could not have helped but notice this. Maybe that was what was concerning him.

He sighed.

"How are you feeling, Lieutenant?"

McKenzie had spoken first. I smiled.

"Feeling, sir? Do you really want to know?"

"Good point. I'll re-phrase my question. I'm asking if you're ready for the next battle… I need you to spearhead things again. That's why I've been resting you."

"I'm ready, sir. You didn't have to do what you did…"

"I know."

"But I appreciate it, sir. Being around Captain Poyntz was an education in battlefield surgery."

I didn't say it had also been an education in chess and American slang.

McKenzie made one of his grunts. He had stopped listening now. I could see what his look meant – enough chit chat; time to get down to business.

He pulled a piece of paper out of his pocket.

"General Routine Order No. 2384"

He read the order out loud:

"Classification and disposal of officers and other ranks who without any visible wound become non-effective from physical conditions claimed or presumed to have originated from the effects of British or enemy weapons in action."

"Is that a roundabout way of saying 'shell shock', sir?"

I was feeling nervous now. It felt as if he was about to diagnose me and call in the men who had been hovering outside the door with the strait jacket ready.

"Yes it is, Hunston. That's exactly what it means. Now you are to ignore everything you've previously been taught on this subject… and I'm afraid I've been directed to read it out in full, so shut up and listen up."

He read on:

"Number 1 – All officers and other ranks who become non-effective in the above category, will be sent to the Special Hospital set apart for their reception."

"The Special Hospital, sir?"

"That's right," McKenzie said. "The *Special* Hospital."

"And I suppose that will be near the front, sir, and not back in Blighty…"

McKenzie grinned at me.

It was a logical strategy – the army keeping the cases of simple exhaustion close by, before they were sent so far down the line that they became, in effect, irretrievable. I remembered what they had told us on the Awapuni course; how they had learnt at the Somme that the process of sending men all the way back to England was bad economics. The pieces of meat were needed to fight, not flounder.

"Number 2 – The officer commanding a medical unit, who in the first instance deals with a case needing transfer to the Special Hospital, will not record any diagnosis. He will enter on the Field Medical Card the letters 'NYDN' only. This stands for Not Yet Diagnosed, Nervous."

"Excuse me, sir?" I said, "but isn't it our job to diagnose… as doctors I mean? Isn't that what we trained for?"

McKenzie grinned again.

"Not in the Army, it's not."

"Oh."

"Number 3 – In no circumstances whatever will the expression 'shell shock' be used verbally or be recorded, except in cases classified by the order of the officer commanding the Special Hospital."

McKenzie folded up the piece of paper and tucked it back into his pocket. He looked extremely pleased with himself.

"So in summary, I can't say it and I can't write it, sir."

"Correct."

"Can I still think it, sir?"

"No," McKenzie said, smiling even more broadly now. "Don't even think it."

I realised he felt exactly the same as I did about the directive. That it was balderdash.

"So the decision making has been taken out of our hands, sir."

"Yes it has, Hunston. That's how much the army cares about you."

"How thoughtful of them," I said.

McKenzie's look turned sober.

"Get ready," he said. "This is going to be different to Messines. This order tells you all you need to know about what's going on east of Ypres and what it's doing to men's heads. We move out in three days."

"What shall I do now, sir?"

McKenzie thought about this for a moment.

"Go and see your friends…"

He pointed at my waist where Jennifer's letter was half poking out.

"Write back to your sweetheart…"

He looked over towards the stove where my boots were drying.

"Put some dubbin on your boots if you want. To tell you the truth, Lieutenant, I don't really give a shit what you do."

I smiled, because it was obvious that he did.

Chapter Fifteen

I did all the things McKenzie advised: wrote to my sweetheart, visited Rennie, even put dubbin on my boots.

It is hard to know what to say to people you care about deeply, knowing that the chances of your making it through have become much slimmer. The end is suddenly within touching distance, and anything you say might be your last words. You feel you should probably be saying something profound.

When it came to my 'sweetheart' as McKenzie had called her, I decided to write it there in the Billiard room after he had gone, while the full import of what he had just said was fresh in my mind. Barefoot, I huddled by the stove with my pen hovering over the paper, unable to move. If I had been a statue in a gallery I would have been called, 'the man who left it too late' or, better still, 'the procrastinator'.

In the end I decided not to think about it too much and just write whatever came into my mind, without censorship or reflection. I hoped it would relay the truth.

My darling Jennifer,

Please allow me to call you that. Ever since our meeting in the Brian Boru that night, it is how I have thought of you – as my darling. I'm afraid I write this with a certain amount of dread, as my CO has just told me that we are moving up to the front line in a few days and I'm sure you know there's a battle raging out there the likes of which mankind has not seen before. So this may be the last thing you ever hear from me and that is a thought I find unutterably depressing.

For many years I have lived a kind of hollow life, never really daring myself to enjoy it properly. Rather than beat around the bush, which I don't have time for, I'll explain why to you right now, so that you might understand. In fact, having read the letter you sent me via Rennie in New Zealand, you do understand partially, the Rennies having told you about my brother and what happened. You said some lovely things in that letter, and I have re-read your sentences many times, and each time, the words have given me heart.

Here it is: I felt guilty, Jennifer. For all those years I felt guilty if I was happy, knowing that he should have been enjoying his life too. So I didn't dare. I know now, or am at least vividly reminded, as I see men dying by the hundreds, that how I have lived is a great waste. I once met someone who told me that my brother would have wanted me to be happy. And I'm sure that's true. But it is easier said than done, and although I made some small steps of progress initially, I stalled and stood still. The Rennies have been my only friends in all that time, and I have kept other relationships at arm's length, fearful of what might happen if I start to move forward again. I treated you like that Jennifer and I am sorry, deeply sorry, to have wasted that precious time when it might turn out to have been the only time we had. That is in the past. Right now, I want you to know that I fully commit myself to you. You have my heart in your hands. As long as you are its guardian, my heart is safe. I know I will be happy with you Jennifer, and I want to make you happy too. I hope and pray that I get another chance to prove to you that what I say is the truth. Your love has made me want to live again.

Yours, John

As regards seeing Rennie, I didn't have to think about when I would arrange our meeting – he summoned me. The telegram arrived at Wisques that same afternoon:

LT. HUNSTON. TOC H 5 PM ON 29/9/17. HIGHLY IMPORTANT. CF RENNIE

Not just important, but *highly* important – that certainly had me wondering.

The next day I found him upstairs at Toc H, in his room with the flowery wallpaper.

His feet were up on the desk and he was leaning back on his chair with his hands clasped behind his head.

Handel's Messiah was playing on the phonograph and Rennie was singing along to the music with his eyes closed.

I knocked on the open door.

"Hey there."

Rennie opened his eyes.

"Hello, John."

"Am I disturbing you?"

He lifted his legs off the desk and sat forward. "Not at all, come on in."

I took the spare chair and removed my jacket. Since the stove was hot, I parked my feet in front of it in the hope that I could finish drying out my boots there.

"You looked like you were somewhere else just then," I said.

"Yes… I was. Back with Matty in the garden and she was cooking a hangi. I could almost smell it."

"And what was she saying? Telling you off for not helping, or complaining about your dancing?"

Rennie smiled. But he was sad, I could tell.

In the background the music blared on: *Halleluiah! Halleluiah!*

"You know you're supposed to stand up for this one," I said, trying to cheer him up. "Traditionally, I mean… the king did it once."

"Oh yes," Rennie said. "I remember that. Which king was it again?"

"One of the Georges I think."

Despite what I said, we both stayed sitting.

"I stand and I bow before only one man, John, as you well know."

"Yes… I know."

It looked as if he wanted to tell me something, but was holding back.

I noticed a letter lying open on his desk… Materoa's writing.

"What does she say?"

"She's worried about the boys."

"Is that it? There's a lot there."

"I'm worried too," Rennie said, ignoring me.

I picked up his steaming cup of tea from the desk and took a sip.

"Are there any biscuits?" I said flippantly, trying to change the subject. Something was in the air, I could tell, something deep, and I didn't want to go there.

"John?"

"Yes."

"What was your father like when your brother died?"

"Is this Earl Grey?" I said. "It tastes like it."

"As a friend, I'm asking you, John."

I put the mug on the table and looked at Rennie.

"You don't want to know," I said, my voice suddenly husky, as if my throat was unconsciously constricting. This was an old reaction. Rennie was digging up memories that I preferred to keep buried.

"I do… I need to know."

I sighed.

"How do you think he was? He was never the same again. There are no words for that kind of pain."

Rennie could see in my expression what I couldn't describe.

"A man of sorrows and acquainted with grief?"

"Where's that from? The Bible?"

He nodded. "Book of Isaiah," he said. "Christ's sufferings foretold."

I let out another even deeper sigh.

"Well," I said, "with no disrespect in the comparison, it's a fair depiction of my father's sufferings too."

Tears welled up in Rennie's eyes.

"I don't think I could take it. I don't think I could cope if one of my boys was killed. Materoa either… God help us."

"They're diggers, Sean. They don't go over the top."

It was all I could think of saying and, even as I said it, I saw how irrelevant my words were. Shells didn't care if you went over the top or not.

"Messines," he said. "Seventeen of their battalion killed. How do you rationalise that? Do you console yourself that they dug 5000 yards of trenches? In July, they dug positions and laid down telephone cables with the French and our 3rd Brigade. One killed. The following month they set up wire entanglements on the front near La Basseville. Sixteen killed. For a strip of barbed wire, John… sixteen men were killed."

I picked up his mug of tea and held it out to him. There was nothing to say.

"Anyway, for the last fortnight they've been repairing bridges and roads in Ypres. They're camped out in an old cellar on the Poperinghe Road just west of the city. I walked there myself yesterday to ask them to come here today – squared it with their CO."

This was good news. I hadn't set eyes on the boys since Messines, though I had visited Rennie regularly at Toc H and knew they had managed to see their father a few times.

The music was still going:

For the Lord God Omnipotent reigneth…

"Maybe you shouldn't be playing this, Sean," I said.

He only ever played the Messiah when he was troubled.

"Why not?"

"Well…" I said, searching for an excuse, "for one thing Handel was German."

"Oh… I'm sure no-one will mind. It was 175 years ago."

"Hmm… I suppose."

Rennie sat back and closed his eyes again.

"You know, his career was in the doldrums at the time," he said. "Handel's, I mean. In operatic circles he was fast becoming a 'has-been'. Then a man called Jennens put together some words for an oratorio and, in the depths of his despair, something in that text made Handel sit up. You know what verse it was? He was despised and rejected, a man of sorrows and acquainted with grief. It's a prophecy, John, written seven hundred years before Christ."

"I see."

"Anyway, Handel could relate to those sentiments. He wrote the music in twenty-four days straight after reading that verse – barely ate – just wrote…"

Rennie opened his eyes and took a sip of his tea.

I sat there listening to the end of the chorus respectfully.

Ha-lle-lu-iah!

It was only when the music stopped that it felt all right to talk again.

"So what's going on, Sean?" I said, holding up the telegram. "What's so highly important? Why are we meeting here today?"

"I just wanted us all to be together for a change. I invited Poyntz too."

"I know. I saw him in the square – he was looking for a cake to bring along."

"He doesn't have to do that."

"That's what I told him, but it didn't make any difference. You know these Yanks – they have their own way of doing things."

"Yes," Rennie said. "They're so… independent."

There was a silence. The room was very quiet without the music. There weren't many soldiers at Toc H today.

"Sean, are you all right?"

"This war…" Rennie said, "…it's been a hell of a two months. What gains have we made? A few hundred yards; maybe three quarters of a mile? How many thousands have died? And for what? Some wire entanglements and an enemy trench? You know, John, the generals remind me of men who have only ever known nails and are then given the task of removing a screw from a piece of wood. They make a big effort to pull out the screw by force, and when that doesn't work they just pull even harder. It never occurs to them to try and unscrew the thing… You know, change tactics, and do something original, something surprising. Now at least Messines was surprising."

"That's goddamn right…" said a voice.

Rennie and I both looked out to see who had spoken.

At the table in the adjoining room was a soldier with a book, a man of about thirty with short cropped blond hair. His cap must have been on the floor of the library upstairs as insurance for the book he had borrowed. His accent was American and the metal insignia on his collar – U.S. – confirmed his nationality.

"Oh, you shouldn't listen to me, sir," Rennie said, "I'm no military man."

"Well, it's about the most sense I've heard about the state of play out here so far," the American said, closing his book and coming over to the doorway of our room. "I'm sorry," he said, "I couldn't help but overhear your conversation once the music had finished… I'm Captain George Patton of the AEF."

We both stood.

"Oh… you're a Padre," Patton said, seeing Rennie's dog collar. "Sorry about the 'Goddamn'…"

"You are forgiven, Captain," Rennie said, smiling good-naturedly. They shook hands.

"I'm Reverend Rennie and this is my good friend, Lieutenant Hunston of the New Zealand Medical Corps."

"Nice to meet you, Captain," I said.

He had a bone-crusher handshake, like Westbourne's had been back in Thames, but twice as powerful.

"Good God!" Rennie said. "While we're on the apologies, I hope you weren't offended by our earlier comments on your countrymen. How very embarrassing."

"No, not at all. You were right there too, Reverend. Independent is a good word for it. The founding fathers thought the same thing."

Rennie pointed at the book.

"I trust you found something interesting in the library?"

"Elephants," Patton said.

"What's that?"

"Elephants… I've been studying Hannibal and his battle tactics. The equivalent now is tanks, but the principle is the same – overwhelming power, speed and surprise. Just like you were saying… I'm going to change the way battles are fought in the future. Forget the nails and screws – I'm gonna knock the whole goddamn wall down… Oh, I'm sorry Reverend. There I go again with my cussing."

Just then, Poyntz came up the stairs, holding a gateau.

"Ah, Poyntz," Rennie said, waving him over, "we've found a fellow American to keep you company. Captain Patton this is Captain Poyntz, another old friend and medic, and one of your country's best surgeons."

Poyntz put the cake down on the table, saluted Patton and shook his hand.

"Captain," he said.

"Captain Poyntz."

"Wait a minute," Poyntz said, evidently remembering something, "are you the same Patton who raided the Mexican hideout last year? The man I read about in the *New York Times*?"

"The one and the same."

"Gentlemen," Poyntz said, addressing me and Rennie, "Captain Patton here conducted America's first ever motorised assault against a group of notorious Mexican bandits – he attacked the ranch of Julio Cardenas, one of Pancho Villa's most trusted men. You were charged by three of the Villistas on horseback, weren't you, Captain?"

"Yes, that's true… at the San Miguel ranch… May 14th last year. The odds were in our favour mind you… ten of us and only three of them. There was a big shoot out… and pretty soon all three men were dead. Cardenas was one of the three… fought to the bitter end, despite being shot through four times. He was still firing at us until my scout put in the tira gracia."

Rennie frowned: "Tira Gracia?"

"It means the 'mercy shot', Reverend."

"Oh… my goodness me…"

My friend backed into his study to retrieve his cup of tea.

"Anyway," Patton said, "when we counted up Cardenas's cartridge belts, we worked out he'd fired thirty five shots.

Poyntz came back into the exchange.

"The papers said you strapped the bodies of the bandits to the hoods of your cars and drove them back to General Pershing. Is that really true?"

This question started off a coughing fit from Rennie.

"Yep," Patton said. "They were good cars too…"

His coughing fit over, Rennie – fearless as ever – came back into the fray: "Tell me, Captain… doesn't your conscience trouble you for killing a man?"

There was a moment's silence as the question hung in the air. Rennie sipped at his tea, as if he had just asked about the weather.

"It does not, Reverend," Patton said. "I feel about it as I did when I got my first swordfish… surprised at my luck."

Rennie choked on his mouthful of tea.

"Patton here likes tanks," I said to Poyntz, changing the subject.

"Is that so? You in the Tank Corps?"

"Not yet, but I'm thinking of joining 'em, Poyntz; thinking of doing it pretty soon. Got me a desk job at the moment on General Pershing's staff and I'm getting fed up with just sitting on my ass. There's a colonel in charge of a tank project for the AEF and he's asked me to head up the light tank school. I'm giving the matter some serious consideration."

"You know enough about that kinda thing?"

"Yup… for a start the project will be based in France and I speak French; always gotten on with Frenchmen. I know machine guns well enough and I'm the only American who's ever made an attack in a motor vehicle – last year down in Mexico, when chasing those bandits…plus lately I've had the distinct feeling that fate is tapping me on the shoulder and telling me to do it."

"You mean you're following your instinct?" I said.

"I suppose you could call it that, Doc, though I prefer to think of it as fate, coming from somewhere else. Don't you ever get that feeling?"

I thought about his question for a moment. Perhaps there had been a time in my life where I had listened to fate – seeing the job advert for a post out in Western Australia and acting on it and leaving my life in London behind – that had felt like being 'tapped on the shoulder'. I had listened to that small voice in my conscience deep down inside and ignored what convention said I should be doing. In retrospect it had been one of the best decisions in my life. At the time it had *felt* so obviously to be the right option.

"You mean, like a steersman?" I said.

I caught Rennie's eye, aware that we had spoken of the same thing on New Year's Day.

Patton clapped his hands together in delighted agreement.

"That's damn right, Doc – a steersman who tries to reach out and touch you at crucial points, to guide you on your way. I think a lot of people ignore that feeling – they say, 'Go away' or 'I don't know you' – but I want to hear what he has to say, listen to him and follow my true destiny. A man needs to know what he was meant to be."

I understood this Patton, or at least this boldness in his character, which others might have construed as a foolhardy and rash. That's what my colleagues had thought when I had left Harley Street for the Australian hinterland.

Rennie would understand Patton too, though he would call it 'listening to God'.

"You need a kind of fearlessness to follow your intuition like that" I said, remembering how I had felt.

"Damn right, Doc. If a man has the guts, he'll follow it."

"Well, Captain," Poyntz said, "it certainly sounds to me like the tank job's yours if you so choose."

Patton stood proud as he heard Poyntz's validation, hands on hips. His demeanour was more Wild West Cowboy than Great War Soldier.

I noticed a distinctive ivory-handled revolver in his holster.

"Captain Patton," I said, "you might be interested to know that Poyntz here used to play chess with Wyatt Earp."

Patton's eyes lit up.

"No kidding?"

Poyntz laughed. "Yes, it's true, Captain. A long time ago, over in Nome, Alaska, during the gold rush days. And I can let you into a little secret…" he said, winking and leaning his head towards his fellow countryman, "…Earp was a better shot than he was a chess player."

Laughter erupted.

"But even Earp admitted that, when it came to marksmanship, he wasn't a patch on Doc Holliday."

More laughter. Patton was clearly impressed with Poyntz.

I pointed at the ivory-handled revolver.

"Are you a good shot with that thing?"

"Yes, sir, I believe I am. Placed fifth at the 1912 Olympic pentathlon. Might've been higher but the judges said I missed the target in the shooting round since they only counted seventeen holes out of the twenty bullets fired."

"And you hadn't missed?"

"No chance; the bullets went through a big hole I had already made."

"Didn't that happen to anyone else?"

"No. See, I had a .38 compared with the other competitors. They were using a .22. But that's a sissy gun and there was no way I was going to compete with that. Anyway, the .38 bullets ripped a gaping hole over the bull's eye, so big you could have driven a truck through it unchecked, let alone three other bullets."

Poyntz, Rennie and I laughed, slightly nervously.

Patton drew the revolver.

"Wanna closer look?"

"May I?"

"Certainly, Lieutenant Hunston…"

He put it in my hand.

"Colt .45," he said, "aka, the peacemaker."

The intertwined initials 'GSP' adorned the right side of the grip. The left side had an eagle engraved on the ivory. Two grooves were at the neck of the stock.

"That's a shame – the ivory's been scratched here."

"No," Patton said. "I made those… after the bandit attack last year."

I looked up at him and immediately gleaned what he meant. I had seen the Australian sniper doing the same thing after killing the Uhlan.

I handed it back.

A fearsome confidence radiated out from the American like the blazing heat from the stove. This man was the ultimate Type 2, an American version of Lord Desborough, *my* ultimate example of the English 'Empire man'. Patton really was a 'big shot', not some pretender. There was no veneer; the man we were seeing was the original with no affectations or pretence. No wonder we were all stood there in awe of him.

"Aaah, my boys," Rennie said, as Kahu and Manu appeared at the top of the stairs.

They each came over to grasp their father's hand warmly, pausing long enough to do the hongi – nose on nose. Then they turned to me and did the same. Their breath smelt of wood smoke.

Rennie made the introductions to Poyntz and Patton.

"Gentlemen – these are my two sons, Kahu and Manu. Since their mother Materoa is Maori, they serve in the Maori Pioneer battalion. Boys, this is Captain Poyntz, an American surgeon. Before you were born, both he and John saved my life. I was moribund with typhoid fever, you see… but the good Lord had the grace to entrust my care to the very best men."

Poyntz shook the boys' hands.

"Captain Patton here is soon to be a famous American tank soldier," Rennie said, continuing. "I'm sure, from what I've already heard, he'll be as famous as the great Carthaginian General Hannibal one day."

This comment elicited a proud smile from Patton.

"Kahu, Manu," he said, shaking each of their hands. "I've studied Maori military history… outnumbered, outgunned but never conquered. You are the first Maori I've ever met and I want to take this opportunity to express my admiration for the warrior spirit of your people."

"Thank you, Captain," the boys said in unison.

Patton peered closely at the decorations on Kahu and Manu's uniforms.

"Military Medals," he said. "May I ask for what action?"

"We were members of a wiring party at La Basseville in early August, Captain," Manu said. "A lot of machine gun fire and shelling that night, but we finished the job."

Rennie had turned pale.

"Damn brave," Patton said. "And I see you both have Moko tattoos on the right side of your faces – showing your mother's ancestry, I presume."

The boys glanced at one another, impressed at this American soldier knowing so much.

Manu spoke again. "Captain Poyntz, Captain Patton… this is truly an honour. My brother and I would like to show our respect for you both in the traditional way. Please come outside into the garden."

We all followed the boys downstairs to the ground floor.

A few soldiers were sitting around the piano in the conservatory. Rennie's batman Pettifer was in the kitchen, busy stirring a large vat of soup with a steel ladle.

There were a dozen Maori Pioneers around the billiards table. They must have all decided to come along to see Toc H with Kahu and Manu. I recognised their CO from Messines.

Manu spoke in Maori to them, gesturing towards Poyntz and Patton as he talked. Then the group opened the double doors to the patio, stepped outside and lined up in two rows on the lawn a few yards away from us, shaking out their arms and legs like prize-fighters warming up in the ring.

I had seen the haka dozens of times over the years, and the Pioneers didn't hold back on this one. Their blood up, some of the Maori started poking out their tongues and opening their eyes up widely before the performance even began. Manu had taken the role of leader of the haka, and was strutting around among the group, booming out the words from the top of his lungs. You could probably hear him all over Pop.

> Ringa pakia
> Uma tiraha
> Turi whatia
> Hope whai ake
> Waewae takahia kia kino

Manu was giving orders to his fellow performers, gearing them up for what they were about to do:

> Slap the hands against the thighs
> Puff out the chest
> Bend the knees
> Let the hip follow
> Stamp the feet as hard as you can

Prowling between the two ranks of his men, yelling these words in Maori, it appeared that Manu had suddenly turned into a furious caged tiger. Then, just as the initial refrain was ending, all of the Maori sank to a half squat and crossed their arms so that one was parallel above the other. Their hands were quivering, symbolising the 'life force' running through them, like an electric current.

Then they started shouting together: deep bass roars, their faces and bodies full of power.

It was so intimidating that Patton instinctively reached for his holstered Colt, before checking himself. His hand hovered there, as if he was in a stand-off at the OK Corral.

Ka mate! Ka Mate!
Ka ora! Ka ora!
Ka mate! Ka mate!
Ka ora! Ka ora!
Tenei te tangata puhuruhuru
Nana nei i tiki mai whakawhiti te ra!
A upane! Ka upane!
A upane! Ka upane!
Whiti te ra! Hi!

As they shouted and slapped their thighs and stamped their feet in time, even the ground shook.

You couldn't help but react when faced with this war dance – some just froze in shock at the sheer aggression of the outburst, the blood draining from their faces, wanting to run away. Some could see it for the spectacle it was, watching on like anthropologists, eyebrows raised and mouth open – a little bit of fear but mainly a feeling of exhilaration combined with deep respect. I was one of those people. I loved watching it. Then there were the sorts who rose to the challenge – in their own way just as aggressive as the Maori warriors. They would nod and smile and say to themselves, 'Bring it on, bring it on…', clenching their fists and straining to take a step forward, ready to fight to the death if necessary. It was obvious that the American fell into this latter category.

When it was all over, Patton finally relaxed his shooting arm.

He walked up to the Maori, put his fists on his hips and said, "Well, gentlemen, I gotta tell ya… that's the most visceral damn thing I've seen in my whole Goddamn life."

We all sat down together at a long table and Pettifer served out the soup.

The table was noisy – the haka had really livened things up. Poyntz and Patton were talking about America, Wyatt Earp and tanks, the Maori men around them laughed and told the Americans what the words of the haka meant.

It was a little quieter at my end of the table where Rennie and the boys were; they had picked up on his tension.

To try and lighten the mood I showed them Dobbs' photograph of myself, Rennie and Materoa from 1901.

"Mum's no different. Look at you, Pa" Manu said laughing. "You had hair."

"Tenei te tangata puhuruhuru…" Kahu said.

The boys laughed.

"For this is the hairy man…" I said, looking at Rennie as I translated the line. "It looks like you're in the haka now."

He didn't respond in the way I had expected, he just kept staring at the photograph, probably at Materoa.

Manu stopped laughing and looked more closely too.

"John," he said, his expression thoughtful, "I saw someone who looks a lot like you do in this picture… young, I mean."

I turned to face him, my relaxed good humour draining away.

"Where was this?"

"Near the village of Woesten, to the north."

"When, Manu?"

"July… we were stationed there with our 3rd Brigade and the French. One day I was passing a group of soldiers… 3rd Rifle Battalion I think. They were all staring at me because I was carrying an aerial torpedo towards a trench mortar forward position. It was on my shoulders and I think they were worried I might drop it. Anyhow, for a split second I thought you were sitting there in the group of soldiers, John – I almost called out your name, that's how sure I was. The man wasn't you, though he looked a hell of a lot like you, especially the way you look in this photograph. A young version of you."

"Did you say anything to him?"

"I did – I told him he looked a lot like someone I knew."

"And what did he say to that?"

"Nothing. He was smoking. He just shrugged his shoulders and made a face like this."

Manu imitated what the man had done and it was then I knew for sure that he had seen Harry Ingram. The gesture was just like the one I had seen Mad Dog make at the RAP in Messines and just like Freddie too, a sort of 'so what?' body signal. Freddie had driven schoolmasters half mad with that gesture.

At least I knew now that Ingram hadn't died at Messines.

As I absorbed this news, a thought occurred to me: Friendship's Corner, the noticeboard at Toc H. Some weeks had gone by since I had last checked it.

I left the table and went out into the hall.

Sure enough, my message was gone, and there was a note in its place.

I pulled it out and read:

Lt Hunston. I am LCpl Ingram of the NZ 3rd Rifle Battalion. I hope we can meet to discuss the family matter you mention. We are assembling today in Pop, but go up the line tomorrow to the east of Ypres so it looks as if I will unfortunately miss you. 26/9/17

I looked at the date. Three days ago.

Harry had gone towards Passchendaele and there wasn't anything I could do about it. He was in the deadliest place on earth – probably the most dangerous place in all of history. What had Frickleton said? 'The bugger's got more lives than a bloody cat.' I wondered how many of them he had used up by now.

Back at the table, Rennie was the only one who picked up on how fraught I had now become, largely because he was the only one feeling the same way. I looked at him and didn't have to say anything. I held up the message for him to see and gave one shake of my head, a final small gesture which seemed to prod him into action.

Still holding my eye, he stood up and knocked against his glass gently with his spoon. The chatter in the room died away.

"Friends, sons… it is good to have you all gathered in this place, this haven away from all the horrors out there…"

Rennie stopped to clear his throat and picked up the picture which was still lying on the table in front of him.

"My good friend Lieutenant Hunston here was just showing us this old photograph. It's from May 1901. Believe it or not, that's me there," he said, pointing himself out.

A few of the audience laughed.

"There's Lieutenant Hunston there…" Rennie said, before breaking off again.

He composed himself.

"The pretty one is my wife Materoa… and before you say it, yes I know, I'm a very lucky man."

Some more laughter.

"There's something I have to say now that won't please everyone at the table, but I am afraid that I have to say it. In this photograph, my wife was pregnant with my sons. You can't really see it – she was only two months gone. For the mathematicians of you out there, you might have already worked it out. My sons were born in November 1901."

Shocked, I glanced across at the boys.

Manu and Kahu both wore thunderous expressions, as though they might go into the haka again at any moment.

"Yes, it means that my sons are even now not sixteen years old."

The room was deathly silent.

"I sense you can all realise the implications. Believe me, I do not say this lightly. I am all too aware of the import of my words. But I must speak. I have tried to live with their wish to come out here and do their bit and it's been a miserable time for me. But now I have reached the end of the line and cannot in good conscience allow it to continue. I see their Commanding Officer is here today and I hope he will forgive me for not having said anything earlier."

The CO nodded gravely at Rennie from the other end of the table.

"May God forgive me… My sons are worthy Maori warriors already – you all know this. Their medals are a testament to that. Their fellow Pioneers have seen first-hand that they have no fear. Gentlemen, the fear is in me, not in my sons. These boys are my life. I have watched them grow and become strong… I…"

Rennie's voice was rising in volume as he struggled to contain his emotions.

"I DON'T WANT TO WATCH THEM DIE OUT HERE… THEY ARE TOO YOUNG TO SERVE… CHRIST, THEY ARE TOO YOUNG TO DIE…"

With that shout he slammed his fist down on the table with all his might. Nine months of pent-up frustration – slowly building ever since our Christmas Day talk on Orokawa beach – came out in that strike. The cutlery jumped and the wood of the table split down the middle.

As he did it he let out an odd cry – a kind of half sob, one of fulminant rage combined with utter despair. Almost a howl. I had heard that kind of sound once before in my life, when I had telephoned my father on 1st June 1900 to tell him Freddie had died. The noise he made on the other end of the line was sudden – as if he'd hit his thumb with a hammer – but it wasn't all just angry pain. There was a mournful note to it too, his heart ripped out through his throat, all the stranger sounding for my never having heard him cry before. That had been it – a second's outburst before he had come to his senses – but I had never forgotten. Anyway, it was the same sound Rennie had made just then.

Rennie stood there shaking, the bones in his right hand broken and misshapen, his knuckles bleeding.

"I'm sorry, boys," he said, his voice quiet now, "but I want you to go home. You kept half of your faces clear of Moko in my honour… and so I hope you will obey me, just this once."

Slowly, the boys stood up.

I could hardly breathe.

I had never seen Rennie like this, never. And neither had they.

"We'll go home, Pa," Manu said, in little more than a whisper.

Kahu went over and hugged Rennie like a bear, being careful to avoid his damaged hand.

"Yes, Pa," he said, "we'll go home."

I knew why he had asked about my father now. The way I saw it, there were a set of scales in Rennie's mind and quarter ounce weights had been piling up on one side for months, causing it to lower by tiny increments. My earlier response about my father's pain had been just another weight. Jesus, he'd even made the same bloody wail my father had.

A man of sorrows and acquainted with grief.

It wasn't just my father who fitted the description.

Perhaps it was when I had returned to the dinner holding Ingram's note, knowing Freddie's son was in all likelihood going to die. I was the perfect embodiment of the line from Isaiah. The look on my face had been the last quarter ounce weight causing Rennie's scales to lurch irreversibly downwards.

In that moment I think he glimpsed a possible future version of himself mirrored in my expression and that was when the scales had finally clunked down. I remembered what Materoa had said about the Mokomokai.

Everyone has a breaking point. They say that even God tore the temple curtain in two after Jesus died.

Chapter Sixteen

2ⁿᵈ October, 1917, Near Ypres

"Blimey… Wipers is getting it proper tonight," our driver said.

She was looking through the rain and mud-spattered windshield at the light-show out to the east, and from my seat in the back of the ambulance truck I could see what she meant – lightning seemed to be concentrating on a single point on the horizon, with the thunder of the detonations reaching us several seconds later.

We were on the seven-mile straight section of road from Pop to Ypres, driving without headlights because of the risk of being fired upon by one of the big German guns on the far ridge.

Halfway across, our vehicle slowed to a crawl as we became caught up behind traffic, mostly other ambulance trucks, all heading into town. A soldier on traffic detail flashed a torch at our driver and told us to have our gas masks ready.

Ten minutes later, we were dropped off at the western edge of Ypres, next to a road sign which read: 'POPERINGSEWEG'.

Our unit chose to hole up in the ruins of a large white house set back from the road. In pre-war times it must have been a fine place, with its gravel drive and sweeping front lawns; the residence of a respectable Ypres family.

There was a decent sized cellar, accessible by a spiral staircase from the rubble strewn ground floor and this became our temporary HQ. As we descended we met the cooler air, musty with the smell of storage, which struck me as a welcome change after the stench of war. Free of the whiff of cordite and the manure-tinged muddy odour permeating the whole area, the underground room was an oasis amongst the desolation. The walls on all four sides, from floor to ceiling, were lined with bottles of wine, hundreds of them, maybe even thousands. And incredibly, bearing in mind the almost continual bombardment of the last three years, not a single bottle in the cellar had been broken. A small circular table and rickety chair occupied the centre of the room and on the table stood a lone wine glass next to a corkscrew, still buried in a cork. The bottle was nowhere to be seen. Old sediment, like tiny pieces of dried blood, was visible in the bottom of the glass, the remains of that last drink enjoyed God knows how many months ago. The occupant had probably been sitting down here sampling a bottle from his extensive collection when the order had come to evacuate. I could imagine him taking his last sips before the shells started landing too close for comfort. Perhaps he had taken the rest of wine with him, swigging from the bottle as he headed west with a few belongings, to help numb the ordeal. It's what I would have done.

I picked up the nearest bottle from the wine rack, wiped off the dust and read the label: Château Lafite-Rothschild, 1870. I picked out another from the row above: another Château Lafite-Rothschild 1870.

I showed McKenzie and raised my eyebrows.

He checked the labels and smiled.

We left the rest of our unit down in the cellar and, taking the two bottles and the corkscrew, climbed back up the staircase to what had once been the sitting room. A fallen beam lay across the floor, and there were large shards of glass under the window openings, blown in with the shelling.

In front of the hearth were two armchairs made of brown leather, the material cracked with white lines and the arms marked with small wine spills. Perhaps, in better days, the owner had brought chosen vintages up here to share with his wife or well-to-do friends.

Mice had bitten through the leather and strands of horsehair and straw poked out of holes in the backs and sides of the chairs. Tell-tale droppings were scattered about.

McKenzie and I sat on the chairs, and drank straight from the bottles. Every time I swigged, the taste detonated in my mouth, then in my throat, and then advanced towards my chest, like a creeping barrage of warmth. We sat there in a comfortable silence, staring ahead at the empty hearth and smoking my Navy Cut. In the fire grate were some pieces of charcoal and ash, again signifying the comforts of a bygone time. It was a little like Freddie finding the hydro camp: '...*I had to clear out the old ash from the woodsmen's fires of years ago...*'

Carved neatly into the wooden mantelpiece were the words 'PRO ARIS ET FOCIS'. It meant 'for God and country', though neither McKenzie nor I saw fit to comment further. The Latin reminded me of the jabbering soldier I had met on the pier at Netley. I wondered where he might be now – not far away at the front waiting in a trench for the next big attack perhaps, or in some 'Special Hospital' somewhere. For all I knew he was still sitting there on the pier, talking at the moon. Most likely, he was already dead.

The shelled-out sitting room was illuminated by a ghostly pale moonlight, the occasional flashes of shelling and the more protracted glow from flares – all light sources entering through the blasted windows and a large cavity in one wall.

We were in a gentlemen's club from hell – where the Devil had seen fit to provide our palates with the very best of wines, with the condition that they be imbibed on site, in a black and white world of destruction.

My thoughts returned to Rennie and the events at Toc H a few days before.

We had taken him back to Poyntz's Casualty Clearing Station and X-rayed his hand, the film revealing three fractured metacarpals. Luckily there was no gross bone displacement necessitating surgery and one of Poyntz's nursing assistants had fitted a plaster-of-Paris cast. We did it all hush hush, making no record of his treatment, because there was the remote possibility the injury might be construed as a self-inflicted wound by some bureaucratic idiot. Even though Rennie was a padre, and the circumstances not in any way suggestive of SIW mentality, we weren't taking any chances. I had seen how pernickety the army could be. Back in Bloemfontein, I had once asked for some extra supplies from a quartermaster and he had made me fill out a form in triplicate, not fussed about the need for urgency and the fact that men from his own side were dying in unnecessary squalor. It was the same mentality here. Soldiers were essentially pieces of meat, there to be used up and thrown away. General Routine Order 585 had come into effect at the beginning of 1915, decreeing the presumption of innocence did not apply in cases of desertion. Guilty until proved innocent – frightening but true. The army was like some Contrarian Corporation where everything normal got switched around. So, a man breaking his own hand and leaving his place of duty, even if it was for an X-ray, could theoretically end up getting shot at dawn by a firing squad. It could be mis-construed so easily, some weary pen-pusher unfamiliar with the circumstances filling out a form and writing in the space: 'cowardice' or 'deserting his post'. Stranger things had happened.

Kahu and Manu had been honourably discharged by their CO straight after Rennie's dramatic announcement. Their calm acceptance surprised me – they did not fight or argue against it in any way. I think they were still in shock at what their father had done, just as I was.

They were probably at Boulogne by now, waiting for an outbound hospital ship to take them back. All being well, they would be home by Christmas, fishing and arguing in the boat off Orokawa as we had all been doing the year before.

Thinking this made me smile.

Poperingseweg: the boys had been in a house on this road. I remembered what Rennie had told me, how he had walked here to summon them to Toc H. Maybe it had even been this house, maybe the boys had been sitting in these same chairs when their father showed up, red faced from his seven mile march.

If the Pioneers were here, they had respectfully left the wine alone.

I started feeling guilty for raiding the cellar. The owner had probably put down the wines for his children. But then I took another swig and the creeping barrage of warmth started up again and I didn't feel the guilt anymore.

I wondered if Rennie had known beforehand what he would do at the meal; whether he had planned it all out, or if he just acted on the spur of the moment. I knew he had been agonising about the boys for months

– ever since they had joined up – but right up to the Toc H dinner, I don't think he had worked out a way of persuading them to go back home.

Until that moment he had been leaving it all in God's hands – hoping that the Almighty was guiding and protecting the boys. Rennie had been able to steer his thoughts away from the risks his sons were taking, going along with it because it was God's will.

In my wine-clarified mind, I started to conduct an enquiry with myself.

Something was nagging at me.

Had he really done what he did because of his own worries about the boys?

It didn't make sense with the Rennie I knew; because he had faith in God's plan. Up until then he had trusted it.

So why had he made such a violent gesture?

The answer hit me.

Her letter had been on his table at Toc H.

He had been staring at her in the photograph at dinner just before his speech.

"I want you to go home now," he had said.

He had done it for Materoa. He had struck out and altered God's plan to save her from a lifetime of heartache, to save her from having to see the Mokomokai – the dried heads - of one or both of her sons. When he had asked about my father, Rennie had been trying to imagine his wife's grief, not his own. More than his own pain, he would not have been able to bear Materoa's pain if the boys had been killed, God's plan or not.

After watching his sons perform the haka, I think he realised they would only respect strength and power. His fist smashing display at the table was his way of making the boys listen – a type of Rennie haka. It had worked – and they had heard him at last.

McKenzie had become tired of staring at the empty fireplace and was now studying a map with his torch.

His bottle was three quarters empty.

He pointed out through the craggy hole in our sitting room wall, open to the elements.

"According to this map, the town's insane asylum is just over there."

Thirty yards away, on the far side of the back garden, was a largely undamaged brick wall some eight feet high.

"Lunatics, Hunston… on the other side of that wall."

I took another swig from my bottle and realised I had already finished it.

A blast went off in the neighbourhood and dust rained down on us from the ceiling plaster.

"Lunatics," I said, my voice soft and lazy.

McKenzie let the map float to the floor and then got up and walked a few paces to the hole in the wall. He stood there looking out towards the asylum.

"I wonder if the lunatics are still there?" he said. "On the other side."

"I very much doubt it, sir… but if they were still there, I imagine that they would be looking at the wall from their side and asking themselves exactly the same question."

The daylight revealed what had become of Ypres.

It was like a wrathful scene from the Old Testament, a Sodom or Gomorrah for modern times. Piles of rubble lined the road where grand brick townhouses had once stood. Not one civilian inhabitant was visible on the streets. There was a complete lack of greenery – not a single blade of grass, not a bush or a tree, just grey or blackened stumps. The Ypres I had known in my boyhood was all gone. Even the moat under the old medieval ramparts where we had taken boating trips was now a fetid stinking swamp. That morning I had to come to terms with the fact that my childhood haunts only existed in my memories.

When you think about it, everything before this very moment is just a nebulous collection of neurons in your brain, firing in fits and starts and giving glimpses of the life you have lived. You might assume the further back in time you go, the sketchier the glimpse, but this is not necessarily so. Some impressions do not lose their lustre, nor suffer the wear of time. Certain memories are as clear as the Château Lafite from the night before. Nostalgia is a strange sensation, because it warps time in confusing ways; making thirty years ago seem like yesterday. Old painful memories can be right up close. One of these days I might try avoiding nostalgia altogether, learn to live only in the present, and avoid all the bloody pain.

Things would never be the way they were before in this town. After the war, the houses might be rebuilt, the moat dredged and cleaned, the trees replanted – but, even then, some of the devastation would remain, like a stain on the fabric of the place. The inhabitants would have to learn to live alongside the ghosts and get on with their daily lives as best they could.

In the northern suburb of the city was the quay of the Yser canal terminus, known as the 'Kaaje'. On warm summer days, Freddie and I had fished for minnows here, perched on the steep canal bank with our home-made rods and worm bait; not catching anything of course, but happy. Together with the Belgian boy and girl, we would devour fresh bread from the bakery like vultures and watch barges coming in from Dixmude to the north. Families on bicycle rides would pass us along the towpath, talking amongst themselves in rapid, incomprehensible Flemish.

Now it was cold.

The Kaaje had once been flanked by large warehouses but in the three year siege every building had been destroyed. The soldiers now called it 'Dead End'.

The road to the Kaaje was one of the most dangerous in the city. It was rumoured among the troops that the shelling had never stopped on a particular bend and so that had become known as 'Devil's corner'.

Even if I had been able to remember where our host family had once lived, it would have made no difference, because the streets around the Kaaje were just indistinguishable mounds of bricks, strewn with pieces of wood and twisted metal.

Our 1st and 4th Brigades were moving up to the front from Dead End along the road that ran east to Wieltje, a village a mile and three quarters distant. For now, the 3rd Brigade – Mad Dog's brigade – was remaining in reserve; hundreds of soldiers housed in dugouts excavated into the canal embankments with the rest our 3rd Ambulance. Compared to their hovels, our white house on the edge of town was like a royal palace.

Even though it wasn't exactly a tourist spot anymore, I was compelled out of my reminiscences to visit the thirteenth century square in the town centre, to see for myself what had become of it.

It looked like a neat archaeological dig, an excavation of an ancient city; the rubble swept into piles, timber struts propping up remaining walls and the roads cleared of debris. All that remained of the Cloth Hall tower and Cathedral were forlorn stone shards jutting upwards from the ground, like worn dentition poking out from the gums of an old man.

Birds had taken over the ruins of the tower, hundreds of them – mainly starlings and doves – and whenever a shell burst on the far side of town, they would rise up in a great cloud before settling once again.

I climbed on top of a heap of bricks, took out my cigarettes and watched a Lewis gun section passing through the square on their way to the front. I could tell they were Australians because their slouch hats were turned up on one side, just like they had worn them in the Boer War.

The trotting horses, the truck engines and the marching soldiers, they all sounded too quiet; and I realised it was because there were no walls to make any echoes. We were basically out in the open.

Near me on the rubble pile, a man was taking photographs of the same view, and as I smoked, I watched him at work – checking the light, adjusting his tripod, pushing the glass plates into the back of the camera.

He stooped down to peer through the viewfinder.

"Bloody fantastic," I heard him say. "That's bloody got it…"

He clicked the shutter and cursed away to himself happily in a strong Australian accent.

Then the camera appeared to jam and he moved over a few paces to where I was and handed his plates to me.

"Hold these a minute, would ya, mate."

I took them without saying anything.

"Come on, ya bastard," he said to the machine, struggling with a lever on the side.

Something seemed to move into position and the problem was fixed, or I assumed so, because he came back over and sat down next to me with a broad smile on his face.

"Got any more of those, mate?"

I pulled out my packet of Navy Cut and passed it over, along with my matches.

"Thanks," he said, lighting up.

He exhaled and pointed the cigarette at the scene.

"What a bloody place... wildly beautiful."

"I suppose that's one way of describing it."

He transferred the cigarette to his left hand and then held out his right.

"I'm Captain Hurley, Australian Imperial Force."

"Lieutenant Hunston, NZ Medical Corps," I said, shaking his hand.

"N Zedder? You sound like more like a bloody pom..."

I laughed at his coarse bluntness.

"Well, I was once."

"Fair point. So was I. My old man was from Lancashire."

We continued smoking together and watching the column of soldiers in the road.

"So, you're an official photographer I take it – for the Australians?"

Hurley nodded.

"They're warriors with guns; I'm a warrior with a camera, embedded with the troops. Already been to Hill 60 and Hell Fire Corner..."

"It sounds like a tough assignment."

"Yeah, but not as tough as my last one," Hurley said. "I was on Shackleton's Imperial Trans-Antarctic Expedition..."

I had read about that in the papers.

"Your ship got trapped in the pack ice, didn't it?"

"Yeah... poor *Endurance*... We had to abandon her and row to a godforsaken place called Elephant Island. Then Shackleton and some others sailed a life-boat to South Georgia to get help." Hurley was chuckling at his own story. "Eight hundred miles of the Southern Ocean those buggers sailed through… and then they crossed an unexplored mountain range. Unbelievable."

"How long were you on Elephant Island before help arrived?"

Hurley had taken the glass plates back from me and was putting them in a canvas rucksack.

"Four and a half months," he said. "Huddled under our upturned boats, freezing our arses off and eating penguin and seal. Men went half crazy. I made a motion picture of the whole thing… called it: 'In the Grip of the Polar Pack-ice'. They might even show it once this bloody war's over."

"You filmed it all?"

"Yeah, the whole adventure, even the part in South Georgia."

"How did you film South Georgia if you hadn't been there?"

"Oh… I went back again there again afterwards – last winter. Got what I needed then."

I coughed on my cigarette.

"You went back there?"

"Yeah… to complete the film. What a place. Dozens of mile high peaks surrounded by ice fields and glaciers. I can hardly believe Shackleton and two of the men got across it, especially in the state they were in."

We smoked for a while in silence.

When he spoke again, Hurley's voice was quiet, as if letting me into his confidence.

"Later, after he'd picked us up, Shackleton told me something strange about that mountain trek in South Georgia… Said he'd felt the presence of a fourth man, even though there were only three of them there. The two men with him both said the same thing. These are the toughest buggers there are, and they all felt it. Some kind of bloody ghost or guardian angel or something…"

Hurley was looking straight at me, his frizzy hair moving in the breeze, the smoke from his cigarette dispersing into the air as he exhaled.

It only seemed right to tell him after he had shared his tale.

"I had a similar experience once," I said.

"Yeah? What happened?"

"Well, I was alone in the Nullarbor desert on a bicycle…"

"You were on a bicycle, alone in the Nullarbor? Jesus, and they call me mad…"

"It's a long story… I was dehydrated and exhausted. Alone… then suddenly someone else was there with me. It's hard to explain, but they were speaking to me, encouraging me to keep going. After a while the feeling went… but by then they had saved my life, because I found a water station. It was something profound, but because it didn't make any sense I decided to put it down to a hallucination in the end."

Hurley looked to be gripped by my tale.

"It felt real at the time though?"

"As real as sitting here talking to you."

"Strewth. Were you spooked?"

"That's the funny thing," I said. "At the time it felt like the most natural thing in the world."

The Australian infantry column was gone now. Hoof prints, foot prints and tyre tracks marked the muddy road.

"I'm not afraid," Hurley said out of the blue.

"Not afraid of what?"

"Dying. And I've seen a lot of it in the last month. The soldiers here think I'm a mad bugger – taking my pictures with the shells dropping and the German snipers taking pot shots. They call me 'the mad photographer' to my face. The crew of the *Endurance* thought I was mad too – at the risks I would take in getting a good shot, climbing up the mast, diving down into the icy waters to get my glass plates from the sinking ship. It's not madness though, Doc. People spend their lives in fear of dying. I'm aware of death, but I'm not scared by it. It's a bloody certainty that we're going to die, right? We might as well commit while we're here…"

Hurley was almost whispering now, a kind of low growl.

"What's the point if you don't fucking commit?"

Early on 4th October, our 1st and 4th Brigades attacked the first of two spurs leading to the Passchendaele Ridge, at a place called Gravenstafel. It was raining and windy – miserable weather to be fighting in. Come to think of it, any type of weather was miserable to be fighting in. It could have been a beautiful sunny day, and it would have been just as bad.

From our house in Poperingseweg, we heard the artillery bombardment start at 6am. The barrage was heavy, as loud and intense as the guns at Messines, but without the initial knockdown punch of massive exploding mines.

Though the objectives were achieved by lunchtime, they came at a cost: hundreds of NZ dead, including the former All-Black's Captain Dave Gallaher, a loss affecting the morale of the whole division. Even a Padre was killed – the Rev Bryan Brown – caught in shelling as he buried German dead outside an RAP.

The bearers we saw resting at Dead End later that day looked as though the life had been sucked out of them. It was the mud that had done it – six of them were needed to carry a single stretcher case, so for each wounded soldier relayed from the battlefield, a total of eighteen bearers had to be used. The Maori pioneers came to the rescue, switching roles and becoming bearers too. With them, it only took four per stretcher, and sometimes they even carried the injured men in their arms like children.

On the 5th October, the weather cleared enough for the backlog of injured to be cleared from all the forward RAPs and the ADS at Wieltje, and that night the NZ brigades were relieved by the British 49th division.

By the 6th, the rain and the high winds were back.

McKenzie and I sat shivering in our armchairs, covered in blankets and drinking more of the Château Lafite-Rothschild. We knew we were next up. The waiting was the worst thing: I just wanted to get it over with. It had been the same in my rowing days before big races. Once you were in the boat, things were much better – at least it was happening. But the waiting was complete torture, since it allowed you time to contemplate the outcome, and that was when the mind could play tricks.

I couldn't say why, but although it was safer in the cellar, we preferred to take our chances upstairs in the sitting room. It felt as if we had been there forever.

As the days passed we lost all semblance of hierarchy. I stopped calling him 'sir' and McKenzie finally shed the last parts of his officious exterior, becoming as much a friend as Rennie and Poyntz.

A double row of empty bottles had formed on the floor next to our chairs.

On the night of the 9th of October, we got stinking drunk, more than any other night so far. The phrase from the *Wipers Times* advert selling 'the Salient Estate' – the one saying that it could be a 'home for inebriates' – had become true in this place.

The rain was coming in through the hole in wall, being blown in by the prevailing wind.

"Jesus, you've got to feel sorry for those poor fuckers of the 49th, haven't you?" McKenzie said, shaking the contents of his second bottle as he waved his hand in gesticulation. He swore even more than usual with alcohol in his veins.

"I do… I do."

When I was drunk I just agreed with everything he said.

"Yorks and Lancs Regiment I think," McKenzie said.

He staggered over to the hole in the wall and let the rain soak his face.

"God, they're out there in this shit," he said, raising his voice to be heard. "Poor fuckers."

He came back to his chair and fell into it.

"And you know what, Hunston? We're bloody well next. As soon as those boys are all used up, we're going."

"I know. We're going…"

"Christ almighty… how much of that bloody stuff have you been drinking? You've turned into a bloody parrot again."

"A bloody parrot… Yes…"

We started laughing and couldn't stop.

Ha, ha, ha.

The bearers down in the cellar must have thought we had lost it, but they were busy making their way through the wine supplies too and probably didn't care.

"You've got to feel sorry for those boys in the 49th," McKenzie said again, before bursting out into hysterics.

Ha, ha, ha.

We were crying with laughter.

It wasn't funny, but we were happy. It was all right to be happy. We weren't hurting anyone. Christ, we were happy just to be alive.

I tried to talk about something serious.

"What do you know about that new gas, H?"

The Germans had been using it in the last few months, but I had yet to see a case close to, as I had been parked up in the rear. They had used it so much around these parts that some of our soldiers were calling it 'Yperite'.

"From HS," McKenzie said, slurring. "Short for 'Hun Stuff'. Smells like garlic, some say mustard, attacks the skin – especially the moist areas… the eyes, armpits and groin. Soon you can't see a bloody thing. Burns its way into the victim and leaves agonising blisters. Seen the skin on a man's genitals slough right off… Lungs get fucked too, obviously."

"Obviously… obviously," I said.

"Penetrates all clothing," McKenzie said, blundering on with his drunken analysis. "I forgot to mention that part. Some bastard's invented it, you know? Been to University for years to learn Chemistry, then they've sat with their test tubes in their laboratory and come up with this bloody potion – dichlorated ethyl sulphide. That's how messed up the world is, Hunston, when even the clever bastards do things like that. They'll probably give him the Nobel Prize."

"The Nobel prize," I said.

Ha, ha, ha.

Tonight, it felt as if the Germans had released laughing gas, and not H, over Ypres.

McKenzie was the first to be able to talk.

"You know what I said to an Australian soldier I met?"

"No… what did you say?"

McKenzie was already starting to laugh.

"I asked him if he'd come here to die?"

"What did he say?"

"He said: 'Nah mate, I came here yester-die…'"

Ha, ha, ha.

McKenzie's joke made me think of the estaminet near Toc H, which had a sign out front, saying: *'English Spoken, Australian Understood'*.

"You know I bumped into some," I said. "Australians I mean – out near Messines on Z day."

"How did you know they were Australian?"

"By their accents."

"Know how you can tell for sure?"

"No."

"You just look for the lobotomy scar…"

Ha, ha, ha.

"Tell you what though," I said, my laughter abating, "I wouldn't have told that joke to the boys I met. They were bloody deadly."

McKenzie waved my comment away.

"Oh, they would have been all right about it. Christ, if anyone can take a joke, it's the Aussies."

We spent the next morning nursing our hangovers, drinking hot tea and eating tins of corned beef, the joking of the night before a distant memory. In the afternoon, we readied all our gear and when that was done we sat in the chairs, dozing and thinking, largely silent.

I wondered if the family who had lived here would ever return; whether the house would be flattened and rebuilt from scratch, or if they would try and salvage something from the ruins.

I imagined coming back here as an old man, driving into town and parking out the front of the house. I would knock on the door and tell the family I had stayed there in the war. I would have several crates of wine with me to reimburse them for what McKenzie and I had taken from the cellar. They would ask me in for a drink and listen to my stories and I would sit in an armchair in front of the fire. I would try not to talk too much about the war. Instead, I would crack some jokes and make them cry with laughter, just as McKenzie and I had done on our last night in Ypres.

Chapter Seventeen

Evening, 10ᵗʰ October 1917

McKenzie laid out the map on the cellar table and leant over it so that the rest of us had to peer over his shoulder to see, like medical students watching a great surgeon at work.

Except for flickering candle light, it was dark in the cellar, and I had to strain my eyes to make out the shadowed features on the map. Next to me one of the stretcher bearers ran his cigarette along the seams of his shirt to get rid of lice. I took a small step away from him.

"Now listen up," McKenzie was saying, "I'm going to make this very simple, so that even an idiot can understand…"

Although he was still bent over the table I felt as if he was addressing me directly, remembering my map reading at Messines.

"The village of Passchendaele sits on a ridge five miles from here; and coming off this ridge are two west facing spurs… like a back-to-front 'C' – Gravenstafel Spur to the south – captured by our 1ˢᵗ and 4ᵗʰ Brigades last week…" He pointed to the relevant part of the map. "Just here…" We all nodded at him with serious looks on our faces, keen to show we were paying attention. "And the Bellevue Spur to the north… right here. And that's where the Germans are presently dug in. The lower land between the two is the Ravebeke River Valley. This blue line here, that's the river itself, more of a stream, really. But as you know, it's been raining a hell of a lot… which means that there are three types of ground in this area: lightly flooded, flooded and heavily flooded …"

"Sounds miserable," someone in the group said.

"Hundreds of stretcher cases in two days," McKenzie said, confirming the misery, "each journey taking around four hours. You'll be carrying for longer than that…"

There were a few low whistles in the room.

McKenzie jabbed his finger onto another square on the map.

"We have two RAPs in that valley facing the Bellevue Spur – both in captured pillboxes. Here, at 'Waterloo Farm', just south of the Ravebeke – that's the RAP for our 2nd Brigade. Five hundred yards northwest is 'Kronprinz Farm'… here, just north of the river. This is the RAP for our 3rd Brigade – all four Rifle Battalions – and we're headed there tonight, to relieve the British. The ADS is here, at Wieltje – we'll pass it on our way up to the front. In two days' time, our 1st 2nd and 3rd Rifle battalions are to attack. The 4th battalion is already moving up to hold the existing front line… tonight. After the other battalions attack, they'll follow through and form defensive flanks."

McKenzie was looking at me now.

"Same rules as before… don't let me down, and don't die… Questions?"

The last part was said in a way that did not invite a reply.

Twenty minutes later, we moved out for Kronprinz.

The road to Wieltje was so rutted that I thought our vehicle would rattle itself to pieces, but the poor contraption was saved that fate after only a mile when we were forced to stop because a shell had blasted the road away.

Maori Pioneers were hard at work, throwing chunks of debris into the crater for infill, but even so, it would be at least an hour until the road was useable.

There was nothing else for it but to climb out of our vehicle and continue on foot.

Within minutes my boots had soaked through and the cold was moving up my legs, the exact opposite effect of the Château Lafite-Rothschild – a creeping barrage of cold.

I focused my attention onto the men in front of me. A spectral light from the continuing glimmer of gun flashes and flares was cast on our unit. We were trudging along the muddy road in a sad silence, heads down, each caught up in his own thoughts. The road was lined by the broken silhouettes of blasted trees. If you stared at them long enough, they turned into men… a row of silent watchers on the road to doom.

At the Wieltje ADS, a group of vehicles heading towards Ypres had built up, delayed by the damaged road behind us. From the open windows of the cabs, came grey trails of cigarette smoke, as the drivers sat and waited for the route to re-open.

The ADS was in an underground gallery one hundred yards long. It had two curtained openings which led out onto the road; from one, stretcher cases were exiting the dressing room and being placed into the queue of ambulances. The other opening was at the base of a steep incline. Injured soldiers were first being stripped of their clothing by men in gowns, masks and rubber gloves before being lowered down by ropes.

I turned to McKenzie.

"What's going on?"

"New protocol," he said. "It's the H gas fluid… it sticks to the clothes. A few weeks ago, all the doctors and orderlies inside the ADS were contaminated. So now all clothing gets removed."

Beyond Wieltje at 'Spree Farm', we came across a refreshment booth, with a YMCA volunteer serving out hot tea from a large vat. I think that in the whole of my time in Flanders, there was no sight so uplifting as this, despite the desperate surroundings.

Though he couldn't have been more than twenty years old, the volunteer was saying the same thing to everyone:

"Here you go, son, get that down you… be lucky."

'Be lucky'. You had to admire the Tommy spirit – or was it a sense of humour?

We stood around the booth, drinking the brew and watching another Maori working party clearing the ground of debris and erecting tents for what was to be a 'walking wounded' collecting post. Hard looking soldiers on their way to the front were stopping to pick up tea. Tall men, with latent power and menace – so much so that I felt glad they were on our side. I checked their insignia – they weren't from Harry Ingram's battalion.

A heavy gun being brought forward by the artillery was stuck in the mud, the eight horses dragging it sunk to their bellies. We all stared in awe as the Maoris – perhaps twenty strong – performed the haka and pulled the gun carriage out of the quagmire using ropes tied to the axles.

From Spree Farm, a duckboard track led us over the newly conquered ground, though the term 'ground' was a loose one, just as we had been warned. When a flare went off, it illuminated a bleakness that was shocking in its scale: a huge bog dotted with shell-holes half full of water, stretching for miles in every direction. Not the green fields, buildings and woods McKenzie's pretty map had suggested.

Other than the ones at Wisques, I had only ever walked the duckboards in the sand-dunes of Waihi Beach before and the noise our footsteps made on these sounded just the same. Here too the path twisted and turned haphazardly just as if it were skirting clumps of sea grass. If I concentrated on the familiar sound and shut out the insidious cold, I hoped that I might be able to transport myself back home to the dunes and away from this miasma.

A slip jolted me out of my daydream – these were great shell-holes we were avoiding, not tussocks of waving grass, and they were filled with stagnating, foul-smelling water. Even more depressing were the gaps in the duckboard, created from recent shell blasts; each time we came to one, we had to drop down into the ooze, sink waist-deep, and then clamber out up the slimy banks to the next intact section.

After an hour of this I was spent. At one point I found myself limp and exhausted at the foot of a disgusting slope of mud, implanted with shreds of fabric and body parts, like a ghoulish piece of fossilised strata, detailing the history of the man-made carnage. It took four of my team to haul me out.

At 'Dump Farm' there was a bearer-relay post, but this time there were no jokes when we passed through: no cigarette swapping and no banter, not like there had been at Messines when I had been searching for 'Spring Street'. Messines had been a summer holiday compared with this. The bearers stood at the doorway of their pillbox and watched us in a funereal silence – to them we were just another set of shivering, dejected mud figures, probably making a one-way trip.

Nearby, a Mark IV tank was stranded in the glutinous mire, pockmarked by bullets, although none appeared to have pierced the armour. The machine was dead, listing to one side like a ship run aground on rocks. Even the Maori Pioneers wouldn't be able to extricate that.

There must have been a hell of a battle for Gravenstafel Spur the week before.

'Calgary Grange' – another relay post – was a few hundred yards further on, its name dating from 1915 when the Canadians had held the same ground.

Then the duckboards ran out and we struggled on, each footstep heavier as the mud stuck to our boots and the fatigue grew ever worse. We must have been on a half-submerged corduroy track, as we didn't sink all the way down. I got so cold and tired that I started to cry silently, fuming with anger and frustration at my predicament and the sheer bloody futility of it all, but also out of utter exhaustion. I was completely spent and the battle hadn't even begun.

Stray Tommies from the 49th Division were coming the other way – the walking wounded with muddy bandages wound around their limbs and heads. They staggered like marathon runners at the finish line, unsure on their legs and practically directionless. Some wore wraps over their eyes and had to be guided by the man in front, joined by a string tied around their waists.

Knowing what I had just been through, I feared for them on their journey back behind the lines and doubted many would make it, instead finding a watery grave at the bottom of a shell hole.

Someone behind had slipped off the path and this created a hold-up while half a dozen of our bearers struggled to fish him out. A small group coming the other way had to stop and we all huddled there waiting together. I started up a conversation with one of them. I couldn't tell his rank because he was completely caked in mud.

"What's your regiment?"

"East Lancashires," he said, looking down at the ground. The soldier was shivering violently, his voice hoarse and his nose streaming mucous from a heavy cold. "You?"

"New Zealand Medical Corps."

He coughed in reply.

"You sick?" I said.

He hunched his soldiers.

"Plenty of dead men back there who would bloody love to have my cold."

"How bad is it?"

It was a stupid question, but to his credit the soldier didn't take it that way. He was still looking down.

"The hun have MGs... took out most of my company..." He waved his hand in the air at the dozen men in his group. "We're all that's left. Been stuck in a water-filled crater for the last twenty four hours with a Lewis gun. Rain never bloody stopped."

I looked out at the wasteland and tried to think of some way of connecting with this man.

"The East Lancashires, you say? I had a brother who fought alongside the Royal Lancaster Regiment at Spion Kop. He was in the 2nd Middlesex Regiment..."

The Tommie, who up until that moment hadn't really been paying attention, turned to face me.

"He was at the Kop? Christ..."

Seeing his reaction made me proud to have shared Freddie's act of bravery with a fellow soldier from this current conflict. It felt good that he wasn't forgotten. That was one of my biggest fears, that no-one would even know he had existed.

"Won a medal for leading a fixed bayonet charge... his regiment lost forty-two men that day, and he lost his leg..."

I didn't go any further. I didn't want him to hear the really bad ending.

He shook his head. "Fixed bayonet charge – that's what we did, day before last. Fat lot of good a bayonet is against a null-acht-funfzehn..."

"A what?"

"Oh, sorry… an MG 08/15… cha… cha… cha… cha… cha… cha… That's all I heard for the last twenty four hours. My ears are still bloody ringing with it…"

He gave a short laugh.

"What's so funny?" I said.

"Our bloody relief… two hours ago. We're sitting there and I hear voices behind me. These three tall figures come out of the darkness. I said: 'Who the hell are you?' and one of them replies: 'We're the Aussies, chum. We've come to relieve you,' and they jump down into the shell-hole… Naturally, I'm delighted. But it's a lousy handover – I tell him there are no trenches, no ammunition, no rations, though I do have a map if he wants any references on our position… You know what he said to me?"

The soldier was chuckling now.

"What?" I said, amused at his laughter.

"He says: 'Never mind about that chum, just fuck off.'"

We both started laughing.

McKenzie and some of the other medics had heard too and were smiling at the story.

Our bearers had managed to drag our man out and the duckboards had cleared again. The soldier's company started to leave.

"They didn't seem the least bothered," he said, as he moved away. "The last I saw of them they were squatting down, rifles over their shoulders, and all three of them were smoking. They just didn't care!"

It rang true, from my experiences with Australians. My old friend Tom Dudley had been exactly like that. In fact, as the soldier had told the story I had even imagined the Australian's voice being Dudley's. After what had happened in the Boer War, Dudley had said he wasn't afraid of anything, but from what I knew of him, it was evident he had always been like that. There really did seem to be a character trait of fearlessness amongst Australians and New Zealanders… almost a gene for it.

It had been raining for the entire journey, but as we crossed the Ravebeke – the small stream between the Gravenstafel and Bellevue spurs – the intensity increased a notch further. The wind picked up too, becoming so strong you had to lean into it. If I looked up, the tears and rain on my cheeks were blown back into my ears; so I bowed my head instead and listened to the rain being pelted against my steel helmet. Christ – after the drudgery of tonight I would never have to worry about any journey I undertook again. Nothing could be as bad as this.

The stream itself had been shelled into a marshy morass, in no way resembling a watercourse, but fortunately the engineers had been considerate enough to lay down some cocoa-nut matting to help with the footing and we made it through. It was like the 'Slough of despond' from *The Pilgrim's Progress*. I had read the book as a child and could remember it being the deep bog Christian falls into after leaving the City of Destruction. Bunyan must have been a prophet of some kind, because he had foreseen the Ypres sector very accurately when he had written that.

'Kronprinz Farm' was a two room pillbox.

Captured the week before by our 4th Brigade, the structure had largely withstood the artillery bombardment, despite the concrete in some sections having been torn off like an outer skin, exposing the reinforced skeleton of railway irons and steel bands beneath. Through the darkness, I could make out dozens of dead soldiers, horses and mules, just lying around in the mud outside the pillbox, a sight so bizarre that, for a second, I thought they were all playing a joke on me, as if it were a children's game of statues.

The outgoing British RAMC captain made tea while we recovered from our four hour ordeal. I sat on an oilskin and leant back against the wall, wondering if I would ever be able to get up again. My legs were numb and I could not stop my teeth from chattering. Without meaning to, I kept biting my tongue and could taste the blood in my mouth. The cold was right in my core. My hands had turned a bluish mottled colour and it was hard to make fists with them.

A few stretcher cases were lying on the ground – two British soldiers from the look of their uniforms, and there was a German too.

Another bandaged soldier was crouching against the far wall and watching me with what looked like curiosity. He had a sheepskin jerkin over his uniform, held shut at the front by three fastenings, like rucksack straps. The wool of the jerkin was so brown with battlefield mud that that it looked more like the pelt of a Grizzly bear.

"There are still British out there in no man's land," he said. "And we can't get to them. In the day, the snipers shoot you for fun and by night we can't see a damn thing. This place is too exposed. The 'Jaegers' are holding the ridge."

I frowned. "Jaegers?"

"Crack machine gun regiments."

The wounded German soldier on the stretcher spoke to me.

"You know zis word... Jaeger?"

I shook my head.

"In English it means hunter... die Jaegers sind bereit... What I mean to say to you is... they are ready. Messines war ganz unerwartet... you understand? For us, Messines was big surprise. Here... no... not a surprise. For your commanders to attack now... sie sind verruckt... ja?"

"I think he's saying our commanders are mad," I said to the English soldier.

"Well," he said, "This Fritz may have a point. Two days ago when we attacked, the machine guns on the ridge stopped us all within two hundred yards. The Jaegers are just sitting there in their pillboxes waiting for the next wave. Their barbed wire is still uncut... Maybe Plumer and Gough know something we don't – or perhaps your lot are bulletproof?" I thought of Rennie's metaphor about the generals trying to get a screw out by pulling ever harder instead of just unscrewing it. Fritz was damn right.

The RAMC captain knelt down and poured the brew of tea into our mugs.

"Sorry, gents," he said, "the cooker flame keeps blowing out and I'm afraid it's lukewarm."

It was hot enough. I drank it in large gulps and waited to feel its effects – unfortunately it didn't make much of a dent on my ice cold core, but through my shivering, I had just enough energy to smile. Only an Englishman would apologise about the standard of his tea-making in circumstances like these.

The captain wanted to take the two most serious stretcher cases back with him when he left, so McKenzie allowed him ten of our bearers to help carry them as far as the first relay post at Calgary Grange. It was a mark of their character that our bearers unhesitatingly accepted their order. I couldn't have walked another ten yards, that's how heavy my legs were, and the relief I felt in not being one of their party was immense.

The English soldier with the sheepskin volunteered to help out too, saying his injury wasn't causing him too much bother. When you included the RAMC captain, this made up the team of carriers to six per stretcher.

Before leaving, the soldier came over to where I sitting and gave me his sheepskin jerkin.

"I'll only sink in the mud with this on," he said, "and you look like you could do with it."

He emptied out his haversack and put a bottle of HP sauce on the ground next to me and a tin of Fray Bentos corned beef.

"It's not much, but the HP makes it taste half decent."

Along with the tea, this was a real feast.

"What have I done to deserve this?"

"You're English, aren't you? Originally, I mean…"

"Yes, that's right. I was brought up there, went to Oxford… Went to South Africa with the RAMC in 1900 as it happens."

"I know."

I frowned. "How do you know that?"

"Your photograph is on the wall at the Blue Boar Club in London, alongside the other veterans. I thought I recognised you when you came in. It's John Hunston, isn't it?"

I nodded and shook his outstretched hand. This was surreal.

"I'm Lieutenant Worsley," he said.

"The only pictures I remember from the Blue Boar were those Spy cartoons from Vanity Fair."

Worsley smiled.

"They're still there… but when I first joined and was made Club Secretary, I made it my mission to put up photographs of all members who had served. I've been staring at your picture for the last five years, wondering why you never showed up. You were a rowing blue weren't you?"

"Once upon a time…" I said. "1896, '97 and '98."

"1911, '12, and '13." Worsley said, beaming. "We were coached by a chap called Gold."

"Harcourt Gold? Why I rowed my three boat races with him. He was a Magdalen man, wasn't he?"

"That's right, sir."

It was odd that Worsley called me 'sir', even though we were the same rank. I think he was saying it as a compliment because I was an old Blue like him.

I laughed.

"Good old Gold… a great stroke man… had a rhythm from the gods."

There had been a Spy cartoon of Gold on the wall of the club, near to the one of William Grenfell. He was wearing his Blues outfit with a pair of brown brogues and a white scarf, hands in pockets with the thumbs showing. *With the thumbs showing* – it was funny, the details that stuck in your head. "Leave it all on the water," Gold used to say before our races. "No regrets. Win or lose, we can walk away with our heads held high."

Despite where I was, in a forward RAP in Passchendaele and chilled to the bone, I actually felt rather pleased to have made it onto the wall at the club, even if it was just an RAMC mug-shot.

In the shadows behind us, I could see McKenzie rolling his eyes and shaking his head.

"He coached our 1912 winning Olympic crew too," Worsley said. "In fact, eight of the nine were Magdalen men… rowing for Leander, of course."

'Magdalen' referred to one of the Colleges in Oxford. Leander was one of the top rowing clubs in the country and a place where the top Oxford oarsmen trained when the University term was over.

"Last I heard, he'd joined the Royal Flying Corps – probably buzzing around up there right now looking for the Red Baron…"

As he gazed out into the darkness his expression changed.

"Already lost one of my Olympic team-mates earlier this year; chap called Kirby. He was Oxford President in 1909."

"I'm sorry."

But Worsley wasn't hearing me anymore.

"And I fear the worst for the 1910 Oxford President too, sir… chap called Mackinnon. An old team mate from my Oxford 1911 eight, and another Magdalen man; Olympic gold medallist from 1908. Damn fine oar… Scots Guards… not been seen since yesterday…"

Worsley was somewhere else, still rowing in Elysium with his dead team-mates.

"Lieutenant… LIEUTENANT…"

He came back and looked at me.

I held up the sheepskin.

"I'm very grateful for this. Maybe I'll pay a visit to the club when I'm next in town and buy you a pint of ale, how about that?"

"Yes… you do that, sir.'

I had been saving the cognac until the war was finished, but right then I would have happily traded a hundred bottles of Segonzac for Worsley's sheepskin, the Fray Bentos and the sauce, let alone the meagre contents of my flask.

I pulled it out of my pocket and handed it to him.

"For now though… in case I don't see you again…"

We understood each other.

"There's some cognac left in there. It's good stuff… Take it. As a fellow old Blue, for luck and for warmth."

"Why thank you, sir," Worsley said, looking genuinely moved as he accepted my offering.

"I'll be sure to look out for you in the Club," I said. "God speed to you."

He left the pillbox quickly, helping to lug out the stretcher cases with the others.

Olympian or not, I did not envy Worsley one little bit. The return journey he had to make carrying that stretcher was going to be the hardest physical challenge of his life. Calgary Grange was only a few hundred yards away, but it would easily be two hours' agonising journey. He would be able to pass on the case to the bearers there, but even then it was still a long way back to town. By my estimate, poor old Worsley wouldn't be back in Ypres for another six hours at best.

His sheepskin soon took the edge off my chill and I managed to doze fitfully on the pillbox floor near a low window facing the lines. I dreamt of the days when I had been an English gentleman, rowing Boat Races for Oxford and lounging around in the Blue Boar Club. It had felt so easy to slip back into that old life during my chat with Worsley, if only for a few moments.

All through the night, German flares lit up the inky darkness and I could see the huddled forms of our soldiers manning a line of shell holes at the front a hundred yards away. They had tried to dig in as best they could, although the idea of 'digging in' was a relative term – you couldn't really dig anything in this mire. How on earth they were managing out there, God only knew. I wondered what had gone through the minds of the mapmakers as they had marked on the red, blue and green lines signifying objectives, nice and neat. They had probably whistled to themselves as they worked, warmed their hands by a pot-bellied stove, sipped tea and jauntily gone about their task, blissfully ignorant of the reality on the ground.

October 11th passed quickly.

Our bearers arrived back and then after an hour's rest, six of them took away the German.

McKenzie and I prepared the RAP with blankets, oilskins, medicines and field dressings. It was basic, but there was enough space to hold around twenty-five men.

All day he teased me: "I rowed with him... that's right, sir... A Mogadon man, he was," he would say, laughing.

"It's Magdalen not Mogadon."

"I say, Mr Blue Boar, hand me those field dressings will you? There's a good chap."

At least McKenzie had the name of the club right.

As we shivered and made good our station, I vowed to myself that if I did make it out of here, I would go to the Blue Boar Club and bloody well have that pint; drink it next to the warm fire, while eating one of the club sandwiches under the pictures on the wall. Once, I had tired of the place and its haughty members, but now it was symbolic of civilisation – the polar opposite of the barbarity we were living through. That night, in snatched bouts of sleep, I dreamt I was inside the rowing clubhouse of my old college in Oxford, at a point in time far off in the future…

The sun was beating down – it was the Saturday of 'Eights Week', the grand finale of four straight days of racing.

On the wall of the clubhouse, photographs of the pre-war teams were gathering dust in the shadows. The images of the men in blazers and caps – one row seated, the other one standing, with the college quadrangle as the backdrop – were all faded with age. Newer team photographs had assumed prominent places on the wall.

Students were standing below the old records of the past, shouting and laughing in their drunkenness and then staggering out onto the balcony to watch their friends row up the river. The crowds outside were packing the towpath and the beer was flowing as freely as it had always done.

I stayed in the clubhouse, unseen and unnoticed.

When everyone had gone home and it was dark, the ghosts of the old crews came and joined me. Those who had died in the war still looked young, but others had aged and had clearly lived out their whole lives.

I was a ghost like them – but didn't know to which group I belonged. I didn't want to know.

Chapter Eighteen

Zero hour came at 05.25 on the morning of the 12th October.

It didn't bode well. The artillery barrage was weak and patchy and many of the shells just slapped into the mud without exploding. Not only that, but in places the barrage fell short of the German lines, landing in the middle of our own troops and cutting many soldiers to pieces.

Our 2nd Rifle battalion attacked first.

It was soon clear that our barrage had done little to destroy any of the German emplacements because our men walked straight into a withering blanket of fire. The machine guns seemed to be almost belching out the bullets – as if they had eaten too many – the continual clatter coming from at least two directions along the ridge.

This was the sound of death: *cha… cha… cha… cha… cha… cha;* just the way the English soldier from the Lancashires had described. It was a noise which made the killing sound like an objective exercise, devoid of human feeling, each 'cha' mechanically counting off a life like a number. After each burst, an echo rang out around the valley.

Worsley had been right – unless you were bullet proof, this was sheer madness. The Jaegers were wreaking havoc. This wasn't even hunting, as their name suggested, this was more like a duck shoot.

The men of the Rifle Battalion were falling by the dozen, but somehow as a body they still kept moving forward up the gentle slope of the Bellevue Spur.

"Christ Almighty," McKenzie said, awestruck, "if that's not bravery then I don't know what is."

Within an hour, our RAP contained more than fifty men and the overflow of stretcher cases was spilling out into the open to the rear of the pillbox; meagre cover at best.

We were repeatedly hit by shells, the impacts filling the pillbox compartments with dust and acrid vapours and driving down heavy pieces from the concrete ceiling onto the huddled wounded below.

Close by one of the low windows, a lieutenant colonel of the 3rd Rifle battalion was trying to direct the movements of his men as they took over the advance from the beleaguered 2nd battalion.

He was sitting on the floor, hemmed in by the wounded. Then a shell landed outside and a bearer who had been crouching in the doorway was hit in the neck by a flying fragment. A fountain of blood gushed from his wound, deluging the battalion commander. I tried to save the bearer, uselessly pressing a dressing against his neck, but he bled out within a minute.

His last word was, "Water."

I managed to pull out the wooden stopper from his bottle and give him some before he died. It was something, I suppose.

From what we could see from our vantage point at Kronprinz, most of the soldiers of the 2nd and 3rd battalions were either dead or taking cover from the machine guns in the shell holes of no man's land. Less than an hour later the 1st Battalion joined them.

Some of the injured managed to crawl back to the RAP and word reached us that a composite platoon of all three battalions had managed to capture a German strong point in a cemetery at Wallemollen on the brow of the spur; at least twenty Germans had been killed and four machine gun posts captured.

The news lifted spirits in the aid post – our boys *had* made an impact.

I overheard one of the injured men who had been at the cemetery say the words, "Mad Dog," in his morphine-fuelled mumblings. I rapidly scanned the RAP for Harry Ingram, hoping he might be one of those who had made it back, but he wasn't there.

My heart was beating hard, my head busy thinking of a tenable pretext for abandoning my post and heading out to the cemetery to search for him, but it was impossible to leave. For a start, any movement outside was met with a hail of bullets from the Jaegers on the low ridge.

By mid-morning, a tenuous line had been reached on the spur which ran from the cemetery to a point slightly beyond a wood called 'Wolf Copse', some five hundred yards further than our original line. On our right, in the Waterloo Farm RAP sector, the 2nd Brigade had only gained two hundred yards, their advance meeting with complete annihilation in the area of the Ravebeke river valley known as 'Marsh Bottom', though it should have been renamed 'The Valley of the Shadow of Death'.

Any further progress was impossible – banks of barbed wire remained intact and dozens of pillboxes studded the ridge behind. The Germans had become so confident they had even moved their machine guns onto the top of the pillboxes. "Kommen auf Neuseelander!" they were saying. 'Come on New Zealand!'

At one in the afternoon I noticed a group of battalion commanders looking grim-faced at the Brigade Major, who had just come off the telephone in our RAP.

"We're to renew the attack at 3pm," he said.

After the major had gone, the commanders huddled in a conference, talking in desperate tones, like surgeons in an operation that was going badly wrong.

"Are they bloody joking? The MG fire isn't just from in front of us, there's enfilading fire too… We're getting slaughtered out there…"

"Orders are orders."

"Bugger the orders."

"Then you get shot anyway."

"Better me than a hundred of my men."

"I know it's a suicide mission, but we've got no choice."

"Fuck this fucking war and all the fuckers running it."

The tension was eased with that comment and the commanders chuckled.

"I'm with you on that."

In the end, realising that obeying the order was the only real option open to them, they left the RAP to prepare their men for certain extinction.

'Enfilading fire' was army speak for gunfire coming from the flanks, so that it hit you obliquely. Soldiers were getting hit from all directions – the poor sods had even had it from behind earlier, from the messed-up artillery barrage. The ground outside the RAP was a complete death zone. And somewhere out there was Harry Ingram.

Just before 3pm a call came through and runners sprinted out of the RAP to pass on the message before it was too late; the order had been rescinded.

I could imagine the harassed commanders reading the pencilled and muddied message forms and nodding, not exactly happy – not on a day like this – but at least satisfied that someone back at Divisional Headquarters had finally seen sense.

Through the blur of treating that day's casualties, one in particular stood out for me, largely because of the unorthodox manner of his arrival.

In the late afternoon, we saw a soldier approaching the RAP, pulling a rolled-up groundsheet with a solid lump within it. He dragged his burden slowly and relentlessly towards us, oblivious to the gunfire. It seemed a miracle, but the man didn't fall. Maybe the Germans were impressed by this act of altruism and had decided not to target him.

When he was twenty yards away the ground rocked from a shell-burst and the man was veiled momentarily with a curtain of mud, but as it fell back, he appeared again, crawling on his hands and knees now and still somehow dragging his package. At last, we were able to help him into the shelter of the RAP.

"Found this bugger… up on the ridge near the cemetery," the exhausted soldier said, gasping for breath.

He nodded at the groundsheet, torn up by barbed wire and bullet holes.

The lump inside was indeed a man.

A bullet had torn through his right eye and part of his forehead and blood from that wound covered his face, like a gored matador. His remaining eye stared out at me and it was only when the eye blinked that I realised he was alive.

I performed a quick external exam.

"Where else did you get it?"

His lips moved, but I could not hear his reply.

His arm was shattered and blood was oozing from his torso. He wouldn't last much longer if that kept going. His one eye asked me to do something.

My thoughts crystallised into a single, simple aim: If I can stop the bleeding, he might survive.

I stripped off his jacket and shirt and saw the source of the blood in his side – with a bandaged lead pencil, I probed back his lung and plugged the wound with a field dressing. Then I fixed a tourniquet and bound his arm to a piece of spare duckboard. While I was at work an orderly dressed the head wound like an Egyptian mummy – completely covering the soldier's face, and leaving just the remaining eye and his mouth free. I gave him morphine and anti-tetanus, scrawled letters on the bandaging, and went to another case. When I came back to him a little later, to my surprise he was still alive. As other soldiers at the RAP died around him, this man hung on. I thought of him as 'MAT', since those were the letters I had written on his head bandages.

It rained heavily that night and was intensely cold.

At midnight McKenzie came over to where I was sitting next to my incredible survivor. I had rolled up the sheepskin jerkin and put it under his head to make a pillow.

McKenzie's map was out.

"I want you to do what you did at Messines," he said. "I want you to make a forward RAP. Here…"

He pointed his blood-stained finger on the page.

"At the cemetery… apparently some of our boys up there are still alive. It's our front line and I want you there."

Harry Ingram was my first thought. I might be able to get to him.

"Yes, sir!" I said with a certainty that surprised us both. "Any bearers you want me to take, sir?"

"No… We need every bearer here to help move this lot out. Your mission is a palliative one, Hunston. They might be dying, but we can still take away some of their pain… I'll come and find you when this is all clear. Hold on until I get to you."

He shook my hand and gave me a haversack with several steel containers of morphine phials and hypodermic syringes.

I glanced at 'MAT' and hesitated.

McKenzie looked at the soldier I had managed to save and then back at me.

"I'll take care of him," he said. "Don't worry."

I left the RAP, pausing briefly to smear mud on my face for camouflage. Then I crept and slithered my way through the morass of the battlefield. The mud threatened to suck my boots off – sometimes it was knee deep, sometimes it was waist deep – but it always held you down, as if this part of Flanders wilfully desired to absorb your body and turn you into a physical constituent of the soil, a bedfellow with the worms, clay, rock particles and other organic remains.

I remembered McKenzie pointing to the cemetery in his map briefing of two nights ago. Straight up the slope of Bellevue Spur from Kronprinz.

I couldn't miss it.

The gunfire was only sporadic now – just a few pops and cracks in the distance – but I knew Jaeger snipers were probably scouring the field, listening out for strange noises, watching for moving shapes, so I kept low and stayed paranoid.

I shredded my uniform on barbed wire and the arms tore in several places. Large pieces of cloth came away so that my Dayfield armour vest showed through from underneath.

As I moved up the shallow slope I chanted the words, "Mad Dog," in a hoarse whisper to keep myself going. This was my chance to honour my promise to Kate Ingram, a chance to make Freddie proud of me. It never occurred to me that Harry might be dead, not after the stories

Frickleton had told me. He was indestructible, protected by a Guardian Angel. Freddie's boy was out there somewhere and I was going to find him.

There were hundreds of our soldiers on the Spur, most of them dead, a few still calling out. With a jolt, I realised it was the premonition I had experienced on the Orokawa track on Christmas day the year before, when I had run in terror from the Grey Lady. She was here now, I sensed, moving among these dying soldiers. Come to take them away.

I went from man to man – if one called out in pain, I gave him a dose of morphine and drew a large 'M' on his forehead with the skin pencil, in case he was picked up later. It was quicker and easier to write on a head instead of the wrist – besides in many cases soldiers had lost their hands and arms. I treated at least twenty men in this way during my journey to the cemetery. They had been out there for fifteen hours already. Fit and highly-trained men didn't die easily or quickly. If I hadn't been so exhausted I would have been burning with resentment that generals could sanction such appalling and meaningless carnage, but as it was, I just dealt with each case and automatically moved on. A few times, the men died holding my hand, their grip easing only when they went to the next place.

After two hours of this, I saw a gravestone.

I had finally arrived.

There were soldiers here, but I saw none alive, a testament to the ferocity of the fighting from earlier in the day. Some had black triangles on their sleeves… the 3rd Rifle battalion. I checked for Mad Dog and stumbled on, tripping and falling over the bodies and then getting up again.

It was too dark to see more than a few yards ahead.

I was just beginning to entertain the thought that the next dead man might be him when, without warning, I found myself up to my neck in water.

In my confusion I started to panic; struggling and thrashing around to get out. All that happened was that I sank deeper still. The watery mud came up over my chin and I had to tilt my head back to breathe. The Dayfield vest weighed me down.

Jesus Christ, I thought. *I've walked straight into a shell hole and I'm going to bloody drown.*

Then my right foot suddenly struck something hard at the bottom of the hole and I was able to stand on top of it and stop myself from sinking any further. The shell had blasted open a grave and my guess was that I was balancing on the edge of a coffin.

My breathing was fast and ragged, more from the fear than the cold.

With great effort, I brought my breathing under control, like an athlete composing himself for a race.

Focus.

I thought it had been silent in the cemetery but now I had stopped crashing about, I could hear sounds – feeble whimpers and moans. Turning my head from side to side I could see the huddled shapes of men nearby, moving ever so slightly, their lives ebbing away.

With a huge effort, I lifted my left hand out of the slime, pulling up a piece of wood which had been floating just beneath the surface. It was a strip of the coffin lid – a decent length – perhaps six foot long, and I was able to wedge it against the sides of the hole, like a roof rafter. I tried to pull myself up with my left arm but it was useless. I had no strength left. So I brought my right arm up and grabbed the wood with both hands, but it cracked and started to give way and I almost lost my footing on the edge of the coffin.

I can't get out.

Irrational thoughts crowded into my head – I felt angry with myself; for letting McKenzie down, for missing that planned drink in the Blue Boar Club, for missing out on the chance to argue about God with Rennie again, for the possibility that Jennifer would end up marrying some bloody idiot like Westbourne.

Jesus, I can't bloody get out.

I rested my chin on the broken stay and licked the face of my watch so I could see the time. It was just after two in the morning.

So this is where it ends, I thought. *The irony of it… buried in a graveyard before I'm even dead.*

The air became colder and my breath fogged in front of me.

That was the moment I saw them: not the shapes on the ground of the dying soldiers, but other shapes. There were figures standing in the cemetery, dozens of them, standing over the stricken soldiers. Frantically I swept my eyes from side to side.

Death was here.

My heart almost stopped. The grey figures were watching the men on the ground, waiting for them, just the way the Grey Lady had stood at the end of my brother's bed the night he had died.

I thought I was too terrified to call out, because no sound came, but that was the moment I think I lost my voice. It was probably a good thing that I couldn't turn my head all the way around to see if a grey figure was standing behind me. Even if I had been able to, I don't think I would have looked, because just like in my boathouse dream the night before, I didn't want to know.

I must have passed out, held in suspended animation by the mud, because the next thing I remember, I was looking at dawn's first flecks in the sky above. My entire body was numb by now, but I hadn't sunk, so I must have stayed standing on the coffin, even though I could not feel my feet.

Time to sleep.

I saw that the birds were migrating. A great flock of them, wheeling and circling in the sky above, being joined by other groups and mobilising for the long flight south. I wondered if the group from the Cloth Tower in Ypres was with them, having finally decided that enough was enough.

I closed my eyes.

Hold on, John.

It was Freddie's voice, just as it had been out on the Nullarbor when he had talked to me seventeen years before.

I opened my eyes again.

They're coming. Hold on.

'You've got a son, Freddie,' I said wordlessly. 'You've got a boy and I'm sorry I couldn't save him.'

Just hold on John. Don't give up now. Never give up, John… Never, do you hear me…

"Fuckin' 'ell, Ted, this one's still alive. Either that or he's died with his bloody eyes open."

A man was grinning down at me.

He was soon joined by another British stretcher bearer.

"Fuck me… he bloody is too."

Together, they managed to lasso a rope around my head and push it down over my shoulders before pulling it tight. Then they hauled me out.

I lay in the mud like a stillborn calf, not moving, virtually paralysed by my night in the shell-hole. But at least I was still breathing.

"What's your name, son?" one asked, crouching down.

I tried to reply but nothing came out of my mouth.

He grabbed my cardboard identity disc and peered at it.

"Turned to fuckin' mulch…" he said, muttering the words with a frown.

My name's John Hunston.

They both stared back at me. My mind had thought it, but my mouth hadn't said it. Instead of speaking, I think I must have made some kind of facial contortion, akin to panic, because the other bearer knelt down too and patted my shoulder consolingly.

"Not to worry – we'll get you back, mate," he said.

He pulled off my soaked, ripped tunic and Dayfield body vest and wrapped a dry blanket around me. Two others came and joined them and, taking a limb each, they lifted me onto a stretcher.

"He's the only one alive, from what I can see," one said.

In extreme anxiety, I sat up and tried to tell them to look for Harry, but again, the only sound to come out of my mouth was the heavy sound of my breath. I must have looked like a madman.

I tried again.

Harry Ingram – you've got to find him…

Not a sound.

What the hell has happened to me?

"Calm down, mate," the bearer said, pushing me back down on the stretcher. "You're all right now – we'll get you back."

It was only then that I realised we were moving around the cemetery freely in the daylight.

Yards away, half a dozen of the German Red Cross, clad in Gabardine coats and gumboots, were moving around and looking for their own dead.

"There's been an unofficial truce, mate," one of my bearers said. "So we can collect our dead and injured. Only for us, though. If you're not carrying a stretcher or wearing a Red Cross brassard, old Fritz over there will blow your bloody head off."

I followed his gaze to the pillbox beyond the cemetery, surrounded by intact belts of barbed wire.

German snipers were standing on top of the pillbox and calling out to our bearers to tell them where their victims lay: "Hier sind sie!"

They were pointing at the barbed wire where some of our men from the Rifle Battalion were hanging, like meat in a butcher's window.

"Kommen sie!"

When I saw the dead soldiers caught up in the barbed wire, I felt sure we would win the war.

Nothing on earth could stop commitment like that – not bullets, not shells, not even the spectre of death itself. To use the photographer's inimitable expression, they had 'fucking committed'. Those dead men were a terrible inspiration.

Chapter Nineteen

Professor S was looking at me incredulously.

"You really saw those grey shapes… really?"

"Yes."

"What do you think they were?"

I paused for a moment, almost scared to say it.

"Angels of death."

Professor S let my conclusion hang in the air. He wasn't buying it. Perhaps he was waiting for me to say something more sensible.

"I've seen one before," I said. "Remember me mentioning her? Standing by my brother the night he died in 1900… the Grey Lady… an angel of death who haunts this very hospital. After several years I thought I might have dreamt it, and that she hadn't really been there. I nearly managed to convince myself of it too… then in the cemetery at Passchendaele, I saw dozens of them, all waiting to escort the dying soldiers into the next world…"

He shook his head in denial of this. This kind of thing simply didn't fit into the professor's scientific worldview.

"Are you sure they couldn't have been stretcher bearers searching for the wounded, or soldiers on reconnaissance?"

"No. There were too many; and they were standing too still."

"Well, it's possible you may have hallucinated. As a doctor I must entertain that possibility. As a doctor yourself, *you* must entertain that possibility."

"It's possible" I said.

"You were in shock, after all. Come, come, Doctor. Ockham's razor – the simplest explanation is usually the best. Do you concede that?"

"Yes, I agree. The simplest explanation *usually* is the best."

I could tell he didn't care for my emphasis on the word 'usually'.

"Or you could have been dreaming" he said. "A hypnogogic vision – you mentioned passing out soon after."

"That's possible too."

"And then your brother's voice… just like before, coming at a time when you were in extreme peril. A similar experience to Shackleton's in the mountains of South Georgia. Now it's very interesting, I grant you that… very interesting. Something saved you out there – kept you hanging on. That something seemed to know help was on its way. But I suspect it was simply your instinct, your in-built stone-age survival mechanism. Your own brain, in other words, picking up on the sounds of the approaching bearers. Never underestimate the power of the mind."

The professor didn't believe me, but I was fine with that.

"You're right of course, there's no way I can prove it, Professor. But you can't change my mind."

I wanted to go on, to ask him how we could really prove anything. If he had a wife and a child he loved, could he provide me with proof of his love for them? Or did he expect me to take his love on faith, just because he said so? I wanted to go on, to ask him how we could really prove anything. I recalled a conversation I'd had with Rennie many years ago, one in which he had challenged my scientific faith with these same points, backing me into a corner until I had become exasperated and blurted out: 'I just know it to be so' – something that had really delighted him. He saw my unprovable yet strong statement as partial admission to a kind of faith – and he had rammed the point home by telling me there were 'unknown quantities which we shouldn't expect to be able to define'. I could have tried 'the Rennie method' now with the clever Professor S, and pushed this line of logic, but I was tired of talking now and left it alone.

"Tell me," he said, after a brief pause in the conversation, "why did no-one know you were from New Zealand?"

"Human error, I think."

"Explain."

"Well, my uniform was already torn and shredded and what was left of it was encrusted with mud. The British bearers wouldn't have been able to recognise anything. They jettisoned my ruined tunic when they found me. My cardboard identification tags had turned to pulp in the water. At the ADS, the rest of my uniform – my trousers and boots – were stripped off before I was taken in for examination…"

"In case the clothes had any H gas fluid on them?"

"Precisely… and since I could not identify myself, the MO just assumed I was British because British stretcher bearers had brought me in. It was a reasonable guess, because there were still plenty of the 49th Division coming in from the battlefield. The MO was very busy, so he quickly wrote 'Unknown British Soldier, NYDN' on my ticket – Not Yet Diagnosed, Nervous – and passed me down the line."

The professor was nodding.

"Yes… yes… I can see how easily it had happened. Assumption can be dangerous. When you assume, you make an ass out of u and me," he said, grinning at his clever piece of wordplay.

"I was taken to a Casualty Clearing Station at a place nicknamed 'Bandagehem' – one of the special centres that Poyntz mentioned. They observed me there for a week and, when it became obvious I wasn't just suffering from exhaustion, they shipped me back here; just another British soldier with shell-shock."

There was a knock at the door.

"Are you all right in there, Professor?"

It was one of the MOs.

"Yes… we'll be out presently."

"Very good, Professor."

The sound of footsteps receded.

Professor S stood up. It was a bright November morning outside and the room was bathed in light.

Somewhere in the distance, bells were ringing.

I checked my watch, the only object that had survived my ordeal.

Eleven o'clock. November 11th… a Monday. It was a strange day for bells to be ringing.

"I'm sorry about Ingram," he said.

"Me too."

I shook my head, thinking back to the carnage I had seen in the cemetery. He must have been there, with one of the angels of death standing over him. How would I ever be able to face his mother again? Knowing Harry was gone, together with the thought of Kate Ingram's agony made me want to retreat back into the bowels of D block and never come out. That was what I had been doing for the last year – hiding from the world. But it hadn't helped. It had just paused things for a while. It was a bereavement I was going to have to face now.

"He was a very brave young man by the sounds of it."

"Yes," I said. "They all were."

"Indeed."

Tactfully, the Professor changed the subject.

"Well, at least you're cured now," he said, holding up a key. "Do you want to do the honours and let yourself out?"

I got to my feet quickly.

"With great pleasure," I said, taking it from him.

I went over and unlocked the door to the electrical room.

"I'll go and write up your notes," he said. "Talk to the doctors here and square things away. As far as I'm concerned, you're free to go. Good luck to you, Doctor."

Briefly, he took my hand.

For the professor, I was 'case solved', and it was onto the next.

I watched him walk away down the corridor of D-block.

Then he surprised me. He stopped and half turned.

"Ghosts," he said, scratching at the wall gently with his finger.

For several seconds he stood there silently, staring at the flaking paint on the wall. "Angels of Death" he said, nodding to himself as he patted the wall and walked away.

I think that was his small concession – that he was at least willing to consider that I may have encountered something from another world. He was taking all possibilities into account, no matter how remote those possibilities were. Just this one time, he was allowing his beloved Ockham's razor to become slightly blunt.

Type 2, but with a brain, I thought to myself, making my own spot diagnosis.

****

Late November 1918, Royal Victoria Military Hospital

I was sitting at the end of the pier and smoking.

The hospital had given me some clothes from the 'lost and found' section in the laundry; a tweed jacket (some well-to-do visitor must have taken it off in the summer and then forgotten all about it), a pair of tan moleskins which went well enough with the jacket (how someone had lost those was anyone's guess) and a pair of brown Oxford brogues, heavily scuffed and one size too large.

The D-block doctors had only signed me out the day before. The bureaucracy had been infuriating; they had not released me until receiving telegram confirmation from McKenzie that I was who I said I was. That was where the delay had happened – it had taken them several days to track him down.

The telegram had finally arrived from a town called Le Quesnoy in North Eastern France.

I checked the newspapers to find out why he was there.

Occupied by the Germans for four years, Le Quesnoy had been liberated by the NZ division on the 4th November, in what would turn out to be their last major action of the war. The 3rd Brigade had captured the town – the same Rifle battalions which had been in action that day at Bellevue Spur, though I doubted there were many veterans left from that battle. Rather than flattening the place with an artillery bombardment, the NZedders had scaled the ancient town wall using ladders and forced the German surrender. The medieval style of the assault had captured the public imagination and been widely reported – the acceptable face of the end of the war. The press steered away from the other reality; how at an arbitrary hour the mass slaughter had suddenly been halted like a football referee blowing the whistle for full time.

McKenzie's reply had been brief and to the point:

CONFIRM LT. JOHN HUNSTON M.O. IN NZ 3rd AMBULANCE. MIA SINCE BATTLE OF BELLEVUE SPUR 12.10.17. PLEASE INFORM HIM I WILL ATTEND IN PERSON THIS WEEK FOR DEBRIEF. CAPT. MCKENZIE

My most powerful emotion on seeing the telegram – far overshadowing the relief at getting out of D-block – was the knowledge he had made it through the war. 'Debrief'. Christ, I wondered how many swear words that would involve.

While waiting for McKenzie to arrive, the RAMC authorities transferred me to a four bed side ward in C-block – the officer's section of the main hospital. Because their injuries were purely physical, the other men there did not scream in the night – a luxury compared with the large communal ward on D-block. Their higher social standing meant they kept to themselves and did not mix much, an aloofness I did not resent. After a year of being mute, I was happy to be quiet for a while longer, rather than filling the airspace with meaningless trivialities. That was one thing I had noticed in my time as a listener – ninety nine per cent of what came out of people's mouths was utter tripe.

I was smoking my last cigarette when I heard footsteps on the pier. I had started the habit on this pier as my war began, and so I was going to stop on the pier too, now that it was all over.

McKenzie was walking towards me, carrying a long package and a bag which I recognised as my haversack from Kronprinz. I had left it there before leaving on my night mission to the Wallemollen graveyard.

"Christ Almighty, Hunston…" he said, launching straight in, "I thought you were bloody well dead… for an entire bloody year."

"I'm sorry, sir."

"I had to write to that girl of yours, tell her you were missing, presumed dead on the Spur, that you were probably one of the hundreds of bodies which just sank into the mud and disappeared without trace. Had to admit to her that I sent you out on a suicide mission. Had to break her heart. Quite a bloody palaver, I must say, and all because of you, Hunston."

"I'm sorry, sir," I said again.

"Hmmm… Here's all your shit, which I've been lugging round all that time."

Despite the rollocking, I could tell he was happy to see me.

McKenzie held up the long package.

"And why I kept your bloody spear, I have no idea."

I took one final drag of my cigarette and flicked it away into the water. Both hands were needed to take the object and remove all the brown paper he had wrapped it in.

It was indeed the Uhlan's lance, smaller and less menacing than I had remembered.

"Thank you for bringing this, sir," I managed to say.

"Yes, well… the British customs officer gave me the third degree, I can bloody tell you. You've no idea of the hassle I had to go through to get it here."

"I really appreciate it, sir," I said, laying the lance on the floor and smiling.

It was good to see McKenzie alive.

"You can stop calling me, 'sir'," he said. "I'm out. Back to being that strange breed called a civilian."

He was wearing a greatcoat and because of that I hadn't noticed he was out of uniform.

"You're out?"

"That's right – handed in my commission the week after the Armistice, just after I received the telegram from this place about you. My war's over Hunston. I've got a three year old son who needs me. I've done my bit… it's someone else's turn now. General surgery is going to be a bloody dream compared to what we were doing out there."

"I want to say sorry… about what happened at Bellevue Spur, about my losing my speech and letting you down."

"Don't be."

"I feel bad about it," I said.

"Well… you did exactly what I ordered you to do, Hunston – it didn't matter they weren't in the graveyard. In fact, I found some of them the next day, during the truce. I saw for myself you had been there and written on their foreheads. You brought those men comfort in the most bloody uncomfortable place on earth. I gave you a hell of a mission, Hunston and you succeeded in carrying it out. Here…"

He rummaged in his coat pocket for a moment and then held out a box.

I opened it up to see the object inside: a silver cross held on a white ribbon with a blue central stripe. My first thought was how 'religious looking' it was.

"A medal?"

"That's right – the MC – you were awarded it posthumously for your action that night."

"Who recommended me for that?"

McKenzie looked down at his feet and then out at the water.

"Me," he said, so quietly I could hardly hear him.

"What was that?"

"It was me, Hunston."

I grinned. It was good to see McKenzie looking so bashful.

"Impressed you, did I?"

His voice was quiet again.

"I suppose so."

"I can't hear you."

"YES, HUNSTON, you bloody impressed me. After I found how many men in the mud had 'M' written on their foreheads, I was impressed. Know how many you eased into the next world that night, Hunston?"

"No, I have no idea."

"Thirty… I made the count myself the next day, in the ceasefire. You gave thirty men a dignified and comfortable death."

"You make it sound as if I saved them all."

"Well, it was thirty one actually… one made it back – he managed to crawl into the RAP before dawn – big bloody M on his head. Said how you'd crawled around the spur, giving injections to all his wounded fellows, holding their hands, saying a few comforting words before moving on, 'like some bloody angel' – his exact words."

He took the medal from the box and pinned it onto my tweed jacket.

"Not bad, Hunston – makes you look almost respectable. And it's damn nice to be able to rescind the posthumous part."

I picked up the spear and thumbed the point instead. It was still sharp.

"What happened to that soldier who was dragged in on the groundsheet that afternoon? Did he make it?"

McKenzie hunched his shoulders.

"No idea… but he made it through the night. Early next morning a team of Maori bearers came and took him away."

I weighed the spear in my right hand, holding it in the middle of the shaft like a javelin thrower.

"What was the rest of the war like?"

He laughed and in his eyes I saw a myriad of painful recollections stirred up by my question.

"Still shit," he said eventually, "though Bellevue Spur tops the shit list. The official figures say 842 killed that day… in that cursed bloody rain, and a lot more afterwards. The Canadians relieved us on the 18th and managed to reach the ruins of Passchendaele a week later – nothing more than a smear of broken bricks on the muddy landscape. By then, even Haig realised his strategy was going nowhere and, with winter coming, he simply closed down the offensive. It was all for nothing."

"We did win in the end, sir."

"Tell that to the families of all the New Zealanders who died, I'm sure they'll be bloody delighted. They reckon around 16,000 of our boys have been either killed in action or died of their wounds. And more are still dying. I reckon there'll be a couple of thousand more who'll be pushing up the daisies in the next few years, well before their time."

I could believe it. I knew all about soldiers who died even though they were away from the fighting. What a waste.

We watched as three swans flew low over the water, making their way gracefully south towards the Solent. Seeing them go by made me feel better for some reason. Despite everything, it was still a beautiful world. I continued to follow them until they were specks in the distance.

Then, holding the lance level with my ear, I ran to the end of the pier and, with a snap of my arm, launched it skywards.

It arced out for thirty yards and fell into Southampton Water, disappearing with barely a ripple.

McKenzie ran up to the pier rail and looked over at the water and then at me.

"Now, why in Christ's name would you go and do a thing like that, Hunston?"

"I didn't want it anymore."

I am tired of the fear. My God, for eighteen years I've been afraid.

Poyntz would have understood.

McKenzie shook his head and leant against the railing.

"Sometimes I worry about you, Hunston... I really do. You mad bloody bastard."

The Blue Boar Club had not changed; the same Spy cartoons on the wall, the same carpet on the floor, the same butler even – he had been old in 1900, now he was positively ancient.

One thing that had changed was the dress rule – if you had been in the war you didn't have to wear a black suit as long as you wore your medals. So I was still in my tweed with the medal McKenzie had given me. The only other difference, as far as I could see, were the photographs on one wall of club members who had served in conflicts. Mine was there, just as Worsley had said it would be.

'Dr John Hunston, RAMC 1900, Oxford Rowing Blue 1896-8' read the caption underneath.

I hardly recognised myself. For a start it was before Freddie had died – and that felt like another lifetime altogether.

The photograph had been taken in the barracks just before I shipped out for South Africa. My uniform looked too big, but it was my expression which made me want to laugh; leering out from under my RAMC cap as if I owned the place. God forbid I should ever look that way again.

I sat and waited for Rennie in my old corner chair, looking out of the window at the view. The trees in Green Park were shaking in the winter wind, the rain falling in sheets, obscuring the distant buildings. The scene was as exactly as it had always been.

The old waiter had not appeared to recognise me – not surprising really, what with my tweed jacket and the grey hairs at my temples, most of which had appeared in the preceding twelve months. Still, he was respectful enough, my MC showing I had fought for King and Country with distinction.

When I asked about Worsley, the waiter said, "He's not been in today, sir." A reply cheering my spirits, as it meant that he was alive.

The Blue Boar was the only place in London where I could think of meeting Rennie.

I had telephoned him at Toc H the week before.

Although 'Tubby' Clayton had long since resumed his responsibilities there, Rennie had kept close links and was conducting a thanksgiving service in the attic chapel when I called.

It was Pettifer who had answered the phone, and he had sounded pleased to hear my voice. "Padre Rennie will be very, very pleased to hear it's you, sir." In his deadpan delivery 'very, very' was an ecstatic statement. It occurred to me that poor Pettifer must have been witness to Rennie's grief on a daily basis for over a year.

On hearing my voice on the telephone, Rennie had burst into tears, but before doing so had managed to shout the words, "Christ Almighty," down the earpiece.

He came into the lounge and, when he saw me, he bellowed out my name – an outburst of such unmitigated volume that I doubted anything like it had ever happened before in the esteemed Blue Boar lounge. Meekly I acknowledged him with a wave as he half ran across the room. When he lifted me up in a great bear hug, I was acutely conscious that the other members were staring.

Despite all the years in New Zealand I had retained strong English character traits, perhaps not enough to complain about luke-warm tea in a front line RAP, but certainly enough to have reservations about public displays of affection.

When we finally sat down he poked at my tweed jacket.

"I like it."

"Thanks."

The waiter appeared at Rennie's side.

"Sir, can I get you anything?"

"Yes, two double whiskies, thank you."

After the waiter had gone, Rennie looked at me.

"What?" he said.

"Double whiskies, Sean?"

"The war's over. You're alive. The boys are alive. This calls for a celebration. We need to let our hair down a little, John. I'd say we've earned that right."

"Fair point" I said.

He looked around.

"What is this place anyway… a museum?"

I laughed.

"In a way it is," I said. "In an ideal world every town would have a Toc H, something alive – with someone like you running it, but this is the best we have in London. It's my old club, believe it or not. I've been a member here since University days."

"Really? When were you last in?"

"June 1900."

Rennie's booming laugh rang out, drawing more looks.

The waiter returned with the drinks and Rennie held up his glass in a toast.

"I never stopped praying, John… never stopped. I think the professor who cured you must have been an emissary of God: 'and looking up to heaven, he sighed, and sayeth unto him, *Ephphatha*, that is, Be opened… and the string of his tongue was loosed, and he spake plain.'"

I nearly contradicted his biblical theory of what had happened, but managed to hold back. I didn't want to spoil this reunion with an argument straightaway. Instead I nodded at him and said: "Mark, Chapter 8… 'he hath done all things well: he maketh both the deaf to hear and the dumb to speak'."

Well, I don't think I had ever seen my friend so happy.

We touched glasses and drained them straight down.

As the liquor burned its way to his stomach Rennie thumped his chest a few times and went a little cross-eyed.

The biblical talk had reminded me of something I had read:

"So, I heard our boys fought at Armageddon," I said, "just the other month."

"They did."

"But it wasn't the end of the world?"

Rennie shifted in his chair.

"It didn't seem to be," he said.

We stared at one another, guardedly but with humour in our eyes. Things had picked up right where they had left off. Surely it wouldn't hurt to have just a *small* argument.

"I thought that Armageddon meant a second coming… with you know who coming in the clouds with much power and glory. Isn't that what you told us all in the garden back in Waihi last year?"

"Yes, I think I do remember that… but I also think we never quite finished that particular conversation…"

He reached into his pocket and pulled out his bible, leafing through it until he found what he wanted.

"Let me see," he said, playing his part well. "Aha… here we are… '*But of that day and that hour knoweth no man, no, not the angels which are in heaven, neither the son, but the Father.*'"

He slammed the book shut again in triumph. "In other words, John, no-one knows except God, so it's pointless trying to work out dates and timetables. Now, I grant you this, Mark 13 is one of the most difficult chapters in the New Testament for modern men to understand and a lot of it is because Jesus clothes the idea of his second coming in language and imagery from those times. But essentially, all you need to know is that he foretold he would come again. *What I say unto you I say unto all, Watch…*"

He leant forward and pointed at me when he said it, like Kitchener in his recruitment poster – with a serious look. I wanted to say something clever and quote Prometheus; tell Rennie how the Titan had placed in mortals 'blind hopes' to stop them foreseeing doom, but again I didn't push it. I thought it wise to keep quiet. We both knew where the boundaries lay in our discussions, or at least I did.

It was definitely time to change the subject.

"So, Sean… how are the boys doing?"

He put the bible away and smiled at me broadly.

"Good. I had a letter from Materoa last week in fact – they're out fishing a lot… lots of rugby… the usual."

I remembered the Maoris at Passchendaele.

"You did the right thing, you know," I said, "getting them to go back. How's the hand, by the way?"

Rennie massaged his malformed fracture.

"It aches on cold days."

"Well, it was worth it… I'm still amazed you changed their minds."

"It wasn't just my table breaking display," Rennie said.

"Really?"

"No, I talked to them some more in the hospital afterwards, while we were waiting for the result of the X-ray… when we were alone."

"What on earth did you say, Sean?"

Rennie lounged back lazily in his chair, looking to the all the world like he was a Blue Boar regular.

"You remember the story about Maui I told that day on the Christmas fishing trip… the one about the giant fish and the formation of New Zealand's rugged mountains?"

"Yes."

"Well, I told them another story… about Maui dying."

I hadn't heard this one. I inhaled the fumes of the whisky before putting the empty glass down on the table.

"I'm all ears."

Rennie was cradling his whisky glass as if it were a crystal ball which showed the old Maui legends. "In Maori mythology death is a goddess called *Hine-nui-te-po*, who has eyes of greenstone and whose hair is kelp. She is said to have the mouth of a barracuda, with an icy breath. And… and…"

He looked a little embarrassed.

"Go on," I said. "And what?"

"Well, in the place where men enter her, there are sharp teeth of obsidian."

"Hang on a minute," I said. "You mean…?"

"Yes, down *there*…"

"Oh… right, I see… pardon me. Please continue."

"Well, despite Maui having been warned by his father that Death could not be conquered, he was brash enough to think he could outwit her. He came up with an audacious plan and set off to find her, along with a large group of bird companions. As he drew closer to the sleeping goddess, the temperature dropped. He reached the forest clearing where she was and spoke to the birds: 'My friends, there she lies asleep – *Hine-nui-te-po*, the Great Mother of the Night. I ask you to remember my words, for my life is in your hands. I'll kill the goddess by entering her from down below and exiting from her mouth while she is asleep.'"

I couldn't help but laugh at the imagery.

"That's exactly what Maui warned his friends not to do." Rennie said. "He told them that on no account must they laugh until he had passed right through and come out of her mouth. If they laughed before that happened, then he would die. The birds begged him to give up his plan, but Maui scoffed at their fear. He took off all his clothes. The goddess was sleeping with her legs apart and he could see the sharp flints set between her thighs. With a mocking smile he stooped down and quickly made his way, head first into her body. Soon his shoulders and his upper torso disappeared inside. The birds were choking back their laughter as Maui continued his antics, thrusting his head into the throat of the Death goddess. Then, with a heave he pushed upwards so that his face suddenly appeared in her mouth. The absurdity of it all was too much for the fantails who couldn't help themselves from laughing out loud. The goddess woke up, and realising what was happening, closed her thighs on him, and cut his body in two."

"Blimey, Sean, that's pretty graphic stuff."

"Yes, indeed," Rennie said. "Because of Maui's failed attempt, we all continue to tread the dark path to *Hine-nui-te-po*."

"That's it?"

"Yes," Rennie said, "that's the story I told them. I said not to tempt death anymore… to stay well away from her. Not to wake her up."

I nodded at Rennie though I was not seeing him. I was seeing Wallemollen cemetery - his story had catapulted me right back there.

I remembered sinking up to my waist and then my neck in the shell hole, with the cold water sucking the life out of me. I had seen birds too, high above and preparing to migrate. Lucky for me they had been silent that day and not laughed and woken Death. That night I had visited the death goddess and survived; at least for a while longer… we all tread the dark path in the end.

"John… JOHN!"

I came back into the Blue Boar Club, leaving my dark memories behind.

"Yes?"

"What are you going to do now?"

"I'm going to get on with some living."

"Oh? What exactly does that involve?"

"Well. Number one, we have a few more drinks here and get well and truly drunk. Then, number two, I go and find Jennifer. The last I heard she was working in the NZ General Hospital down at Brockenhurst."

This was good news to Rennie. He rubbed his hands together and went cross-eyed with excitement.

"Just make sure you wait until you get back to New Zealand until you marry her, or Materoa will never forgive you."

I laughed for a few seconds and then stopped.

"You know, Sean, I was thinking about staying here."

"What, in the club?"

"No, in England I mean. I think it's time for a new direction. In a funny way, it feels like I'm home."

Rennie stared at me for a few moments, and then slowly nodded, accepting my decision.

"You're alive," he said. "That's good enough for me."

Suddenly he was frowning.

"Materoa will understand. That shouldn't be a problem… we'll get the best photographer and send her a dozen pictures. But shall I conduct the service or be your best man? I'm not sure I can do both at the same time."

I laughed.

"Don't get ahead of yourself. She hasn't said yes yet."

"As good as… I saw her face that day, John. It's inevitable, but best man or officiator… that's the real matter at hand here."

As Rennie mused on the wedding dilemma, two well-heeled men in black suits – one short and one tall – entered the lounge and took up positions at the bar.

They were talking loudly about the British Garrison entering the Rhineland on the conditions of the Armistice. I had been reading about it in the newspaper just before Rennie's arrival. The previous day, on the 3rd December, the British had gone into Germany, crossing the Belgian frontier and occupying the town of Malmedy.

"Listen to this," the short man was saying, quoting directly from the same paper, "…notices have been put into the windows of the shops and houses: 'Citizens are earnestly requested to maintain great calm and order on the entry of the Entente troops into our city and to receive them with courtesy and dignity.'"

He raised his eyebrows as he read on.

"'… Apparently native troops are heading to the border too, to be part of the Garrison… a Maori Contingent is marching towards the Rhine.'"

"Good God… The Maori… Really?" the tall man said. "Not to worry, I'll make sure our High Command sees sense. I'll have them sent back home. Savages keeping check on fellow Europeans – that just won't do…"

Without pausing, Rennie called over to the men, "Excuse me."

"Yes, Reverend," the tall man said, noticing the dog collar. "Can I help?"

"As a matter of fact you can. You can help me by exercising some decorum in your conversation. My two sons are half Maori you see, winners both of the Military Medal. I take it as a slur that you refer to them disparagingly as savages, and an even greater slur that by inference you are insulting my wife who is a full Maori. I would have addressed you both as gentlemen, but obviously that would have been inappropriate, since you have behaved in a most ungentlemanlike manner."

The two men stood in shocked silence for a few seconds, until the taller one, who had made the comment about 'savages', managed to gather his wits.

"I say! Do you know who I am, Reverend?"

Rennie stood up from his chair and raised his voice.

"No… I don't know who you are and at this moment I don't care. What I do know is that my sons and plenty of their comrades served the British Empire for the last four years. That alone deserves your respect. So what I suggest is that you apologise to me right now… and we can all forget about this and go about our day."

"I most certainly shall not," the man said, his face red with rage. "I have never, ever been spoken to in such a way. It is you, Reverend, who will do the apologising… this instant… or by God, I'll have you thrashed to within an inch of your life."

Rennie had made fists with his hands.

"'By God', you say! 'By God', you say!"

The threat of the thrashing had gone right over Rennie's head, but the tall man had made a big mistake invoking God's name like that. Now I could see that Rennie was about to do something he might regret. I didn't want trouble for him, not in his position as a Minister. If he hit this man he would be remorseful about it for years to come.

I wouldn't though.

Sighing, I got to my feet.

"Now you've gone and dragged me into this…" I said, becoming part of the stand-off.

The tall man looked down at me disdainfully. He was only an inch taller. No obstacle at all.

"Who the hell are you?"

"I, sir… am the Reverend's friend… you probably don't know an awful lot about friendship, so let me explain. What you say to him, you say to me. By my calculations you now have two apologies to make – one for insulting the Maori and another for insulting my friend with your crass threat, which I am completely certain you lack the courage to carry out."

I walked up to the man until my face was inches away from his own. I breathed my whisky breath on him. Intimidation like this was something I had learnt from McKenzie.

It was then that he noticed my MC, and when he did he swallowed hard.

Beads of sweat had collected on his upper lip. I saw the fear in his eyes. I had been in the belly of the death goddess and survived. This was all just child's play. This was nothing at all.

The short man was edging his way down the bar, as if to dissociate himself from the scene. He definitely wouldn't be backing up his friend, I could see that.

The walls of the club closed in on the tall man and me.

I wanted to break my fist on his face the same way Rennie had broken his hand on the table at Toc H.

I was almost snarling at him.

"I'll ask you one more time," I said. "Apologise now."

"Do it," said another voice from across the room. "Apologise, or you're barred."

I looked over to see Worsley framed in the doorway. Arriving unnoticed, he had been watching the whole drama unfold.

He marched up to us and glared at the tall man.

"Or you are barred… *permanently*."

In the world of the English gentry, that was about as big a threat as you could make.

The man hesitated for a moment and then caved in, his shoulders slumping in defeat.

"I… I… unreservedly apologise gentlemen, both for what I said about the Maori and for threatening you, Reverend."

"That's good to hear," Rennie said, "so very good to hear. You are forgiven. '…Father, forgive them; for they know not what they do.'"

Catching Worsley's eye, I bit my lip to keep myself from smiling.

The tall man looked confused.

"Luke 23.34," Rennie said. "And please allow me to say sorry for getting a bit hot under the collar… most uncharacteristic of me. That's the last time I try whisky… Good Lord above… it's the Devil's brew."

"It's all right," the man said, shaking Rennie's hand limply. "It's quite all right."

Ashen faced, he and his short friend retired to a table at the far end of the room.

I looked Worsley up and down – the first time I had seen him without his face being smeared with Flanders mud.

"Crikey, Worsley – you have some clout around here, don't you? I was about to lose my head before you walked in. You hold a lot of respect as club secretary."

He smiled.

"Ah… I used to be the secretary, but I've been the president since 1914. Now, if I remember correctly, old chap, you were going to buy me a drink."

Chapter Twenty

New Forest, December 1918

I approached the NZ No.1 General Hospital, crunching my way up the gravel drive in my borrowed brogues.

The words 'Balmer Lawn Hotel' were only just visible up on the roof, the pre-war sign blending with the grey tiles and the dark wintry skies behind.

The train ride had been straightforward enough. At Waterloo station a long line of soldiers had been on the platform, not waiting for a train but queuing at a kiosk under the notice: 'French money changed here for soldiers and officers in uniform'. They were all in their greatcoats, Lee-Enfield rifles shouldered, and helmets strapped onto the back of their packs. Most were smoking. The banter sounded happy; the chit-chat of demobilised soldiers on the winning side.

A few hundred miles away in Germany, I imagined there were similar groups of soldiers standing about on station platforms, relieved it was all over, even if they had lost. Most would just be glad to go back to their homes and pick up from right where they had left off in 1914. But maybe not all of them would be so accepting. Some might be bitter about what had happened. There was definitely an unfinished feeling to things – it had been so sudden – almost a stale-mate, rather than an outright victory. Though the Allies had taken control of the Rhine there was to be no occupation of Germany itself. The rumour was that Lloyd George had wanted to drive the German Army all the way back into Germany, so they would know they had been well and truly defeated, but he had been talked out of it by his cabinet colleagues.

You had the sense that the end of the Great War had merely been postponed for another time.

I waited in the main entrance of the hospital while a call went out for her. Watching the patients drifting past me in their 'hospital undress', I felt a close affinity towards them, even though I was wearing civvies now.

Of course I wasn't just turning up out of the blue. To spare us both from the emotional shock – her fainting at the sight of me, and my standing there with a stupid smile on my face, dumbly expecting everything to be fine – I had written to her to break the news that I was alive. In a way, it had been a harder letter to write than the one telling her I was going to the front and that I might not make it through alive. To tell someone you had come back from the dead wasn't easy. As Rennie would testify, even Jesus had a hard time trying to convince the Apostles it was really him after he had been resurrected.

My biggest fear was a selfish one – that thinking me dead she had 'got over it' and found someone else. What if her heart had moved on? It was hard to imagine a worse feeling than having made it through the war only to find I had lost her. So I wrote the letter with even more dread in my spirit than I had felt before Bellevue Spur, so much so, that I did not dare to write 'darling' or say anything presumptuous at all:

> *Dear Jennifer,*
> *I am alive. I know my CO told you the opposite and he said what he thought was true. It is a long story, borne of severe trauma, but one which I will explain if you will allow me to do so…*

I explained about the night on the Spur; of the dying men and the ghosts and of my being trapped in the flooded grave, half in this life and half in another. I wrote of my mutism and of the incarceration at D-block, only ten miles from her the entire time. Finally, I described the strange Professor S and his electricity treatment.

The last paragraph was the one I struggled with the most:

I would like to come and see you, if that is acceptable. I am worried you will run from me as if I am a ghost, but I am not one Jennifer. I am whole again. Please allow me to come.
Yours, John

I received a reply by the next post, a short one, almost a written version of Rennie's first response:

John
I cannot believe it. I cannot stop crying. Please come down as soon as you possibly can. I am waiting for you.
All my love, J

Not married to some other idiot then, by the sound of things. The writing was even stained with tears. 'All my love' made it pretty obvious I had still stood a chance.

She appeared on the stairs – first a pair of legs in black stockings and shoes, then a light blue-grey dress with an overlying white apron, set with matching white collar and cuffs. A short scarlet cape was draped over her shoulders, making for a dramatic splash of colour. And lastly her face; I noticed every detail – branding it onto my mind so that I would never forget this moment.

Despite wearing a white veil headdress, some of her hair was still showing at the sides. It was the colour of autumn – I had always thought that – the same russet brown the leaves turn in an English October. She had a few tiny freckles on her nose and the stark white headdress contrasted with her pale skin.

She walked across the hall easily until there she was, right in front of me.

"Hello there, John," she said, in a matter of fact manner.

It was a bit surprising how 'cool' she was being. Was this just an act for her patients? Her way of being stoic?

"Hello, Jennifer."

I had forgotten quite how beautiful she was. More specifically, I had forgotten how beautiful she was when she smiled. And she was smiling at me now.

The shape her face was making as she smiled was so enchanting that, without thinking, I kissed her left cheek right there and then, an action drawing a few whistles from some of the patients in the hallway.

Jennifer exuded a new found confidence and bearing; compared to the distracted and frightened girl I had last seen in Thames a year and a half earlier.

"Now look here," she said, pretending to be cross, "what do you take me for?"

"The prettiest girl I have seen in England."

"Just England?" she said, without missing a beat.

"Sorry, I meant to say the entire world."

For an instant her face was serious, and then she threw back her head and laughed.

"I have to hand it to him," she said to the spectating patients, joshing and playing hard to get, "he knows how to shower a girl with compliments."

Then she turned to me. "But we all know actions speak louder than words, John."

"You tell him, Nurse," one of the patients said.

I could tell that Jennifer was a different person; it must have been her work here that had given her the self-assurance I had not seen before. With me and Westbourne that day at the *Brian Boru* she had been miserable, but not now. She was radiant. This was my second chance and I wasn't going to muck it up. I decided to take her at her word, picking up on the last thing she had said.

"Would you like to come for a walk with me?"

She moved her face closer to mine and whispered into my ear, "Yes."

Someone in the crowd made a wolf-whistle, and as we left the building, another of the onlookers called out to us, "You look after that nurse, mate; she's the best girl here."

As soon as we were out of sight of the building I reached for her hand and she held mine, and for a few steps we walked without talking, just enjoying the electricity of touching. That was when she started to cry – a strange, nervous release, her breathing fast and shallow – almost as if she were scared.

Fumbling around, I found my handkerchief in my pocket and held it out, just like I had done for Kate Ingram after telling her Freddie had died. It was strange how similar Jennifer looked now, even though her tearfulness was for the exact opposite reason. She didn't take the handkerchief, so I dabbed gently at her eyes myself, trying my best to clean her up.

"I never stopped hoping" she said, ignoring the handkerchief, "never."

She was smiling and crying at the same time now, and it was the sweetest sight I had ever seen. The best I had ever felt. I hugged her tight and said, "I will never let go of you."

Her eyes were still watery and her cheeks shiny with tears.

"You can kiss me properly now."

Her lips were soft and warm.

Once I had thought myself an ice man, trapped out on top of a mountain and frozen in suspended animation for thousands of years. I had always thought I would remain that way.

But now Jennifer's warmth filled me – *I want to take you closely in my arms and give you all my love and strength*, she had once said, and now it was really happening. God, it was good to be alive again after all this time.

We sat on a bench in the hotel gardens and told each other our war stories. She became very quiet when I talked about my fruitless search for Harry Ingram. I think she sensed my disappointment and didn't want to dwell on it at such a time.

The sun went down and it became too cold to stay out any longer, but before we went back I tried, in a faltering way, to explain why losing Freddie had made me distant.

"It was like a curse."

Jennifer listened, her eyes fixed on mine.

"I loved you anyway, you stupid thing… I love you now too."

It was easy to make a simple choice now and love this woman back. I realised that's all it had ever needed – the ability to let go and trust that all would be well, to flip the switch in my head and allow it all to happen. In a single second, our entire future together fluttered through my mind and it was all good. Fate was tapping at my shoulder and yelling into my ear: 'GO ON THEN, BLOODY ASK HER' it was saying. I didn't need telling twice.

"Will you marry me?" I said.

Jennifer looked at me seriously: "You're not joking?"

I shook my head. "No joke."

"Well then… yes," she said.

I walked her back to the hospital and was just turning to leave, when she said she would take me somewhere special the following day: "Just a nice place I know," she said casually. "You'll like it, I'm sure. Will you come?"

"Of course I'll come… where are we going?"

She moved her mouth next to my ear, just like she had done earlier, and whispered again: "Be patient, John – it's a secret."

****

The following day

We emerged from the forest and walked out onto the shingle, holding hands. I could hardly let go of her.

An ambulance girl had driven us here by way of Beaulieu, in all a ten mile trip from the hospital. After being dropped off, we had walked through Marchwood forest and soon reached the western shore of Southampton Water. Directly across from us, some three hundred yards away, lay the Royal Victoria Military hospital and the pier. It was odd to see it all from this side. I had always hoped I would get a different perspective on my last night with Freddie and the aftermath, and here it was.

"Is this the special place?"

Jennifer smiled at me.

"Do you like it?"

"I do… it's far better than being on the other side."

I was just about to clear a spot for us to both to sit when I noticed a man fishing on the shore some fifty yards away to our right. He was sitting on a long, bleached fallen tree-trunk right by the water's edge.

I ambled slowly towards him, thinking I might ask if he had caught anything.

The fisherman was wearing a bulky jacket on his upper half and I could tell just by looking at his posture that he was young. The winter sun, low on the horizon, was bathing him in a weak golden light.

Something stirred vaguely in my memory, some kind of recognition, but I didn't know quite what it was – probably the fact that someone was fishing and the knowledge that back home, Manu and Kahu would be doing the same.

Full of bonhomie from being with Jennifer, I called out as I approached.

"Have you caught anything, lad?"

"No," he said, standing and turning towards me. "Not yet."

I felt Jennifer squeeze my hand more tightly.

Now we were closer and he had stood up, I could see it was a sheepskin jerkin he was wearing, and underneath, hospital blues. The sheepskin had seen better days, the wool a tea brown and stained darker in various places, but still serviceable. A black patch covered the man's right eye.

He looked at me carefully.

"Do I know you?" he said.

It felt as if this was some kind of fantastic dream. When I spoke, my voice felt detached from my body. It was if I had been switched to an automatic function because the shock was too overwhelming for my system. My castle walls were taking another big hit.

"Jesus… that lump of meat in the groundsheet was *you?*"

That seemed to spark his memory.

"You were the doctor who looked after me that day" he said, "... the day I was injured?"

"Yes."

I remembered how his good eye had begged me to help him.

"You're Harry Ingram," I said, just to confirm it.

He nodded, still not fully understanding.

The healed skull wound was hidden under his hair and somehow he did not look disfigured. If anything, the patch gave him a distinguished piratical air.

He saw me staring at his injuries.

"I don't mind it," he said, putting his hand to his head self-consciously. "There were plenty of others who lost more than an eye. They fitted me with an artificial one, you know... but I prefer to wear the patch. I didn't chuck it out though, it's in my sock drawer in case I ever need it."

Jennifer laughed.

I realised then she already knew who Ingram was – she had been looking after him in the hospital all this time.

Everything fell into place - *this* was her surprise.

"He always fishes here," she said to me now. "He walks all the way from Brockenhurst. We have to drive out and collect him most evenings. Today I told him he would be having a surprise visitor."

Harry Ingram was studying me with suspicion, no doubt noticing our facial resemblance.

"How do you know my name?"

"It's... I... um... the reason..."

I was stumbling badly over the answer, not quite knowing how to tell him – there was too much to say. I hadn't expected this at all.

Harry decided to try another question, a simpler one.

"What's your name?"

"John... John Hunston."

"John Hunston," he said, frowning and repeating the name.

Pausing, he reached into his trouser pocket and pulled out his wallet. He extracted a small card and held it up – it was the note I had left for him at Toc H, from more than a year and a half ago.

"So you're the one who wrote this?"

"Yes, that was me."

"I saw it when we assembled in Pop for Third Ypres," he said.

"And I found your reply," I said. "I missed you by a few days."

He read it to me:

"Lt John Hunston NZ Field Ambulance, c/o NZ Stationary Hospital, would like to meet LCpl Harry Ingram, 3rd Battalion, NZ Rifle Bde. An important family matter."

"So what's it all about?" he said, putting the note away again. "This important family matter?"

I still didn't know quite how to begin. In the end I started my explanation in a sort of chronological order:

"Your mother asked me to look out for you in the war."

"Why? Is she your girl?"

I looked at Jennifer and then back to Harry Ingram.

"No, nothing like that."

"So how do you know her?"

I hesitated for a split second. In Belgium, before Bellevue Spur, I had imagined that if I did find him, I would tell him somewhere cosy and intimate, perhaps over a beer in one of the estaminets in Poperinghe. I had thought we might laugh about it together and get drunk. Instead, here we were on a cold English shore-line in winter, completely sober.

"She asked me, because I'm your uncle."

Harry Ingram frowned again.

"That can't be... she doesn't have any brothers."

"I meant... I'm your father's brother."

His good eye blinked in surprise and I could see from his expression that he knew it was true. We were clearly related. Looking at me must have been like looking at an older version of himself – that's how similar we were.

"His name was Alfred," I said. "Freddie..."

Visibly struggling with my revelation, he nevertheless managed to keep going with the conversation, his voice very quiet.

"I... I know. My mother told me about him. Wouldn't reveal his surname, though."

Harry looked back down the path which led out from the forest and then back at me.

"Where is he?" he said, his voice becoming louder. "Is he here with you?"

I put my hand on his shoulder.

"No, Harry."

"Then where is he?"

His misunderstanding – that there might be another big surprise in store – almost brought me to tears.

I think he already knew the answer to his question before my reply.

"Freddie died a long time ago, back in 1900…"

He sank back down onto the sun-bleached tree-trunk, and for a while the only sound was the soothing, gentle breaking of small waves on the shingle beach.

I sat down beside him and pulled out my new brandy flask. Not filled with Segonzac but Hennessey, which the barman at the Blue Boar had kindly provided, free of charge, after seeing I was on good terms with the club president. It tasted just as good.

"Here," I said, holding it out.

Harry accepted the flask and took a swig and I followed suit.

Jennifer sat next to me, nestling her head in the crook of my neck and shoulder.

I started to speak, haltingly at first, keeping my gaze on the water's edge near my feet.

"Just before leaving New Zealand I met your mother by chance, Harry… and I had to watch her cry when I told her… she had never found out what happened to him either, you see."

"I understand," he said.

"I've been in pain too, believe me, and to see both of your reactions cuts like a knife…"

I broke off to regain my composure.

"Anyway, as your newfound uncle, your mother entrusted me to look out for you… a hard ask, since from what I could gather, you and your mates were charging down machine gun posts like a bunch of immortals."

He smiled at hearing that, and the mood lifted a little.

"I was the MO in Messines too… the one who helped your friend Frickleton in the aid post."

Harry nodded as he began to remember that day too.

"Because of all the dirt on your face, I had no idea who you were," I said. "And now I find out it was you again at Kronprinz, covered in blood. Both times I failed to recognise you. Instead I was sent on a suicide mission to Wallemollen Cemetery and gladly took it, hoping I might finally get to save you…"

"Wallemollen…" he said. "That's where I got shot in the head. I was told someone dragged me back to the RAP, though I don't remember it. What I do remember is lying in that concrete bunker; feeling like half my face was hanging off. I remember watching you and thinking there was something familiar about you. Then you gave me this sheepskin for a pillow… I should probably give it back to you."

He made a move to undo it.

"No, no. It's yours, Harry."

"Thanks," he said, not arguing the point. "I think of it as my good luck charm."

"I couldn't believe you had survived, and my senior said you made it through the night too…"

Harry was hugging himself now, as if to try and hold his body in one piece still, in case it started to unravel itself again like it had that day, with bits hanging out, parts broken and organs missing.

"Yes, the head medic kept an eye on me… swore a lot, I remember. Then a team of Maori came and took me away the next morning. Four of them… all the way back to the ADS. I was driven to a head injury hospital at Mendinghem where some Yank patched me up. Luckily the arm was a clean break – healed up fine."

Harry Ingram stopped talking, unclasped himself and rested his elbows on his knees.

His hands were shaking slightly, and tears were filling his good eye and threatening to breach the lid barrier. He was the fearless 'Mad Dog', a twenty-one year old hard man who had cleared out German machine gun nests and probably killed dozens, but now he was just a young lad who had lost his father.

"So his name was Freddie Hunston…" he said simply, his voice quiet.

The tears spilled over and ran down his stubbled cheek.

"He didn't know about you, Harry," I said. "He promised your mother he would make something of himself – make some money – and then come back for her. So he became a soldier like you. He fought for the British in the Boer War. He was injured out there… lost a leg… and then went down with typhoid fever, the same as me. I'd gone over to South Africa too you see, for the same reason I came over here for you… to try and look out for him. We were both shipped back to that place." I pointed out across Southampton Water at the huge hospital. "That's where he died, of pneumonia…" I pulled out the photograph of the two of us on the hospital pier, the one Kate Ingram had seen back in Waihi. I had kept it carefully within a leather wallet at the bottom of my haversack, alongside the picture of me, Rennie and Materoa.

"That's us after the war, sitting on that pier over there."

Harry Ingram studied the photograph, seeing his father for the first time.

"I've been fishing here and staring at that pier for the last year."

"He's buried in the hospital grounds. If you want I'll show you his grave."

"I'd like that."

"He's proud of you, Harry…"

Harry looked at me, as if to say 'you really think so?' or maybe it was because I had spoken about it in the present tense.

"I'm not just saying that to make you feel better… I've never really been what you would call a religious man, Harry, but strange things have happened… which have led me to believe that somehow… well… put it like this: I'm sure that his spirit lives on, in some way we can't comprehend…"

I was starting to sound like Edgar Allan Poe.

My voice was cracking as the memories of Freddie's eerie encouragement in the Australian desert and the Passchendaele cemetery threatened to overwhelm me.

I took a deep breath, exhaled slowly and put my hand on his shoulder.

"What I'm trying to say is that I think he knows what you have become, Harry… A brave soldier… a good man…"

Harry was staring down at the photograph again.

"My father…"

The onshore breeze carried his words off and I watched as he wiped his eye and swept his hands through his hair. Then he looked over and smiled at me – the most honest, disarming and genuine smile I ever saw; of a kind that suggested he was on the road to an inner peace. I hoped so anyway.

For a time, we all watched the waters of the Solent in silence as the sun's rays played on the shimmering, rippling surface. Along with the present company, the sparkling, dancing lights made me feel very good about the world.

Eventually, Jennifer spoke: "Tell us about him, John."

I looked across to the hospital pier and cast my mind way, way back. Then I closed my eyes and listened to the sound of the water on the shore and the repetitive gentle splashes it was making as the small waves rolled in.

It was water that I went back to, specifically the river we had rowed on back at school. Soon, the images started to come through clearly and I remembered it all. To the fore came the sight of the bow of Freddie's single sculling boat, surging forward as the hull cut through the water with increasing speed, the repetitive stroke, smooth and rhythmic – graceful you might say – but with a relentless power too. I was out in front and he was coming up fast. His back was to me. That's how it was with rowing – most of the time you were looking to where you had come from, and not to where you were going. Out beyond the stern of his boat were a parallel set of puddles imprinted on the otherwise dark flat surface, those furthest back slowly fading away into the body of the river so that you would never know a boat had passed through. Occasionally he would turn his head, just a glance within the continual rowing motion – to make an adjustment to his course if needed, and to see where I was. Then he would turn back round, knowing what he had to do, and keep on coming. That's what we became out there – entities on the surface of the river, cutting our bow waves through it the best way we could. It was like moving through time in a way; you were in the present, but you were able to see the past, and every so often snatch small glimpses of what the future might be.

Life could be cruel, but on some days and in some moments it could feel truly beautiful and eternal.

Of all the memories of my brother, the fleeting image of him propelling a sculling boat through the early morning mist was perhaps the most precious.

When I opened my eyes again I realised that Jennifer and Harry were still sitting there on either side of me, patiently waiting for my response.

Putting an arm around each of them, I started to talk.

Author's Notes

As with *The Sudden Metropolis* (GWL Publishing, 2017), the historical setting of *The Long White Cloud* involved extensive research. The full listing of sources is available on my author website, but some notes are set out below:

Philip Hoare's *Spike Island: The Memory of a Military Hospital* (Fourth Estate, 2010) describes D-block life, electrical therapy and the Grey Lady ghost, and a visit to the Royal Victoria Country Park helped to get a sense of the place and where things were, such as the pier. The hospital is gone, but the war cemetery and Chapel both remain.

The first public use of the term 'shell shock' was in: Myers C.S. *A Contribution to the Study of Shell Shock*, Lancet, February 13th 1915: 316 – 320. Cobb, the traumatised soldier, is partly based on a 19 year-old private called Preston and the original film record of him hiding under the bed to the word 'bombs' can be viewed on: https://www.youtube.com/watch?y=AL5noVCpVKw (second case shown). Hunston's bitterness at the D-block doctors writing up their findings in the Lancet is based on the paper by Hurst and Symns: *The Rapid cure of hysterical symptoms in soldiers* (Lancet, August 3rd 1918, 139 – 41). A description of the 'Ueberumpellung' system appeared in the *BMJ*, Dec 23rd 1916, 2: 882. Also useful was: Kevin Brown's *Fighting fit: Health, Medicine and War in the twentieth century* (The History Press, 2008).

Medics being instructed to use the phrase NYDN instead of term 'shell shock' did indeed happen ('General Routine Order No. 2384' on 7/6/17), as told in Lynn Macdonald's *The Roses of No Man's Land*

(Michael Joseph Ltd.1980). All the NYDN cases were taken to the 'Bandagehem' CCS during Third Ypres.

Poyntz's boss, Harvey Cushing (1869 – 1939) was an American Neurosurgeon working on the Western Front whose work involved removing shrapnel with magnets. He wrote *From a Surgeon's Journal 1915 – 1918* (Boston, Little Brown and Company, 1936) describing his war experience. The predicament of men not being identifiable is noted by Cushing: '…the wretched tags, insecurely attached to the button of the wounded soldier's uniform, are often lost or become rumpled and completely illegible. There are two poor aphasic chaps who were necessarily listed as 'unknown' since all ID marks had been lost in transit.' At the end of the novel, when Harry Ingram describes a head injury hospital at 'Mendinghem' he is referring to the No.46 hospital where Cushing operated on head wounds. On 13/10/17, when Harry Ingram has his surgery, Cushing's operating list included a soldier from the 3rd NZ Rifle Brigade with a 'frontal gutter wound… had gone 1000 yards when wounded…'

Regarding Maori culture, the 'haka' is best seen live (https://www.youtube.com/watch?y=AnlFocaA64M), but the words used come from Dave Clements' *The Story of the Haka* (The Haka Book Ltd 1998). H.G. Robley's *Maori tattooing* (Dover Publications 1896) details Moko tattoos, their use as signatures, and Mokomai.

E.O. Wilson's *On Human Nature* (Harvard University Press, 1978), in the chapter 'Aggression', tells of the Musket wars and the tale of warriors turning up to battle and being equally related to both sides. The 15 year-old Maori enlisting is from James Cowan's *The Maoris in the Great War: A history of the New Zealand Native Contingent and Pioneer Battalion: Gallipoli, 1915, France and Flanders 1916-1918* (Auckland, 1926). Cowan likens a fieldwork near Rotorua (built in 1867 by a Maori war-party) to the trench systems cut by the Pioneer Battalion in Flanders in WW1.

The demigod Maui stories were from Alistair Campbell's *Maori Legends* (Seven Seas Publishing, 1969).

Descriptions and facts of the Coromandel Peninsula (including the 'Hydrocamp', Kauri logging activities and the strange giant egg shaped mountain - Tauranikau) are largely based on the author's own experiences from living there in 2006 -7, but two books in particular were very useful: Marios Gavalas' *Day walks of the Coromandel*, (Reed Books, 2001) and Michael King's *The Coromandel* (Tandem Press, 1993).

In Hunston and Rennie's chat on New Year's Day, the politician objecting to the war is Peter Fraser, future Prime Minister, who was imprisoned for 12 months for anti-war comments in December 1916.

Freddie's ghost telling his brother to 'Get up!' in the Australian desert is based on a phenomenon experienced by people in acute danger (in: John Geiger's *The Third Man factor: surviving the impossible,* Cannongate Books, 2009) and is the same as 'the fourth man' effect, which Capt. Hurley later describes in relation to Shackleton.

The rebellious way Harry Ingram wears his hat 'fore and aft' was inspired by a photograph of men from the NZ Rifle Brigade taken in 1917 (in: Wayne Stack's *The New Zealand Expeditionary Force in World War I*, Osprey Publishing 2011). This book was very useful for other uniform details such as the black triangle sleeve flash for the 3rd Rifle Battalion, NZ Rifle Brigade, and what the Maori Pioneer uniforms looked like.

Professor S is based on Dr Lewis Yealland (1884 -1954) and his electric shock treatments during WW1. The original source was used: Yealland and Farquhar, *Hysterical disorders of warfare* (Macmillan London, 1918).

Hunston's treatment is loosely based on that of 'Case Ai' (a private, 24 years of age, suffering from mutism of 9 months duration). In chapter 21 of her novel *Regeneration* (Viking, 1991), Pat Barker refers to the very same case. My aim has been to present Yealland's work in a more positive light since it can be argued his methods, although brutal, were highly successful. Between 8/12/15 and 7/3/19, he treated 196 cases of 'functional disorder' (basically shell-shock) at Queen Square, London. A 2013 retrospective survey of all the patient files concluded

88 were cured, 84 improved, and 24 remained in status quo (In: Linden et al. *Shell shock at Queen Square: Lewis Yealland 100 years on*. Brain 2013 June; 136 (6): 1976 – 1988).

The earthquake disturbing Rennie's service is a reference to the Tauranga earthquake of Nov 22nd 1914 (magnitude 7.3). Continental drift theory was first published in Germany by Alfred Wegener in 1912, in a paper entitled: *Die Entstehung der Kontinente.*

I tried to follow dates for real troopship transports. Kahu and Manu's ship, the *Ulimaroa* (His Majesty's NZ troopship - HMNZT 74), departed NZ on 21/1/17 with the 13th Maori contingent. Hunston and Rennie's transport, *Navua* (HMNZT 78), carrying 2,123 troops, left NZ on 15/2/17 and arrived at Devonport, Plymouth on 26/4/17. The BBC presenter James May brilliantly explains dazzle camouflage (available on YouTube).

Details on the interchange with Almroth Wright (1861 – 1947) were from: Leonard Colebrook's *Almroth Wright: Provocative Doctor and Thinker* (William Heinemann, 1954). Also useful was Frank Diggins' *The Life and times of Almroth Wright* (Biomedical Scientist. March 2002, 274 – 276) which revealed that Wright's son Edward died from a self-inflicted revolver wound to the chest in 1913. Wright's griping about the 'statistician' refers to Karl Pearson (1857 – 1936) whose findings were eventually published in 1904 (K. Pearson *Report on certain enteric fever inoculation statistics*, BMJ, 1904, 3:1243 – 46). The eminent surgeon with whom Wright has differences, was Sir William Cheyne (1852 – 1932), President of the Royal College of Surgeons. 'The surgeon must believe…' is a quote from Cheyne's *The Treatment of War wounds*. BMJ 1915-16, 3: 427. Alexander Fleming (1881 – 1955), worked with Wright at Boulogne and wrote the paper: *On the bacteriology of septic wounds* (Lancet, 1915; 2: 638 – 643) during his time there.

Poyntz's descriptions of Contrary Indians are from John Plant's *The Plains Indians Clowns, their Contraries and related phenomena* (Vienna, 2010) and Thomas Berger's *Little Big Man* (Eyre and Spottiswoode, 1965).

Most Toc H detail comes from an author visit to the site, including the story of a chess tournament in late August 1917 with an unknown gunner simultaneously playing 14 games. Paul Chapman's *A Haven in Hell* (Pen & Sword, 2000) backed up my knowledge. The original sign described still hangs outside Talbot House in Poperinghe. It is a remarkable place – a living museum – where guests are warmly welcomed and offered mugs of tea, much like the soldiers of old. Rooms are available on the site for overnight stays (www.talbothouse.be). Although 'Tubby' Clayton was in charge for most of the war, Padre Humphrey Money (CF, NZEF) did stand in for him temporarily in 1917. Poyntz describing the evacuation chain on a chessboard was based on information gleaned from a visit to the Army Medical Services Museum at Aldershot, as were descriptions of war medals. Another visit (to the Memorial Museum Passchendaele 1917 in Zonnebeke, Belgium) afforded details of the underground bunker, including the latrines. The advert from the *Wipers Times* – 'for sale, the Salient estate' – appeared in the March 20th 1916 issue. Battle detail on Messines was from Alexander Turner's *Messines 1917: the zenith of siege warfare* (Osprey Publishing Ltd, 2010). Turner notes the Messines detonations as being the world's largest man-made pre-nuclear explosion.

Words from the poem 'Into Battle' by Julian Grenfell (1888 – 1915) were from *The Penguin Book of First World War poetry* (Penguin Books, 1979). His parents were the famous socialites William Grenfell (1855 – 1945) and Ethel Grenfell (1867 – 1952), also known as: Lord and Lady Desborough.

A.D. Carbery's *The New Zealand Medical Service in the Great War 1914 – 1918* (Whitcomb & Tombs Ltd, Auckland 1924) provided most of the information on the training of Medics and their activities in Messines and Passchendaele. Peter Doyle and Julian Walker's *Trench Talk: words of the First World War* (Spellmount, 2012) and Lorenzo Smith's *Lingo of No-Man's land: A World War I slang dictionary* (First published 1918) helped with nicknames of the shells, as well as British Army signalese.

A long white cloud over Messines Ridge is based on description of a painting (*Battle of Messines* by Charles Wheeler) in Peter Pederson's book *The Anzacs: Gallipoli to the Western Front* (Viking, Penguin group

2007); 'the sky has been lit by the explosions, smoke from which hangs over the ridge'.

Hunston's Messines experience is loosely based on that of Capt. Nelson, NZMC (in: Carbery). 'Fricks' is based on Samuel Frickleton (1891 – 1971) who won the VC for his actions that day. Part of the citation reads: '…*Although slightly wounded, LCpl Frickleton dashed forward at the head of his section, rushed through a barrage and personally destroyed with bombs an enemy machine gun and crew, which were causing heavy casualties. He then attacked the second gun, killing the whole of the crew of twelve…During the consolidation of the position he suffered a second severe wound. He set, throughout, a great example of heroism.*'

Capt. Patton is based on George S. Patton Jr (1885 – 1945), later the famed General of WW2. In September 1917 he was deciding whether or not to join the fledgling Tank service (Capt. Dale Wilson's thesis: *The American Expeditionary Forces Tank Corps in World War I: from creation to combat* Temple University, Philadelphia 1988). The story of the shoot-out with Cardenas was in the New York Times, May 23 1916. The swordfish quote is from Michael Keane's *George S. Patton: Blood, Guts, and Prayer* (Regenery Publishing, 2012). Patton's mention of fate tapping him on the shoulder and of 'having the guts' to listen, was in Karl Hollenbach's *Patton: Many Lives, Many Battles* (Venture Inward Magazine, Sept – Oct, 1989). The Olympic story and the carving of grooves into the stock of his revolver are supposedly true, however it is not known if Patton ever visited Toc H.

Capt. Frank Hurley (1885 – 1962) was an Australian photographer with the Australian Forces and his film 'In the Grip of the Polar pack ice' exists: http://main.wgbh.org/imax/shackleton/sirernest-two.html.

Hunston's comment about the German chemist inventing 'H' gas - 'they'll probably give him the Nobel Prize' - is based on fact also; Fritz Haber (1868 – 1934) receiving the Nobel Prize in 1919.

Kahu and Manu's Military Medals are based on the actions of Privates T. Brown and J. McAndrew (of the Maori Pioneers 'A' company) who were both decorated for their wiring work at La Basseville on the night of 6th - 7th August, 1917 (in: Cowan).The Maoris performing the haka to free a gun from the mud is recalled by Bert Stokes (NZ field artillery): https://nzhistory.govt.nz/media/sound/bert-stokes-remembers.passchendaele. Lyn Macdonald's *They called it Passchendaele* (Michael Joseph 1978) contains: 'never mind about that, chum, just fuck off…', words spoken by Lt. King (East Lancs Regiment) when relieved by Australians on the night of the 11th October 1917. 'Jaegers' are described in a letter home by Private Hart on 19 Oct 1917. He also mentions the unofficial truce, when German snipers left the stretcher bearers alone, and of how: 'dozens got hung up in the wire'.

Dave Gallaher (1873 – 1917), the All-black from Katikati, died soon after the battle of Gravenstafel Spur on 4/10/17 and is buried at Nine Elms British Cemetery, near Poperinghe. Lt. Worsley is loosely based on Leslie Wormald (1890 – 1965), Oxford Blue 1911-13 and Olympic Gold medallist in eights 1912, who served in the Royal Field Artillery and was awarded the MC in 1918. The Kronprinz RAP was actually manned by: Capt. Benham NZMC and Lt. Baxter NZMC (in: Carbery). Though the meeting at Kronprinz is fiction, I wanted to establish a rowing connection, consistent with Hunston's rowing background. Harcourt Gold (1876 – 1952) was an Oxford Blue from 1896-99 and a successful coach thereafter. In WWI he served in the Royal Flying Corps. Alister Kirby (Oxford Blue 1906-9 and Olympic Gold medallist in eights 1912) died of illness on 29/3/17 and is buried at Marseilles. Duncan Mackinnon (Oxford Blue 1909-11 and Olympic Gold medallist in coxless fours 1908) was killed on 9/10/17 near Passchendaele. His name is listed at the Tyne Cot cemetery.

'He dragged his burden…' is partly based on Cpl Lording's recall of his injury at the Battle of Fromelles, July 1916, while fighting with the ANZACs (in: Pederson). Lording describes a fellow soldier - 'Stan' - rolling him up in a groundsheet and dragging him back to the trench. 'Fit and highly trained men didn't die easily', comes from Sidney Stanfield (Wellington Infantry Battalion): https://nzhistory.gov.nz/

media/sound.sidney-stanfield-remembers-passchendaele.The fighting at Armageddon refers to the Battle of Megiddo 19 – 26th September 1918 (in: Pederson).

The front cover of Norman Stone's *World War One: a short history* (Penguin Books, 2008) provided the image of the Uhlan lancer from 1917 inspiring that scene. The analogy of 'men who have ever only known nails' is also mentioned in Stone, as is Lloyd George's prophetic warning from the end of the war: 'if peace were made now, in twenty years' time the Germans would say what Carthage had said about the First Punic War, namely that they had made this mistake and that mistake, and by better preparation and organization they would be able to bring about victory next time.'

Abbreviations:

ADS	Advanced Dressing Station
AEF	American Expeditionary Force
ANZAC	Australian and New Zealand Army Corps
AT	Anti-tetanus
Bde	Brigade
Capt	Captain
CCS	Casualty Clearing Station
CF	Chaplain to the Forces
CO	Commanding Officer
H	Short for HS – Hun Stuff, also called 'Yperite' or mustard gas
LCpl	Lance Corporal
Lt	Lieutenant
M	Morphine
MC	Military Cross
MG	Machine gun
MM	Military Medal
MO	Medical Officer
Pop	Poperinghe
NYDN	Not Yet Diagnosed Nervous
NZEF	New Zealand Expeditionary Force
NZMC	New Zealand Medical Corps
RAMC	Royal Army Medical Corps
RAP	Regimental Aid Post
SIW	Self-inflicted wound
Toc H	Talbot House
VC	Victoria Cross

24834187R00195

Printed in Poland
by Amazon Fulfillment
Poland Sp. z o.o., Wrocław